DEADLY

BUSINESS

Other Titles by Award-Winning Author
Anita Dickason

Operation Navajo
"The first page thrusts readers into a tangled world of high-powered politics and global finance."

Not Dead
"Not Dead sits firmly in the top five books I've read this year (and I have read piles of them)."

A u 7 9
"I wasn't quite ready for the dizzying speed when the storyline took off and the action didn't stop. I loved it!"

Going Gone!
"If you like action-thrillers, this one has murders, covert agents at risk, car chases, explosions, ex-special forces good and bad guys, paramilitary action, gun battles, etc."

Sentinels of the Night
"It started with a bang and kept the momentum and intrigue going to the very end."

anitadickason.com

Deadly Business

Anita Dickason

Mystic Circle Books

Copyright © 2021 Anita Dickason

Publisher: Mystic Circle Books
Cover Design: Mystic Circle Books & Designs, LLC
Editor: Jennie Rosenblum

ISBN
978-1-7340821-5-9: Paperback
978-1-7340821-6-6: Hardback
978-1-7340821-7-3: eBook

Library of Congress Control Number: 2021907781

Acknowledgments

To my daughter

Christy Kay

I couldn't have done it without you.

To my friends

Pat Pratt

Beth Vansyckle

Thank you for taking the time to read the manuscript. Your comments and critiques were invaluable.

Embedded in the hard ground, the sharp edges of rocks dug into her thighs as she inched forward. Stalks of weeds, impatiently thrust aside by a brush of her hand, tickled her nose. Alongside her, Davy scooted, pushing his body and rifle until he reached a gap in a thicket of small trees. It wasn't the best of cover, but they'd had worse.

Davy's arm stretched to flip out the folded legs of the bipod. He leveled the rifle on the rough ground before tucking the stock tight against his shoulder.

While her partner settled into position, Piper propped her elbows and brought the farmhouse into focus through the small collapsible binoculars. Her earpiece crackled. A raspy voice echoed in her ear. "McKay, status?" Her head swiveled toward Davy.

He quickly nodded and thumbed off the safety.

"Ready," she answered.

Earlier, they'd tossed a coin for who would be on the rifle. Piper lost. She'd handle the communications.

Barely visible in the early morning fog-laden air, the farmhouse appeared to be abandoned. A weed-infested yard, a porch with missing and broken slats, cracked and peeling paint, and missing roof shingles were proof of the toll from neglect and time. Still, she searched for any movement at the windows before turning her attention to the dilapidated barn. What she couldn't see was the black pickup parked behind it. The truck had been spotted during the flyover and matched the description of the last one stolen.

Three days earlier, Harvey Benton, a violent psychopathic killer, had escaped from federal custody. Convicted for the brutal murder of a federal judge, Benton was on his way to death row when the prison van was run off the road. Two men, Benton's brother, Charlie, and a cousin, Dario Mata, overpowered the two U.S. Marshals. One was killed. The other was still fighting for his life, and the outlook was grim.

Benton's escape galvanized the law enforcement community. A massive manhunt ensued. Pictures of the men had been broadcast on every news channel, and a hotline was set up.

While she studied the terrain around the farm, Piper couldn't help remembering the shock that ripped through her when the news hit her office. It could have been her, either dead or on life support systems. She'd been on the schedule instead of Tom Harper, the marshal killed during the attack.

At the last moment, her boss, Supervisory Deputy Luke Purdy, pulled her off the detail. As one of the unit snipers, she occasionally helped train officers for the local law enforcement agencies. She was walking out the door, headed to the range when Luke got the call.

The three men had left a bloody trail as they systematically hijacked cars, killing drivers and passengers. By the time one vehicle was found, they'd stolen another and managed to stay one step ahead of the officers tracking them. Their plan had succeeded until yesterday afternoon.

A call came in on the hotline from a convenience store in Tipton, a small town near the Texas and Oklahoma border. The store clerk reported seeing one of the men. Piper and Davy were in Lawton where the last vehicle had been hijacked, a black Ford F-150. They immediately headed to Tipton.

Inside the Hop and Sack, a grungy-looking teenager sat on a stool behind the counter. As the bell tinkled over the door, he looked up from the cellphone in his hand.

Piper pulled out her badge case, flipped it open and extended it toward the kid, who didn't look old enough to work in a store that sold beer. "I'm Deputy U.S. Marshal Piper McKay. This is my partner Davy Fenwick."

As he hopped off the stool, the kid's face beamed with excitement. "Oh, man! You're here about my phone call. You really think I saw one of them?"

"Maybe," Piper answered. "Are you Billy Massey?"

He gulped. "That's me."

From the file folder he held in his hand, Davy spread six pictures across the counter. Mixed in were three fake photos. Gesturing with his hand, he asked, "Do you recognize any of these men?"

"Yeah!" Billy stabbed a finger at one. "That one! That's the one. He came into the store."

Piper and Davy peered down. It was Charlie Benton.

"What happened?" Piper asked.

Billy bounced from one foot to the other. "I ... I ... just can't believe this. It's freaking unbelievable. Oh, man! Wait until the guys hear about this."

Her tone sharp, Piper said, "Billy! Tell us what happened."

"Okay ... okay. This truck pulls up to the pump. A guy jumps out from the passenger side. You see, you have to pay for the gas upfront, cash or credit card. The boss had too many customers drive off without paying." He took a deep breath. "So, this guy," pointing to the picture, "walks in. Man, he was a mean-looking dude. Gave me the willies just lookin' at him. He tosses a couple of twenties on the counter. Never said nothing. Just turned around and walked out."

"Did you see anyone else in the truck?" Piper asked.

"Yeah. Two men. The windows had a dark tint, so I couldn't really get a good look at them."

"What happened next?"

"After he pumps the gas, I thought they'd leave, but they didn't. The guy leans into the truck, talking to the men. Then he walks back inside. This time he grabs bread, lunch meat, and a twelve-pack of beer. I ring up the stuff and bag the food. He hands me the money. After I give him his change and receipt, he picks up the stuff and leaves."

"What time did this happen?"

Billy scratched his face as he thought. "Before my lunch break, maybe elevenish or so."

"Why did it take you so long to call?"

"I was surfing my phone, and the article about the jailbreak popped up. That's when I seen the pictures."

"What kind of truck?"

"Uh … black, Ford F-150. Looked new."

Piper picked up the fake photos and the one of Charlie Benton. "Have you ever seen these two men around here?"

Billy looked at the remaining pictures again before shaking his head no.

She handed him a business card. "If you remember anything else, call me."

The kid cradled it in the palms of his hands and stared at it in awe. "I will!"

Despite the grim reason they were in the store, Piper had to smile. She figured she'd just made Billy's day, though he was damn lucky Benton didn't kill him. Her hand on the door, she paused to look over her shoulder at the kid with the goofy grin. Why didn't Benton kill him?

Outside, Davy was on the phone. He motioned to her. When she stopped in front of him, he said, "It's Luke. I've already told him what we found out from the store clerk." He clicked the speakerphone. "Luke, Piper's listening."

Her boss's voice echoed. "Anything else, Piper?"

"What's the status on the background for the brother and Mata?" she asked.

"We're still digging, but so far, nothing that would give us an idea where they might be headed."

"This could be a long shot. Look for any relatives or ties to Tipton."

Luke said, "All right. But why Tipton?"

"Because Benton didn't kill the clerk."

"Tell me why it isn't just good news."

"I may be grasping at straws here, but they've tried to eliminate everyone who has seen them. Why not the clerk? Is it because they didn't want cops snooping around Tipton?"

"You might be onto something. Stay in the area. Talk to other people in town."

A wry look crossed her face as she viewed the deserted street and boarded-up buildings. "Sure, boss. Just don't hold your breath. The population is 847, at least according to the city limits sign."

Luke just grunted and disconnected.

Piper ambled toward their parked car. "Davy, you heard the man. Let's see if we can find someone to talk to."

Over the next hour, they queried employees and customers at the few businesses in the tiny community. No one recognized the three men. It wasn't until they stopped at a small wood-frame house on the outskirts of town that they hit paydirt.

An elderly man, wearing faded and worn overalls and a long-sleeved shirt, sat in a rocker on the porch and watched with interest as they approached.

A large hound dog crawled out from under the steps. Mournful eyes looked up at them for several seconds before the dog flopped on his side.

The man leaned over the edge of the rocker. A stream of black spit hit the ground near the dog. He swiped at a dribble of chewing tobacco sliding down his chin, then wiped his hand on his overalls.

Piper flipped open her badge case. "Piper McKay, U.S. Marshal. We'd like to ask you a few questions. What is your name?"

A rusty chortle erupted. "Well now, if that just don't beat all, a pretty girl like you a federal marshal." He looked at Davy. "Guess you're one too."

Davy grinned and held up his open badge case.

"I'm Jedediah Wilson, though most folks just call me Ole Jed. Gotta be something important to bring two feds to Tipton."

"How long have you lived here?" Piper asked.

"Plus or minus, about ninety-two years. Born on a farm about ten miles from here."

"Plus or minus?" Piper questioned.

"Don't rightly know the year, no birth certificate."

Davy handed him the photos. "Do you recognize these men?"

Rheumy eyes narrowed as he studied the images. "I'll be damned. These are the yahoos everyone's chasing, killed a few people from what I saw on the news." He handed back the pictures. "I can't say I've ever seen them."

"Did a family named Benton or Mata ever live around here?"

He leaned to spit another stream of tobacco juice, this time barely missing the dog. "Yeah. The Mata family has a farm north of here. Old man Mata still lives there. The old coot's older than I am."

He grinned, flashing his nicotine-stained teeth.

"What can you tell us about the family?" Piper asked.

"Not much. The wife's dead. The son took off for greener pastures years ago. The old man mentioned the boy had married and had a couple of kids, but I've never seen any of them. Let me take another look at those pictures."

Davy handed them to him.

The dog sighed. The chair creaked as the old man rocked and shuffled the photos. After a few seconds, he slid one on top before handing them to Davy. "That one could be Mata's kin. Something about the eyes. But couldn't swear to it."

A look of excitement flashed between Davy and Piper. The picture on top was Dario Mata.

"Where is the farm?" Piper asked.

Ole Jed gestured with his hand. "That road will take you to Buck's County Store. Turn north. When you get to an intersection with a water tower, turn west. The road curves, and right after the curve is the Mata place. Can't miss it."

"We appreciate the information." She turned to walk to the car, then looked back. "It would be best if you didn't mention our conversation to anyone. This is a ruthless gang who won't hesitate to kill anyone who gets in their way."

A gleam sparked in the old man's eyes. "Missy, already figured that one out." He spit. It splattered across the dog's butt. The tail just thumped as the man roared with laughter. "Got ya."

Her phone call to Luke about Jedediah's information set the events in motion that ended with her and Davy lying on a slight rise overlooking the Mata farmhouse.

A medivac helicopter had been commandeered for the flyover, though the pilot was a marshal. Once the pilot spotted the black truck, teams of men and equipment left Oklahoma City.

Assigned the task of finding a location for the staging area, one that wouldn't draw attention to their arrival, Piper and Davy found a roadside park about twenty miles from town. They made one more trip to visit Ole Jed. This time when they left, they had a diagram of the interior of the Mata house.

Before the sun had risen, officers crowded around a conference table inside the tactical van to study a plat map, along with the house diagram. There wasn't an easy approach. Flat, empty fields surrounded the place. Using the trees along a stream that bordered the property offered the best protection. The team's exposure would be limited. Piper and Davy set up across the road.

Through her earpiece, voices sounded as the tactical unit moved into place. Coming in at dawn, her boss hoped the men would be asleep. Her gaze shifted to the trees. In the dim light, she could see the dark shapes of the entry team. At a steady pace, they started across the open field. Her gaze turned back to the house as she scanned the windows. A shot from inside the house cracked, then a second.

"Pull back!" Luke shouted. "Nolan's been hit!"

Fear ripped through Piper. Powerless, her fingers tightened around the binoculars. Several of the agents returned fire as they moved backward. Nolan's body hung over the shoulder of a teammate. Their worst scenario had just become a reality.

Luke's voice echoed in her ear as he ordered the driver of the tactical van to move up. The hostage negotiator would take over the communications. The other piece of information Ole Jed had provided was Mata's telephone number.

From her position, she could see one side of the house and most of the front. Her eyes shifted from window to window. Davy would be doing the same, looking for a target through the rifle scope.

Tim's voice, the unit's hostage negotiator, sounded over the tactical van's loudspeaker. "Federal Marshals. Answer the phone."

The front door opened. A frail, elderly man was shoved forward. His hands helplessly flapped the air. Behind him, Harvey Benton had one arm wrapped around Mata's neck while the other held a gun to the side of the old man's head.

Piper's chest tightened at the sight of Mata's seamed and unshaven face, bleached white with fear, his mouth open as he gasped for air. Every detail was magnified by her binoculars.

"Front door," she said.

"I see it," Luke answered.

Davy said, "No shot."

Benton shouted, "Stay back. We're leaving. If I see a single cop, I'll kill the old man." He jerked the man back, slamming the door shut.

"Piper, do you have eyes on the truck?" Luke asked.

"No."

"We can't see it either."

Piper knew, just as everyone else did, it had to end here. No options, no giving three killers a chance to escape.

The only way to get to the truck was to move past the house and double back. She could use the trees for cover until she had to cross the road. If anyone looked out that side of the house, they'd see her. The entry team was on the other side. If this was going to work, Luke would have to create a distraction to keep the three men on his side of the house.

"Luke, I can get to the truck. Try to keep them occupied."

He clicked the mike to acknowledge.

Davy said, "I'm coming with you. I can't cover you from here."

Piper folded the binoculars and slid them into a pocket. They both eased backward. Once they were out of view of the house, they stood. Trotting, they weaved around the trees, paralleling the road until they passed the house.

While Piper watched the farmhouse, Davy dropped to the ground, crawling until he was in a position where he could see the barn. "Ready," he told Piper, then keyed his mike. "Now!"

Shots rang out. Piper, her gun held tight in her hands, ran flat out until she reached the side of the barn.

Luke's voice crackled in her ear. "Davy?"

"She's in place," he answered, his gaze tracking her through the scope.

Piper stepped next to the truck and aimed. Two shots hit the front tire, then she locked onto the rear one, firing two more. The tires collapsed.

Davy's voice rang out in her earpiece. "Behind you!"

Piper whipped around to see two armed men charge across the yard. She fired. The lead man stumbled, then fell. Even as she swung her weapon toward the other, she knew it was too late. The barrel of Charlie Benton's gun was aimed at her face. Time seemed to slow. Piper heard the shot. Astonished, she watched Benton topple forward. The thud of his body hitting the ground galvanized her. She ducked back, using the side of the barn for cover. There was still an active threat inside the house.

Piper said, "Two down."

Luke's voice followed, telling the entry team to go. Somewhere in the back of her mind, she wondered how her hands could be so steady while she kept the gun aimed at the back door. From inside, doors slammed and shouts erupted.

Once Luke called the all-clear, she moved toward the men lying motionless on the ground. It didn't take a check of their pulse to know they were dead as she holstered her gun and finally felt a tremble. This had been close, too damn close.

Davy, his rifle slung across his shoulder, ran toward her. Agents streamed out the back door. Luke walked over and stared at the bodies of the Benton brothers and the guns lying near them.

"There wasn't any other way this was going to end," Luke said.

"Nolan?" Davy asked.

"Alive," Luke told him.

While they waited for the county sheriff, coroner, and ambulance to show up, everyone clustered around the tactical van. Dario Mata was handcuffed and seated in one of the marshal's cars. His great-grandfather was inside the house where he'd collapsed. The team's medic was keeping an eye on him. Nolan was inside the van. He'd taken a round in the thigh and had already been patched up, at least enough to get him to the hospital.

Between moments spent rehashing the confrontation and endless cups of coffee brewed inside the van, everyone was riding an adrenaline and caffeine-driven high.

Piper said, "Damn glad you had my back."

"Hey, you did the hard work. I had an easy shot."

"Maybe so, but for an instant, I thought I was a goner."

Luke stepped out of the van and motioned to Piper. She followed him back inside. Usually, his face glinted with humor. This time, his grim look set off a tingle of uneasiness.

"Piper, my office got a call from Grady Estes."

Her heart jumped. Grady was the foreman at her grandmother's ranch.

Her voice, almost a whisper, "What happened?"

"Your grandmother is in the hospital. It doesn't look good."

"Why?"

"According to Mr. Estes, her horse threw her. She suffered severe head trauma."

Agitated, Piper shook her head. "No! No! That can't be true. My grandmother is an experienced rider. There isn't a horse in the whole damn county that could throw her. It's not possible."

The look of sympathy on Luke's face was almost her undoing. "I've already authorized an emergency leave for you. You and Davy head out. If there is anything I can do to help, anything at all, let me know."

Her mind reeling, she mumbled something before stumbling out of the van. Luke followed her, motioning to Davy.

Piper stared about her in confusion as she tried to assimilate what Luke had told her. It didn't make sense. With an inner shake, she pulled herself together. The first priority was to get to Texas. Standing around in a daze wasn't solving anything.

Once they were on the road, she checked her phone. She'd missed several calls from Grady. When she tried calling back, his phone went to voice mail. She left a message telling him she was on her way. Her next call was to the hospital in Sulphur Springs. After confirming she was next of kin, all she learned was that her grandmother was still in intensive care, and there was no change in her condition. She told the nurse she'd be there in a few hours and left her number if someone needed to contact her.

It took less than two hours to reach Oklahoma City. When breaking the speed limit, it helped to be in a vehicle with U.S. Marshal Service plastered on the car doors. Davy dropped her off at her apartment. After reassuring him several times that she didn't need him to drive her to Texas, he finally left.

Propelled by a sense of urgency, she took a quick shower and washed her hair. Dressed in jeans, her favorite hiking boots, a long-sleeved shirt and jacket, and her wet hair twisted in one long braid, she grabbed clothes from the closet, stuffing them in a suitcase. The Glock 19 lying on the dresser was shoved into the holster on her leather belt.

As she headed to the door, rolling the suitcase behind her and her backpack slung over her shoulder, she paused. Not sure why the thought popped into her head, she walked back to the bedroom and grabbed a duffel bag from the closet. It contained additional ammunition and an assortment of tactical gear. She added tactical clothing, the gun belt she'd worn earlier, and her combat boots.

Everything but the backpack was tossed in the trunk that already contained her sniper rifle and gear she removed from Davy's car.

She made good time, not as good as Davy, but still managed to pull into the hospital parking lot in a little over three hours.

After identifying herself to the receptionist, she was directed to the intensive care unit, where another nurse greeted her. The news wasn't good, no change in her grandmother's condition, and she hadn't regained consciousness. Until the doctor gave permission, Piper wasn't allowed into the ICU.

She wandered into the small waiting room. The aroma of freshly brewed coffee wafted in the air. Holding a cup, she walked to the window. The depressing view from the back of the hospital didn't help her mood.

What the hell had happened? She just couldn't envision Jennie Layton flying off a horse. As a young woman, she'd lived up to her name, Jennie Storm. Billed as Jennie, the Rodeo Belle, she'd been a champion barrel racer. Awards and ribbons filled the bookcases in Jen's home office.

The rodeo circuit is where she met Sam Layton, a bronco and calf roping rider. They married and continued to follow the circuit until a horse rolled over on him, breaking his hip. It ended his rodeo days. They quit and bought an 800-acre cattle ranch near Sulphur Bluff, about thirty miles northeast of Sulphur Springs, the county seat for Hopkins County. When her grandfather dropped dead from a massive heart attack, Jennie took over running the ranch. Hardly a day went by that she wasn't on a horse.

Behind her, footsteps sounded. She turned. A man in blue scrubs strode toward her.

"Ms. McKay?"

"Yes."

"I'm Doctor Henderson."

Puzzled, she stared at him.

"Uh … is something wrong?" he asked.

Collecting herself, she said, "No. It's just, well, I'm sorry. I expected Doc Able. He's been the family doctor for years."

"Ah, I see. Dr. Able was here earlier. I'm the neurologist. Won't you have a seat?" He motioned toward a chair.

The cup clutched tight in her hands, Piper perched on the edge of the chair. "A neurologist? How bad is it?"

"When she fell, Ms. Layton cracked her skull. I had to operate to relieve the pressure on the brain and repair the damage. While it was successful, it is still very much touch and go. The next twenty-four hours are crucial. Her vitals are strong, and according to her medical records, she is in good health. Dr. Able described her, and I use his words, as one tough cookie."

"May I see her?"

"Yes, but just for a few minutes. It would be best for you to go home. There is really nothing you can do here. If anything changes, I will call you immediately. Do we have your contact information?"

"Yes. I gave it to the nurse."

"Good, follow me."

The inside of an ICU wasn't a new experience. She'd been in several since she became a marshal. Still, she wasn't prepared for the sight of her beloved grandmother lying motionless in the bed. Tethered to multiple machines that beeped and flashed, her small frame seemed to disappear under the white sheet. Her ghostly white face blended into the white bandages circling her head.

As Piper stepped to the side of the bed, tears clotted her throat and blurred her vision. She reached to gently stroke the back of the frail-looking hand lying alongside her body. "Jen, I'm here. I won't be leaving until you get well. I love you."

She leaned over and brushed her lips across Jen's cheek.

"That's all for now," the doctor said.

After another light stroke of her finger over her grandmother's face, she turned and walked out. By the time she reached the car, Piper couldn't hold back the tears. Sliding inside, her forehead rested against the wheel as deep sobs racked her body. She didn't understand how this had happened. From a box in the console, she grabbed a handful of tissues and wiped her face. It was time to find a few answers.

As she drove, memories of her first trip to the ranch surfaced. Piper was ten when her life changed. Her parents were killed in a car crash. Jennie Layton had flown to Boston for the funeral. When she left, Piper went with her. She'd never been to Texas, and the day before the funeral was the first time she'd met her grandmother.

Her mother never went back to where she grew up. She often joked about leaving the dust of Texas behind and never looking back. A talented violinist, Amy was a member of the Boston Symphony. As a teenager, Piper's grandfather gave her mother a violin as a Christmas gift. After high school, Amy attended the University of North Texas at Denton. Music wasn't a career option. In fact, her mother enrolled in business management courses. One day, while practicing in a courtyard outside her dorm, Henry Wainwright, the head of the music school, walked by. Unaware he listened, she finished the concerto she was playing. Impressed by the talent he heard, Wainwright had encouraged her mother to pursue a career in music. While Amy's father supported her decision, Jennie didn't.

After Amy graduated, Wainwright contacted a friend, who happened to be the conductor for the Boston Symphony and arranged for an audition. It led to her mother moving to Boston, where she met Piper's father at her first practice session. When Sam Layton died, Piper's grandmother wanted her daughter to move back to Texas, but Amy refused. Their estrangement became permanent.

Piper remembered watching out the car window after they left Sulphur Springs. Where were the people, the houses, cars? Her home in Boston had been on a street with large trees. She could ride her bike on the wide sidewalk and visit her best friend, who lived next door. Where would she ride a bicycle here? There were no sidewalks, nothing but flat land and cows. It scared her.

Sullen and rebellious, those first months were difficult. Piper wanted her mother and father. She missed her friends. The only time she saw other children was at school. Since she still wore the dainty dresses that had been sent to Texas, not jeans and boots like the rest of the kids, they laughed at her.

Piper didn't know the woman who was her grandmother. Even what to call her became a source of contention. Finally, they'd compromised, what was to be the first of many. While everyone else called her grandmother Jennie, for Piper, it was Jen. Looking back, she knew she had tried Jen's patience more than once.

It didn't turn around until a mare had a foal. For Piper, it was a miracle, better than a dog or cat. Realizing what had happened, Jen gave her the colt, but only with the understanding that Piper had to keep the stall clean for it and its mother. Later that week, Piper asked if she could get a pair of jeans and boots. Another turning point in her life.

The sight of the large sign, Layton Ranch, mounted on the fence alongside the gate, pulled her out of the trip down memory lane. When she drove into the yard, the motion detectors triggered the floodlights. She parked, stepped out, and looked around. Not much had changed over the years. A wide front porch encircled the front and sides of a large, single-story brick ranch house. Nearby, a large paddock connected two barns. A man walked out of one as she popped open the trunk.

"Piper."

She spun and ran toward him. His arms wrapped around her. Choking back the tears, she buried her head in his shoulder.

"Ah, little one." His hand patted her back. "It will be all right. Jennie's a strong woman. She wouldn't like to see you this way."

Piper gulped and stepped back. "I know. But it was so hard seeing her lying there, not moving. Oh, Grady, what happened? I don't understand."

"Come into the house. I've made a pot of soup."

"Let me get my suitcase and backpack."

"You go on in. I'll take care of it."

Inside, the earthy aroma of onions and spices teased her taste buds, reminding her that she'd eaten nothing since before the pred-awn briefing. After a quick visit to the bathroom and the splash of cold water on her face, her tension eased. She couldn't change what had happened, and her grandmother's life was out of her hands. What she could do was what she did best, find out why.

In the kitchen, a bowl of salad was on the large plank top table, along with a glass of wine and a bottle of beer. The room was large, built to accommodate the family and cowhands. While they used the formal dining room for holidays and the occasional special event, the kitchen was the day to day hub for meals.

Grady stood in front of the six-burner gas stove, ladling soup into bowls. He glanced over his shoulder as she walked in. "Sit."

She sat, picking up the wine. Over the rim of the glass, her gaze scanned the man who'd become a surrogate father over the years.

He'd worked the rodeo circuit as a clown. One of the more dangerous jobs, his responsibility was to distract the bulls so a rider could get to safety. After Grady lost his wife and baby during childbirth, he decided to turn in his clown suit. He followed his best friend, Sam Layton, to Texas.

Grady wasn't a large man, only a couple of inches taller than Piper's five-foot, six-inch frame. Lean but muscular, he could handle any job on the ranch. The faint limp was a holdover from being gored in the leg by a bull. Deep lines gouged his weather-beaten face. His dark eyes under bushy brows usually held a twinkle, but not now.

"Grady, what happened?"

He turned to set the bowls on the table. "Early this morning, Jennie rode out to check the gates. When her horse came back without her, I took one of the UTVs and went looking." He eased onto the chair. "I found her on the ground near the east gate, her head covered in blood. She was breathing but just barely. I called 911. Once the ambulance left, I came back here, then headed to the hospital. I tried calling, but your phone just kept rolling to voice mail. When I couldn't reach you, I called your office."

"We had a raid this morning, and I turned the phone off. We'd just finished when my boss told me you'd called. I can't believe Jen's horse threw her."

"Yup," he said and took a swallow of soup. "That's what the sheriff's deputy said. He showed up just after the ambulance arrived. That's all I know."

Piper dipped a cracker in her soup and munched it before she said, "I don't believe it."

"Didn't figure you would. All the years I've known your gran, not once did she ever come off a horse when she didn't mean to."

For a few minutes, she ate while she thought about what he said.

When she finished, Piper pushed the bowl aside and leaned back. "For argument's sake, what would cause her horse to act up?"

He shoved the last forkful of lettuce and tomato in his mouth. A thoughtful look crossed his face as he chewed. Swallowing, he said, "I wondered when you'd get to that. She was riding Bess, and that horse never spooked at anything."

"Bess! She was on Bess?"

"Yup."

"Is Bess injured?"

"Scratches on her front legs."

"From what?"

"It could have happened if Bess stumbled and went down."

At the odd note in his voice, she leaned back. "You don't think so." It wasn't a question.

"You take a look. See what you think." He swallowed the last of his beer. "Been a few problems lately." He fiddled with the empty bottle.

She waited. Grady didn't often talk about problems around the ranch. He could be as tight-lipped as her grandmother.

"Twice now, we've lost some cattle, including Leopold."

"Leopold!" she declared, her spine rigid with shock. "Why didn't she call me?"

Leopold was Jen's prize bull. He'd won numerous awards at the local cattle shows and was why Layton cattle brought a premium price at the auctions.

"Probably figured you had enough on your plate without worrying about a few stolen cows. A deputy came out, took a statement."

"It must have broken her heart to lose Leopold."

"It was a bitter blow. It's why Jennie was checking the fence. If you're done, let's get this cleaned up, then look at Bess."

They gathered up the dirty dishes, stowing them in the dish-washer. For Piper, helping him with the simple kitchen tasks brought an unusual sense of comfort. Grady was a good man. Whatever was wrong at the ranch, she knew he wouldn't back down.

She followed him outside. Pinpoints of lights sparkled in the night sky. A sight that still packed a punch, though as a kid, it took a while to appreciate how bright the stars were when they didn't compete with city lights.

Grady flipped the switch for the barn lights. Three heads, King, Tapper, and Bess, popped over the doors to the stalls. King was her horse. His sire, Breakaway, had been the colt she raised many years ago. Jen entered into a stud fee contract with a neighboring rancher. Piper got the first foal. Not long after that, Breakaway died. King nuzzled her arm as she stroked him.

Tapper belonged to Grady and happily tossed his head in the air with a long whinny at the sight of the man. He stopped to rub the horse's head before turning to Bess's stall.

When he opened the door, she butted him in the shoulder. "Yes, yes, you're a sweetheart," he murmured as he guided her back. His hand ran over her neck, his voice whispering in the tone he always used to calm an animal.

Piper stepped next to him, running her hand down Bess's head before kneeling to examine the cuts that scored the horse's legs. "Did the sheriff's deputy look at Bess?"

"No. He never said anything about wanting to look at the horse."

"If Bess had stumbled and gone down, I could see the damage to the knees, but what caused the cuts lower down." She leaned closer. "Grady, would you get me the flashlight from the tack room?" While she waited, Piper ran her hand down Bess's leg, calming her when the horse flinched. The tip of her finger gently touched the edges of the cuts.

Grady knelt beside her and handed her the flashlight. In his other hand, he held a tube of salve.

She aimed the beam at the cuts, studying each one, then did the same on the other leg. "These are too symmetrical to be random, which is what they should look like if Bess had stumbled." She snapped off the flashlight and stood. "I think someone cut her legs before they sent her running back here."

He opened the tube. Using a finger, he smeared the ointment on each of the cuts. "I had the same notion but thought I was overreacting."

Her eyes narrowed as she stared at the horse's legs. "If we're right, this wasn't an accident."

Grady followed her out of the stall. His grim expression matched hers. "What do you figure on doing about it?"

"Find out who and why someone tried to kill Jen, and I'm starting in her office." She handed him the flashlight.

"I'm calling it a night. It's good to have you home."

Piper hugged him, then watched while he slowly limped to a staircase at the end of the two-story barn. Grady lived in an apartment on the second floor.

After grabbing a can of soda from the refrigerator, Piper walked into her grandmother's office. The rocker still sat in the corner of the room. One of Piper's favorite places in the house, she'd curl up with a book while Jen worked on the ranch accounts. The desk faced the large front windows. Even though it was slightly off-center in the room, Jen never cared. What mattered to her was the view of the pens and barns through the window. Next to it was a large four-drawer file cabinet. Shelves on one wall held books and awards. On the opposite side, family pictures adorned the wall.

Piper's gaze roamed over them, reliving the memories some held. In many, her grandfather, with his larger-than-life image, stood next to Jen. Others were taken as Piper grew up. Her grandmother hadn't changed much over the years. While her hair was whiter now than blond, she still had the same slim build. Over the years, friends had commented on the close similarity between Jen and Piper. Even though Jen was in her early seventies, she still had the look of a younger woman.

Another picture rose in her mind, Jen lying in that hospital bed. Along with it, the flare of hot anger she'd felt when she looked at Bess's legs and knew—someone had tried to kill her grandmother.

She spun and dropped into the chair. Fingers jabbed the keyboard, opening files and emails. She didn't find much, but she hadn't expected she would. Jen was still old school when it came to using a computer. She relied on paper copies, which is where Piper went next, the large side drawer in the desk. Jammed inside, hanging file folders bulged with paper. Dismayed by the sheer volume of material, it dawned on her this would take more time than she realized.

Nevertheless, as daunting as it looked, she had no choice. The reason behind the attack on Jen had to be connected to the ranch. Somewhere, in this ream of material, there had to be something that would tell her why.

After wading through the fourth file, this one containing receipts for hay, grain, and a multitude of other ranch supplies, she had to wonder if Jen ever threw anything away. She'd saved even the scraps of paper with notes, telephone numbers, and names.

The next file, labeled cattle sales, wasn't as thick. Inside were several stapled documents and an unsealed envelope with *Jennie Layton Copy* typed across the front. She opened the envelope, removing several folded pages. It was a contract with Jarvis Livestock and was dated about four weeks back. As she read, her incredulity grew. This wasn't possible. Her grandmother would never sign a contract like this, but Jennie Layton was scrawled on the signature line when she reached the last page.

In stunned disbelief, she went over it a second time. The sinking feeling grew worse. It didn't make sense. Why would her grandmother sell every head of cattle she owned?

After a fitful night of worrying about her grandmother and the devastating contract, Piper finally gave up. The sun was a narrow gleam on the horizon when she tossed aside the covers. Seated on the edge of the bed, she called the hospital but was told there was no change. Despite the disheartening news, she planned to stay there as long as they would let her.

Dressed in jeans, boots, and a long-sleeved shirt, she slid her gun and holster on her belt. On her way out, she grabbed a lightweight jacket and the backpack.

The door to Jen's bedroom was ajar. Piper pushed it open and walked in. Overwhelmed by a rush of memories, tears glinted in her eyes.

Neat and pristine, a faint aroma of wildflowers, Jen's favorite perfume, clung to the air. Piper's fingers trailed across glass globes on the dresser. Several were ones she'd given Jen over the years. The wedding ring quilt, a gift when Jen and her grandfather were married, still covered the bed. In the corner, Jen's handbag hung on the chair in front of a small desk. She opened the bag and scanned the contents, a wallet, a small notepad, brush, extra pair of reading glasses, and other sundry items. Typical of Jen, there was also a notice of a cattle auction. When she pulled it out, she spotted a note stuck to the sales ad. On it was a name, Cade Tanner, and a telephone number. She tucked the flyer and note into a pocket on the outside of the backpack.

In the kitchen, she wasn't surprised to see Grady cooking breakfast. He was usually up at the crack of dawn. Bacon popped and splattered in a skillet as he poured scrambled eggs into another pan.

"Fresh coffee. Grab a cup."

When she reached to get one from the glass-fronted cabinet, he noticed the gun on her belt. "Do you always wear it?"

Her thoughts elsewhere, she said, "What?" then noticed where he was looking. "I'd feel naked without it."

"Never thought you'd take on a law enforcement career."

"Neither did I, but I'm glad I did. Grady, who is Lane Jarvis?"

"A cattle broker. Moved into town a few months ago. He sold some of her cattle?" He flipped the bacon.

"He did?"

"He came by the ranch one day. Told her he could get a better price for her cattle than she could get at a livestock auction. As proof, he offered to sell ten head on consignment with a reduced commission. If Jennie was satisfied with his service, they'd talk about future sales. She took him up on the offer."

"Did he sell them?"

"He said he did." He stirred the eggs." A couple of men showed up to load the cattle. I'm not sure about the sale price, though Jennie seemed satisfied at the time."

"Did something happen to change her mind?"

"A few days back, she mentioned she still hadn't received the check and planned on contacting Jarvis."

"Was that the only time she did business with him?"

"She never mentioned anything else. Is there a problem?" He put the bacon on a paper towel.

"I'm just getting a handle on her affairs." She decided not to mention the contract she'd found until she knew more. It wasn't that she didn't trust Grady, but he had a lot on his plate right now. It was up to him to keep the ranch going. He didn't need the additional stress. "Before I leave for the hospital, I'd like to take a ride out to where you found Jen."

"Already got the horses saddled."

Piper chuckled. "I never could get one step ahead of you."

He scraped the eggs into a bowl. "Just don't forget it, even if you are a gun-toting fed." He set the bowl on the table along with the plate of bacon.

The pot of coffee in her hand, she laughed, then said, "Don't forget, you're the one who taught me how to shoot. Wouldn't it be faster to take one of the UTVs?" She refilled her cup.

"We could, but I figured you might enjoy the ride. Did you call the hospital?"

"You know I did. No change. Besides the hospital, I've another stop to make."

"Anything you want to share?"

She set the cup in front of her plate and slid onto the chair. Her tone grim, she said, "Not yet."

Grady mumbled, "Just like your grandma, tight-lipped."

Once they cleared away the breakfast dishes, they headed outside. When the horse tied to the gatepost spotted Piper, he whinnied, prancing from side to side.

Her hand reached out, and King pushed his head under her arm. "You devil. I'm happy to see you too." Slipping the reins off the post, she stepped in the stirrup and vaulted onto his back with ease. Still prancing, he circled the yard.

Grady, astride Tapper, leaned over to open the gate. King trotted through it, and Piper eased up on the reins. Feeling the lack of restraint, the horse broke into a light lope. The rush of morning air across her face sparked a deep sense of contentment. She loved the ranch. It was why the decision to apply to the Marshal Service had been difficult. Piper knew she'd have to leave.

Grady caught up with her. They gave the horses their head, letting them work off their excess energy as they galloped across the wide-open flat land. When Grady pulled back on the reins, slowing Tapper, Piper did the same.

He motioned with his hand. "Up ahead is where I found Jennie."

In an instant, the contentment vanished, replaced by the fear she'd felt since Luke told her about the phone call. When King stopped, her eyes scanned the terrain. Ahead, the fence line weaved its way through the trees. A gate led to the narrow road that ran along the side of the property.

She wheeled King around, looking across the acres of open land. As far as she could see, cattle grazed.

Grady dismounted. Once the horses were tied to a nearby tree, he walked toward the fence. Piper followed. When she saw the bloodied rock, she abruptly stopped. Knowing and seeing were two different emotions. Right now, she couldn't let the grief and anger at the sight of her grandmother's blood override her senses. She took a steadying, deep breath, then knelt to look at the jagged edges of the rock—black with dried blood.

"Judging by the bloodstains on the ground, her head was close to the rock," she observed.

"About a foot or so."

"Was she lying on her back or facedown?"

"Facedown."

"Which way did she face?"

His face puzzled, he said, "Toward the rock. Is it important?"

"Hmm … could be," she said as she studied the pattern of stains. She stood. Her steps slow, she circled, looking at the rock and stains from every angle. Despite the heavy trampling of the ground, a picture began to build in her mind. She intently scrutinized every rock and blade of grass in ever-widening circles before walking back to the bloodstains.

"Grady, do you know what I don't see? Any stones that would have caused the injury to Bess's legs."

Grady's eyes scanned the area. "My god, you're right."

As she spoke, her voice vibrated with anger. "Isn't it convenient that a rock, the only one around here large enough to injure her, just happened to be in the right spot when she fell? Here's another point. This rock hasn't been here long. Look at the grass around it."

She squatted, picking it up. "The grass is flattened but not dry and lifeless as it would be if that rock had laid here for a long time." She laid it down and stood. "Over here."

She walked several yards away and pointed. Clumps of dirt and dried grass edged an irregular depression. "The shape matches the rock. Jen didn't fall. Someone dug it up, then bashed her head with it."

Piper pulled her phone from her pocket and began snapping pictures of the depression, rock, and bloodstains on the ground. She had Grady tip the rock on its side so she could take pictures of the soil and grass underneath it.

Before they left, she walked along the road. If there had been any evidence, the ambulance, paramedics, and anyone else who arrived at the scene had destroyed it.

As they mounted their horses, she asked, "How would someone know Jen would be out here? This wasn't a spur-of-the-moment attack. It was planned. What happened before she left?"

"We had breakfast as usual. Jennie said she wanted to take care of some paperwork before checking the fences. I asked if she wanted me to come along. She said, no."

"Do you know if she talked to anyone before she left or planned to meet anyone?"

"Come to think of it, I remember hearing the phone ring as I was finishing up in the kitchen, but I didn't see your gran again. By the time I finished mucking out the stalls, she'd already left."

"When we get back to the house, I want you to either write or type up a statement of everything that happened, starting with what you just told me. Make sure you give me every detail of what you saw and did when you found her."

The ride back was grim and silent. For Piper, one thought was all-consuming. Why hadn't the sheriff figured out what happened? His office was her first stop.

Back at the house, they unsaddled the horses and wiped them down before putting them in their stalls. Once she had King squared away, Piper led Bess outside and took several pictures of the horse's injuries.

After transferring the pictures from her phone to her computer, she printed off copies before calling Luke. Since she was about to stick her nose into Sheriff Horne's business, it was a good idea to keep her boss in the loop. She explained what she'd discovered. His response was surprising. Did he need to contact the sheriff, and did she want any help? While grateful for the support, she declined the offer.

The comment Grady made about a phone call reminded her she hadn't checked the answering machine. Grant Sheffield had left a message. She knew him. He owned the local livestock auction. She didn't recognize the other caller, Mack Huber. A thought struck her, where was Jen's cellphone?

When Grady walked in, she said, "Do you know what happened to Jen's phone? Would she have had it with her?"

"She never left the house without it. I expect it's at the hospital."

"Grady, that call, was it on the landline or Jen's cellphone?"

"Her cellphone. She still uses a snippet from Texas A&M's war hymn as the ringtone. You can't mistake it."

Located in a building near the downtown, the sheriff's department was about a half-block from the county jail. A row of marked patrol vehicles and two prisoner vans were parked on one side of the building. Piper pulled into a visitor's spot. As she strode toward the front door, she still hadn't decided whether to identify herself as a U.S. Marshal. Despite her call to Luke, this was personal, not official business.

An older woman, fiftyish, sat behind a desk in a small reception area. A few chairs lined the walls, and a low table was covered with magazines. She looked up from her keyboard as Piper approached.

"Good morning. May I help you?"

"I'm Piper McKay. I'd like to speak to Sheriff Horne."

"For what reason?"

"It's about the Layton investigation."

A puzzled look crossed the woman's face. "I'm not familiar with a Layton investigation. Are you sure you're at the right place? The police department is in the next block."

Piper glanced at the name plaque on the desk. "Yes, Ms. Taylor. I'm at the right location."

"I'll check to see if Sheriff Horne is available. And please, your name again?"

"Piper McKay."

The woman walked into a hallway where sounds of laughter could be heard. When she returned, she said, "Sheriff Horne is in a meeting but will be with you shortly."

The laughter from the hallway continued for several minutes

before a man walked into the reception area. Attired in a uniform, his name tag and stars on the collar proclaimed him as the sheriff. Around five-ten, slightly overweight, with a ruddy complexion, his eyes darted toward her. His hand brushed what appeared to be crumbs from the front of his shirt.

"I'm Sheriff Horne. You want to speak to me about an investigation?"

"Yes. I'm Piper McKay, Jennie Layton's granddaughter."

"If this is about the missing cattle."

Interrupting, she said, "Sheriff Horne, may we continue this discussion in your office?"

"We can, but I'm not sure what I can tell you."

"No, it's about what I have to say to you."

Startled, he stared at Piper for a few seconds before turning and striding through a doorway at the back of the reception area.

She followed and closed the door behind her. A frown crossed his face.

"What's this all about?" He sat in the chair behind the desk.

When she sat, his frown deepened. Piper pulled a file folder from the backpack before setting it on the floor. "Yesterday morning, my grandmother was injured on her ranch near Sulphur Bluff. Sound familiar?"

"Yes. One of my deputies responded to the 911 call. It was an accident, so why are you here?"

"It wasn't an accident. Someone tried to murder my grandmother."

The frown disappeared as a look of astonishment flashed across his face. He leaned forward. "Just how did you come to that conclusion?"

She pulled the pictures from the folder, stood and spread them on the desk in front of him. Her finger tapped each one as she explained the relevance of the image. She finished by saying, "Someone struck my grandmother with that rock, then cut the horse's legs to make it appear the horse stumbled to its knees."

She sat back down and watched while he picked up the pictures. He gave each one a brief look before tossing it aside.

"I don't see anything here to support your accusation. These pictures could show any number of possibilities, not a murder attempt." In a condescending tone, he added, "It's my experience that whenever a tragedy such as this happens, family members try to find an explanation, a reason to justify why the accident happened."

As he spoke, her phone beeped. She pulled it from her coat pocket and glanced at the screen. It was a text from Grady, *no cellphone*. Sliding it back into her pocket, she said, "Her cellphone is also missing. According to her ranch foreman, she had it with her."

"Ms. McKay, again, there could be a simple explanation. Maybe she lost it while riding. I'm sorry about what happened to your grandmother, but I can't help you." He glanced at his watch. "I do have other matters to attend to."

"I'm not finished. There have been several thefts of Layton cattle, including a prize bull. What is the status of the investigation?"

Not bothering to hide his irritation, his voice clipped, he said, "It's still an open case."

"In other words, your investigation went nowhere."

"Ms. McKay, we're done. I really must leave." He pushed back his chair.

"Sheriff Horne, I want a copy of the theft reports and the report on the injuries to my grandmother."

"There was no report on Ms. Layton. The deputy who responded ruled it accidental. As for the cattle thefts, the investigation is still incomplete. I can't release any details."

A slow fuse of anger built that she didn't bother to disguise. "Sheriff Horne, I'm certain you are aware of the Open Records Act. I am entitled to a copy. I also insist on a full investigation of the attack on my grandmother."

"Young lady, you're not in a position to demand anything."

She had no choice. Piper pulled her badge case and flipped it open. "I'm a Deputy U.S. Marshal. I am telling you someone tried to kill my grandmother. I fully intend to investigate with or without your assistance. Please contact me when the reports are ready. I'll pick them up."

She stood and pulled a business card from the badge case. Piper tossed it on the desk, then gathered up the pictures.

Horne spluttered, "Why the hell didn't you identify yourself?"

"I hoped to gain your cooperation without making it appear as an official request. Since that didn't happen, I'll handle it."

She picked up the backpack and shoved the pictures inside.

"Who the hell is your boss?"

"Luke Purdy. He can be reached at the number on my card."

She turned, opened the door and walked out. Ms. Taylor stared at her with a wide-eyed look.

Before driving out of the parking lot, she called Luke. When he answered, she told him to expect a call from the sheriff, then asked for a trace on Jen's phone. As she headed to the hospital, the questions continued to pile up. She needed to talk to the ambulance personnel.

Since she hoped the medics were on duty, she parked near the emergency room entrance. Inside, people in various states of emotional distress milled around the waiting area. The nurse behind the desk had a beleaguered look.

When Piper walked up, she said, "If you're here about the car crash, please have a seat. I don't have any information on the status of the victims."

"No, I'm not. I'm Piper McKay, and my grandmother Jennie Layton was transported by ambulance yesterday. Can you tell me the names of the medics and how I can contact them?"

Evidently relieved it wasn't a question about the accident, she said, "I sure can." She stepped to a desk behind her and searched through a stack of folders. She pulled one out and looked inside.

"Nancy and Hugo were on the Layton run. If you follow that hallway," she motioned with her hand, "there's a door to the EMS office. They should be there."

After thanking her, Piper followed her instructions. The door labeled Hopkins County EMS opened into a large room. Several men and women lounged in chairs or on an L-shaped couch as they watched a wall-mounted television. A young man seated near the door asked if she needed help.

"I'd like to speak to Nancy and Hugo."

The medic hollered, "Nancy, someone wants to talk to you and Hugo," then nodded toward the couch. "That's Nancy."

The woman rose and walked toward her. "How can I help you?"

"Could we speak outside?"

"Sure."

Another man followed as they stepped into the hallway. Nancy looked over her shoulder. "This is Hugo."

He leaned against the wall with his arms crossed.

"I'm Deputy U.S. Marshal Piper McKay. Jennie Layton is my grandmother."

"Oh, the woman who fell off her horse. How is she?" Nancy asked.

"She's still in critical condition. I'd appreciate it if you could answer a few questions."

Nancy shot a look at Hugo, who shrugged his shoulders. "I guess it will be okay."

"When you arrived, tell me what you saw?"

"The gate was open. Grady Estes, the man who called 911, was kneeling beside Ms. Layton. She was lying facedown. Blood stained her face and the ground. Mr. Estes had stripped off his shirt and used it as a pressure pad to stop the bleeding from a wound on her head. A rock was nearby. It had blood on it."

"What did you do?"

"I had him keep the pad in place until I was ready to replace it. After I had the new one in place, Hugo slid a brace around her neck. Then he brought over the stretcher, and we moved her onto it. Once we had her in the ambulance, Hugo hauled ass back here. I wasn't certain she'd make it, but she held on."

"Did you move the rock that struck her head?"

Nancy stared at her with a puzzled look before saying, "No, we didn't. It wasn't in the way, so there wasn't a reason to move it."

"Where was the wound on the head?"

"On the back, but with the heavy loss of blood, I couldn't see the precise location. I would say, though, it was near the top of her cranium."

"Who else showed up at the scene?"

"A deputy sheriff, Evan Clarkson." A brief look of dislike crossed her face.

Piper wondered why. "Did he help?"

Nancy tossed her head and shot another look at Hugo. "No."

"Was there a reason?"

Her face closed down. "You're a cop. You know how it is. Some are better than others. He was only there for a few minutes anyway. As soon as Mr. Estes told him about the horse, he said it was obvious she fell and left."

"Were there any personal effects with her?"

"No. I checked her pockets once she was in the ambulance, but there was nothing, not even a tissue. Is something wrong? Why all the questions?"

Piper kept her response vague, knowing what she said would become grist for the local rumor mill. "Just trying to get a complete picture of what happened. My grandmother was an experienced rider, and it's hard to rationalize that her horse threw her."

The puzzled look on the faces of the two medics disappeared. "We understand," Hugo said. "Unfortunately, accidents on ranches around here are commonplace."

"If it hadn't been for what Mr. Estes did, I don't think she would still be alive," Nancy told her.

After thanking them, she walked out to her car. The medic had confirmed her suspicions. The deputy didn't investigate, and whoever struck Jen took the phone. Grady had also not told her everything, though she wasn't surprised.

A beep sounded, an incoming text from Luke. The track on Jen's cellphone was negative.

Piper stepped off the elevator and spotted Grady as she passed the doorway to the waiting room. At the nurse's station, the nurse told her there was no change, but the doctor was making his rounds.

Grady looked up from the magazine in his hand when she walked in. He laid it on the table beside him. "Any news?"

"No. Her condition hasn't changed." She slid the backpack off her shoulder and set it in a nearby chair before settling into the one next to Grady. "The new doctor, Henderson, is here."

Piper slipped her arm around Grady's shoulder and leaned closer to kiss his cheek. Before she pulled back, she gave his shoulder a hard squeeze.

Astonished, he said, "What was that for?"

"You didn't tell me everything that happened. I talked to the medics. One said you probably saved Jen's life."

Embarrassed, he turned his head. His voice raspy, he said, "Aw, hell, I just did what anyone would have done."

Piper patted his knee. She saw the glint of tears before he turned away.

He cleared his throat. "What else did the medics tell you?"

"Jen didn't have a phone on her. I also had a meeting with Sheriff Horne. He blew me off, even after I told him the phone was missing. Insists it was an accident. Since he wasn't willing to do his job, I told him I would."

A wry smile crossed Grady's face. "From what I know of the man, I bet that ticked him off."

"Yeah, it did, but I don't give a damn."

"So what now?"

"I'm staying until I can see her. When I get home, I'm taking another look at Jen's records."

When she spotted Henderson headed their way, she grabbed Grady's hand.

"Ms. McKay, Mr. Estes."

They stood to greet him. "Any change?" Piper asked.

"Yes, and for the better."

Piper's legs weakened as relief swept through her.

Henderson added, "Her vitals have improved, though she is still unconscious. If she continues to progress, I hope to move her into a private room tomorrow. I assume you would like to see her?" He glanced at Grady. "I can only allow one visitor."

"That's okay," Grady told him. "Hearing she's getting better is all I need to know."

Piper followed Henderson into the ICU.

He said, "Only a few minutes. Once Ms. Layton has been moved, you will be able to stay as long as you like."

"Thank you," Piper murmured as she stepped to the side of the bed. Her eyes anxiously studied her grandmother's face. She seemed to have a bit more color. They'd removed the tube, and she was breathing on her own.

It was all she could do to hold back the tears. She lightly stroked the back of Jen's hand, careful not to disturb the needle, while she whispered, "Come on, Jen. Wake up. I'm here, and everything is okay. Grady is outside. They won't let him in until you're in a private room. It's time to come back. Doc says you're doing good."

When Henderson tapped her shoulder, she looked up.

"Time to leave," he said.

Piper leaned over and kissed Jen's cheek. "They won't let me stay any longer, but I can come back later. I love you."

Grady waited in the hall, an anxious look on his face.

"She looks a lot better. I don't want to leave yet."

"I'll stay too. I don't have a reason to rush back to the ranch."

Throughout the rest of the day, they waited. Whenever the nurse signaled, Piper was allowed to see Jen for a few minutes. In between times, thoughts rolled in her head. The Jarvis contract was a ticking time bomb waiting to go off. She needed to talk to Jen's attorney and Grant Sheffield. When she asked about Mack Huber, Grady told her the man was a local banker. He was another person she needed to contact. Grady didn't know a Cade Tanner.

His cell phone rang. He glanced around to be sure no one could hear before he answered, "Yes."

The man on the other end said, "Everything's in place. You shouldn't have a problem."

He exclaimed, "I wouldn't count on it. Layton's still alive."

"Damn. My man was certain she was dead," the caller said.

"If she lives—"

Interrupting, the caller said, "Don't worry, I'll make sure it doesn't happen."

"That's not all. The granddaughter's making waves."

The caller snorted in derision. "So what? She won't be around long enough to cause a problem."

"She's a U.S. Marshal."

On the other end, the man sucked in his breath. "Why the hell didn't we know that?"

"You damn well know why. We discussed it. The woman's been gone for several years. Since we figured all she'd do is close out the estate, it didn't matter what she did for a living. She's been to see Horne. Claims someone tried to kill her grandmother."

The caller said, "We can't afford to have any scrutiny."

His voice hissed with anger. "Don't you think I know that! She's a problem we need to fix and fast. Make sure it looks like another accident."

The caller said, "I'll handle it."

Outside the windows, the last of the sunlight had faded away when the nurse walked into the waiting room. "I just received a call from Dr. Henderson."

At the anxious look that flashed across Piper and Grady's faces, she hastened to reassure them there was no cause for alarm. "The doctor has changed her status from critical to stable. He said you should go home."

Relieved by the good news, Piper slung the backpack over her shoulder and followed Grady into the elevator.

On the way down, he said, "I'm stopping at the grocery store. Do you need anything?"

Occupied by her thoughts, she shook her head no.

During the drive to the ranch, Piper replayed what she'd seen and heard. What possible reason could someone have to kill her grandmother? Then a horrifying thought struck. Fear raced through her. Someone wanted Jen dead, and she wasn't. Would they try again? My god, she couldn't risk it. She turned and sped back to the hospital.

Before going inside, she punched Grady's number. When he

answered, she told him she'd be late, and she'd explain later.

A look of surprise crossed the nurse's face when Piper walked up.

Her hand, holding the open badge case, extended toward the nurse. "I'm a U.S. Marshal. Jennie Layton may be in danger. I need to find out how secure the ICU is. How many doors are there?"

The surprise turned to shock as the woman stared at the badge case, then Piper. "Uh, uh," she stammered. "Just two. There's an emergency exit. If the door is opened, an alarm goes off. Why would your grandmother be in danger?"

"Her fall wasn't an accident. Is there a nurse in ICU at all times?"

"Yes. Two at night. They don't leave. During the day, there are usually three or four, depending on the number of patients. Do I need to call security?"

"I'd appreciate it."

While she waited for the nurse to make the call, she leaned on the counter, assessing where and how an attempt could be made.

The nurse hung up the phone. "The security director has already left for the day but is on his way back."

"What checks are there on anyone entering the ICU?"

"If the person isn't part of the staff, they must be monitored by a doctor or nurse. Hospital personnel must have their ID visible." Her hand gestured to the ID card with her picture pinned to her uniform.

Too restless to sit, Piper paced, pondering her options. It took about thirty minutes before an older man in a rumpled suit rushed toward her.

"Are you Marshal McKay?"

Piper showed him her credentials.

After a brief look, he said, "I'm Arthur Nelson, head of hospital security. What is going on? How could a patient be in danger?"

"My grandmother, Jennie Layton, is in ICU. Someone has already tried to kill her. There could be a second attempt. Can an unauthorized person gain access to the ICU?"

"Marshal McKay, is it possible you're overreacting? According to Ms. Layton's records, she fell from a horse and hit her head."

"An investigation is underway." She didn't think it was necessary to inform him that she was the one doing the investigating. "I can't go into the details, but someone struck her in the head. She didn't fall from a horse."

"Oh, my, I see. To answer your question, the ICU is one of the most secure areas in the hospital. Due to the critical condition of the patients, access is limited and supervised."

"I've been told that she will be moved, maybe as soon as tomorrow, to a private room. Please notify me before she is moved. I want to be here."

An impatient look crossed his face. "Of course. I'll make sure Ms. Layton's file is flagged with your request though I don't believe she's in any danger in this hospital."

He headed toward the nurse's desk, shaking his head. Piper could hear the instructions he left with the nurse.

Weary, she tossed her backpack on the seat before sliding behind the wheel. Jen was safe for tonight, but she was vulnerable once she was moved to a private room. Piper tapped the speed dial for her boss.

"I know it's late, but I do need your help. I'm concerned someone might make another attempt to kill my grandmother." She detailed what happened with the sheriff, his lack of cooperation, and her concerns about hospital security.

"I understand why you're concerned about the sheriff. Horne called. He was quite adamant he didn't want any interference from you. In polite words, I told him to stuff it. Let me get something set up, and I'll call you back. If Horne gives you any more grief, let me know. I don't mind calling the Attorney General."

Reassured, she pulled onto the street, unaware that two men watched from a truck parked on the far side of the parking lot. It wasn't until she turned onto the road leading to the ranch that she noticed a vehicle rapidly gaining ground behind her.

Ahead were several hairpin turns, and she eased off the gas. The curves had proved deadly to many drivers with a penchant for speeding.

"Idiot," Piper muttered as the driver moved into the oncoming lane to pass. She braked to let the truck get ahead of her. Instead, the driver slowed to match her speed, then swung toward her car to force her off the road.

Her foot stomped the accelerator, and she raced past him. The high-speed training she received at the academy paid off as the car hugged the curves. When she reached the straightaway, she punched it.

Even though she had the pedal to the floor, the advantage she'd gained in the curves was soon lost. The truck was about to overtake her again. So much for saving money by buying an economy-sized vehicle.

Piper lowered the window, then unbuckled the seatbelt before jerking the gun from the holster.

In the side mirror, she watched the driver move into the opposite lane. The truck was coming up fast. As it came alongside, she spotted the gun sticking out the open passenger window. It was pointed at the front of her car.

The tire! Her foot hit the brakes. Piper's hand swept up. She shoved the gun toward the window. Unable to react in time, the driver sped past. She fired, then a second time. Deafening blasts resonated inside the car.

The driver's reaction to hit the brakes sent the truck fishtailing. Piper goosed it, racing past him, narrowly avoiding the corner of the truck's rear bumper. As she sped by, she had the satisfaction of seeing a shattered rear window. Her gaze flicked between the rear-view mirror and the road. When the driver slowed and turned to head back to town, she thought, *bastards, guess you don't have the stomach for a gunfight.*

It wasn't until she neared the driveway, her body relaxed. She'd stirred the pot today, more than she realized. Parked in front of the house, she took a deep breath. Her body still throbbed from the jolt of adrenaline along with the ringing in her ears. The front door opened. Grady stood in the doorway, probably wondering why she was still sitting in her car.

Exiting, she slid the gun into the holster and grabbed the backpack.

"Been wondering when you'd get here," he said.

"I had a slight delay."

Her stomach growled when she inhaled the aroma that greeted her. "Chili!" she exclaimed. While Jen did most of the cooking, there were a few dishes she refused to make. One was chili. She always claimed hers would be a poor second to Grady's.

"It's ready to be dished up."

She dropped her backpack on a chair and stripped off her jacket. "Be right there," she said and headed to the bathroom. On the way to the kitchen, she heard her phone. It was still in her jacket, and she rushed to get it.

The caller was Luke. "Davy and Tony will be leaving here in an hour or so. I've already made reservations at a hotel. Do you want one of them to go to the hospital?"

"No. As long as Jen is in the ICU, she's safe. I can meet them at the hospital in the morning. If they prefer, they're welcome to stay here instead of a hotel."

"We discussed it, but they both felt it was better to be closer to the hospital."

"I had another problem tonight." After she explained the details, she added, "Someone doesn't like that I'm involved. Since the sheriff is the only one who has objected, I have to wonder if there is more behind his insistence it was an accident."

"You may be right. I sure as hell don't like it. Davy said he'd call once they were on the road. I'll let him know. Where are you now?"

"At home. Luke, thank you."

He grunted. "No thanks needed." The line went dead.

When she walked into the kitchen, Grady had a bowl in his hand.

"Before you start chowing down, tell me what happened."

"Someone tried to run me off the road."

The bowl smacked the table. Splatters of chili flew.

"Aw, hell, now see what I've done," he said, grabbing paper towels. "Better tell me the rest." He quickly wiped up the spills.

"Not much to tell," she said as she pulled out a chair. "A truck tried to force me off the road. When that didn't work, the passenger decided to shoot out my front tire. I popped off a couple of rounds, broke a rear window. Last I saw of the truck, the driver was high-tailing it back to Sulphur Springs."

"Are you going to report it?"

"My boss knows. He just called. After my reception from the sheriff, no, I'm not. My visit to him is what I figure triggered this. Tomorrow, I'll check some of the repair shops." Crushing several crackers in her hands, she dropped them in the bowl, dusting the crumbs from her palms.

Grady eyed the crackers in disgust. "Never saw anyone who could ruin a good bowl of chili the way you do," he quipped.

"Hell, Grady, it's the only way I can eat it without burning my gut."

The food had their attention for several minutes. After swallowing the last spoonful, Piper let out a long sigh. "It's been a long time since I had your chili. I'd forgotten just how good it is."

He picked up his bowl and utensils, setting them in the sink. "Why were you late leaving Sulphur Springs?"

"It suddenly occurred to me that if someone made one attempt to kill Jen, they might try again."

Grady's head whipped around as he stared at her with a look of shock. "Good lord, you could be right."

"It's why I called my boss. Two agents, Davy Fenwick and Tony Kline will be here in a few hours. From what I learned when I went back to the hospital, as long as Jen is in ICU, she's safe. The danger will come when she's moved to a private room. Davy and Tony will rotate shifts."

A look of relief spread across Grady's face. "Are they staying here?"

"No, at a hotel by the hospital. I'll meet them in the morning. What's on your agenda tomorrow?"

"I need to check the fences and cattle before I head to town."

She rose and picked up her dishes. "Do you need help before I leave in the morning?" After rinsing them, she dropped them into the dishwasher.

Grady said, "No. It'll only take me a couple of hours."

Physically and emotionally drained, Piper said, "I'm headed to bed. I wanted to look through the rest of Jen's records, but it'll have to wait until tomorrow."

Her first thought when she woke was Jen. She called the hospital and was told no change. The nurse also didn't know when her grandmother would be moved, though she did confirm she had instructions to call Piper. Her next call was to Davy.

His voice groggy, he said, "Is the sun even up?"

"Quit complaining. What time did you and Tony get here?"

"Um … somewhere around one a.m."

"Let's meet at the hospital cafeteria. I'll be there in an hour."

"I'll call Tony." He disconnected.

In the kitchen, she found a note. Her breakfast was in the oven. Grady was already up and at work. She quickly ate. On her way out, Piper grabbed the keys for Jen's truck. From now on, if these guys wanted to play rough, she'd have the horsepower under her.

The nurse spotted her as soon as she stepped off the elevator. "Ms. McKay." When Piper approached, she said, "I received an order from Dr. Henderson to move Ms. Layton this morning. We'll be ready in about an hour."

"Thank you. I'll be in the cafeteria. If that changes, would you please call me?"

Davy and Tony were already seated at a corner table. She

grabbed a cup of coffee and headed their way. In amazement, she eyed the plates piled high with scrambled eggs, bacon, and fried potatoes. Tony even had a side dish of biscuits and sausage gravy.

She grinned. "Did you leave anything for someone else? This isn't your last meal, you know."

"Hey! Guard duty can be strenuous. We need to keep up our strength," Davy quipped and bit into a slice of bacon.

While they chowed down, she drank her coffee and studied the two men. Both were good friends. Davy was leaner and shorter than Tony, though no less muscular. His dark hair was cut short, military-style, while Tony's longer blond strands were barely within agency regulations. The jokester in the squad, Tony always had something going. Davy had been her partner for the last three years, shortly after she joined the unit. When David Jr. was born, Davy and his wife, Susan, asked her to be David's godmother.

"Luke filled us in. Sounds like you've got a hell of a mess on your hands," Davy said before shoving another piece of bacon in his mouth.

Her lips thinned as she thought over the events of the last two days. "I sure do."

Tony said, "Talk."

She started with Jen, pulling out the pictures. She spread them across the table. As they ate and listened, they studied each one.

Davy picked up one. "You're right." He pointed to the close-up of the rock. "It was placed to make it look like she hit her head on it." He handed the picture to Tony.

Tony asked, "Do you know where she was struck on the head?"

"The medic said near the top. To be sure, I'll ask the doctor."

"What I see," Davy said, "is an injury consistent with a downward blow, not one caused by landing on the rock."

"What else?" Tony asked.

"Did Luke tell you about the attack last night?"

"Yes, but he didn't have many details." He forked up a piece of biscuit smothered with gravy.

"There's not much. The driver tried to run me off the road. When it didn't work, the passenger planned on shooting my front tire. I shot first, broke the rear window."

Davy said, "That's interesting. Someone's getting nervous. Any ideas?"

"No, but I'm going hunting. I might get lucky. Maybe someone is dumb enough to take the truck to a local repair shop. As for why, I don't have a clue, but I suspect what triggered the attack was my visit to Sheriff Horne. He was most unhappy when I left his office. Even called Luke to complain."

Davy pushed his plate aside. "You think he might be involved?"

She shrugged. "I don't know. There's something else. There have been two cattle thefts at the ranch. I asked the sheriff about his investigation. All he said was it was still an open case."

Tony finished off the last of his coffee. "I wonder how it ties into what happened to your grandmother?"

"That's the problem. I've got more questions than I do answers. The kicker is a sales contract I found in her files. A cattle broker, Lane Jarvis, purchased my grandmother's entire herd. It doesn't add up. I can't believe she would even consider it, let alone sign a contract. I'm taking it to our lawyer."

Tony asked, "Do you want us to start a background on Jarvis?"

"That would help. Give me an idea of who I'm dealing with."

She looked at her watch. "We'd better get back. They're getting ready to move her. We might have a chance to talk to the doctor."

They picked up their dirty dishes and set them on the conveyor belt before heading to the elevator. As they stepped out on the second floor, Dr. Henderson stood at the nurse's desk. As they walked up, he said, "We should be ready to move Ms. Layton in just a few minutes."

Piper said, "Would you have a few minutes to talk to us?"

"Yes, I can spare five minutes or so."

"Let's step into the waiting room."

A curious look crossed his face as he followed her. Tony and Davy were right behind him.

Piper introduced the two agents.

After shaking their hands, he said, "It's not often I'm surprised these days, but I must admit you've managed it. Is there a reason the two of you are here?"

Piper answered, "My grandmother's injury wasn't an accident. Someone tried to murder her. Tony and Davy are here to make sure someone doesn't try again."

A thoughtful look settled on his face. "I see. What prompted this idea?"

"What I found at the location where she was injured isn't consistent with a fall from a horse."

Henderson rocked on his heels. "This is exceedingly disturbing. I wondered, but Sheriff Horne assured me it was an accident."

Piper's body tensed. "You talked to the sheriff?"

"Yes. He called yesterday afternoon. Wanted to know Ms. Layton's status."

"Doctor Henderson, where exactly was the wound on Ms. Layton's head?" Davy asked.

"That is what was bothersome. If, as it was explained to me, Ms. Layton struck her head by a fall onto a rock, I would have expected the injury to have been lower on the skull, side or back, not near the top. Her injury was here," he patted his head, "near the top and slightly to the side."

"Where was the crack in the skull?" Piper asked.

He bent his head and used a finger to trace the line. "It ran from side to side near the top. A portion of the skull on top was crushed."

His description added weight to Piper's belief someone struck her grandmother with a downward blow.

"You really believe Ms. Layton is in danger?"

"Yes, sir, I do. Until I get this sorted out, I'm making sure someone doesn't try again."

The nurse stepped into the room. "Ms. McKay, we're ready."

Down the hall, both ICU doors swung open, and two attendants rolled out a bed. They gently turned it in the opposite direction from the main elevators.

"Where are we going?" Piper asked the nurse.

"There is a larger elevator at the end of this hall."

Piper stepped alongside the bed while Davy and Tony followed. Looking down, she couldn't stop the jolt of fear. Jen was so still. "Has she shown any signs of coming out of the coma?"

"Not yet," the nurse answered.

Once they wheeled the bed into the elevator, there wasn't enough room for Davy and Tony.

Davy said, "We'll be right behind you. What room number?"

The nurse told them 314.

On the third floor, the attendants pushed the bed into a room near the end of the hall. At the other end was the nurse's station.

It took a few minutes to get the bed in place, and the monitors reconnected. Once the ICU nurse and attendants left, another nurse walked in.

After introducing herself, then Tony and Davy, Piper added, "One of us will be staying with Ms. Layton."

"Will you need a cot?"

Davy spoke up. "No, the chair will do nicely."

The nurse quickly checked the monitors before picking up the clipboard hanging on the end of the bed. After making a few notations, she said, "If you need anything, just let us know." As she walked out, Grady stepped into the room.

He stopped beside the bed. "How is she?" His hand gently touched hers.

"According to the doctor, she is a lot better."

When Piper introduced the two agents, Grady eyed them with approval. "Don't rightly think anyone will get by the two of you."

Tony laughed. "We'll do our best. Piper, we flipped a coin. Davy has the night shift. I'm on days. We're going to vary our times on shift changes, just in case someone is looking for a set routine."

"That's a good idea. No one will be sure when you will arrive or leave."

"Don't worry."

"Grady, are you staying or going?"

He looked toward Jen. "I think I'll settle for a while."

The bank had just opened as she strode into the lobby. Tellers were getting into place. One looked up at her approach. "I would like to see Mack Huber," Piper told her.

"Do you have an appointment?"

"No. I'm Piper McKay, Jennie Layton's granddaughter."

"We heard about your grandmother's terrible accident. How is she doing?"

"Better, though she has a long recovery."

"That is such good news. Ms. Layton is a favorite with us. We always enjoy seeing her. I'll tell Mr. Huber you're here."

A few minutes later, a portly man with a ruddy face walked toward her. His hand extended, he greeted her. In a sympathetic tone, he said, "Ms. McKay, I'm Mack Huber. I'm so sorry to hear about your grandmother's accident. How is she?"

"Better, thank you."

A look of surprise flashed across his face. "That is good news since I'd heard Ms. Layton wasn't expected to recover. What can I do for you?"

"I have several questions." She looked at the tellers, who didn't bother to hide their avid interest.

He noticed the direction of her glance and said, "Please come to my office. Can I get you anything, coffee or a bottle of water?"

"No, thank you," she said as they walked along a short hallway, then entered an office.

A woman seated behind a desk looked up from her computer as they walked in. Huber said, "Maisie, hold all my calls."

He walked through a second door and motioned toward a chair in front of the desk. After settling into a sizeable executive-style chair, he asked, "Now, how may I help you?"

"You left a message on my grandmother's answering machine. Would you tell me the reason?"

"It was about her loan."

Puzzled, Piper said, "What loan?"

"Several weeks ago, your grandmother contacted me about a loan on the ranch. I was in the process of setting up the paperwork when I heard her bull had been stolen. Since the bull is the reason for the loan, I wanted to find out if she wanted to cancel the application."

She leaned forward. Jen had paid off the original note on the ranch several years ago and had sworn she'd never take out another. "Why did she need a loan? What did Leopold have to do with it?"

"Ms. Layton planned to market the bull's semen. The loan was for the startup cost of the equipment. I take it you didn't know anything about this?"

"No, I didn't. Did you talk to Jen?"

"As a matter of fact, I did. She called back that same day and asked me to put the loan on hold. She had a possible lead on the whereabouts of the bull. I told her I could keep it open for thirty days. Beyond that, the financial data would have to be resubmitted."

"Did she say anything else?"

"No, she didn't."

"When did you talk to her?"

A look of curiosity crossed his face. "It was the day before she was injured. Why? Is it important?"

"Probably not, but I'm trying to learn the status of her financial affairs. Any information is helpful. Would you give me a copy of the loan application and the supporting documentation?"

"No, I can't. I must have Ms. Layton's authorization."

"I have her power of attorney." She reached inside her backpack. She'd made several copies of the original. Piper handed him a copy.

A frown formed as he studied the document. "It seems to be in order, though I should have the bank's attorney examine it."

His statement caught her by surprise. "Mr. Huber, our attorney, Arnie Larson, prepared the document. His signature is on the second page. I can't see any possible reason you would have to question the legitimacy of a notarized document. Do I need to call him?"

He cleared his throat. "Oh, no. It won't be necessary. I'm probably just being overly cautious. Do I need to make a copy of this?"

"No."

He pushed a toggle switch on a speaker on his desk. "Maisie, make a copy of the pending loan documentation for Ms. Layton and bring it in."

Piper pulled her badge case from her pocket, opening it to get a business card.

"You're a federal officer?"

She looked up. "Yes. A Deputy U.S. Marshal. Is there a

problem?" she asked. She wrote her cellphone number on the back before handing it to him.

He gathered himself, saying, "Oh, no, not at all. I didn't know. From your appearance, it is rather surprising." He rotated his head as if his collar had tightened. "Your job must be exciting."

"It has its moments."

His secretary opened the door and walked in. She handed Huber an envelope, then left.

After checking the documents inside it, he stood and handed it to her. "Everything is here. If you have any questions, please let me know."

Occupied by her thoughts, Piper didn't see the worried look on the secretary's face as she walked past the woman's desk. As she left the building, she pondered Huber's odd reaction. Was he, as he put it, being overly cautious, or was there more to it?

In the truck, she pulled up a list of repair shops on her phone. Over the next couple of hours, she went from shop to shop. No one had brought in a black pickup to have the rear window replaced. Frustrated but not surprised, she thanked the manager at the last one on her list.

As she walked across the lot, a sheriff's car pulled in. Horne exited and strutted toward her. He stopped and hooked his hands around his gun belt. "I got a call about you. Said you were looking for a black pickup. Why?"

Piper's eyes gleamed with disdain. "Just doing my civic duty."

"I don't like your attitude. If this has anything to do with your grandmother, I demand to know it."

"If I decide you need to know, I'll tell you."

"You're on my turf, so you'd better watch your backside."

Piper stiffened. "Is that a threat?"

"Take it any way you want. Stay out of my investigations."

She smiled sweetly before saying, "How can I interfere in something that doesn't seem to exist?" She turned and walked to her truck. As she opened the door, she glanced over her shoulder. He watched her with a baleful look. "I still haven't received a call about those reports I asked for."

He turned and stomped to his car.

She had to wonder who called him. Not once, at any of the repair shops, had she identified herself as a U.S. Marshal. So, why the interest?

ir, tainted by the pungent stink of manure, smacked Piper in the face as she stepped out of the truck. Livestock yards were the worst. Like the stench of blood, once you smelled it, you never forgot.

Sheffield's Livestock Auction, the largest sale barn in Hopkin's County, ran thousands of animals yearly through the auctions. Today, the parking lot was near empty, though many pens were filled with cattle. The owner, Grant Sheffield, a longtime friend of Jen and Grady, had left a message on Jen's answering machine.

Seated behind a dinged and scratched metal desk, Grant's low voice rumbled in disgust as he stared at his computer. Piper rapped on the doorjamb. His head swiveled around, and a flash of surprise crossed his face.

"Dang me if it isn't Piper McKay!" He popped out of his chair, rushed around the desk, and grabbed her in one of his infamous bear hugs.

It had been a couple of years since she'd seen him. The mustache still drooped around his mouth, but most of his hair was gone, and his belly was a bit larger.

Laughing, she pushed back to give him a kiss on the cheek. "Grant, you haven't changed one iota. Still hugging the ladies."

"Always, darling, always."

She motioned toward the computer. "Having problems?"

A grimace crossed his face. "Aw, it's all these damn forms. Every time a new one comes out, it's more complicated than the last. Say, I heard about Jennie. Terrible, just terrible. How is she?"

Piper's smile slipped away. "I came close to losing her, and she's still not out of the woods, though her condition has improved."

"How the hell did she get thrown? Something I never expected could happen to her. She's too good of a rider."

"I know. I'm still trying to sort it all out."

"I remember when you were just a kid, running around and getting under everyone's feet. Never would have believed you'd turn into a federal officer. Jennie's mighty proud of you."

Tears sparkled in her eyes. "Thanks, Grant."

"Hey now, didn't mean to get all emotional here. How about a cup of coffee? Got a fresh pot going."

"I'll pass, but thanks."

"Have a seat. What brings you my way today? Not that I'm not glad to see you."

"I'm trying to get a handle on Jen's affairs. I found you'd left a message on her answering machine and wanted to find out why."

"I did, but she never called back. It was just a follow-up about the flyer for Leopold. Jennie dropped one off, asked that I send it out on the livestock auction network. I was letting her know it had been sent."

"Do you have a copy? I don't remember seeing one in her files."

"Sure. I made several copies to hand out." He opened a desk drawer and pulled out a sheet of paper. "Damn shame, best bull in the county, maybe in all of Texas." He reached across the desk to hand it to her.

Her eyes flicked over it, widening in astonishment. "A ten thousand dollar reward! That should get someone's attention. This mentions a DNA profile." She folded it and slipped it into the backpack.

"Jennie said she had a DNA report and planned to register it. I was surprised. Several times, we talked about getting the bull's DNA profile, but she never seemed to have any interest."

"I'll need to find it then, just in case I get a call."

She pulled out a business card. On the back, she jotted down her cellphone number before handing it to him. He dropped it into a tray on his desk.

"There's an auction tomorrow. If you have time, stop by. You'll probably see a few old friends in the crowd. Might pick up some information."

She reached down, picking up the backpack. "If I get a chance, I will." She rose. "I'll get out of your way. Thanks for taking a few minutes." After another hug, she strolled outside.

While she'd talked to Grant, activity in the parking lot had picked up. Trucks waited to unload their cattle. One was backed up to the ramp. On each side of the trailer, men, dusty and disheveled, used paddles and prods to keep the cattle moving onto the ramp.

The sight brought back memories as Piper stopped to watch.

Straddled atop the fence, a cowhand holding a clipboard closely scrutinized each animal, looking for signs of disease as it passed. Piper knew the man also counted them.

Once the last one trotted out, the driver pulled forward to let the men at the back close and lock the trailer gate. Herded into the wide alley connecting the pens, a man on horseback kept them moving.

The cowhand jumped down as the driver walked up. After a brief conversation, the man tore off a sheet of paper and handed it to the driver, who headed to the sales office.

He hung the clipboard on the fence post and stripped off his gloves. He spun, looking around as if he sensed someone watched. Whip-cord lean, blue jeans molded his narrow hips and long legs. A t-shirt, tucked into the jeans, stretched across his impressive chest muscles. A belt buckle, the size of a small dinner plate and engraved with the Texas flag, adorned the leather belt. Without the scuffed boots, he'd easily top out at about six-foot-two.

Under the brim of a frayed cowboy hat, grey eyes gleamed. The rough stubble of his beard emphasized a stubborn jaw and chiseled cheekbones.

As she stared, his gaze raked her. Lips twitched into an insolent smile. He shoved his gloves in his back pocket, then reached for his hat. While he slapped it against his thigh, the wind whipped his long black hair.

The ping of an incoming text brought her to her senses. What the hell was she thinking, standing here like a love-struck teenager gawking at the man? Shaking her head in disbelief, she turned and walked toward her truck. A glance at the message pushed any thought of the cowhand out of her mind. *Jennie headed for CT scan.*

The bed was gone when she rushed into Jen's room. From a circle of chairs, three sets of eyes stared at her.

"What happened?"

Grady shook his head. "I'm not sure. One of the monitors started beeping. The nurse ran in. A few minutes later, they wheeled her out. When the nurse came back, she said the doctor ordered a CT scan. It would take a while." His foot nudged an empty chair. "Sit."

She did, and with a deep breath, pushed back on the fear, forcing herself to focus on what she'd learned.

Davy helped when he asked, "Did you find out anything?"

"I didn't find the truck, but I didn't expect to. Though I had another interesting encounter with Horne. He showed up as I was leaving the last place on my list. Someone called him. I'd sure like to know who since I never identified myself as law enforcement."

Tony leaned back in his chair, stretched out his long legs, crossing them at the ankles. "What did you tell them?"

"I kept it vague, information about an accident. But that's not the only piece of news."

She relayed what she discovered at the bank. "Grady, did Jen mention a loan?"

"She's been looking into the artificial insemination procedures. The equipment is expensive, but I didn't know she planned to get a loan."

"According to Huber, after Leopold was stolen, she told him to put the loan on hold, that she had a lead about where Leopold might be found. Know anything about it?"

"Not a clue."

"Any thoughts on how she might have come up with something?"

"It could have been anywhere. Jennie seldom missed a sale at the auction. She was always stopping by to visit other ranchers."

As much as she hated to broach the subject, she had to find out if Grady knew about the contract. She leaned forward, her arms rested on her knees. "Did you know about a second contract with Jarvis?"

He shook his head. "No. Hell, Piper, you know your grandmother. Sometimes, she's tighter than bark on a tree when it comes to her affairs."

"I know. She never told me about any of this. Jen sold the herd to him."

Bewildered, the man scrubbed a hand across his face. "I don't believe it. She'd never sell. The herd is the lifeblood of the ranch."

"It's a consignment sale, no money until he sells the herd, but he owns the cattle."

His protest was loud and forceful. "No! It's not possible. Jennie wouldn't do it."

"Is Arnie Larson still our attorney?"

"Yeah, why?"

"I want to discuss a restraining order on the Jarvis contract."

Grady whistled. "I always knew you were a smart one."

Davy, who had quietly listened, piped up. "Just how valuable is your grandmother's ranch?"

Piper told him, "Three million or so when you add the land, buildings, and herd. Grady, what do you figure Leopold is worth?"

"About 200,000."

"My god, 200,000 dollars for a damn cow!" Tony exclaimed.

Grady chuckled. "No, not a cow, a prize bull."

She looked at Tony and Davy. "Did you find anything on Jarvis?"

Davy answered, "Enough that I called Luke. On paper, Jarvis appears to be on the up and up. He buys and sells cattle and markets a service to manage the herds for ranchers. What disturbed me was what I found. A Colorado rancher lodged a complaint with the local cattlemen's association. A couple of weeks later, he's killed in a car accident. The complaint was dropped."

"I'll pass that on to the attorney. It might be something he can use. Grady, what do you know about the DNA report?"

"Where did you hear about that?"

"Grant Sheffield."

"Where'd you run into him?"

"I stopped by the auction house to find out why he called Jen. He gave me a copy of the reward notice. It mentioned a DNA profile."

Grady said, "A few weeks before Leopold was stolen, we took a sample of his blood and sent it off to a lab in Austin. Jennie was pretty excited when she got the report back."

"So far, I haven't found any DNA paperwork."

"There is a file labeled Leopold. It's probably there."

"I don't remember seeing it. I'll look for it this evening."

"What about the contract?" Davy asked.

"I've got it in a plastic bag. I plan to send it to Luke. I want it checked for prints and for someone to take a look at her signature. It may have been forged."

"Good idea," Davy said.

The door opened, and Henderson walked in, his expression serious. After a quick glance at the three men, he focused on Piper. "I was hoping you'd be here. Fluid is building in Ms. Layton's brain. I operated and put in a shunt to drain the fluid. I'm going to keep her in ICU for a few hours before we bring her back here."

"Is she still in a coma?" Piper asked.

"Yes, though I am hopeful once the pressure on the brain has subsided, she will regain consciousness." At the worried look on her face, Henderson added, "While this seems to be a setback, it's not unexpected with a severe head injury. I will call you if anything changes."

After the doctor left, Davy stood. "I've got the night shift, so I'll head to ICU. Why don't the rest of you leave? I'll keep you posted."

Tony said, "I'll keep you company for a few hours before I head to the hotel."

"I'll talk to the two of you tomorrow," Piper said.

In the parking lot, Grady told her, "I'm going to be right behind you. No one's going to try to run you off the road tonight."

She patted his shoulder and grinned. "Yes, sir. Got it."

The drive back was uneventful, giving Piper plenty of time to think. Parking in front of the house, she leaned her head back for a few minutes. It seemed she'd been stuck in high gear since her boss told her Grady had called. Another long evening was ahead as she planned to have another go at Jen's records.

At the tap on the window, she opened the door.

"You okay?" Grady asked.

"Yes, just thinking."

"Well, set it aside for the time being. Let's get something to eat. Then you can get back to it. Got enough chili left to make another meal, that is, if you think you can handle it."

"Bet your bottom dollar I can," she quipped back.

"Come on then. Quit dithering out here."

After they cleaned up the kitchen, Piper called the hospital. No change in Jen's condition, still in ICU. She thought about calling Davy, but if he had anything to tell her, he'd call.

Grady had made a fresh pot of coffee. Since Piper planned on spending the rest of the evening in the office, he figured she'd be up late. Piper set the cup on the desk and settled into the chair.

She picked up the bank envelope she tossed on the desk when she got home. Pulling out the loan papers, Piper quickly scanned the documents. Nothing out of the ordinary popped out at her, but what did concern her was that she hadn't found Jen's copy of the loan papers. Not unless it was in the large file cabinet.

Piper dropped them in a tray on the desk. A couple of bills had arrived. From the center drawer, she removed the business check ledger. After writing the checks, she laid them aside for Grady to sign. Jen had added him to the account several years back. Before closing it, she entered the amounts in the transaction section. Idly, she glanced at the deposits. Something pinged in her mind, a comment Grady made. It took a few minutes before she realized what it was. There wasn't a check from Jarvis.

If Jen had signed another contract, it was probably in the file for cattle sales. After the mind-boggling discovery of the Jarvis contract, Piper hadn't gone through the rest of the documents. Sure enough, she found another one from Jarvis Livestock for ten head of cattle. It was dated about six weeks ago. Jen had written a date and $2000 per head on the sticky note stuck to the front. Evidently, the man didn't waste any time. He'd sold the cattle about two weeks later.

She quickly scanned the terms. Basically, it stipulated Lane Jarvis would sell ten head of cattle, with a reduced commission of 2%. Jen had the final authority on the sales price. The date of the sale was two days before the date on the second contract.

"Grady," she hollered. "You got a minute?"

He walked in, drying his hands on a dishcloth. "What do you need?"

"You said something about Jen not getting a check for the sale of the cattle. Is there a pile of mail somewhere I don't have?"

He motioned to a tray on the desk. "That's where all the mail goes."

"I've looked there. There is no record in the checkbook she got the payment. When did Jarvis pick them up?"

A thoughtful look crossed his face. He finally said, "Somewhere around four weeks ago. I bet she made a note of it in her calendar."

Piper found it under a stack of papers. She flipped pages until she found the entry. "You're right. Four weeks ago, she approved the sale for $2000 per head, and Jarvis picked up the cattle. He still owes her the money."

"Did you find the file on Leopold?"

"I haven't looked for it yet."

He stepped to the large four-drawer file cabinet near the desk. "It's in the top drawer. It's so big, you can't miss it." He pulled out the drawer. A look of shock crossed his face. "It's gone!" He looked at Piper. "Registration papers, award certificates, veterinarian records, calving data, genealogy, everything is gone!"

"When did you last see it?"

He thought. "She had it out the day before she was attacked. She was working on the registration for the DNA results. It's gone too."

"Then someone did break into the house. I checked all the files in the desk drawers the night I got here. It's when I found the contract. While I didn't go through any in the file cabinet, I did look inside. I sure didn't see a file like you described. Jen's file on the bank loan is also missing. How did they get in?"

"Jennie's keys!" Grady exclaimed. "Why didn't I think of it before?"

"What keys?"

"Both of us always carry a set when we're out on the range. It's not just the house. It's the keys for all the locks."

"They're missing along with her phone. The locks will have to be changed."

"I'll have someone here tomorrow. As for tonight, I'm bunking in the house."

"Grady, it isn't necessary."

A look of determination settled on his face. "Maybe not, but I'm not taking any chances. Don't forget someone tried to kill you too."

Knowing it was a waste of time to argue with him, Piper turned her attention back to the missing file. "Where is the lab located? I'll contact them to get another copy."

"Ringtail Labs outside of Austin. They specialize in animal DNA reports. I'll get my gear and be back in a few minutes."

The next time she saw him, Grady was headed to the spare bedroom with a semi-automatic in one hand, a shotgun in the other. She guessed it was his definition of gear.

It was shift change. A low buzz of voices filled the air as medical personnel crowded the halls. The elevator dinged. Piper stepped inside. The third-floor button was already lit. When the door opened, several people followed her out.

Before she left the ranch, Davy had sent a text that Jen was back in her room. As she walked in, he looked up from the laptop on the table next to the chair.

"I was expecting Tony."

"I'm your relief until he gets here." She stepped to the side of the bed. What little color Jen had regained was gone, her face pasty white. Her chest barely moved. "Has the doctor been by?"

"Not yet," Davy told her.

Not bothering to disguise her worry as she settled in a chair to watch Jen, Piper leaned closer to Davy. In a low voice, she said, "Someone broke into the house," then explained about the missing files and keys.

"Why would someone steal the files? It doesn't make sense."

"I wish I knew. Go get some sleep. We can talk about this later."

He closed his computer, then placed it in his computer bag. "See you."

From the file folder in her backpack, she took out the pictures. While she kept an eye on Jen, she slowly studied each one, searching for something she missed. Nothing. She laid them aside and pulled out her notebook. Inside was the note she'd found in Jen's purse. *Might as well call and find out who this guy is,* she thought.

She quickly tapped the numbers into the phone.

A woman answered, "Texas & Southwestern Cattle Raisers Association." Taken aback, Piper hesitated, then said, "I'd like to speak with Cade Tanner."

"I'm sorry, but he is out of the office. May I take a message?"

"Yes. Have him call U.S. Marshal Piper McKay," she said, rattling off her number. "Do you have any idea when I might expect a call?"

"No, I'm sorry, I don't."

"What is his position at the association?"

Her voice sounded surprised. "Cade Tanner is a Special Ranger. Is there anything else?"

"No, thank you."

A thoughtful air settled over her face as Piper slid the phone into her pocket. This was an unexpected twist, a Special Ranger. While she'd never had any dealings with them, she was familiar with their function. On the same level as Texas Rangers, Special Rangers investigated crimes dealing with livestock and equipment. Why would Jen have his number? Was he the source of the lead on the bull?

Her next call was to the DNA lab, but no one answered. She left a message on the automated recording.

The door opened. Henderson's voice broke into her musings. "Marshal McKay, good morning. I didn't expect to see you here."

Piper jumped to her feet as he stepped to the side of the bed. He checked the monitors, then flashed a small light into Jen's eyes before removing the chart at the end of the bed. Once he finished making notations, he turned toward her.

"Your grandmother is reacting well to the shunt. We did another CT scan before she left ICU, and I am pleased with what I saw."

"Has she come out of the coma at all?"

"Not yet, but I am hopeful it won't be too long."

The door opened, and Tony walked in. He greeted the doctor and stepped toward the chair.

"Looks like your reinforcement has arrived. I'll check on her later this afternoon." He nodded to the two of them as he left.

Tony set his coffee cup on the table. "I saw Davy in the parking lot. He told me you were here. He also said you had an update."

As she gathered up her files, she brought him up to speed. "Once the locks are changed, Grady will probably stop by."

"Where are you headed?" he asked.

"To see an attorney."

Arnie Larson's office was in a small building near downtown. She parked on the street, dropped several quarters into the parking meter, then strode inside. As a child, she'd been to his office a few times. She remembered sitting in the corner reading a book while she waited for Jen. Before they left, Arnie would say hello and hand her a lollipop.

The woman seated behind a desk greeted her. When she identified herself, the woman said, "I'm Hester Mitchell. How's Jennie doing? We couldn't believe it when we heard about her accident."

"She's improving. I'm hoping Arnie might have a few minutes."

"I'll let him know you're here."

She picked up her phone. "Ms. McKay would like to see you."

A man strode out of an office in the short hallway. His round face and eyes lit up when he saw her. "Piper, my gosh, it's good to see you. It's been a few years. Come on back to my office. Would you like a cup of coffee or maybe tea? I have both."

"I'll take the coffee."

"Cream, sugar?" Hester asked.

Piper told her, "No, just black."

"Hester, make it two cups."

At the look of disapproval on the woman's face, he added, "I know. I've already had my quota for the day, but I think we can forgo the restrictions this time."

Piper followed him into a small office as he explained, "The doctor has limited my caffeine intake along with several other dietary restrictions. It's a pain in the ass. Please, have a seat and tell me how Jennie is doing. Is she able to have visitors yet?"

Hester walked in, setting two mugs on the table. "Anything else?"

"No, that should do it, though please close the door."

Before answering his question, Piper took a sip of the hot brew while she waited for Hester to leave. "She's still in a coma."

"An unbelievable accident," he said.

"That's the problem, Arnie. It wasn't an accident. Someone tried to murder her."

Stunned, he sat back in his chair. "I'd say you're kidding, but coming from a U.S. Marshal, I seriously doubt you'd throw out that type of accusation without proof."

She pulled the file folder from her backpack, removed the photos she'd taken and handed them to him. As he perused them, she explained what she'd learned.

"Have you given this to Sheriff Horne?"

"Some of it. When I talked to him, Horne wasn't receptive to reopening the case. Insists it was an accident. His attitude and lack of investigation are disturbing. Why didn't he find the same evidence I did?"

"Some of the ranchers around here aren't happy with him either.

There's been a number of cattle thefts. What are you planning on doing with this information?"

"Right now, I'm investigating. Two more marshals arrived last night. They're handling the guard duty. I'm afraid whoever tried to kill Jen will try again."

"A wise precaution. What do you need from me?"

"Do you know Lane Jarvis?"

"I've met him a few times, though, between you, me, and the gate post, I don't have much use for the man."

Piper handed him a copy of the sales contract. "I found this in Jen's files after she was attacked."

As he read, a look of disbelief grew. "Your grandmother never signed a contract that she didn't clear with me first. I don't understand."

"I'm not sure Jen did sign it. She had her keys with her. They are missing along with her phone. I believe someone broke into the house and planted that contract."

"This is unbelievable!"

"I sent the original along with another document with Jen's signature to my boss in Oklahoma City. I want to know whose prints are on it and if the signature was forged. Can I get a restraining order against Jarvis to stop the sale of the cattle?"

Before he answered, he scanned the document again. "Not unless you have proof she didn't sign this. The terms are ironclad. Jarvis owns the herd. Jennie is responsible for their upkeep until such time as Jarvis sells the cattle. All she gets is thirty percent of the sale price. This is nothing short of highway robbery. Can I keep this?"

"Yes."

"How soon do you think you will hear back on your analysis of the contract?"

"Hopefully tomorrow or the next day."

"I'll prepare a motion and have it ready to file with the court. I'll need a notarized affidavit attesting to the evidence. I'm sure you're aware that if you can't prove the contract is a forgery, Jennie's denial won't carry any weight in court. It's her word against his, and he has a signed contract."

"I know. Somehow, I have to find the proof. You mentioned Jen never signed a contract you didn't approve. Did you see the one she signed about six weeks ago with Jarvis? It was for the sale of ten head."

"Yes. She sent it to me. Why?"

"He hasn't paid for the cattle. But Jarvis sold them for $2,000 per head, and he picked them up."

"Do you want me to take action on the default of the payment?"

"Not yet."

He cleared his throat. "You've got another major problem, the loss clause in the contract, your missing cattle, and Leopold."

A bleak look crossed her face. "If I've read it right and Jarvis activates the loss clause, it could bankrupt Jen."

"Were the cattle and Leopold stolen before or after the date of this contract?"

"According to Grady, after. I asked Horne for copies of the reports. So far, he's refusing to provide them."

He pointed to a section on the page in front of him. "The contract stipulates a value of one million dollars for Leopold and a half-million for 200 head of cattle. The bull is valuable, though not to the tune of one million bucks."

He pulled a calculator from the center drawer. "Since Jarvis gets seventy percent from the sale of the cattle, if there's any loss, Jennie is liable for the seventy percent. Right now, she owes him $700,000 for the bull unless it's recovered. How many head were stolen?"

Piper said, "Fourteen."

He tapped the calculator. "That adds another $24,500. You lose anymore, it's going to add up. The entire herd would amount to $350,000. Between the herd and Leopold, Jennie could end up owing Jarvis over a million dollars."

A sick feeling rolled through her. "Jen doesn't have that kind of money. She'd be forced to sell the ranch. That's not all. Whoever left that contract stole the documentation on Leopold."

"Why would someone steal the documentation? They can't use it."

"Right now, I don't know. But Jen may have found something." She told him about her visit to the bank, the loan, and Jen's comment about a lead on the bull's whereabouts. "Did you know about her artificial insemination project?"

"Yes. She talked to me about it several weeks ago. Jennie needed a sales contract. At the time, she didn't have the DNA results."

"The DNA report is missing too. I'm waiting on a call from the lab. They should be able to provide a duplicate."

"I can help with the missing file. I have a copy of the pertinent documents for Leopold. Jen thought it wise that I have a set considering the value of the bull."

He stood and walked out. When he came back, he said, "Hester is making a copy for you."

A look of relief crossed her face, one less worry.

He reached for one of the business cards in a holder on the desk. Flipping it over, he wrote on the back. "This is my cellphone and home phone number. Call if you need help. It doesn't matter what time of day or night." He handed her the card. "In all my years as an attorney in this town, this is beyond belief."

Piper slid the card into a pocket on the backpack, then stuffed the file folder inside the bag. "Thank you, Arnie."

On the way out, Hester handed her two large stuffed envelopes.

"This is everything Jennie gave us on Leopold."

In the truck, Piper leaned her head back. Devastated by what she'd learned, her thoughts were a tangled mass of fear that threatened to overwhelm her. Somewhere, in the depths of her mind, she pulled on her innate sense of determination. Right now, she was all that stood between her grandmother and the loss that would destroy her. She took a deep breath and stiffened her spine and shoulders. She resolved that no matter what she had to do, she wouldn't let it happen.

Piper pulled out her phone. The lab still hadn't returned her call. She tried again, this time a man answered. After identifying herself, she explained why she was calling.

He transferred her to another number. When a woman answered, Piper repeated the reason for her call.

Her tone flustered, the woman said, "I don't know if I can get you a copy. We had a fire at the lab. A lot of our records were destroyed."

A chill raced over Piper. "When did this happen?"

"Night before last."

"Do you know what caused it?'

"Initially, the fire inspector thought it was faulty wiring, but now he suspects arson. It seems unbelievable. Why would someone destroy our lab?"

"Is the lab where all the DNA records are kept?"

"Yes, not only the samples but also the submission documents. Once the analysis is complete, the results and documents are scanned into the client's file on the computer. I'm sure Ms. Layton's sample and the original documents were destroyed. What I need to check is the status of her client file."

"I'm not sure I'm following you."

"We have a secondary system that is housed in our

administrative office. Every two weeks, the laboratory system uploads the completed client files to the administrative system. If Ms. Layton's file wasn't transferred, the report is gone. This will take a few minutes. Do you want to hold, or I can call you back?"

"I'll hold, please." Piper wasn't taking any chances on the woman getting distracted and forgetting to call her back.

Impatient, fingers tapped the steering wheel to the beat of the music that blared over the phone. She didn't like coincidences, and red flags smothered this one. It didn't take much of a stretch of her imagination to connect the theft of Leopold's file to the destruction of the lab that ran the DNA analysis.

"Ms. McKay, we do have Ms. Layton's client file with the analysis."

"Could you fax me a copy?"

"Sure, give me the fax number."

Piper suddenly realized she hadn't seen a fax machine in Jen's office. "Hold on." She pulled out Larson's business card and gave the fax number to the woman.

"You should have it in just a few minutes. Do you want me to mail another hard copy?"

"Yes. Please send it to the Layton Ranch."

After disconnecting, she stepped out of the truck and walked into Larson's office. Hester looked up.

"I have a fax coming to your number."

A ring sounded. "That's probably it now." She swiveled her chair, reaching toward the machine behind her. Once it stopped, she collected several sheets of paper.

"Please make a copy for Arnie," Piper said. "Is it alright if I talk to him again?"

"You bet. Go on in."

Piper tapped the doorjamb. When he looked up, she said, "I just talked to a representative at the DNA lab. Night before last, a fire destroyed the lab. The blood sample from Leopold and Jen's original submission documents are gone, but they did have a copy of the report. I had it faxed here. Hester is making a copy for your records."

Arnie said, "Convenient. Leopold's file goes missing, and now the lab is destroyed. I don't like it."

"Neither do I. It sounds like someone is trying to erase Leopold's identity, but why?"

On her way out, she glanced at her watch. There was plenty of time before the start of the auction to make a stop at Jarvis' office.

Located on the opposite side of town, his office was in a new business area. On one end of the block was Starbucks. On the other end, a discreet sign over the front door read—*Jarvis Livestock*.

The door opened into an upscale interior that was a dramatic contrast to Arnie's office. Her boots sunk into the thick pile carpet. Leather chairs graced the waiting room. Against one wall, a coffee bar with a high-end Keurig machine offered a variety of coffee blends. Soft music emanated from overhead speakers.

The receptionist, seated behind a heavy, wood-grained desk, certainly enhanced the room's elegant ambiance. Attired in a deep blue suit, lace gathered at her neckline, and her blond hair was wound into a chignon at the nape of her neck. Discreet makeup emphasized her eyes, cheekbones, and lips. Even her long fingernails only had a hint of color.

"May I help you?" she asked, even as her patronizing gaze skimmed over Piper, taking in the scuffed boots, faded jeans, flannel shirt, and canvas jacket.

Piper smiled as she approached. "I would like to speak with Lane Jarvis."

"Do you have an appointment?" she asked.

You know damn well I don't, Piper thought. "No."

"You will need to make an appointment. Mr. Jarvis is unavailable."

Piper said, "Oh, I think he will see me. Tell him Piper McKay, Jennie Layton's granddaughter, is here."

She hesitated, then rose.

Piper walked to one of the chairs and sat, sinking into the soft leather.

From across the room, the woman said, "Mr. Jarvis will see you."

She led Piper down a hallway to an office twice the size of Arnie's and even more plush than the front lobby. A magnificent set of polished Texas longhorns, the tips bronzed, hung on the wall behind a desk. Texas landscapes, and she suspected they weren't prints, adorned the other walls.

Lane Jarvis stood and stepped around the desk to greet her. Brushed back from a broad brow, heavily gelled dark hair glistened under the overhead lights. From her research, she knew he was fifty-four years old. His tanned complexion, starched white shirt, sharply creased blue jeans, snakeskin boots and matching belt fit the persona of a successful Texas rancher—at least, his perception. She wasn't impressed, though Piper hid her instant dislike.

His voice boomed, and he extended his hand. "Ms. McKay. I am so delighted to meet you. May I call you Piper? How is your grandmother doing? What a terrible accident. Please have a seat."

Sinking into another leather chair, she set her backpack at her feet. "She's doing much better."

"Really? I'd heard otherwise, but that's wonderful news."

"Just proves, don't believe everything you hear."

A hardy laugh erupted. "So true, so true."

She noticed he didn't make an offer of coffee. Despite his bombastic attitude, his eyes had a guarded look.

"I'd heard you're a U.S. Marshal. Odd. A pretty young thing like you choosing such a difficult profession."

She leaned back and folded her hands in her lap. None of the distaste she felt showed, though Jarvis' blatant chauvinistic attitude gave her an idea. If he believed she was clueless about running a ranch, he might be more forthcoming.

"I assume you're here because of my contract with Ms. Layton?"

"Yes. I was quite surprised when I found it."

"She hadn't told you?"

"No. I don't get home often. I have a few questions if you have the time to answer them."

"Of course, I do."

"The contract stipulates the Layton ranch is responsible for the cattle's upkeep. There is no time limitation in the contract. When do you expect to sell the herd?"

"I discussed that very issue with Ms. Layton. As uncertain as the cattle market is these days, I don't want to sell the herd until I know I can get top dollar. Ms. Layton assured me it wasn't a problem. Since she is in the hospital, I hope it hasn't become an issue."

"Until my grandmother can manage her affairs, I'm responsible. I have her power of attorney."

Surprise flashed in his eyes. Had she not been watching closely, Piper would have missed it. She'd bet Jarvis hadn't planned on that complication.

"In the years since I moved away, a lot has changed. I'm attempting to get a handle on the details."

"Well, of course." He relaxed. The wary look vanished, replaced by one of disdain. "I fully understand. A ranch this size is a big responsibility."

Her tone slightly disconcerted, she said, "I need to order feed, hay … I'm sure you know more than I do," pandering to his inflated ego.

A wolfish grin crossed his face. "Now, I don't want you to worry your pretty little head about any of this. I'll stop by later this week and go over the contract in detail. By the time we finish, I'm sure you won't have any questions. I want you to be absolutely comfortable with the arrangement so you can concentrate on your grandmother."

As difficult as it was, she managed to keep the smile on her face and not grit her teeth. "Thank you, Mr. Jarvis. I don't suppose you've heard anything about our bull that was stolen?"

"Please, it's Lane. No, I'm afraid I can't give you any good news about Leopold. Another piece of bad luck for your grandmother. I remember how upset she was when she told me what happened. You do understand that the bull and the other stolen cattle are part of the contract?"

She played dumb. "I was under the impression the cattle were stolen before the contract was signed."

"No. The thefts happened after your grandmother signed the contract, which means the herd's value has decreased. If you haven't reviewed the terms, you might wish to do so."

"Good lord, can this get any worse?"

"Let's hope not," he said with a gracious tone. "Since I haven't sold the herd, I have held off on activating the loss clause and demanding the money your grandmother owes me."

Resisting the urge to kick every one of his pearly white teeth down his throat, Piper said, "A wise precaution."

"Oh?"

"Yes. I am confident the stolen cattle will be recovered."

His eyes turned cold. Gone was the verbose attitude.

"Considering my interest in the matter, I've spoken several times with Sheriff Horne. He hasn't reported any progress." A toothy grin appeared. "If the sheriff hasn't had any luck, I seriously doubt there is any chance the cattle will be recovered."

"But … I'm not the sheriff, am I?" Her jaw ached from smiling. "There is another matter. In going through my grandmother's records, I discovered she's never received your check. The one for the sale of ten head of her cattle."

"Hmm … I do believe I mailed a check." He opened a drawer on the side of the desk and drew out a large checkbook. "Let's see." He flipped pages. "Ah, yes. Here it is. Ten days ago, I sent her a check."

"May I see that?"

"No, I'm sorry. Other transactions are private."

"Can you tell me if the check cleared your account?"

"I couldn't say until I've had a chance to check my account activity."

Her anger grew, and she fought to keep her self-control.

"I'd appreciate any help you could provide. It should be an easy matter to resolve. My attorney is handling some of her affairs. If you can't reach me, you can contact him, Arnie Larson. I'm sure you know him."

"We've met. As soon as I know, I'll call you. How long do you plan on staying?"

"I'm not sure. My grandmother still has a long recovery, and I'm investigating how she was injured."

"I thought her horse threw her."

"There is some question about it, but I can't discuss the details." She smiled. "I'm sure you understand."

She picked up the backpack and walked out. Seething with

anger, she managed to keep the smile plastered on her face until she was out the door and out of sight of the windows.

She was certain that if she'd had a chance to look at his damn checkbook, she wouldn't have seen a check. Lane Jarvis was in up to his trimmed eyebrows in whatever was going on.

beehive of activity, filled with people, horses, and cattle, the scene was a slice of time from a bygone era, an aura of the old West.

No fancy shirts, designer blue jeans, or flashy boots here. Instead, heavy-duty shirts, canvas jackets, worn jeans or overalls, and scuffed boots were the norm. In many back pockets, leather work gloves protruded.

Piper wandered among the buyers and sellers who milled around the cattle pens. The buyers were easy to spot. A bid card stuck in a pocket, a buyer's tally sheet and pencil in hand, they studied the animals making notes for prospective bids. Judging by the number of animals, the bidding would be fast. A buyer had to be prepared.

She knew most of the buyers represented the meat companies. Ranchers would be looking for animals to improve or increase their herd. It wasn't all cattle. She spotted a few horses.

Walking inside, her pulse quickened. There was a buzz in the air, a keenness she'd never encountered anywhere else. Bidding was an art, a game of knowing when to up the bid, when to fold. Unlike a card game, it was a game of business. Whether sellers or buyers, what happened in the sales ring had very real consequences for the ranchers. It could make the difference between ending the year in the red or in the black.

In front of the sales ring, tiered rows of bench seats formed a half-circle. Behind the ring, Grant was seated at a raised table. When he spotted her, he waved.

She waved back, then climbed the stairs to a spot about midway up the rows of seats. As she gazed around, an uneasy sensation tickled her nape.

A voice rang out. "Piper, Piper McKay!"

Turning, she spotted Henry Miller, a local rancher, rushing up the steps.

"Dang girl, how long has it been since I've seen you?"

"A couple of years or more, Henry. It's good to see you again." The Miller ranch was only a few miles down the road from her grandmother's place. In the excitement of greeting an old friend, the uneasiness slid away.

He stood near the sales ring and had spotted her the moment she walked in. How could anyone miss seeing her? At least any red-blooded male. A single long braid of golden brown hair swung down her back. Under the brim of a worn cowboy hat, high cheek-bones accented her almond-shaped dark eyes. After his first glimpse of her the day before, he decided her face, while not classi-cally beautiful, was more—what he'd term captivating. From her attire, canvas jacket, boots and jeans, she was obviously comforta-ble in this setting.

When Sheffield energetically waved, he figured she must be a local girl until he heard Miller's booming voice. Evidently, the woman had left town. She didn't appear to be a buyer, so what was she doing here? He had a name. It wouldn't take long to find out.

Sheffield rang his bell, the signal the auction was about to start.

Clusters of people broke up as they took their seats. For now, he shoved his curiosity aside. Frankie Hillard, another handler, opened the gate on the opposite side, and the first batch of cattle rushed into the sales ring.

From her perch above the ring, Piper watched the action. Grant went into his fast spiel, the specialized chant of an auctioneer. Other personnel on the stage pointed toward buyers who waved their bid cards. A sign mounted above Grant's head warned—*Don't wave if you don't mean to buy.* Though she was nothing more than an observer, she still felt the addictive urge to bid, to win out over everyone else.

Once Grant hit the table with a mallet and shouted, "Sold!" a handler on the exit side opened the gate. When he turned, Piper recognized him, the man she'd seen astraddle the fence the day before. Interested, she watched. After the last animal ran out of the ring, he closed the gate, grabbed a clipboard hanging on a metal post and made a notation.

Even though she tried to concentrate on the rest of the sale, her gaze kept straying back to him. He waited with a foot propped on a rail and his arms resting on top of the gate. Despite his rugged good looks, she wasn't sure why she felt intrigued. After all, she worked with hunky guys. But not once had she felt this tug of awareness. There was just something about him. The ring of the bell broke into her musings. The auction was over, and she'd missed most of it.

Voices swelled as people rose. Some stopped to say hello and ask about her grandmother—each offering their help. The ranching community was a tight-knit group. If help was needed, everyone pitched in.

She took her time, answered their questions about Jen, and

promised she would indeed call if the need arose. She also inter-jected a few comments about Leopold, the reward, and asked about the cattle thefts. While she didn't learn anything, she knew that word of her interest would spread.

The crowd had thinned by the time she made her way outside. Loading the cattle into trailers had already started. Piper stopped to watch. At the tap on her shoulder, she turned.

Grant said, "Find out anything?"

"Not really, but I let it be known about the reward for Leopold."

Over his shoulder, she spotted two men talking. She nodded in their direction.

Grant turned.

"Who is the man with Henry Miller?"

"Ron Pollard. I hired him about two months ago. Why?"

"Just curious." She grinned at him. "It's me, being a cop. I didn't recognize him. Grant, what do you know about Lane Jarvis?"

His gaze turned wary. "Not much I can tell you. He moved into town several months ago. Promotes himself as a mover and shaker, promises to get a rancher top dollar for their cattle, just sign on the dotted line." As he talked, he strolled toward the two men.

At the sound of their footsteps, Pollard looked around. The flash of awareness in his eyes when he caught sight of Piper was quickly suppressed.

"Henry, you remember Piper McKay?"

"Sure do. Sat next to her during the auction."

After introducing Pollard, Grant turned back to Henry. "I hoped to catch you before you left. Did you pick up your sales receipt? I thought I saw it lying on the front desk."

As she listened, Piper was aware Pollard intently watched her.

Henry chuckled and slapped the side of his thigh. "Dang if I didn't forget. My memory's just not as good as it used to be. Thanks for reminding me. It saved me a trip back here. I'll go get it."

He looked at her. "Piper, now don't you be a stranger around here. Stop by the café some morning, and I'll buy breakfast."

"Thanks, Henry. I may take you up on the offer." The Sunset Café was the local watering hole where the ranchers gathered, usually early in the morning.

Before Grant followed Henry into the building, he told Piper, "If you're still in town, there's another sale coming up."

She rose to her toes and kissed his cheek. "Since I don't plan on leaving anytime soon, I'll stop by." She turned to walk to her truck.

Pollard stepped alongside her. "Are you from around here?"

She glanced up at him. Her estimate was close on, easily six-two. "I grew up here."

"I wondered why I'd never seen you before."

"I don't get back much these days."

"Where's home now?"

"Oklahoma City. How about you? Where do you come from?"

"Up north."

She reached her truck and opened the door. "Nice meeting you, Mr. Pollard."

"It's Ron. If I wanted to get ahold of you, how would I do it?"

She gave him a cool look. "I imagine we'll run into each other again."

He didn't plan on talking to her until he spotted the bulge of a gun under her coat. It piqued his interest and why he followed her. Still, as he watched her drive away, a thought crossed his mind. What he'd just done fell under the category of grade-A stupid. Whatever the reason for the gun, McKay was a distraction he couldn't afford.

As she stepped onto the porch, Grady opened the door. His eyes had a worried look. "Did you talk to Henderson?"

"Yes. He said he is pleased with Jen's progress." Piper followed him inside the house. The heady aroma of garlic and basil set off a rumble in her stomach. "You made spaghetti. Meatballs?"

Grady glanced over his shoulder. "Of course. Wash up. I'm putting it on the table."

"You're going to spoil me with all these meals. Usually, I live on takeout."

He laughed. "I don't mind. Cooking helps keep my mind off what's going on."

Since spaghetti was one of her favorite dishes, eager anticipation lightened the bone-deep weariness and sent her spinning toward the bathroom, then into the kitchen.

Piper piled pasta on her plate from the large bowl on the table and ladled extra sauce from a second bowl. In the middle, she nestled two fist-sized meatballs. "A lot happened today."

"Eat, then we'll talk."

Grateful for the respite, she didn't waste any time. After a second helping, she eased back in her chair. "Oh, that was so good."

"I picked up a chocolate cake at the store. If you remember, baking is not my thing."

"I couldn't eat another bite, so maybe later."

He picked up the dishes, and when she rose to help, he waved her back to her seat. "I'll take care of this. You start talking."

While he spooned coffee into a filter, Grady listened to what she'd discovered from the attorney. When she reached the part about the money, she couldn't sugarcoat it. His lips thinned in anger, and his hands trembled. After scattering ground coffee across the counter, he tossed the spoon down and marched out the back door.

Anxiety squeezed Piper's chest as she followed.

His hands braced on the porch railing, he stared across the paddocks and fields. Piper stopped beside him.

"What in hell is going on? I feel so damn helpless. If Jennie loses …," he choked.

"I know." Since she had the same feeling, there wasn't much she could say to reassure him.

Grady straightened. "What happens if you can't get the restraining order?"

"Since I'm not sure what Jarvis is up to, I don't know. But I'm concerned about the herd."

Grady thought for a minute. "With the time we've spent at the hospital, we've been leaving this place wide open. It might be a good idea to take on an extra hand. We've always gotten by with temporary help, never needed someone full-time, until now."

"Grady, that's a damn good idea. I know who to get. That is if I can arrange it."

"What about the DNA report?"

"I've got it, though I found out a fire destroyed the lab night before last."

"How did it happen?"

"According to the woman I talked to, it's arson. Leopold's blood sample and the documents Jen sent were destroyed. But the report was in another computer."

"Holy hell! Do you think it's connected to the theft of Leopold?"

"That's what my instincts are telling me. I had the report faxed to Arnie's office. He also had copies of Leopold's documentation."

"That's good news, not much, but better than nothing. Come on. Let's go back inside. Have a cup of coffee and a piece of cake."

Not wanting to disappoint him, Piper agreed, though, after what she'd just eaten, she didn't know where she'd put it. But if it made Grady happy, she'd stuff it down.

Pollard strolled around the lot, checking the gates on the pens near the building. Then he hopped in the UTV and drove around the outlying pens. A couple of weeks earlier, a gate had been left unlocked. Cattle wandered onto the road in front of the auction house. While it had been hilarious to watch cops herding the animals with their squad cars, it was dangerous. If a vehicle hit one, the animal could end up in the driver's lap. Grant had never found out who was responsible for the open gate.

He parked the utility wagon in a large shed, then strode toward the office door. On the way, he passed Grant's secretary leaving.

"Is Grant busy?" he asked.

"Dick's with him, talking about numbers."

Inside, he checked the break room, hoping to grab a cup of coffee before he left. No luck. The glass pot was in the sink.

Down the hall, Pollard could hear Grant and Dick's voices. Though he couldn't make out the words, from the tone, Grant was pissed. Dick Crowley was the accountant. According to Frankie, the man had worked for Grant the last ten years or so. Wondering what was going on, he moved closer.

"I knew we shouldn't have tried this. We're moving too fast," Grant exclaimed.

Dick said, "It won't be a problem. No one noticed."

"Someone might. I don't have to tell you what could happen."

Dick muttered something in a low tone. Pollard strained to hear. Grant said, "Just fix it."

"I'll take care of it," Dick told him. A chair scraped the floor.

His steps light, Pollard trotted back to the front door, opened it, then let it slam.

Dick strode out of the hallway leading to Grant's office and brushed past him with an irritated look.

Grant's voice called out, "Who's there?"

"Ron," he hollered before stopping in the doorway.

"What do you want?" Grant demanded in an angry tone.

"Just letting you know I checked all the gates."

"Good. I got lucky before. If a car had hit one of those damn animals, I had liability hanging out my ass. Come on in." He waved toward a chair. "You've been here for a couple of months. Any problems?"

Pollard sat and crossed his legs. The conversation he'd overheard buzzed in his mind as he studied Grant's face. The redness had started to fade. Was there a way to find out what had sparked Grant's ire?

"Nope. It's a good job. Everyone seems to work well together."

Grant eyed him. Pollard was a cut above the typical type of barn laborer he usually employed. He'd quickly caught on to the routines and paperwork. After his first week, Grant had wondered why the hell he was pushing livestock in and out of pens for a living. He'd done some checking, found out Pollard had a criminal record. Probably the reason the man was working in a low-end, go nowhere type job.

"You've caught on fast."

His lips twitched with a wry grin. "Been around cattle all my life. Not that difficult."

"It shows." Grant shifted in his chair. "Have you decided to stay in the area?" When he hired him, Pollard had been upfront, told him he wasn't looking for a permanent job.

"Been giving it some consideration," he drawled. "I kinda like the town." Maybe it was time to give Grant a prod. "I noticed something odd today." When Grant didn't respond, he added, "Miller's cattle. The count was off."

"You certain about it?"

A grin split Pollard's face. "Oh, yeah. I've got a good memory when it comes to numbers. I tallied his cattle when they arrived. The count when they came out of the sales ring didn't match what I tallied."

"Damn, it's happened again."

"What's the problem?"

"Computer program. I've told Dick to get it fixed. Did you mention it to anyone?"

"Nope. Told you, other than that, it's none of my business."

"Good. If this got out, I don't need the aggravation it could cause. I run anywhere from 70,000 to 80,000 head through here a year. Mistakes happen. I'll let Dick know."

He stood. "I'll be on my way." While the explanation seemed reasonable, Pollard wasn't buying it. The problem went beyond Miller's cattle. He wondered how he could turn it to his advantage.

Instead of turning toward his house when he drove out, Pollard headed to a local bar across town. Red's Bar & Grill was a favorite hangout for many of the cowhands after the auction. Not only was the food good, but he'd discovered he could tune into the rumblings and gripes floating in the rumor mill.

A smoky aroma of fried meats and onions filled the air as he walked in. Nothing fancy, other than the large flat-screened TVs conveniently mounted on walls. Wooden tables sat atop the nicked and stained thick wood plank floor. In one corner, a small buffet table held an assortment of salad fixings. Attached to the wall behind the bar, flashing neon signs advertised a variety of beers. No waitresses here. Place your order at the bar, then pick it up.

A low rumble of voices from the customers, mostly men garbed in rough work attire, pervaded the room. There was only one dress code, park your hat on one of the hooks by the front door. After finding an empty hook, Pollard strode toward the bar and eased a hip onto a stool. A beefy red-faced man, wearing a red apron, greeted him.

"What's your pleasure?"

Not surprising, the barkeep was the owner. Pollard pointed to one of the beer handles. Red grabbed a mug from the counter behind him. Tipping the lip of the glass under the tap, the golden brew flowed into the mug. His hand twisted with a slight flourish as he topped it off with only a tiny fringe of foam and slid it toward Pollard. "Anything else?"

For a moment, he studied the menu mounted on the wall. "A number two."

"How do you want your steak?"

"Medium rare and load the potato." While he waited, he twisted until his back was to the bar, sipping his beer as he glanced around.

At a table in a corner across from him, two of Lane Jarvis' thugs, Quinn Giles and Jack Sloan, huddled over their beers. Focused on their conversation, they hadn't noticed him. Not wanting to draw attention to himself, he didn't let his gaze linger. He'd already had a run-in with Giles. The two men had shown up at an auction. He'd found them in an area behind the sales barn that was off-limits to anyone but the employees. When he politely asked them to leave, Giles turned ugly. Sloan pulled him away, but not before Giles made a few threats.

On the other side of the room, Dale Hanson, Henry Miller's fore-man, waved his hand, motioning toward an empty chair. Pollard picked up his mug, slid off the stool, and weaved his way around the tables. He scooted the chair back, then eased his long legs under the table as he sat.

Dale said, "Ron, do you know Harley and Jerry?"

Nodding, he greeted the two men.

"We were just talking about the sale today," Dale told him. "A lot more cattle than we've seen before."

"Is it unusual?" Pollard asked after taking a swig of the icy cold brew.

"There have been upswings in the past, but it's usually when the yearlings come up for sale. What seems odd is that Henry has talked about cutting back until beef prices improve. I would think the other ranchers would feel the same," Dale told him. He shrugged his shoulders and changed the subject. "How do you like working for Sheffield?"

Not one to gossip about his boss, he just said, "It's a good job."

The resounding clap of a cowbell, Red's way of letting a customer know the food was ready, interrupted the conversation. Pollard looked up to see the bartender pointing to a plate of food. When he stepped up to the bar, Red asked, "Want a refill?"

Pollard looked at the invoice and pulled a twenty from his wallet. "One's my limit," he said, handing him the money. He pocketed the change, then picked up the plate and utensils next to it. As he turned, he caught a glimpse of Giles and Sloan staring at him. He shot them a hard look before turning to walk to his table.

While he dug into the thick chunk of charred meat and baked potato, he listened to the three men talk about an upcoming rodeo and stock show. In between bites, he made an occasional comment.

Then Jerry mentioned Leopold. "Damn shame Leopold won't be in the show this year, but it opens the door for someone else to win the grand prize bull award."

Pollard laid the knife and fork on the empty plate and wiped his mouth with a paper towel before saying, "Leopold?"

"The bull stolen from the Layton Ranch," Harley said. "I'm surprised you haven't heard about it."

"I heard about the theft, but no one mentioned the bull's name."

Dale said, "That bull has won every prize in the state and beyond for the last few years."

"Any leads in the investigation?" Pollard asked and took the last swallow of beer.

"Not that I've heard. It's like the damn animal just disappeared into thin air. Then Ms. Layton was almost killed. Someone said she's barely hanging on."

Harley asked, "Did you meet her? She seldom missed an auction even if she wasn't selling any cattle."

Pollard shook his head. "Haven't had the privilege. What happened to her?"

Jerry said, "Her horse threw her, which I find difficult to believe. That woman can ride, a barrel racing champion for many years. It's hard to imagine a horse could unseat her."

Harley said, "Her granddaughter was at the auction."

Jerry said, "I heard she was in town."

At the questioning look on Pollard's face, Dale said, "You met her today, Piper McKay. I saw her talking to my boss."

His face cleared. "Yes, I did, though I didn't know the connection."

Dale added, "I've known her since she first came to live with Ms. Layton after her parents were killed. She was always underfoot when she came to the auction with her grandmother. Damn, who would ever believe what she'd end up doing for a living?"

Uncertain why he had a deep sense of foreboding, he asked, "What does she do?"

"U.S. Marshal. Isn't that a kicker?" He shoved his chair back. "Time to get on the road."

Stunned, it took Pollard a few seconds to collect himself. Curses floated in his mind. It never occurred to him it was the reason she was wearing a gun. He figured it'd be easy to steer clear of the local cops, but a fed, and one who had a vested interest, spelled trouble. The type that could prove deadly.

On the way out the door, he snatched his hat. In his truck, thoughts tumbled as he stared at the front of the bar. He had to stay away from McKay, but was it even possible? Their paths were bound to cross. Sloan and Giles walked out. The dilemma of McKay faded from his thoughts. When they both climbed into Sloan's truck, his interest spiked. It was late. Why would they be together?

Since traffic was sparse, Pollard waited, letting Sloan build up a lead before he pulled out. It didn't take long to figure out they were headed to Jarvis' office, and he eased off the gas. His speculation proved to be right. Sloan came to a stop in front of the building. Pollard turned onto a side street, then doubled back. A block away, he parked in front of a closed bookstore.

A late-night meeting. A closed office. Pollard's fingers drummed the steering wheel as he thought. It was a hell of a risk but an opportunity he couldn't pass up. If he was discovered, he could try to talk his way out by telling Jarvis that he'd seen Giles and Sloan walk in. He just figured it was a good time to hit Jarvis up for a job. If it didn't work, he had no illusions about what would happen. He could end up dead in a pasture somewhere.

His decision made, he grabbed his set of lockpicks and a small flashlight from inside the console. He shoved his Glock 22 in his waistband. The lightweight jacket he wore would cover it.

At a fast pace, one that wouldn't call attention to himself, he headed to the entrance to the alley behind the office. Pollard gave the street one last glance before darting toward the back door. He'd already done some snooping and discovered the lock wouldn't keep an enterprising ten-year-old from breaking in.

Before he inserted the lockpick, he gently twisted the doorknob. *I'll be damned*, he thought. It turned. The lockpicks went back into his pocket. He pushed the door open, just enough to peer into a dark hallway, then stepped inside. Leaving the door slightly ajar, he glided along the hall. The thick carpet muffled his steps.

In front of him, street lights faintly lit the reception area. Pollard stopped, his back to the wall as he peeped around the corner. Another hall branched off from behind the receptionist's desk. Light spilled out of an open doorway.

Jarvis' angry voice rang out. "You both screwed up. I don't give a damn why. She's already told Horne someone tried to kill the old lady. Horne couldn't fob her off. She's investigating. Jesus H. Christ, a damn fed!" Jarvis said.

"We can try again. She drives the same road every night," Sloan said.

Giles growled, "My opinion, a bullet to the head takes care of it."

"Quinn, you couldn't kill an old lady with a damn rock," Jarvis exclaimed in a derisive voice. "I told you this had to look like an accident."

Giles said, "I thought she *was* dead. I couldn't feel a pulse."

His tone calm and unruffled, Sloan said, "Boss, Quinn may have a point. McKay will be on her guard now. We have to do this another way."

As he listened, a chill tightened Pollard's chest. They'd tried to kill both McKay and her grandmother and planned to try again. While he'd pegged Giles as nothing more than a hot-tempered bully, it was Jack Sloan who kindled a sense of trepidation. Sloan was the dangerous one. Pollard had come across his type before, no emotion.

"Damn! Alright. Jack, get rid of her. I don't care how. She's a loose end. I can't make the shipment until I know there aren't any left. Next is the …"

Outside, horns sounded, and lights flashed in the window. Pollard moved, even as Jarvis said, "Quinn, check outside."

In a flash, he was out the door, quietly shutting it behind him. Across the alley, a narrow walkway separated two buildings.

Pollard headed for it rather than risk using the sidewalk. Once he was clear, he broke into a trot. As he slid behind the wheel, a trickle of sweat rolled down his back.

Not wanting to drive past the office, Pollard took another direction out of town. For most of the drive, he was on autopilot, pondering what he'd heard. Equally troubling was when Jarvis was interrupted. What was he about to say?

Lane Jarvis was already high on his list of suspects for the cattle rustling, but Pollard hadn't planned on murder. This changed everything.

In keeping with an image of a down-and-out drifter, he'd rented a small, furnished frame house on the edge of town. Its only advantage was a lack of close neighbors. He pulled to a stop in the driveway.

As he exited, his gaze scanned the front of the house lit by the dim porch light. Before opening the door, Pollard looked for the small trap he'd left, a tiny piece of paper. Reassured he hadn't had any unwanted visitors, he unlocked the door and stepped inside.

After flipping on the living room light, he strode into the kitchen. From the apartment-sized refrigerator, he grabbed a can of beer. He popped the top, took a deep swallow, then a second before reaching for his phone.

A man answered, "Yes."

"Cavalry," he said. His only contact was the burner phone. If his boss, Nick Rawling, didn't hear the code word, he'd immediately hang up.

"Cade," Nick acknowledged. "Where are you?"

"Home. I overheard a conversation tonight between Jarvis and two of his men. As we suspected, Jarvis is behind the rustling, but it's become a lot more complicated. He tried to kill a local rancher and a U.S. Marshal." After he covered the gist of the conversation in Jarvis' office, he took another swallow of beer.

"How'd a marshal get involved?"

"The rancher, Jennie Layton, is her grandmother."

"That explains it. You got a call from a U.S. Marshal, Piper McKay."

When they set up the undercover operation, any calls for Cade Tanner were routed to Nick.

"Did you talk to her?"

"No, she just left a message to call. How do you want to play this?"

Frustrated, he exclaimed, "Damn! If I break cover to warn her, it could all go down the tubes."

Only one person knew he was Ron Pollard, and that was Nick. He planned to keep it that way—the more people who knew, the greater the risk.

He pitched the empty can in the trash. "From what little I've seen, McKay's not the type to be satisfied with a vague warning. She'll want to know every why and how. I can't risk her digging around. How the hell did she get my name in the first place?"

"I don't know. Do you want me to call her?"

"No, not yet. Let me work it from this end. The stolen cattle are being run through Sheffield's sales barn. I still don't know who is involved. Hard to imagine Sheffield wouldn't know."

"There was another theft over in Cass County. A rancher was killed."

Cade said, "I'll be in touch." As he headed to his bedroom, one thought consumed him. He had to warn McKay, but how the hell could he do it without blowing his cover?

When she arrived, the early morning crowd had already packed the café parking lot with vehicles. Piper finally found a spot about a block down. The backpack over her shoulder, she meandered along the sidewalk, enjoying the light breeze brushing her face.

As she stepped inside, her gaze swept the busy room. Near the front window, Pollard sat, digging into a pile of scrambled eggs. He never looked up, though she felt sure he would have seen her when she walked in.

At another table, two men caught her eye. Their gaze riveted on her, the eyes of one man held a hard assessing look while the other leered. A sense of disquiet arose. They seemed to know her, but she'd never seen them before.

A voice hollered, "Two and four up." The cook slid two plates of food under heating lamps mounted over a wide shelf in front of the smoky kitchen at the back of the room.

Henry Miller, seated at a table with another longtime friend, Brad Dexter, stood and waved to get her attention. Piper strode toward him, working her way around the tables.

Henry waited, holding her chair. He scooted it forward when she sat, then destroyed the moment of old-fashioned courtesy by slapping her on the back. "Dang, glad you decided to come by. I was just telling Brad that I saw you at the auction yesterday."

A waitress walked up with a coffee pot in her hand. "Coffee?" When Piper nodded yes, she flipped over a cup on the table, then filled it before topping off the other cups. "Anything else?"

After glancing at the handwritten menu on the chalkboard, Piper said, "Number four."

"Bacon or sausage with those pancakes?"

"Just the pancakes."

The woman nodded and walked toward the kitchen. After writing on a pad, she tore off the sheet and clipped it on a wire above the warming shelf. She hollered, "Number four, naked."

Brad asked, "How is Jennie doing?"

Piper swallowed a gulp of coffee. "Much better. She's been moved from ICU into a private room."

"Can she have visitors?"

She shook her head. "No. She's still in a coma."

"What a freakish accident. I would never have believed a horse could throw Jennie," Brad said.

Piper didn't enlighten him that it wasn't an accident. Instead, she shifted the conversation to cattle. "The auction yesterday did a good business. Is it typical?"

Brad said, "The last few months, it has improved."

"That reminds me," Henry said. "I need to swing by there on my way home. The count on my receipt was off. I was shorted."

Brad said, "Four, maybe five weeks back, I had the same problem. Grant claimed it was a glitch in the computer."

"Seems to be an unusual mistake," Piper observed.

"It is since the count is verified when the cattle are unloaded and again after the sale," Henry told her. "I check my count when I load the stock and make a note of it in a notebook I keep in the truck."

"Has anyone else had the same problem?"

Henry answered, "Not that I've heard."

The waitress set the plate of pancakes in front of her and refilled the cup. Piper waited until she walked off, then asked, "Don't you get a receipt for the cattle once you get to the sales barn?"

"I get a computer printout of the tally, but I like to keep another record," Henry told her. "Once the sale is complete, I get a second printout with the details of the sale."

Interested, Piper asked, "Were both computer printouts wrong?"

"No, just the final one. I double-checked the printout of the tally. It was correct."

The conversation turned to breeding issues. Since Piper didn't want to raise suspicions with too many questions, she listened and ate while the two men talked.

Then Brad said, "There was another theft of cattle over in Cass County, north of Hughes Springs."

Henry said, "I hadn't heard about that one. When did it happen?"

"Two nights ago," Brad told him. "Yesterday, I stopped at the courthouse in Linden. I ran into the sheriff. He and I go back a ways. He told me ranches across East Texas and even down toward Houston have been hit hard. Small batches, five to ten, though he did say the numbers are adding up. This time an owner was killed."

"Good lord, how did it happen?" Henry asked.

"He was shot. A ranch hand found him dead in the pasture," Brad said. "The sheriff figures he tried to stop the rustlers."

Piper spoke up. "Did the sheriff have any idea who's behind the thefts?"

"No, and none of the stolen cattle have been found."

Brad asked, "Have you had any news on your cattle or Leopold?"

She pushed her plate back. "Nothing yet. I talked to Sheriff Horne. He said he's still investigating."

Brad said, "Since Jennie planned on getting into the artificial insemination business, it's a damn shame she lost that bull. I loaned her a couple of books on the subject."

Instantly alert, Piper asked, "When?"

He scratched his head as he thought. "Two, maybe three months ago. She'd been researching the topic as a source of income. Jennie wanted to know more about collection procedures, startup fees, generally trying to get a feel for what it entailed. She knew I used artificial insemination on my herd."

"That's interesting. I don't know much about the topic."

"It's all about DNA. Big business. Stop by my place sometime. I'll let you have the books I lent to Jennie."

"Thanks, Brad. Someone else asked me about Leopold, Lane Jarvis. He's new in town. Where'd he come from?"

Brad said, "Colorado, I've heard. He sells on consignment, though I haven't had any business dealings with him." He stood, dropping several dollars on the table. "Well, I need to get going."

Piper also rose. When she reached into her back pocket, Henry objected. "My treat. Don't be a stranger while you're here, though I know you've got a lot to handle right now."

When she turned toward the door, Pollard hadn't budged. Though he still didn't acknowledge her presence, she was certain he kept his eye on her as she walked to the door. Piper was used to men coming on to her, but his interest didn't seem to fit the typical pattern. Her instincts told her to be careful. Despite his rugged good looks, he had a dangerous aura about him.

The two men who ogled her had left. Curious, Piper knew it wouldn't take long to learn their identity.

Outside, Brad slipped his arms into his jacket. As she walked out, he stepped alongside her. She looked down at the diminutive man who had to be pushing seventy. Five-foot-five, maybe 150 pounds dripping wet, bowed legs, and leathery skin, he was the quintessential old-time cowboy. Tougher than a boiled boot.

"Brad, who does the count at the end of the sale?"

"For one, the man on the exit gate in the sales ring. As the cattle are herded out, he counts and notes it on a clipboard. Not sure who else, why?"

"Just trying to get a handle on who does what. It's probably not important."

In a low undertone, he said, "Watch yourself. Whoever is behind the cattle rustling plays rough. It may not have any connection to Jennie, but just be careful. Don't forget about those books." He split off, walking to his truck on the other side of the lot.

She wondered about his seemingly odd warning as she watched him saunter away. Had she detected a strange reaction when she dropped Jarvis into the conversation, or was it just her imagination? Then, there was his comment about a bull like Leopold. While her visit to the café had raised more questions, she did learn about the irregularities in the tally, and Pollard was the man on the gate. Another tick in the column of possible suspects.

Piper's phone rang as she pulled into the hospital parking lot. It was Luke.

"I don't have good news."

Her heart sank.

"Still nothing on the phone. I suspect it's been destroyed. The handwriting analysis is inconclusive. While the analyst believes it's a forgery, he says the evidence isn't strong enough to take into court. The only fingerprints were yours."

"Damn. That's a setback."

"He did say if this was a forgery, it was one of the best he'd ever come across. On the positive side, I've arranged for you to meet with

Edna Spence in Denver, Colorado. You've got an hour or so before the jet lands at the airport in Sulphur Springs. Someone from the Denver office will meet you and drive you to the Spence home. When you get on board, there will be a packet containing the reports on the case. It's about a two-hour flight, so you should be able to get back to Sulphur Springs tonight. Anything else I need to know?"

"Yes." She filled him in on what she learned about the lab fire.

"Send me the name and location. I'll have someone follow up on it, talk to the arson investigator."

"What about Jarvis?"

"Nothing yet. Call me after you talk to Mrs. Spence."

Before entering, she tapped on the door to her grandmother's room, then opened it. Tony was seated in the chair.

After greeting him, Piper's gaze shifted to her grandmother. It didn't appear there was any change. She stepped to the side of the bed, picking up her grandmother's hand. For several minutes, she talked before kissing Jen on the cheek.

Motioning for Tony to step into the hallway, Piper filled him in on her trip. "When Davy gets here, let him know. I didn't want to wake him."

A worried look crossed his face. "Do you need one of us to go with you?"

"No. I need the two of you here. This will be a quick trip. I should be back tonight."

"I don't like it. Call when you land at the airport."

"No one knows I'm leaving or when I'm coming back. I shouldn't have any problems." She glanced at her watch. "I've got to go."

Disturbed, Tony watched her walk away.

On the way to her truck, her phone rang. The caller ID showed unknown. "McKay."

A muffled voice said, "Be careful. There will be another attempt to kill you."

The call disconnected.

Stunned, she stopped. Her first thought was, how did the caller get her cell phone number? Then the warning raced in her mind. Certain it was a man, he'd said, another attempt. How did he know about the first one?

Disturbed more than she cared to admit, she debated whether to call Tony. No, he'd insist one of them should go with her. It was more important they stay to guard Jen.

The pilot's voice came over the speaker. "We'll be landing in about ten minutes. Please fasten your seat belt."

Piper pulled the belt in place as she stared out the small window. The only passenger, she'd taken advantage of the lack of distractions. First, she'd gone over the packet of reports Luke had sent. There weren't many details. One was the accident report on the crash that killed Bill Spence. It happened on Interstate 70, about five miles west of Byers. According to the Colorado Highway Patrol, a front tire blew. The vehicle collided with a bridge abutment. Bill Spence was dead at the scene. The fact the tire was the cause of the crash immediately sent up a red flag, considering someone had tried to shoot out her tire.

The second report was a complaint Spence had filed with the local sheriff's department. The complaint stated Lane Jarvis failed to pay Spence for fifteen head of cattle. The report was marked closed with a notation, civil not criminal. The last report was a theft of approximately 120 head of cattle from the Spence ranch. It had been filed with the sheriff and the Colorado Brand Division of the Colorado Department of Agriculture ten days after Spence was killed. Value approximately $240,000.

How could someone steal that many head and get away with it? It didn't make sense. The case was disturbingly similar to her grandmother's situation.

The rest of the time, she'd spent on her laptop, researching articles on the use of DNA for breeding livestock. What she'd learned had astounded her. Worldwide, artificial insemination was a multi-billion-dollar business.

One article dealt with the auction of a prize bull, similar to Leopold. The bull sold for one and a half million dollars. In the interview with the new owner, the rancher stated he expected he'd easily recoup the purchase price by selling the bull's semen.

When she shifted to researching cattle rustling, it proved to be just as lucrative. Burglarize a house and steal a TV, it would sell for pennies on the dollar. Steal a cow, the thief could get full value. The multi-billion dollar business's lure enticed everyone from the low-end, single thief looking for drug money to high-end financial schemes.

The pilot's announcement he was on final approach put an end to her reading. Reluctantly, she closed her computer, shoving it back into the backpack. From her window, she watched the ground rush up as the plane landed. It came to a stop near the executive terminal for private aircraft.

The pilot stepped out of the cockpit. He pushed open the door and lowered the stairs. Before she stepped out, he said, "Call when you leave your location. We'll have the plane ready to go as soon as you arrive." He handed her a business card.

"Thank you, Captain Landry."

Inside the terminal, a man in a business suit strode toward her. "Marshal McKay?"

"Yes."

"Marshal Roger York." As they shook hands, he said, "My car is outside. Do you need to stop anywhere?"

"No, I don't. How far is the Spence home?"

"About a thirty-minute drive. Mrs. Spence lives on the outskirts of town."

"I thought she had a large ranch near Byers."

"She did, but after her husband was killed, she had to sell."

Seated in the car, she buckled the seat belt, then pulled her phone from the backpack at her feet. She turned it off while on the plane. Her boss had called and left a message.

When he answered, he asked, "Are you in Denver?"

"Just landed. I'm on my way to the Spence house. Luke, in reading the reports you sent, there is a lot of similarity to what is happening to my grandmother."

"It's why I wanted you to talk to Mrs. Spence in person, not over the phone. If there is something to be found, you'd have the best chance of finding it."

"One more request. I'd like a background on a Ron Pollard. He works for Grant Sheffield, who owns the livestock auction house. This morning, I learned there have been errors in the receipts for the cattle sales. Based on the time frames, it may have begun about the time Pollard started working there."

After she disconnected, Roger asked, "Was that Luke Purdy?"

"Yes, he's my boss."

"A good man. I worked a case with him not too long ago. So what's the deal with Spence?"

By the time she finished explaining, he'd parked in front of a small frame house.

As they walked up the short sidewalk, a woman stepped out. From her research, Piper knew Edna Spence was fifty-six years old, though she appeared older. A look of utter despair emphasized the lines etched on her face.

"Are you the agents?" she asked.

Piper stepped forward, extending her hand. "Yes, ma'am. I'm U.S. Deputy Marshal Piper McKay, and this is Marshal Roger York. Thank you for allowing us to speak with you."

"I don't know what I can tell you, but please come in."

They followed the woman into a small living room, where she motioned toward the couch. "Would you like coffee, tea?"

"No, we're fine," Piper told her as she and Roger sat.

Nervous, Mrs. Spence sat on the edge of a chair, her hands tightly clasped in her lap. "Why would two marshals want to talk to me?"

"I understand you know Lane Jarvis."

Anger flashed across her face. "I know the bastard. I hope he burns in hell!"

Surprised by the outburst, Piper asked, "What happened?"

"My husband met Jarvis at a cattleman's meeting. He's a cattle broker, buys and sells cattle. He convinced Bill that he could get a better price for our cattle than we could at the local auction house. Bill took him up on the offer and sold him fifteen head on consignment. Jarvis picked up the cattle but never paid us. Every time Bill called, it was one excuse after another."

"Did you have a contract for the fifteen head?"

"Oh, yes. Bill even contacted an attorney. Then he was killed. The highway patrol officer concluded a front tire blew out, causing Bill to lose control. I didn't believe it then, and I still don't." Tears glinted in her eyes.

"Why do you think it wasn't an accident?" Piper asked.

"They were new tires. I tried to tell the officer, but he said there might have been a factory defect." She reached for a tissue in a box next to the chair. "Whatever caused that tire to blow wasn't a factory defect."

"I can't imagine how difficult this is for you, so take your time."

"It's been almost a year. I keep telling myself it will get better, but it doesn't. The day after I buried Bill, Jarvis shows up. He's got a contract Bill signed. I couldn't believe it. It gave Jarvis full rights to sell our cattle on consignment. Bill would never sign a contract without discussing it with me. I took it to an attorney, but he said there wasn't anything that could be done."

She stopped and took a deep breath before continuing. "Dealing with Bill's death, I let things around the ranch slide. My son tried to help, but he lives in Seattle and couldn't stay. Our herd was spread out over several acres with plenty of feed and water, so there wasn't much I had to do anyway. We didn't have full-time help. Bill would hire someone when we needed an extra hand. It wasn't until Jarvis showed up to inventory the herd that I discovered most were missing, around 120 head. I filed a report with the sheriff and discovered several cattle thefts had occurred in the area."

Piper said, "One of the reports I have is the theft you reported. Did you ever find out how it was possible to steal so many?"

"The ranch was large with more than one entrance. What the sheriff figured is the thieves used a cattle hauler on more than one occasion. Just drove in and rounded up as many as they could haul. From the house, I'd never see them."

"What happened with Jarvis?"

"He invoked a loss clause in the contract. I ended up owing him money for the loss. I had to sell him the ranch to pay him."

A chill raced through Piper. Jarvis was pulling the same scam in Texas, only this time her grandmother was the victim.

"Bill never signed that contract, but I couldn't prove it. It's why I believe Jarvis killed him."

She couldn't hold back the tears. "I'm sorry. Give me a minute." She stood and rushed out of the room.

Roger, who had quietly listened, said, "I wonder how many times Jarvis has worked this scam?"

Her tone bitter, Piper said, "Well, we know of at least two."

When Mrs. Spence returned, even though her eyes had a bleak look, her voice was steady as she asked, "What else do you want to know?"

Piper asked, "Do you have copies of the two contracts?"

"Yes, I do. Anything else?"

"Another document your husband signed."

"What are you going to do?"

"Compare the signatures to find out if one of the contracts is a forgery."

Hope dawned on her face. "Is there a chance you can put that bastard away for good?"

"Mrs. Spence, I am going to do my *damnedest* to make it happen."

She left the room. When she returned, she handed Piper several documents. "There is a copy of both contracts and a canceled check with Bill's signature. Is this enough?"

Piper quickly scanned them. "Yes. If for some reason we need another signature, either myself or my boss Luke Purdy will contact you." She pulled a business card from her badge case. "If you think of anything else, call me."

"Will you let me know?"

"Yes, ma'am, I will. Do you have any questions for us?"

"I do, but I suspect you won't be able to answer them."

At the door, Piper said, "Thank you again for talking to us."

Mrs. Spence reached for Piper's hand, gripped it hard with both her hands as she said, "No. Thank *you*."

In the car, Piper forced herself to relax. Listening to Mrs. Spence had been more stressful than she'd expected.

Roger pulled away from the curb. "Sounds to me as if you've got the start of a good case against Jarvis. Let me know if I can help. I'd love to nail the bastard myself."

"Thanks, Roger. I will." She pulled out her phone and called Luke. After detailing the results of the interview, she added, "I'll give the documents to the pilot. Let's see what your handwriting expert can do. Anything new on your end?"

Luke said, "The background came back on Pollard, two assault charges, and one charge for theft of livestock. Raised on a ranch in Idaho, he moved to Texas about a year ago. He's worked at a couple of ranches. At his last one, he was fired as the ranch foreman. The next place he shows up is in Sulphur Springs."

He paused.

Piper said, "Okay, what's wrong? I can hear it in your voice."

"It's just a little too pat for my liking. Something's off, but I don't know why. I'm still digging. As for Jarvis, he turned out to be more complicated than I expected. Jarvis Livestock isn't his only company."

After disconnecting, she considered his comments about Pollard. The criminal charges caught her by surprise. Usually, she had good instincts about someone, but in this case, she'd been wide of the mark.

At the executive terminal, Piper made a copy of the Spence documents for herself. The airport attendant rounded up a manila envelope. Piper shoved the papers inside, sealed it and wrote Luke's name on the outside. On the way to the plane, she handed the envelope to the pilot. "When you get to Oklahoma City, there will be a marshal waiting to pick this up."

Low on the horizon, the sun's light gleamed through the

window as the plane banked to head to Texas. Once Captain Landry's voice on the overhead speaker told her she could remove her seat belt, she set her backpack on the seat next to her. She pulled out her copy of the Spence documents and carefully scrutinized Bill Spence's signatures. Even lining up the signature from the check with the contract, she still couldn't tell if one was a forgery. Frustrated, she sighed and stuffed the documents back into her backpack. She sure hoped the handwriting expert had better luck.

What tugged at her mind was the similarity of the two contracts. The Spence contract was nearly identical to the contract Jarvis claimed Jen signed. If she couldn't prove Jen's signature was a forgery, all she could do was to wait for her to come out of the coma. Did she have the time?

The tilt of the plane alerted Piper they were descending. Through the window, she could see heavy clusters of light from Dallas to the west. A slight vibration rocked the plane as the landing gear locked into place. The aircraft lined up to land, and runway lights flashed by.

Once they were on the ground, the plane began a slow turn and then stopped. The cabin lights came on, and Captain Landry exited the cockpit. He pushed open the door, extending the staircase.

He went first, and Piper followed him down the steps. A light breeze ruffled her hair as she stepped onto the tarmac. Dim pools of light at the base of a few lampposts did nothing to illuminate the deep shadows around the buildings.

Landry had also glanced around the deserted airport with a worried look. "Do you have someone picking you up?"

"No, my truck's parked in the front lot."

"I can wait until you're on your way."

Not wanting to delay his return to Oklahoma City, she said, "Thank you, but I'll be fine."

"Are you sure?"

"Yes," she said.

Piper slipped the strap of the backpack higher on her shoulder and started toward the main building. Behind her, she heard the sound of the door closing, followed by the whine of jet engines. She turned to watch the plane as it gathered speed, effortlessly rose, and soon was only a twinkle of light in the night sky.

Once the sound of the plane died away, the silence was unnerving. The warning she'd received flashed in her thoughts. An unexpected wave of uneasiness swept over her. Though she still didn't believe she could be in any danger, Piper took another second to scan the buildings before following the sidewalk around the side of the main office. When she reached the front, she paused. Her gaze probed the parking lot and buildings across the driveway.

Despite her caution, Piper couldn't shake her sense of disquiet. From inside a zippered pocket in her pack, she pulled out her keys. She stepped away from the shelter of the building, rushing toward the safety of her truck. Focused on looking for a hidden threat, the backpack slipped off her shoulder. She twisted to grab it before the bag hit the ground.

Crack! *Rifle* ripped through her mind even as pieces of concrete flew from the impact of a bullet. She dropped and rolled off the sidewalk, scrambling to reach the side of her truck. Snugged against the side of the front tire, she jerked her gun from its holster.

The shot came from behind her, the side of the airport where several buildings bordered the driveway. The shooter must be on one of the roofs, but which one? On the other side of the airport was an open field. At least she didn't have to worry about an attack from that direction.

While the truck afforded some protection, pinned next to it wasn't the safest place to be. For the moment, Piper had cover, but if the shooter moved, he could easily pick her off. She had nowhere to go. If she made a dash to the building, she'd be exposed. It was just dumb luck he'd missed the first time. She looked toward the street. No help there.

Even though she held the gun tightly clasped in her hands, it was useless against a rifle. She couldn't make a move without the sniper seeing her.

A thought flashed in her mind—*the lights*. Unless the rifle was equipped with a night scope, which she doubted, darkness favored her, not the shooter. She crept to the back of the truck and took aim. The bulb on the nearest pole exploded. She shifted and shot again. Another bulb blew. It only took a few seconds to methodically kill the lights in the parking lot.

Then she slid toward the front of the truck. Crouched by the tire, her next targets were the lights in front of the building and on each side of the front door. She'd just evened the playing field.

She bounded to her feet and ran flat out. She skidded to a stop on the side of the building.

The sound of distant sirens grew in intensity. Someone must have heard the shots and called the cops. The roar of an engine overrode the sirens. Tires squealed. Lights from a vehicle flashed across the roadway. It headed away from the approaching police cars and raced out of sight.

When a squad car followed by a second squealed to a stop on the driveway, she holstered her gun and stepped out. Headlights lit up the parking lot. Her hands raised, she walked toward the officers who jumped out of their cars.

One shouted, "Stay where you are! Keep your hands in the air."

When the two officers, guns drawn, drew near, she groaned. Damn, sheriff deputies. The airport must be in the county, not the city. In a loud voice, she said, "I'm U.S. Marshal Piper McKay. I'm armed. My identification is in the front pocket of my jacket."

One deputy said, "Get it out."

Moving her hand slowly, she withdrew the case and tossed it on the ground. While the other officer kept his gun trained on her, the deputy bent over and picked it up.

After he examined it, he said, "She's legit," and holstered his gun. "Did you call?"

She glanced at his name tag. The name, Evan Clarkson, rang a bell. "No. I was too busy trying to keep someone from killing me."

He eyed her with a look of dislike. "What are you doing out here? The airport's closed." He tossed the case at her.

Her hands flew up to catch it. Irritated by his attitude, she barely managed to keep her tone civil. "I just got off an airplane."

When he glanced toward the runway, she said, "It's already taken off."

"It's kind of late for a plane to land here. Where did you come from?"

Saved by the arrival of two other cars, she didn't tell him it wasn't any of his business. A police officer and another deputy walked up. *Must be a slow night*, she thought, or else they don't get many shots fired calls. Cops were notoriously nosy and didn't hesitate to jump another officer's call to find out what was going on.

Another deputy asked, "What happened?"

Ringed by three deputies and one cop, each with an avid look of excitement, she said, "As I walked to my truck, someone shot at me, probably from one of those roofs." She motioned toward the row of buildings.

The cop asked, "What's a U.S. Marshal doing in town?"

"My grandmother, Jennie Layton, is in the hospital."

The last deputy to arrive spoke up. "That's the woman who was thrown from her horse a few days ago."

Piper didn't bother to correct him.

Clarkson's cold gaze never wavered. "Why would someone shoot at you? Maybe it was a car backfiring."

Disgusted, she glared at him. "Deputy, I know the difference.

One bullet struck the sidewalk, and another hit my truck."

As if on a string that tied them together, they turned. Lined up alongside the truck, flashlights beamed across the side.

The city cop pointed. "Here's one. It might be a bullet hole."

Piper stepped toward him to look. It was above the wheel well.

Then they walked to the sidewalk to examine the damage. It was the city cop again who commented, "There's a gouge. It's hard to say what caused the damage."

"You might want to check the roofs," she suggested.

After a brief discussion, the cop and a deputy hopped back in their cars and drove to the next driveway. The other deputy walked into the parking lot. He shouted, "Why is all this glass on the lot? No wonder it's so dark."

"I shot out the lights."

Clarkson pulled out his notebook, and suddenly she realized who he was. This was the deputy who ruled Jen's injury an accident.

"You're the one who responded to the 911 call about my grandmother."

"Yeah, I went out there. Is this your truck?"

"No, it's my grandmother's. I'm curious. Did you actually investigate the incident or just walk up and decide it was an accident?"

His eyes flashed with anger. "I heard about your accusations. I didn't see anything that made me think it wasn't an accident." He flipped his notebook closed.

"I've got enough information for my report. 'Complainant reported an unknown party fired shots at her. No evidence was found to support the complainant's statements that bullets damaged the sidewalk and her truck. Other damage included light bulbs on the poles and building. The complainant admitted she fired the shots that resulted in the damage.' Guess that sums it up. You'd better talk to Scott Adams. He's the airport manager. He's not going to like what you did to his parking lot."

"Is this another example of your in-depth investigations—ignore any evidence? Is that what you've done on the cattle thefts as well? Tell your boss to add your report to the ones he still hasn't provided."

Another look of anger flashed before he turned and walked to his squad car. Tires spun, tossing up dirt and gravel as he tore out of the driveway. The other deputy, who still stood in the parking lot, shot her a curious look before getting into his car.

Piper walked over and picked up the backpack lying on the ground. As she drove out, she saw the officers who'd gone to check the buildings heading back to town. She doubted they'd found anything or even really bothered to look. On the way home, her irritation at Clarkson faded as one overriding question formed in her mind. How the hell did someone know she'd be flying back tonight?

The front porch light was on, along with a small lamp by the front window when she pulled into the driveway. Grady's apartment was dark. She'd wait until the morning to tell him what happened. She couldn't keep him from knowing. The news about the shooting at the airport would spread like wildfire. And his eagle eye would probably spot the bullet hole in the truck.

Inside she dropped her backpack on a chair in the living room. Weary, she collapsed onto the couch. She needed to eat, but first, she had to call the hospital. She'd checked in during the day, but there'd been no change.

Davy answered on the second ring. "Are you home?"

"Yeah. Long day."

"Your grandmother is about the same. The doctor was by earlier this evening and didn't indicate there were any problems. What'd you find out?" She brought him up to date on the meeting with Mrs.

Spence and the documents she'd procured. When she started on the details of the shooting, his voice erupted in anger.

"Dammit! One of us should have gone with you."

"No point in second-guessing. What I'd like to know is how they knew? I plan to go to the airport tomorrow to find out."

"Anyone follow you?"

"Not that I noticed. I'll call Luke tomorrow. Let Tony know what happened when you see him. By the way, how did his shift go?"

"I don't know what it is about him, but he's got all the nurses fawning over him. They bring him coffee and food. I have to beg for it. Damned unfair if you ask me. You sound tired. Try to get some rest."

Davy was right. She was exhausted. Still, she needed to eat. She sighed and dragged herself off the couch. In the kitchen, the note stuck to the refrigerator read, *sandwich inside, eat.* Chuckling, she washed her hands before opening the refrigerator door. She took out a wrapped sandwich along with a bottle of water.

Setting them on the table, she grabbed a bag of chips from the cupboard. As she eased onto the chair, her aching muscles began to relax. She figured there'd be a few bruises in the morning. She took a deep swig of water and unwrapped the sandwich. As she chewed, her mind replayed what happened at the airport. She wasn't about to tell Davy or anyone just how close she'd come to being killed. She'd swear the bullet passed over her head. This was twice someone tried to kill her. An unbidden thought arose, an old saying about the third time being the charm. Not a pleasant thought to take to bed.

It was still dark when Tony walked out of the elevator. A nurse seated behind the counter smiled at him. "Good morning. You're early." He smiled back but didn't bother to tell her that he and Davy had decided to switch out a couple of hours early.

In the deserted hallway, lights were dimmed, the daily hustle and bustle of hospital personnel missing. He double-tapped the door to alert Davy, then opened it. Davy was slumped in the chair. Next to the bed, a man in blue scrubs and face mask held a syringe. The man spun.

Tony hurtled toward him. The man lunged, shoving the needle at his face. He twisted, knocking the man's arm aside. The syringe fell to the floor. Before Tony could recover, the man jammed his shoulder into his chest, pushed past him and bolted out the door. Tony ran after him, shouting for help. The man sprinted to the stairs at the end of the hall.

A woman hollered, "What's wrong?"

Over his shoulder, Tony yelled, "Check Ms. Layton!"

The man opened the door, plunging down the steps. Hot on his heels, Tony followed. At the bottom, his body hit the bar to open the door. It slammed shut before Tony could get to it, and he lost precious seconds. By the time he was outside, the man was across the parking lot. In the dark, he was soon out of sight.

Disgusted, Tony turned to go back and found it was an exit-only door. He ran around the building to the main entrance. As he rushed inside, the security guard at the front desk shouted for him to stop. Ignoring him, Tony dashed to the stairs. The security guard was behind him. On the third floor, he charged through the door, racing toward Ms. Layton's room. Two nurses were inside.

"I'm U.S. Marshal Kline. How is she?"

A nurse turned. "She's fine. What happened?"

Tony looked down. "Where's the syringe?"

The nurse motioned to the table next to the bed. "I found it on the floor." Her tone insistent, she said, "Tell me what happened."

The security guard burst into the room. "What's going on here?"

Tony turned to him and pulled out his badge case. "U.S. Marshal Tony Kline. Someone tried to murder a patient."

"What! How the hell do you know that?"

"Because I walked in as a man planned to inject whatever is in that syringe into Ms. Layton."

Tony turned back to the nurse. "Was any medication ordered for her?"

"My god. No, there wasn't." Horrified, she stared at the needle.

A groan rumbled behind him. Tony stepped to the chair.

Eyelids drooped as Davy stared up at him. His tone groggy, he said, "What's wrong with me?"

The security guard stepped to the side of the chair. "Who's this man?"

Tony said, "U.S. Marshal Davy Fenwick. Davy, look up at me."

"What?" he muttered as he lifted his head and leaned it against the chair.

Bent over to get a closer look, Tony stared at Davy's dilated pupils. He'd been drugged. But how? His gaze locked onto the coffee cup on the table next to the chair.

Frantic, Davy struggled to get up. "Ms. Layton!"

Tony pushed him back. "She's okay. You've been drugged."

Davy shook his head as if to throw off the effects.

The nurses were still checking Jennie. "Did one of you bring a cup of coffee to Marshal Fenwick?" Tony asked.

Blustering, the guard said, "Why are U.S. Marshals here? Nobody informed security." He walked toward the table where the cup sat and reached for it. "Is this what was used?"

"Stop! Don't touch it. It's evidence."

A look of hostility settled on the man's face. "You don't have the right to tell me what to do."

"I'm a Federal officer at the scene of a crime. I have every right. Step outside and wait in the hall!"

"I need to know what happened. I have to make a report."

"I can assure you that your superiors will be informed. Right now, I want you *out* of this room."

"We'll just see about this," he huffed as he marched out the door.

Tony looked at the two nurses, who stared at him with a wide-eyed look.

"Back to the coffee. Did one of you bring it to Marshal Fenwick?"

"Yes, I did."

Tony looked at her name tag. "When, Ms. Butler?"

She glanced at her watch. "About an hour or so ago."

"Where did you get it?"

"From the pot at the nurse's station. Why?"

"Since he's been drugged, I'm trying to figure out how. Tell me exactly what you did."

"I was making the rounds, checking the patients in each room. Marshal Fenwick asked if I would bring him a cup of coffee. I told him I would. It was several minutes before I returned to my desk. I poured a cup and brought it to him."

"From the time you poured it until you gave it to him, did it leave your hands?"

"No." She stopped. "Come to think of it, I did set the cup on the counter and walked into the storage room to get a blanket. I remembered the patient in 302 had asked for one."

"Was there anyone in the hallway or waiting room?"

Her forehead wrinkled as she thought. "Just a maintenance man mopping the floors."

"Did you know him?"

"I'd never seen him before."

"Did you speak to him?"

"No."

From an inner pocket in his jacket, he pulled out a small notepad and pen. "Give me a description." As she talked, he made notes. When she finished, Tony asked, "Was there anything unusual about the man?"

"Not really. Though I was surprised to see him. He was early. The cleaning crew usually gets here later in the morning. And he was here longer than normal."

"What do you mean?"

"It doesn't take long to mop the floors, but the man was taking his time. I just figured he was lazy."

"Who is in charge of the maintenance personnel?"

"I don't know. Someone in the administrative office would be able to tell you."

He gave her his business card, asking that she call if she remembered anything else.

While he talked to Ms. Butler, the other nurse had stepped over to Davy. After checking his eyes, pulse, and blood pressure, she said, "I'll call and get a doctor from the ER."

Davy muttered, "No. No doctor. I'll be fine." He stood, his hand braced on the back of the chair until he got his balance, then he staggered into the small bathroom. When he emerged, his hair wet, Tony guessed he'd doused his head with cold water.

A slight grin crossed his face as he looked at Tony. His voice a little less shaky, Davy said, "An exercise in futility since the drug has to work its way out of my system, but it has psychological value."

He dropped back into the chair and added, "Okay, at least, I'm alert enough for you to tell me what happened."

By the time Tony finished, Davy was muttering curses, and the nurses were done.

"Would either of you like a cup of coffee?" Ms. Butler asked.

Davy shuddered. "I'll pass."

Tony overrode him by saying, "Please, we'd appreciate it. Though I would ask that you make a fresh pot. Before you do, I want to get a sample. Then thoroughly wash the pot before you use it."

"Do you think someone could have tampered with it?" the other nurse asked.

"I don't know, but I'm going to find out."

He looked at Davy. "Don't let anyone throw that cup away."

As he followed the nurses out the door, he said, "I need three plastic bags and two cups with tight lids."

Ms. Butler said, "I can give you urine cups. They have darned good lids."

He chuckled. "How appropriate."

The ring of her phone brought Piper upright out of a sound sleep. Panicked, she scrambled, kicking the covers aside to grab it.

At this hour of the morning, it could only be bad news, which meant her grandmother.

The caller ID was Tony. Her thoughts raced. Why was he calling? Davy was at the hospital.

Tony's first words were, "Don't panic. Your grandmother is fine. There was an attempt on her life."

Her breath caught in her throat as fear clamped her chest. My god, this was what she was afraid would happen. "Tell me."

Holding the phone to her ear, she turned on the light, then pulled clothes out of her closet, tossing them on the bed. Reassured that Jen was okay, her concern shifted to Davy. "You're sure he's okay?"

"Yeah. Still a bit woozy, but he's fine."

"I'm on my way."

She threw on her clothes. From the kitchen, she could hear Grady rustling around. God, she hated to tell him. She adjusted the gun on her hip, slipped into her jacket and grabbed the backpack.

When she strode through the doorway, Grady was setting a pan on the stove. He turned to look at her and froze. The color drained from his face. "What's wrong?"

Just as Tony had done, her first words were to reassure him. "Jen's fine. But there was an incident at the hospital."

"What happened?" he cried.

"Tony called. I don't have a lot of details."

"Tony! Why was he there? It's Davy's shift. Oh, no …don't tell me something happened to him."

"Grady, he's fine. No one was hurt."

He dropped into a chair.

"Are you okay?" she asked.

She could see the effort it took for him to pull himself together.

His shoulders slowly straightened as he said, "Damn right, I'm fine. Don't you worry about me. I'll be right behind you."

When she stepped off the elevator, a cluster of people stood outside her grandmother's room. As she approached, the head of the security department spotted her. His face furrowed by a look of acute anxiety, he rushed toward her.

"Marshal McKay, nothing like this has ever happened in this hospital. I hope you don't believe it is our fault. We take every precaution with our patients. After all, you were the person who took it upon yourself to bypass hospital security."

Disgusted, she gave him a contemptuous look. The man's only concern was whether the hospital would be held liable.

"Mr. Nelson, if you recall, you never offered any hospital security after I informed you of the danger to my grandmother. As a matter of fact, you told me you didn't believe my grandmother was in any danger in *your* hospital. Once I ascertain the facts, I'll make the decision as to whether your hospital is at fault." She stepped around him and quickly glanced at the other men, security guards, before opening the door.

The room was filled with people. Dr. Henderson stood by the bed. A nurse was on the other side and another at the end of the bed. In the corner, a notepad in his hand, a Sulphur Springs police officer talked to Tony and Davy. She nodded toward them as she stepped alongside Henderson.

He glanced down at her anxious face. "She's okay. I can't find any adverse effects. I have ordered another round of tests just to be sure. This is very disturbing that such an attack could occur in a hospital. You were right to be concerned."

He glanced at the nurse at the end of the bed. "Make a note that I also want Ms. Layton checked every hour until I advise otherwise." Then he looked back at Piper. "Do you have any questions?"

"No sir, I don't," Piper told him.

"I'll get out of your way." He glanced at the three men. "I expect you will be busy." He left, followed by the nurses.

The police officer stepped forward. "Marshal McKay, I'm Officer Manning. I do have a few questions for you."

She glanced at her grandmother. "Let's step outside."

Relieved to find the hallway clear of security personnel, she said, "Can it wait? I would prefer to have this discussion somewhere else. And there are details that I don't know yet."

He closed his notepad. "Of course. Please stop by the station. Though I would appreciate it sooner than later. My sergeant is already asking for the report."

"I will."

He added, "I understand this might be connected to what happened last night at the airport."

"At this point, I'm not certain." She hoped her ambiguous answer would keep the local PD out of this. She didn't need any more complications.

When she stepped back inside, she immediately walked to the bed. Needing to be reassured, she held her grandmother's hand while she quietly talked to her. If her grandmother could hear her, she wanted to make sure Jen knew everything was okay. Before she turned, she wiped the trickle of tears from her face.

The door opened, and Grady strode in. His gaze immediately went to Jen in the bed.

"Grady, she's fine. She wasn't hurt. Will you stay here while I talk to Davy and Tony?"

"You go do whatever you need to. There's nothing more important than my being right here." He plunked down in the chair.

Piper turned to the two men. "Davy, if you're up to it, let's go to the cafeteria. Getting some food in your system will help."

Despite the grimace that crossed his face, Davy followed them.

Outside, a security guard sat in a chair. Evidently, Nelson was finally convinced that Jen was in danger.

Once they were seated, Tony had a plate filled with bacon and eggs and Piper a bowl of oatmeal and a container of yogurt. Davy had two slices of dry toast he eyed in disgust, then cast an envious look at Tony's plate.

"Don't be a wuss," Piper told him. "Eat the toast. It's better than all that fried food."

Her face turned serious as Tony began to explain what happened. When he reached the part about the syringe, a chill swept over her. She'd done everything she could, and it still hadn't been enough.

The terrified look on her face spoke volumes as Tony hastened to reassure her. "He failed because you took precautions. What he didn't know is that we varied our routines. Still, this won't happen again. Nothing to eat or drink unless we bring it with us."

She wanted to believe him, but the fear clutched at her mind. Knowing she had to get past it, she changed the subject. "Any ideas on how to analyze the contents of the syringe and coffee since we don't have access to a lab?"

Tony swallowed the chunk of bacon he'd been chewing. "I've given that some thought. I don't want to use the hospital facilities or involve the local PD. As close as we are to Dallas, we can find a lab. I've got a contact in the Dallas FBI office. He might be able to help."

Tony had said the nurse's description of the maintenance man matched the build of Jen's attacker. Piper said, "Here's what I don't understand. If the guy mopping the floor was the one who tried to kill Jen, Davy's cup sitting on the counter was a fortuitous opportunity. He couldn't have planned it would happen. What else did he have in mind? The nurse says he was wearing a maintenance uniform. But when you saw him, he was in scrubs. What happened to his bucket and mop? Before I leave the hospital, I think I'll check a few closets."

"The same thought occurred to me," Tony said. He glanced at Davy, who, despite the scowl on his face, was eating the toast. Satisfied by what he saw, he turned to Piper. "Your turn." Pushing aside his plate, he glanced at her cup. "Do you want a refill before you start?"

When he walked back, he carried three cups of coffee, causing Davy to exclaim, "Hot damn, that's what I need."

Tony didn't point out that it hadn't been that long since Davy had turned his nose up at the thought of coffee.

After Piper covered what happened at the airport, Tony exclaimed, "Someone is getting nervous. Any idea who?"

"None. What I plan to find out is how anyone knew I was leaving town. If I had a tail, I sure didn't spot him."

Tony took a sip of his coffee. "It's the only explanation as fast as that trip came up."

"I'm not sure," she said. At the questioning look on the two men's faces, she told them about the odd call she received, warning her of another attack.

Davy scowled at Piper. "You never mentioned someone called to warn you."

"I knew if I did, one of you would insist on going to Colorado with me."

He retorted, "Yeah, and look how that turned out. You almost got yourself killed."

She glared back. "You would have done the same thing if it had been you, and you damn well know it."

Unrepentant, he grinned. "Yeah, I do."

Tony asked, "How many people have your cellphone number?"

She leaned back. "Good point. It didn't occur to me." She thought for a minute while the men watched her.

"I think three. Mack Huber at the bank, Grant Sheffield, and Arnie Larson, my attorney. I can cross him off."

"It narrows the suspect list," Davy said. "What about the sheriff?"

A wry smile crossed her face at the thought of her tossing the card on his desk. "No. I didn't give it to him."

"Is it possible it was Sheffield?" Tony asked.

"Maybe." She told them about the discrepancies on the tally sheets at the auction house. "Even if he's involved in running stolen cattle through his auctions, he might draw the line at murder."

"Whoever it was, he was right," Davy observed.

She nodded before turning her attention back to the problem at the hospital. "We need to talk to whoever is in charge of the maintenance personnel."

Tony said, "Let's divide. You check the closets, and I'll check with maintenance."

Davy asked, "What can I do to help?"

Piper and Tony said, echoing each other, "Go to bed."

He grinned. "Sounds like a damn good idea."

Tony asked, "Do you want me to call Luke?"

She sighed. "No, I will, since I plan on asking for another agent."

"Why? Between Davy and me, we've got this."

She explained what she'd discovered in Denver and her concerns about the loss clause in the contract. "If there is a plot to steal the herd, Grady is there alone."

"Luke's probably going to want to assign someone to tag along behind you as well when he learns what happened at the airport."

"That's not going to happen. I don't need a chaperone."

Having worked with Piper since she was assigned to the unit, Davy was fully aware of how hard-headed she could be. It would be interesting to see who came out on top in this tussle, their boss or Piper.

"You ready to leave?" Tony asked as he and Davy stood.

"Not yet. I'm going to call Luke."

When he answered, Luke said, "An early call like this can only be bad news."

"I hope you don't have any pressing commitments on your agenda. This will take a while."

"I'm listening."

She started with the airport shooting, then shifted to the attempt on her grandmother at the hospital.

When she finished, he said, "First, start with what you need."

She explained her concerns for Grady and the herd. "Can you spare another person from the unit?"

"Yes, who do you want?"

Her answer was immediate. "JT."

John Thompkins grew up on an Oklahoma ranch and competed on the rodeo circuit during high school and even college. He would fit in, and no one would suspect he was a marshal.

Luke chuckled. "Good choice. He'll be there today. Where do you want him to go?"

"To the ranch. I'll let my foreman, Grady Estes, know."

"Now, who do you want as a bodyguard?"

Since she'd expected his reaction, she already had her arguments lined up as to why it was a bad idea.

After listening, he said, "I don't like it, but for now, I'll go along. I received the Spence documents, and the analyst is working on them. I've uncovered some interesting transactions in Jarvis' financial accounts. He's getting loans on cattle he owns, and so far, I can't find any proof of purchase. He's also moving money that doesn't line up with his loans or purchases. It's a complicated stream of financial activity."

"Since we know he's run a scam on two ranches, is he doing the same elsewhere?" she asked.

"I think it's a good bet he is. Keep me posted, and I mean that, Piper. You've landed in the middle of a hornet's nest down there."

Disconnecting, she couldn't disagree with Luke's assessment. She dropped her dishes on the conveyor belt and considered her agenda. Once she finished at the hospital, next on the list was the local PD, then the airport. After that, she'd do some more sniffing around Sheffield's place. Someone had her phone number, and Piper planned to find out who.

As she passed the nurse's station, she said hello, but kept going. Each of the doors she passed had a room number. The hallway turned, ending at the elevator used to bring her grandmother up from the ICU.

On one side of the short hall was a door labeled supplies. Across from it was the maintenance room. Inside the supply room, racks and shelves held hospital equipment. On one shelf were boxes that contained scrubs, booties, masks, and gloves. It answered how the man got a set of scrubs.

When she opened the door to the maintenance room, Piper immediately spotted a bucket on wheels filled with dirty water. Propped next to it was a mop.

She stepped into the hallway and tapped her phone. When Tony answered, she asked, "Where are you?"

"Talking to the supervisor for the cleaning personnel."

"I found a mop and bucket in a storage room on the third floor. It's full of dirty water. Find out where it's supposed to be."

"I will. I have a fingerprint kit in the trunk of my car. As soon as I'm finished here, I'll grab it."

She didn't have to wait long before the elevators slid open, and a man stepped out. "Marshal McKay?" He extended his hand. "Win Peterson, maintenance supervisor. Show me what you found."

Piper motioned toward the door. "In there."

He took a look and said, "It's not supposed to be here."

"I didn't think so. Do you have any idea who might have left it?"

"Marshal Kline asked the same question. No, I don't. All cleaning equipment is to be returned to the basement."

"Did the description of the man fit any of your personnel?"

"No, but the basement room isn't kept locked. Anyone could have walked out with a bucket and mop."

"How do you schedule the cleaning crews?"

"They are assigned to sections of the hospital. Two women are assigned to this floor." He glanced at his watch. "They should be coming on duty."

Piper had a sinking feeling this was another dead end.

Tony turned the corner carrying a case in his hand. Echoing her thoughts, he said, "It's probably a waste of time."

Tony placed the case on the floor and pulled out a light, a square orange light filter, and rubber gloves. He slipped on the gloves and maneuvered the bucket through the doorway and into the hallway. Then he grabbed several strands of the mop and hauled it out the door.

Peterson crowded close to watch. As Tony switched on the light and picked up the light filter, he explained, "The light is an ALS, alternate light source. If I shine the beam through the filter as I scan an object, I'll be able to see any fingerprints."

He quickly demonstrated as the beam passed over and under the bucket's handle and along the sides. He did the same to the mop handle. The entire process only took a few minutes. He turned off the light and stripped off the gloves. "Been wiped clean."

Once Peterson left, Tony boxed up his equipment. "I'll take this back to my car, then I'll relieve Grady. Where are you headed next?"

"Keeping tabs on me?" she said.

"Someone needs to, but it would be a good idea if you'd keep us in the loop on your whereabouts. Which reminds me, did you talk to Luke yet?"

"I did. Jarvis' financial accounts have red flags all over them. JT will be here today. He'll be at the ranch."

"Who is he sending to babysit you?"

"No one. I wiggled my way out of having a bodyguard."

A roar of laughter erupted.

Fisted hands on her hips, she glared at him. "Okay, what's so funny?"

Still chortling, Tony said, "Bet that was an interesting conversation. So back to my question, where are you going?"

"I've got to stop at the PD. The police officer that was here wants a report. Next is the airport. Someone knew about my trip, but who? Then probably another stop at the auction house."

"Don't be surprised if you get some flak at the PD. The officer wasn't happy that I refused to release the syringe and coffee cup."

Tony was right she thought as she left the PD. The sergeant didn't bother to hide his annoyance about being stonewalled over the attack on Jen. Adding to his grievances was the discovery three U.S. Marshals were on his turf, and he had no idea why. Her vague comments prompted even more complaints. Luke would be getting another call. This time from the police chief.

Having disposed of the issue with the PD, her thoughts shifted to the airport. Every time she replayed what happened the day before, she came to the same conclusion. The leak had to be there.

Barricades blocked the entrance. Forced to park on the edge of the highway, Piper had to step around the barriers on her way to the front door. Two men with large push brooms swept broken glass into piles in the parking lot, while another stood on a ladder replacing a light bulb. At the sight, she couldn't stop the shudder that rippled through her.

Yesterday when she walked in, she'd been greeted by a jovial, friendly person who introduced himself as the airport manager, Scott Adams. Today, he stared at her with a look of outrage.

"Ms. McKay. This morning when I arrived, I was shocked to see the damage to my light poles. At first, I thought it was kids fooling around until I called the sheriff's department and learned otherwise. I don't know what to say. The fact you destroyed all the lights is … well … just incomprehensible. I've already notified my insurance company about the vandalism. They requested your contact information."

Incensed by the false insinuations, she said, "Did anyone at the sheriff's department explain why I damaged your lights?"

"Um … no." His look of indignation turned to one of uncertainty.

"Did you, by chance, speak to a Deputy Clarkson?"

"Evan? How did you know?"

"An educated guess. I destroyed the lights to save my life since someone was shooting at me from a roof on the other side of your entrance."

She pulled out her badge case and flipped it open. "I'm a U.S. Marshal. I can assure you I do not arbitrarily go around shooting lights in a parking lot."

Stunned, he stared at the badge. His voice dropped to a shocked whisper. "Someone tried to kill you? My god, this is even worse. It's unbelievable. I certainly didn't know you are a federal officer. I am so sorry I got the wrong impression."

Clarkson had deliberately misled him, and she wasn't about to excuse the deputy's behavior. "This isn't your fault. If anyone is to blame, it's Deputy Clarkson. It was his responsibility to ensure you were fully informed of all the facts. If your insurance company requires further information, have them contact my office in Oklahoma City." She handed him a business card. "However, I do have a few questions."

Eager to atone for his mistake, he almost stuttered. "Oh my, yes! I'll answer any question, help in any way I can."

"Did anyone ask about me yesterday?"

"No, not at all."

"What about any other inquiries?"

"A man did come in, asking questions."

"What did he want to know?"

"Just general information about flights and planes."

"Can you describe him?"

As she listened, the description seemed vaguely familiar. She pulled out the small notebook she carried and noted the details.

"Tell me what he said."

"Did I do something wrong?"

"I'm just curious about his questions."

"Umm … he asked about rates to hire a plane and pilot. I gave him a brochure."

"Was that all?"

"After looking at it, he seemed surprised the airport could accommodate jets. I told him we routinely had private jets pick up passengers and drop them back later. As an example, I said a jet had landed earlier, picked up a passenger and left. It would be returning later in the evening."

Her suspicions confirmed, she said in a flat tone, "Anything else?"

"No. He just thanked me and left."

"Did you happen to see his vehicle?"

"No, I didn't."

While her anger at the deputy hadn't abated as she headed to her truck, she did discover how the sniper knew when she'd be back. It still didn't answer the perplexing question of how he knew she'd be there in the first place. She was still mulling it over when she drove into the parking lot at the livestock yard. "Aw, hell," she muttered at the sight of a sheriff's car and Horne standing next to it talking to Grant.

They both turned to stare at her as she parked.

As she approached, Grant said, "Piper, I didn't expect to see you today. How is Jennie?"

"Didn't you hear? Someone tried to kill her this morning!"

Horne had leaned against the side of his car, his arms crossed over his chest. The look he shot at her was anything but friendly.

She glanced his way. "Still don't believe someone's trying to kill her?"

He glared at her.

She looked back with a disdainful gaze. "Any progress on finding my grandmother's cattle and prize bull?"

He straightened in anger. "Lady, you coming into town, butting your head into things that are not your responsibility isn't the way to win friends around here."

"Sheriff, that's Marshal McKay to you, and I don't give a damn about winning friends, at least not by your standards."

She looked at Grant. "I just stopped by to see if you received any calls about the reward for Leopold?"

Horne interrupted. "What the hell is she talking about?"

"I sent out a flyer to all the livestock auction barns," Grant told him.

Horne shot an angry glare at Grant. "Why didn't you tell me?"

"Because there wasn't anything to tell."

Across the way, she saw Ron Pollard unloading a stock trailer. He looked at her before turning away.

"Grant, if you've got time, how about a cup of coffee. We didn't really have a chance to talk the other day."

"Why sure, come on in." He looked at Horne. "You staying or leaving?"

"I've got better things to do than shoot the rag with … *Marshal McKay*," he said in a derisive tone. "I'll talk to you later."

Watching the sheriff pull out of the parking lot, Grant said, "Piper, don't let Horne upset you. He's had a couple of cases go south on him. With reelection coming up, he's under a lot of pressure."

"Don't worry. I can handle Horne. I've met others like him."

As they stepped inside, his secretary said, "You've got a call holding. It's about a shipment of cattle that's supposed to arrive tomorrow. There's a problem."

"Oh, hell, Piper. I'll have to take a rain check on the coffee. I need to take this call, and I'm not sure how long it will take."

"It's okay. We can catch up later."

That worked out well, she thought, strolling outside. It was really Pollard she wanted to talk to. She couldn't get around the fact he was in a position to doctor the tally sheets. She spotted him astraddle a fence with a rope in his hands.

Another cowhand shouted, "Move, damn it, move!"

As if simply curious to see what all the hubbub was about, she meandered her way over to an adjacent fence. She stepped onto the lower rail and propped her arms on top as she watched.

Backassward on the ramp, a steer, wild-eyed, flung its head as it loudly bellowed in protest. The horns barely missed the leg of another cowhand astraddle the side of the ramp.

Pollard flicked his wrist. His rope sailed through the air, the noose settling over the head of the animal. His feet braced on the rails of the pen, he strained, pulling the steer's head around until the rest of the body had to follow. Once the steer was headed in the right direction, it trotted down the ramp and into the pen, followed by the rest of the animals in the trailer. Another flick of the rope, and he loosened the noose. It slid off. He quickly coiled the rope and slung it over his shoulder before jumping down.

His hand on the gate, he motioned to the driver. Once the rig was clear of the ramp, he slammed the gate shut, shoving the bolt into place.

The other cowhand, who'd hopped off the ramp once the cattle were moving in the right direction, said, "Damn good toss, Ron."

A grin crossed his face. "Good enough to get them moving, Frankie. This should be the last truckload today."

The driver jumped down and handed Pollard a clipboard. He made a few notations, then handed it back. "Take that inside, and the front office will give you a receipt for the tally." He turned and spotted Piper hanging over the fence. "Enjoy the show?"

She had until she saw the tally sheet in his hand. Piper hid her uneasiness by laughing as she hopped down. Leaning against the fence, she watched him come around the corner of the pen, heading straight toward her. A flutter heightened her senses. One she didn't like. The man was a suspect, had a criminal background. Yet, she still felt a tug when his gaze locked on her, a disquieting contradiction. She straightened, wrapping cold objectivity around her as if it would protect her from an unwanted attraction.

"You're good. Ever work the rodeo circuit?"

"A time or two. I decided getting thrown off the backs of bucking horses wasn't my kind of life."

He draped an arm over the fence, looking down at her. Damn, she was a pretty one with her hair in that long braid. Under the brim of her hat, loose strands nestled around her dainty ears. A faint blush tinted her cheekbones—no heavy makeup here. *Hell, I can't do this*, he thought. He had to remember who he was talking to. Even a conversation could be dangerous.

Even before the remote look shuttered his face, she sensed he'd pulled back.

"As much as I would like to continue this, I need to get back to work. Nice seeing you again."

Piper watched him stride off, moving with a long-legged swagger. Something about Ron Pollard was off. It teased her instincts, especially since she didn't have a clue as to the reason. Across the way, she noticed another man looking at her, the one who helped Pollard. She'd also seen him in the sales ring. He was on the other gate. He turned and walked off. But his stare intensified her sense of disquiet.

Her phone chimed. It was Grady.

"We've got a problem," he said when she answered.

"What?"

"Two of Jarvis' men showed up. They want to inventory the cattle. I told them I couldn't authorize anything without talking to you."

"Tell them no. If Jarvis wants an inventory, he can call me and schedule a time. I'm on my way."

She raced to her truck. Pulling out, she punched it.

From inside the barn, Cade watched while Piper talked on the phone. Whatever was said had her running to her truck and peeling out of the parking lot. Footsteps crunched on the gravel. He spun to pick up a sack of grain. Tossing it over his shoulder, he turned toward the doorway just as Frankie stepped inside.

"What was that all about?" Frankie asked.

"What?"

"McKay? I saw the two of you talking, and then she lit out of here."

"Don't know." He shifted the weight on his shoulder and stepped outside.

Frankie tagged along. "She's one hot-looking babe. What'd she want with you?"

His lips curved in a cheeky grin. "Maybe my body." When Frankie leered at him, he snickered before adding, "What can I say? She liked the show."

"You might want to steer clear of her, considering she's a federal marshal."

Cade shot a sideways glance at him. "Got no interest in her, and there's no reason she'd have an interest in me."

"How about cash? Does *it* pique your interest?"

"Always."

"I do some jobs for a man, helping around the ranch. We might need an extra hand. Pays well if you know how to keep your mouth shut."

Cade glanced at him. "Don't much care what someone does as long as I get paid."

"Good. I'll let you know."

14

Piper screeched to a stop in the driveway, where an ugly scene confronted her. Two men had Grady backed up to the holding pen. One slapped his hand against Grady's chest, pushing him back.

She jumped out of the truck. Her voice vibrated with anger. "Get away from my foreman!"

The two men turned, and she immediately recognized them. They'd been at the café. "Grady, are you hurt?"

"No."

"I'm U.S. Marshal Piper McKay. Who are you?"

Narrow eyes in a weather-beaten face glared at her. "We work for Lane Jarvis. We don't have to answer your questions."

"Then get off my ranch!"

The shorter, heavily built man stepped toward her. His thick lips smirked. "Ah, now, I don't think we can do that either. How could a pretty, little gal like you think she could be a badass cop?" His tongue flicked across his lower lip.

"You are trespassing on private property. Leave, or I will press charges."

The other man spoke up. "We've got a right to be here. Lane Jarvis owns the cattle on this ranch, and we've got a right to inspect them."

"If Jarvis wants to discuss rights, tell him to call me. For the last time, I'm telling you to get off my ranch."

"Jack, maybe we need to teach her a lesson or two," the man with the leering expression said.

As they stepped toward her, she pulled her gun. Grady stepped alongside her, a loaded shotgun in his hands. While they'd been occupied with her, he'd stepped inside the barn and grabbed the gun that was kept next to the door.

They stopped.

In a harsh tone, Piper said, "Get in your truck and leave!"

A look of rage crossed the shorter man's face. "If someone takes a notion to smash your face, you won't be a pretty lady."

"Quinn, shut up," Jack growled. He turned and walked toward the truck parked near the gate.

After another hate-filled look, Quinn turned and followed.

Once they backed out and turned onto the highway, Piper eased the gun back into the holster and asked, "Are you sure you're okay?"

"Yeah, all they did was shove me around a bit. Bastards. If I'd seen them coming, I would have grabbed the shotgun. But I didn't. I heard the truck, and when I stepped out of the barn, they were on me."

Fury overtook her fear for Grady. "Keep that shotgun with you. I'm headed to town."

"Reckon you're planning on a visit to Jarvis' office."

"Got that right. Do you know their last names?"

"Jack Sloan and Quinn Giles."

"Once I'm done there, I'll swing by the hospital."

By the time she parked in front of Jarvis' office, the hot blaze of anger had turned to a cold determination.

Her face grim, she nodded at the secretary who rose from her desk to stop her from entering Jarvis' office. When she stepped inside, Jarvis was leaned back in his oversize executive chair, his feet propped on the desk, and a brandy glass in his hand. Sloan was seated in a chair. The other thug, Giles, leaned against the wall. At the sight of her, Jarvis' feet hit the floor with a thud. He set the glass on the desk.

"Marshal McKay. I planned on calling you. My men just told me there was a slight misunderstanding while they were at your ranch."

"That's why I'm here. To make sure there aren't any ..." she stopped to look at Sloan and Giles before adding, "further *misunderstandings* as you have termed it. Your men assaulted my foreman. The only reason they aren't sitting in a jail cell is because he wasn't harmed. If it happens again, I will file assault charges. So that there won't be any more *misunderstandings,* is that clear enough for you?"

He straightened in the chair. "Now, just wait a damn minute here. You can't walk in here and threaten me."

"Oh, yes! I can. And here's a tip for you, one you need to remember. I don't threaten. I promise. Having cleared up that *misunderstanding,* you will make an appointment with me if you want to inspect the cattle. Do you understand?"

He blustered, "I have the right to inspect my herd any damn time I please."

"No! You don't. I suggest *you* read the contract. Seems you left something out. You or any of your thugs come on my ranch again without my permission, and I can assure you there will be another *misunderstanding.* The next time it will be referred to as criminal trespass."

"It isn't your ranch, and my contract is with your grandmother."

"Must I remind you that I have my grandmother's power of attorney? I am in charge. What is the status of the check for payment of the cattle you sold? I never received a phone call."

"I haven't received a call from the bank yet. I'll follow up on it."

"Not good enough. You've got forty-eight hours to come up with the payment. If you don't, I'll file theft charges."

His toothy grin appeared. "Lady, if you want to play hardball, you'd better think twice. Your grandmother owes me over $700,000. I don't think you want me calling in that IOU."

She stepped to his desk, slammed her hands flat on the top as she leaned forward. "I'm not paying you one red cent. Go ahead, call in that IOU! Take me to court! I'm just itching to get you and your two thugs on a witness stand."

She straightened, turned and shot a scornful look at Giles and Sloan as she walked out. She would have liked to have stayed in the hall to hear what was said, but not with the secretary staring at her with a distinct look of animosity. She opened the door and walked outside.

When she stepped into the hospital room, Piper still fumed.

Tony greeted her. "From the look on your face, I'd say you've been on a tear."

Not wanting to talk about it in the room, she nodded as she stepped to the side of the bed. She picked up her grandmother's hand, leaned over and kissed her cheek. For a few minutes, she quietly talked, mostly about nothing, only wanting Jen to hear her voice. While she spoke, she watched Jen's face, looking for any change. When she mentioned Grady, she felt a slight pressure on her hand.

Hope flooded her system. Had her grandmother moved her hand or had she just imagined it. "Jen, can you hear me?"

The fingers Piper held twitched ever so slightly. My god, she hadn't imagined it. Even though Piper kept talking, there wasn't any further movement. She finally laid Jen's hand down.

When she turned to look at Tony, he shot out of his chair. "What!"

"Oh, Tony. She moved her hand. Not much, but enough that I could feel it. I have to tell the nurse, so she can make a note for the doctor." She rushed out of the room.

When she came back, she said, "Do you want to take a break, even go to the hotel? I can stay here until Davy arrives."

"I think I will run down and grab a bite to eat."

After he left, Piper leaned back in the chair, her eyes locked onto her grandmother, watching for any movement. Her phone rang. It was Luke. When she answered, he asked, "Where are you?"

"In my grandmother's hospital room."

When he asked about her condition, Piper excitedly explained about her grandmother moving her hand.

"Piper, that's great news. I'd say it means she's coming out of the coma. I have news as well. I received the report from the handwriting analyst on the Spence documents. The signature on the second contract was forged."

A jolt of excitement shot through her. They had a solid piece of evidence. As he talked, she stepped into the hallway. "How did he determine it was fake?"

"Trust me, you don't want to know. I asked the same question. When the analyst started throwing out terms like optical transfer, fractal theory, centroid ratio, and vector distance, he lost me in the first thirty seconds. Bottom line, the signature on the contract for the sale of the fifteen head is exactly the same as on the second contract. According to the analyst, no one ever signs their name exactly the same way. There is always a slight variance. This is a digital transference of the signature from the first contract to the second."

"Luke, I've got another contract from Jarvis. Same deal, selling ten head of cattle for which Jen never received payment."

"Send me that contract. I'll bet it'll prove the second one was forged."

"It will be tomorrow before I can send it."

"Okay. We could go ahead with a warrant based on the Spence documents, but there is a lot more going on here than just one contract. There's a nest of vipers, and I'd like to get them all, not just Jarvis. I've got several people tracing his financial transactions. Where is Tony?"

"Cafeteria. After what happened this morning, no food or drinks unless we bring them in."

"I had the lab in Dallas send me the report on the contents of the needle and coffee. The coffee was laced with valium. The needle contained a drug that would cause a seizure. It would look like she had a heart attack."

The same fear she'd felt when she got the phone call that morning rushed through her. Tears clutched her throat.

Sensing her distress, Luke said, "You okay?"

She sniffed. "Yeah, I am. I'll let Tony know when he gets back. I've got two more names to check out. Quinn Giles and Jack Sloan. They work for Jarvis. They tried pushing their weight around at the ranch today." Something occurred to her. "Wait a minute."

She pulled out the notebook to check the description Adams gave her. "Luke, I stopped at the airport. A man was there yesterday asking questions. The airport manager inadvertently told him I'd be returning last night. His description fits Sloan and the man who tried to kill Jen. If Sloan was the shooter at the airport, he had a busy night."

After they finished, she walked back inside, settling into the chair to watch Jen. When Tony stepped into the room, Piper hopped up, grabbed his arm, and pulled him into the hallway.

In hushed tones, she updated him about her conversation with Luke.

"From what you've told me, it could have been Sloan who tried to kill your grandmother. The height and build match," he replied. "I wonder where Giles and Sloan were the night the DNA lab was destroyed."

A surprise awaited when she pulled into the driveway at the ranch. A Ford F350 dually truck with an attached horse trailer was parked alongside the barn. JT had arrived.

A roar of laughter echoed from the kitchen. After dropping her backpack on the nearest chair, Piper stepped into the doorway. The man filled her kitchen. Six-four, 250 plus pounds with thick legs and brawny arms, JT looked like a walking tree trunk. Many a suspect took one look at him and quaked. It wasn't surprising he was assigned to most of the witness protection details.

Across from him, Grady cradled a beer bottle in his hands as he uproariously laughed. The change on his face, alert with color, the ashen grey gone, eased some of the constant anxiety of the last few days.

At the sight of her, JT stood, grabbing for the chair that started to topple over. "Dang," he said. "Good to see you're still in one piece despite the disturbing news I've heard."

Piper gave him a quick hug. "JT, I'm sure glad you're here." She stepped around to Grady, bending down to give him a kiss on the cheek.

JT settled back onto the chair. At the ominous creak, she cringed, wondering how long it would hold up.

"How's your grandmother doing?" he asked.

"Better." She turned to Grady. "I was holding her hand and talking to her. Grady, she moved her fingers."

His eyes twinkled. "Now, that's nothing short of wonderful. What did the doc have to say?"

"I don't know. I told the nurse what happened, and she made a note to tell him. Maybe this means she's starting to come out of the coma."

"You can't get around that it's a good sign."

"So, what have the two of you been talking about?"

JT scowled at her. "I've got a bone to pick with you."

Her eyebrows twitched upward. "Me? Why? What'd I do?"

His finger pointed to Grady. "You never mentioned you knew Grady Estes. My god, gal, don't you know, he's a legend on the rodeo circuit? Saved many a bull rider in his day, including my dad."

She pulled out a chair and propped her elbows on the table, ready to hear one of JT's stories. When he started talking about his rodeo days, the whole unit stopped to listen.

"Nah," Grady protested. "I didn't do anything more than any other rodeo clown."

"Piper, don't you believe it. From the stories I've heard, this man here danced and teased those bulls like a ballerina on stage. His antics kept the bull occupied while the crowd roared with cheers." JT's gaze turned to Grady. "I heard you caught a horn. Is that what ended your rodeo days?"

"No. Slowed me down a bit, but there were other reasons."

Piper knew he didn't like to talk about his past, or his wife and baby's death.

"I don't remember your dad, but over the years, there were many bull riders."

"You might not remember, but he sure as hell does. As he tells the story, he lay on the ground in the arena that day, stunned by the fall. The bull, head lowered, charged toward him. What imprinted in his mind was the sight of horns aimed straight at him. Then legs, encased in floppy, multi-colored pants and boots, danced between him and that bull. You hooted and hollered, waving a flag, darting back and forth, until the bull turned and charged at you. Men ran into the arena and picked up my dad, helping him as he staggered to safety." He paused, then added, "He also said, you damn near bought it that day. The horns barely missed you. Don't be surprised if you get a call from him one of these days."

As if uncomfortable, Grady shifted in his chair. His eyes darted to Piper with an unspoken message.

She changed the subject. "JT, what's with the trailer?"

"I thought it might come in handy to have my horse. I didn't figure you'd have one that's up to my weight."

She chuckled. "You're not exactly a featherweight."

"Tomorrow, I'll take you on a tour of the ranch. We can ride or use the UTV," Grady told him.

"Piper. Luke told me a few details. Said you'd fill in the gaps."

She stood. "Anyone want another?" When both said yes, she pulled three bottles from the fridge. "We're concerned," she nodded to Grady, "we could get hit again by this ring of cattle thieves."

She placed a bottle in front of each. "I'm not telling anyone that you're a marshal. If someone asks, you're an old friend of Grady's."

She twisted off the cap and took a swig before explaining about the thefts, contract, and the impact of the loss clause. "I found out there's been a rash of cattle thefts across East Texas. Since this isn't the type of unsolved crime that's entered in a database somewhere, I'm not sure how to go about researching the problem."

JT grunted. "There is a way. Have you talked to the Special Ranger at the Cattle Raisers Association who is assigned to this area? The Ranger will be your best source to get a handle on the number of thefts. The Association has an extensive database for tracking stolen cattle."

"I think Jen planned to call him. I found a note in her purse with a name, Cade Tanner, and a phone number. When I called, Tanner was out of the office, and I left a message. Since he hasn't called me, tomorrow I'll track down his boss."

She finished off the beer. "Something else you should know. Jarvis has a couple of thugs working for him, Quinn Giles and Jack Sloan. They showed up today, got a little nasty. Even though Jarvis may own the herd, he doesn't have the right to step foot on the ranch without my permission. I informed him of that fact, and if he or his men tried to muscle their way onto this property again, I'd have them arrested for criminal trespass."

JT's lips spread into a wide grin. "Damn, I'd liked to have seen that face-off with him."

Grady chuckled. "When she left here, she had a full head of steam. Takes after her grandmother."

"Were they armed?" JT asked.

"Could have been, but I didn't see a weapon."

Grady stood. "Time to get supper on the table. The grill is ready to go, and I've got three steaks in the fridge and baked potatoes in the oven." He eyed JT's bulk. "I should have added another piece of meat."

Across town, Cade Tanner shifted in the seat. Pushed all the way back, it was still damn uncomfortable. A stakeout was one of the more boring activities in an investigation. He'd spent many unpleasant hours on one as a detective with Houston PD.

The lot was quiet. The cattle had even settled down for the night. Backed in between several trailers parked on the far end of the parking lot, his truck was near invisible to any passing vehicle or anyone who might drive in. Even if they did see it, it wasn't suspicious as several vehicles were scattered around the lot. The cloud cover was a boon as it blocked the faint moonlight.

Since he had plenty of time on his hands, he couldn't keep his thoughts from straying to what he'd heard in Jarvis' office. Cattle rustling was big business, a high-stakes game. A few stolen head of cattle could bring in thousands of dollars. For many, it was worth the risk. However, whatever was going on went far beyond stealing cattle when you figure in murder. Where was the reward for killing a ranch owner and her granddaughter?

At the café this morning, the rumors were running amuck. Everyone seemed to have a different version about the shooting at the airport. The one common fact was that someone took a shot at a marshal. He was certain Sloan was the shooter. At least he'd tried to warn her. Still, he wondered why she was at the airport at that time of night. He'd like to know more, but there wasn't a way for him to find out. After he'd left the cafe, he'd called Nick to let him know what happened. Without any evidence, though, there wasn't much they could do.

Cade's thoughts shifted to the conversation with Frankie. It had caught him by surprise. Frankie's comment about keeping his mouth shut only meant one thing, it was illegal. Who was he working for?

He didn't have a doubt that stolen cattle were being run through the auction. When he first spotted the problem, he began keeping a tally of the incoming cattle. He knew exactly how many head the ranchers unloaded. At every sale, at least twenty additional head were sold that weren't in the original count.

Today, before he left, he'd made a pass by the pens, double-checking his count for tomorrow's sale, no change from the original tally. That meant someone was smuggling them in the night before the sale.

Lights flashed across the parking lot as a truck turned into the entrance. The driver swung wide to back the gooseneck trailer to a ramp.

A second truck with a trailer pulled onto the side of the parking lot. As men exited, Cade grabbed his binoculars. Damn, from his position, it was too dark to get a good look at them. He eased open the door. He'd already disconnected the overhead light. As Cade slid out, he left it slightly ajar.

Engrossed in their tasks, the men never glanced his way as he quietly moved toward the building. He crept forward, hugging the shadows as he slipped around the empty trailers parked on the lot.

Voices grew louder as the cattle were herded into pens. A man shouted, "One goes in with Miller's bunch." He rattled off another rancher's name and how many went in the pen with his cattle.

Cade had no difficulty identifying the voice. It was Frankie Hillard, and he had the pen assignments for the sale the next day.

When he reached the side of the building, he eased forward just far enough to look around the corner. In front of the truck, Frankie used the truck's headlights to read the clipboard.

Another man stepped beside him. Frankie flipped a page. "Four head in Martin's pen." While not surprised to see Jack Sloan, what did surprise him was that Frankie was running the show. Then the third man came into view, Giles.

Once the trailer was empty, Sloan hopped into the truck and pulled it further onto the lot. Giles backed the second trailer in place.

As the last animal ran into the pen, Frankie shouted to Giles, "Make sure the damn gates are locked this time." Within minutes, the men were back in the trucks and driving out of the lot.

Cade ran to his truck. Following them was a risk on lonely, dark county roads, but he might find where the cattle were stashed.

Ahead the tail lights on the trailer were barely visible. When the truck turned onto a county road, Cade flipped on the headlights. He noted the county road number as he turned but had no idea where it might lead. Cursing his unfamiliarity with the area, he was losing ground, but on the dark, empty road, if he got too close, his headlights stood out like a beacon. If he turned them off again, he'd likely end up in the bar ditch, or worse. On the dashboard GPS map, another intersecting county road was coming up. He sped up on the off chance they would turn. As he came over a rise, the tail lights were gone. When he reached the intersection, he stopped, but he'd lost sight of them.

A few more curses resounded as he turned to head back to town—nothing else he could do tonight. Briefly, Cade considered driving around the countryside once it got light. Then rejected it. He had a better use of his time, keeping an eye on Frankie Hillard.

After checking on the horses, Grady had gone to his apartment. JT lugged his duffel bag to the spare bedroom. He said he had paperwork for two of his cases he needed to finish up. Piper had checked in with Davy at the hospital, letting him know JT had arrived.

She picked up one of the envelopes containing duplicates of Leopold's records. She pulled out the documents and flipped through them. With these, Jen wouldn't have any trouble with proof of ownership. Then she remembered the phony contract. Her grandmother wouldn't own the bull unless Piper could prove the contract was forged.

She pulled the first contract from the file and made a copy for her records. Sliding the original into an envelope, she addressed it to her boss. Tomorrow, on her way into town, she'd drop it off at the FedEx office.

Despite a sinking feeling, she refused to allow herself to become discouraged. This wasn't over yet. Energized by a renewed sense of effort, she picked up the DNA report. She wasn't sure what she was reading, but a few statements caught her eye. It seemed Leopold's DNA markers showed an enhanced level for meat production. She really did need to stop by Brad's ranch and get him to help sort all this out. She was in unknown territory here.

Under the DNA report was the reward flyer. This wasn't just some run-of-the-mill bull. Someone had to know something. She wondered if she should increase the reward. Tomorrow, she'd ask Grady. Get his take. There had to be some way to shake the tree, find someone willing to talk. She just had to have the right leverage.

Amazed, Piper stopped in the doorway. Oh, she was so tempted to make a dash to the bedroom for her cellphone to get a picture. By the time she got back, though, the moment would have passed. Poised in front of the stove, JT flipped bacon.

When he turned and spotted her in the doorway with a dumbstruck look, he said, "What! You don't think I know how to cook?"

She laughed, eyeing the spatula that in his large fist looked like a toy. "Somehow, you and a skillet don't compute."

"I'll have you know," he said, waving the spatula at her, "Judy's got me trained. I'm just all sorts of handy to have around the house."

Piper had met Judy on several occasions. The petite woman had her husband wrapped around her little finger. Still laughing, Piper crossed to the counter and poured a cup of coffee. "Where's Grady?"

"Actually, I'm standing in for him. He needed to check something in the barn."

The mudroom door slammed, a breeze of cool morning air rushed in. As Grady walked in, rubbing his hands together, he said, "Bit of a nip in the air. Horses feel it and are raring to go. That's a beauty you've got. I figure he's got to be close to sixteen hands high."

At Piper's look of interest, JT explained, "Ripken's a registered paint. He's got the speed and quickness that makes a good stock horse. I did some bulldogging and calf roping. That horse helped me earn a considerable amount of prize money."

Piper set plates and utensils on the table, then refilled her cup. Grady piled toast on a plate while JT and Piper scooped eggs on their plates, adding strips of bacon.

"What are your plans today?" Piper asked.

"We're going to check the fence lines and gates and move a couple of round bales into the pastures. I'll take another count of the herd. Might come in handy."

Piper washed down the forkful of eggs with a sip of coffee. "That's a good idea. With JT here, it gives us an independent verification. Grady, do you think I should increase the reward money?"

"Might not be a bad idea since we haven't had any takers."

JT asked, "What is it now?"

She told him.

"That's not chicken change."

"I'll type a new flyer before I leave this morning and bump it to 25,000. Grady, how much cash do we have on hand?" Jen always kept a reserve of cash for emergencies.

"I don't know the exact amount, but it's not anywhere close to 25,000. I'd have to check the safe to be certain."

"No, don't bother. It's probably better if I stop by the bank and withdraw the funds. I don't like keeping that much money on hand, but informants are a hinky lot. If someone calls, and I'm not ready with the money, I could lose the chance to find Leopold."

JT asked, "Where else are you going?"

"You're as bad as Tony, wanting to keep track of me."

Unrepentant, a broad smile crossed his face. Waving a fork with a chunk of scrambled eggs, he said, "Damn right."

"The hospital, the bank, and Brad's place." For JT's benefit, she added, "He's a local rancher. I want to talk to him about the DNA report on Leopold. There's another auction today. I'll drop the new flyer off." Piper stood, picking up her plate and utensils. After rinsing them, she placed them in the dishwasher.

While the men finished up in the kitchen, she typed up the new flyer. Piper made several copies and stuck them in an envelope. On the way out, she grabbed a pair of rubber boots from the mudroom and tossed them in the bed of the truck. Tromping around cattle pens was a dirty business. She didn't want to smell like manure the rest of the day.

To her dismay, when she arrived at the hospital, the nurse told her there was no change in Jen's condition. After a quick tap on the door, she pushed it open. Davy was still there, along with Tony. After greeting them, she walked to the side of the bed. Maybe it was her imagination or just wishful thinking, but her grandmother's face seemed more alert, the flaccid look gone.

She turned to the two men. "Has she moved?"

Davy answered, "Not that I saw."

"Has the doctor been here yet?"

"No," Davy told her.

Piper squeezed her grandmother's hand and kissed her on the cheek. After whispering a few words, she turned.

Tony asked, "How'd the first night with JT on the job go?"

"Oh, he and Grady bonded over rodeo stories. Grady used to be a rodeo clown, and JT's dad was a bull rider. JT told the story about how Grady saved his dad's life. It embarrassed the hell out of Grady."

"I'd like to have heard that one," Tony said.

"I sure feel a lot better with him at the ranch."

"What's on your agenda today?" Tony asked.

She chuckled. "JT asked the same question." She told them about upping the reward money and the stops she planned to make.

The door opened. Doctor Henderson strode in.

Piper turned to greet him.

Davy said, "Piper, I'll talk to you later," and left.

"I hope it wasn't anything I said," Doctor Henderson quipped in a dry tone as he shook hands with Tony.

Piper chuckled at the unexpected humor from the normally staid, no-nonsense doctor.

"Not at all," she said. "Shift change."

She waited near the bed while he went through his routine of looking at Jen's chart and his examination.

"I saw your note. Has there been any more movement?" he asked.

"Not that we've seen," Piper told him. "That's a good sign, isn't it? That she moved her fingers."

"Yes, very good. It means she is beginning to be aware of her surroundings. All in all, I am very satisfied with the progress I am seeing. Once she comes out of the coma, we'll be able to disconnect these tubes." He made a couple of notations on the chart, then hung it back on the hook at the end of the bed.

"I'll check on her later today." He nodded to both of them and left.

"Anything I can do?" Tony asked.

"Would you follow up with Luke? I asked for a background on the two goons that work for Jarvis. He's still running the financials. Maybe he's found something new. Tell him JT has settled in at the ranch."

"Will do. I might be able to help with the financial search."

"Thanks, Tony. I'll be in touch."

Piper glanced at her watch as she walked out. Plenty of time to stop at FedEx and the bank before the auction began. After setting up priority shipping on the envelope that contained the first contract, she headed to the bank. Still closed, she took advantage of the lull to check her emails on her laptop. When she saw a man unlocking the front doors, she shut down the computer and hopped out of the truck. A teller motioned to her as she walked in.

After identifying herself, she told the teller she wanted to make a cash withdrawal. The teller slid a withdrawal form toward her. Piper pulled her notepad from her backpack, where she'd written Jen's account number. She filled in the required information and slid it toward the teller.

When the woman looked at it, her eyes widened. She said, "May I see your identification?"

Piper pulled out a copy of her power of attorney from the backpack and her driver's license from a pocket in her badge case. She handed them to the woman. The teller gazed at the badge with an uncertain look before glancing at the legal document. "My supervisor has to approve this." She made a call.

A few minutes later, another woman arrived. After introducing herself, the supervisor studied the power of attorney and driver's license, then the account information on the computer screen.

"I need to refer this to my manager," the supervisor said and walked away.

The response wasn't a surprise. Piper doubted they had many customers who wanted to withdraw 25,000 in cash.

In a few minutes, Mack Huber, along with the supervisor, walked up.

"Marshal McKay. Is this right? You want 25,000 in cash?"

"Yes."

"Humph! This is most unusual."

"Need I remind you that I do have her power of attorney. I'd be happy to call Arnie Larson."

"Oh, no, I'm sure this is fine. I am concerned, though, about the large amount. Carrying that amount of cash can be very dangerous."

She shot him a look of amazement.

Realizing his mistake, he quickly backtracked. "But, of course, you're a U.S. Marshal. You'd be aware of the risks. How do you want that?"

"One-hundred-dollar bills."

The transaction took longer than expected. The teller checked the count twice as well as running the bills through the counting machine. The supervisor stood nearby, which probably added to her stress level. Huber had departed.

Once the money had been placed in two envelopes, Piper stuffed them into her backpack. She certainly didn't want to be seen carrying anything out of the bank.

In her truck, she debated where to stash the money. She didn't want to take the time to drive back to the ranch but didn't want to leave it in the truck while she was at the auction. The best spot was the hospital.

It didn't take long to drive there, where Tony assured her that he didn't mind adding guarding money to his list of duties. With a hearty chuckle, she headed back out the door.

The lot was nearly full when she parked. Not having a reason to carry the backpack, she pulled out one of the new flyers, then dropped the pack on the floor behind her seat. She folded the flyer and stuck it in her coat pocket. Before she walked away, she changed into the rubber boots. She strolled toward the pens, idly glancing at the animals. Her cellphone rang. "Hi, Grady."

"Piper, we've been hit again. By my count, we're ten head short."

A surge of anger rolled over her. "When was the last time you counted the herd?"

"A week or so before Jen was injured."

"Any idea how they got in?"

"JT believes it was through the gate where Jen was attacked. We found tire tracks. I need to check my log for the last time it rained. That might narrow down the time frame. Where are you?"

"Auction house. Go ahead and report it to the sheriff's department. Not that it will do any good." Disgusted, she shoved the phone in her pocket. Next to her, a cow stuck its nose through the metal rails. It let out a loud moo as if protesting its plight. "Yeah, I feel the same damn way," she muttered.

Her gaze scanned the cattle inside the pen before she wandered to the next. As she moved from pen to pen, she pulled on her memory to identify the different breeds. In one, as she stared at them, an odd sense that something was wrong crept into her mind.

An employee, the man who'd watched her the last time she was here, walked by. He asked if she needed any help. She thanked him but told him no.

It wasn't until she reached the last pen that it dawned on her, the ear tags. Ranchers used ear tags to identify their animals, much the same as a brand did. Calves were tagged within a few weeks of their birth. Occasionally, they got lost and had to be replaced. But in this case, in every pen, one or more animals were missing an ear tag. By the time she circled the pens again, she had counted twenty head. She could understand maybe one or two but not twenty. The tags should have been replaced before the animals were brought to the sale.

She glanced at her watch. She had time. In the small notebook she carried, she noted the lot number and owner's name on the paper placard attached to the fence, along with the number of missing tags. Then she took pictures with her phone. She worked her way from pen to pen, documenting and photographing.

As she turned to walk to the building, Ron Pollard was a few feet away from her.

Despite the smile on his face, his eyes had a guarded look. "I see you're checking out the stock. Thinking about buying today?"

She wondered if he'd noticed she was taking pictures. "I might. It's a big sale. Are they usually this large?"

"It runs in cycles. Anything I can help with?"

"No, but thanks anyway. I'd better get inside if I'm going to get a seat."

He stared at her as she walked away. He'd seen her making entries in a notebook and taking pictures. Damn, he'd bet she had spotted the stolen cattle. But it wasn't her actions that set off his misgivings. It was Frankie Hillard. He'd also watched from the shadows of an overhanging roof.

She stopped in the office and dropped off the flyer, asking the woman behind the desk to give it to Grant. Henry spotted her when she stepped inside the arena. He waved to get her attention. She scrambled up the steps as he scooted over.

"Didn't expect to see you again this soon," he said.

The bell clanged, signaling the start of the auction. The gate opened, and the first lot of cattle ran into the ring. She leaned closer and asked, "How many are you selling today?"

"Fifteen head."

She sat back and pulled out her notepad. She flipped pages until she reached the one labeled Miller. She had counted sixteen in his pen, not fifteen, and one had a missing ear tag. She waited to see what would happen. The sale moved swiftly. Grant was an old hand at auctioneering, knew how to keep it on track, despite the occasional glitch of an uncooperative animal.

Henry said, "My lot should be up next." He peered at the buyers sitting in the packed arena as his cattle ran into the pen. During the auction, he watched the bidders, not what was happening in the ring.

When Grant hollered, "Sold," Henry turned to Piper. "The buyer's a rep for a meatpacking plant." By the time he looked at the arena, all that could be seen were the rear ends of the last two animals trotting out.

Since his attention was on the buyers, it was easy to see why Henry didn't notice the discrepancy. She wondered if it was the same for the other ranchers. Piper watched the crowd for the rest of the auction and noted several ranchers who kept an eye on the bidders, not on the sales ring.

The bell clanged. The auction was over. Henry stood, stretching. "These seats are hard on old bones like mine."

Piper spotted Brad walking out. "There goes Brad. I want to talk to him before he leaves. I'll catch you later." Bunched together, people crowded the steps. When she finally made it outside, Brad was opening his truck door. She shouted.

A smile lit up his face as she jogged toward him. "I saw you in the crowd. Good sale today."

Even though she already knew, she asked, "Were you selling?"

He had a satisfied expression. "Yup. I did well. And so did most everyone else. The price of beef is up."

Piper knew ranchers watched the price index for cattle in the same way investors watched the stock market. "How many did you sell?"

"Twenty head today."

"I'm curious. May I see your sales receipt? I'm trying to decide whether I need to bring some of Jen's cattle in."

"Sure, got it right here." He pulled a folded paper from his coat pocket.

She unfolded it and quickly scanned it. She wasn't interested in the sales price, only the number. The receipt was for twenty head. Yet, she counted twenty-two animals in his pen. Two were missing an ear tag.

She smiled and handed it back. "You're right. A good price. Something for me to think about. If you have time, I'd like to come by your place and take a look at those books."

"Sure. I'll be home for the rest of the day."

A feeling of exhilaration coursed through her. She'd bet her last dollar the animals missing the ear tags were stolen. What she didn't know was whether Grant was in on the scheme or was he being duped by someone in his organization? If she hung around for a while, she might find out something else.

The office was abuzz with activity as the ranchers waited to get their receipts. Henry was getting ready to leave when Piper walked up. She asked him the same question. He handed her the receipt. Same as Brad. In this case, it was fifteen head, not sixteen as she'd counted.

"Did you catch up with Brad?"

"I did." She handed him the receipt.

Dale Hanson walked up. "Ready to go, boss?"

Henry smiled and waved his receipt in the air. "Didn't forget today."

Behind her, she heard Grant's voice. He was talking to another rancher. When he spied her, he stepped toward her. "I saw you in the audience."

"A big sale today," she said, her eyes watchful.

"Yeah, it was a good day."

"I dropped off another reward flyer. I increased the reward to

$25,000. I also added another contact telephone number, my cell-phone. Would you please distribute it to all your contacts?"

"Sure. That's a hefty change."

"I'm hoping it will get someone's attention. Grant, I'd like to talk to you about the paperwork on the sales. Since it looks like I will be managing the ranch, I need to learn more about the sales side of the business." Was that uneasiness that flashed in his eyes?

In a voice just a little too hearty, he said, "Sure. I'd be glad to help. I can't do it today, though. I need to sign off on the paperwork for the buyers. I'll call you."

As she wandered outside, she pondered his reaction. She dodged a truck pulling in line to load. An eighteen-wheeler was already backed up to the ramp. She figured it belonged to one of the meat companies. Handlers funneled the cattle into the large trailer. Pollard, atop a horse, herded cattle from a connecting pen. As she watched, the cattle with the missing ear tags trotted up the ramp.

She knew how the stolen cattle were being sold, but what the hell was she going to do now?

eated in her truck, Piper tapped the speed dial on her phone. When Luke answered, she said, "I discovered how the stolen cattle are being sold." She explained.

"Seems like a slick operation," Luke said.

"It is. If someone did spot the discrepancy, it could be explained away as just a mistake. There was a mix-up in the cattle or a computer glitch. The next question is, who's running the show? Would you start digging into the auction house and Grant Sheffield?"

"I'll add him into the mix. What about Pollard?"

"He could be involved. I found out he's responsible for the tally once they're sold. Easy for him to falsify the total. Grady discovered we'd been hit again, another ten head stolen. Some of the stolen animals sold at the auction today may have been from my ranch. When I get home, I'll have Grady take a look at the pictures. He might be able to recognize them. I couldn't."

"What now?"

"Keep flipping rocks to see who crawls out. I upped the ante to $25,000 for information on the bull."

"That should turn some rocks. I finally got a call from the arson investigator. The fire was deliberately set. It started in the room where the samples were kept and the computer room."

"Any suspects?"

"No. The investigator said he'd let me know, though. Jarvis used the Spence contract to obtain a bank loan. That opened up a new level of research. Two more ranches popped up, one in Colorado and one in West Texas. As I get more details, I'll let you know. In the meantime, watch your back. Giles and Sloan have got long rap sheets, drugs, assaults, and weapons charges. I've already passed this on to Tony."

"Did he mention they showed up at the ranch? Tried to muscle their way past my foreman. I warned Jarvis if it happened again, I'd file charges. They don't step foot on the property without my permission."

"I don't imagine that went over well."

"Nothing he can do about it. The contract doesn't stipulate I have to allow him access to the herd."

"I'll be damned. He slipped up there."

"Yeah, he did. I'll catch you later."

As she disconnected, she considered her next step. She needed more information on the other incidents of rustling. She flipped back the pages in her notepad until she reached the telephone number for the Association. She still hadn't received a call from Cade Tanner.

A voice answered, "Texas & Southwestern Cattle Raisers Association. How may I help you?"

"I'd like to speak with Cade Tanner."

"I'm sorry, he's out of the office. May I take a message?"

"I've already left him one. I'd like to speak with his supervisor."

"What is your name?"

"U.S. Deputy Marshal Piper McKay."

"Just a moment, please."

After several clicks, a deep voice said, "Marshal McKay, this is Nick Rawling. What can I do for you?"

"I've tried to contact Cade Tanner. He hasn't returned my call."

"He's out of town at a training conference. Is there a problem?"

"Yes," she told him before launching into the reason for her call. She finished by adding, "There has been another theft of my cattle. I've learned my ranch is not the only one that's been hit. I would like a copy of any other thefts in this area and to talk with the individual in charge of the investigations."

"Let me find out the status, and I'll call you back. What is a good number to reach you?"

Piper didn't bother to hide her annoyance as she relayed the number in clipped tones. After Rawling disconnected, she uttered a few cuss words. She'd just been stonewalled, and she damn well didn't like it. Her tires squealed as she pulled out of the driveway.

He'd spotted her the moment she stepped out of the building. Cade expected she'd leave, but when she hung around, he kept a wary eye on her. As he herded cattle into the pen for loading, her close scrutiny of the animals set off another jolt of uneasiness. Frankie straddled a fence, prodding the animals, but his eyes continually strayed toward Piper. Once she finally walked to her truck, Cade sighed with relief.

Frankie hopped down from the fence. "Pollard," he shouted. "I've got to go inside for a minute. You got this?"

"Yeah." As he watched the man disappear inside the building, his apprehension built. Since he knew Frankie was up to his neck in the cattle rustling, his rushing inside after watching Piper sure didn't bode well.

While he finished loading the cattle, he kept an eye on Piper's truck. She didn't leave. *What the hell is she doing?* he wondered. Then she backed, her tires spun on the gravel as she turned and shot out of the parking lot. *Something sure pissed her off,* he thought.

Once the last of the cattle had been loaded, he turned toward the barn. When he dismounted, he handed the reins to one of the high school kids who worked part-time at the auction.

Cade stripped off his gloves and stuffed them in his back pocket as he meandered toward the sales office. Most of the staff had left, though a couple of men were still cleaning the arena.

Frankie was in Grant's office. When he stopped in the doorway, he heard him say, "Nothing we can do about it right now."

When Grant spotted him, he said, "I'll talk to you about it later. Need something, Ron?"

He stepped further into the room to let Frankie leave. "Wanted to let you know, the loading's done. I'll double-check the pens and lock up the outbuildings. Unless you need me to stick around, I'm out of here."

"No, that should do it for today. Oh, by the way, Piper McKay was here. Frankie happened to mention she was checking out the pens. Any idea why?"

Cade shrugged. "I heard her say something about buying. That it?"

"Yeah, see you tomorrow."

Cade turned and walked out. When Sheffield asked about Piper, his instincts flared. Why would Frankie mention her unless she was what they couldn't do anything about?

Outside, he watched Frankie hop in his truck. His phone rang. He pulled it from his pocket and checked the caller ID—Nick. Before he answered, he walked away from the building, glancing around to be sure no one was within earshot.

"Cavalry," he answered.

"Cade, we've got a problem," his boss said.

"I bet I can guess. McKay."

"I got a call from her. Since she couldn't reach you, she called me. Wants details on our investigations. I stalled."

He chuckled. "I saw her response."

"What?" Nick asked.

"She just tore out of the parking lot spewing gravel. I knew something had ticked her off."

"What's going on?"

Cade had already updated his boss on the delivery of the stolen cattle. "I suspect she's snapped to the fact Sheffield is running stolen cattle through the auction. How I'm not sure, but she was taking notes and pictures. Frankie saw it too."

"McKay said her ranch had been hit again. She's already had two other thefts. I haven't received a report from Sheriff Horne."

"She's not going to like it but keep stalling her. Frankie's offer may be the break we've been looking for. I can't afford for her to get in any deeper than she already is."

"I'll at least send her those reports. That might help keep her at bay, though I've got a hunch it's not going to work for very long."

"As long as she believes I'm Ron Pollard, we should be okay. Have you found out anything more about Jarvis?"

Nick said, "Not yet, but I'll keep you posted."

Giles and Sloan's interest in the auctions had caught his attention. They weren't buying or selling, so why were they continually hanging around? What his boss found on the background check pushed him to look closer at Lane Jarvis. It wasn't until after Cade told Nick about the conversation he'd overheard that Nick started to dig into Jarvis' financial dealings.

He hit the disconnect button and slid the phone into his pocket. A difficult assignment had just become more dangerous.

Cade's prior experience as a Houston PD detective had proved instrumental when the position for a Special Ranger came open.

What he didn't realize at the time, his stint as an undercover narc also played a role in his being hired.

His first day on the job, Rawling brought up the undercover assignment. Cattle thefts in East Texas were on the rise with an imprint of an organized ring of rustlers. The focal point seemed to center around Hopkins County. As the new kid on the block, no one would recognize him. At the time, it seemed a straightforward type of operation, infiltrate the auction house.

As the center of the cattle business in any community, the auction house was a breeding source for rumors. He didn't expect to find that Sheffield's operation was hand in glove with the thieves or that it would turn deadly when a rancher was killed. Then McKay entered the picture, and she was stirring the pot. He'd been keeping an eye on Sheffield and Jarvis. Now he had to add McKay and Frankie to the mix.

Before heading to Brad's ranch, Piper stopped at the hospital. She'd pass on what she'd discovered to Tony.

As she stepped into her grandmother's room, her eyes darted toward the bed.

"No change," Tony told her. "I've been watching to see if she moves."

After standing by the bed for a few minutes, holding Jen's hand and talking to her, she walked to the chair by Tony. A deep sigh erupted as Piper collapsed.

In a low whisper, she said, "Hell of a morning."

A scratchy voice said, "Don't need to whisper. I can still hear you."

"Jen!" she cried. Piper bounded to her feet, rushing to the bed. Jen's eyes were open. Tears ran down her face as she cuddled her grandmother's hand in hers.

"Stop sniveling, nothing to start crying about," Jen said, her voice slightly stronger.

Behind her, Tony said, "I'll get the nurse."

"Who is that, and why is he in my room?"

"Long story." Her hand brushed Jen's cheek.

"What happened?"

"You were injured."

"So tired." Her eyes closed again.

The nurse rushed in.

Fearful that Jen had slipped back into the coma, she said, "She talked to me, then went out again." Piper stepped back from the bed to let the nurse examine Jen.

After a few minutes, the nurse said, "She's asleep, not back in a coma. She'll be fading in and out until her strength builds up."

"Is this normal?"

"Oh, yes, quite normal."

Giddy with relief, Piper braced her hand on the nightstand next to the bed to help hold her upright.

"I've made a note on her chart, and I'll call the doctor. He told us to immediately notify him of any change in her condition."

Sinking back into the chair, she didn't want to take her eyes off Jen.

"Would you like a cup of coffee from the cafeteria? I could use one," Tony asked.

"It sounds good."

After Tony left, Piper walked back to the bed. As she watched Jen sleep, she choked back the tears. The fear that she'd lose Jen finally started to recede.

Tony walked in with two cups balanced in his hand, one on top of the other. She grabbed the top cup and motioned toward the door. He followed her out.

He leaned against the wall. "Okay, tell me what happened."

She took a gulp of the coffee and felt the hot liquid ease the tightness in her throat. Still, she kept her voice low while she explained what she'd discovered at the auction house.

"I'll be damned," he said. "What are you going to do about it?"

"I'm not certain since I don't have any evidence to back it up. Plus, with what Luke is working on, I think we need to keep a lid on it."

She told him about her phone call to the association. "I'm not holding my breath they will be of any help. I'm going to stop by the ranch. I want to put the money in the safe and talk to Grady. If he looks at the pictures, he might recognize some of the cattle. Then I'm headed to Brad Dexter's ranch. He seems to be the resident expert on cattle DNA. I need to pick his brain."

Tony tossed his empty cup in a nearby trash can. "If she wakes up again, what do you want me to tell her? She's going to ask."

"I know. Before she fell asleep, she wanted to know who you were. Limit it to why you're here, a precaution for her protection, nothing about the second attempt on her life or the contract. I need to wait until she is stronger. The one question we have to ask, though, is whether she knows who hit her."

"Got it. I'll let Davy know when he gets here."

She walked back inside. A quick glance showed her grandmother was still asleep. Piper picked up the envelopes containing the reward money and stuffed them into her backpack.

On the way out, her phone chimed. It was the number for the association.

"McKay," she answered.

"Marshal McKay, this is Nick Rawling with the Cattle Raisers Association. I have several reports for you. Give me an email address. Once you've had a chance to look them over, if you have any questions, please call me."

"I appreciate it." After giving him an email address, she disconnected. Maybe she was going to get some cooperation after all.

Anxious to reach the ranch and tell Grady the news, Piper didn't tarry on her way out of town. At the sound of her truck, Grady came out of the barn carrying the shotgun.

When she hopped out, he anxiously asked, "Something wrong? I didn't expect you back this early."

"No, it's good. Come inside, and I'll tell you."

"I'll be right there. I want to put the shotgun back."

Just as she closed the door to the safe, Grady stepped into the office.

"Grady! She woke up. Only for a few seconds, but she talked to me. She knew me."

Excitement lit up his face. "What a relief. So what now?"

"The nurse said it's normal for her to be awake for only a few minutes. But she's not in a coma. She's sleeping. I could almost dance with joy," she exclaimed.

"Did she say anything about the attack?"

"Not yet. Where's JT?"

"Still poking around the east pastures. He wanted a closer look at the truck tracks."

He nodded toward the safe. "Get the money?"

"Yes." She pulled out her phone. "I took these pictures at the auction today. Look at the ones missing an ear tag. Do they look familiar?"

Grady dropped into the chair in front of the desk, slowly scanning each picture. "A few might be ours. What's the deal?"

"I believe Sheffield is running stolen cattle through his auction."

Shocked, Grady stared at her. "Grant! I've known him for years. He's always been on the up and up."

"Either he's in on it, or someone who works for him is running the operation on the sly."

"It just doesn't seem possible. I've known most everyone who works there for years. As a matter of fact, the only ones who are new are Pollard and that Hillard fellow. How did you figure it out?"

"I'd like to wait until JT is here to go over the details. I also told Brad I'd be by his place today. I need to get going. I had my boss run Sloan and Giles. Keep that shotgun handy. Don't take any chances if you see them around here."

His phone rang. After glancing at the caller ID, he waved his hand toward his secretary. "We'll finish the letter later. Close the door on your way out."

Once she left, he answered, "Jarvis."

An angry voice erupted on the other end. "I thought you were going to take care of McKay and the old lady."

"Yeah, well, there were unexpected problems."

"You'd damn well better do something … and fast. McKay's snooping around the auction house, taking pictures of the cattle."

"When?"

"Today."

"Any idea why?"

"No, but there was twenty head of stolen cattle mixed in. She's probably got pictures of them on her cellphone."

"Just because she's got a few pictures doesn't mean she's got evidence that will stand up in court."

"Dammit, man! McKay's a god-damn U.S. Marshal, not some two-bit county cop. And don't forget, if you don't get rid of the two of them, you can kiss that million bucks for the bull goodbye."

"Why don't you do something? But then, you draw the line at actually killing someone, don't you?"

A grunt sounded. "Lane, just do your job. Oh, by the way, she's raised the reward money on her bull to $25,000." The line went dead.

Disgusted, he tossed the phone on the desk. Leaning back in his chair, he thought about how the Layton contract had turned into a major screw-up. As long as two marshals were at the hospital, he could forget about another attempt to get to the old lady. Time, however, might solve his problem. The marshals couldn't protect her forever. Once she left the hospital, he'd find a way.

The bitter taste of bile rose in his throat as he thought of the reason for his failures. *McKay!* She was the thorn in his side. Get rid of her, and it would take care of both problems. With her out of the picture, he'd have a chance to take care of Layton. He had to find a way to get McKay alone, isolate her. *Well, hell!* He had the perfect bait, the bull. It worked once before; why not again?

Straightening, he hit the speed dial. When the call was answered, he said, "Sloan, I need you in my office. Make it fast."

Piper drove up the long driveway that led to a 1940s style ranch house. Since her last visit, the house had undergone a facelift, new paint, and a porch on the side.

Brad stepped out as she exited the truck. He chuckled. "I was sure hoping you'd stop by. I don't get many visitors these days."

She followed him into the living room, which hadn't changed. Hummel figurines still adorned the fireplace mantel. Crocheted doilies covered the arms of the sofa and easy chairs as well as the tops of the tables. A long-ago image of Brad's wife sitting in a chair wielding crochet needles popped into Piper's mind. Even though she had passed away several years back, her memory was still very much alive in this room.

"Have a seat. Would you like something to drink?"

"No thank you."

He settled in an easy chair. "So, how do you like being back?"

"I have to say, I wish it was under different circumstances."

A somber look settled on his face. "How is Jennie doing?"

"Oh, Brad, she came out of her coma. She talked to me."

"That's wonderful news. Your grandmother has been a power-house in the cattle business around here for many years. When your grandaddy died, a lot of people thought she'd go under. How could a woman run a ranch? But damned if she didn't prove them wrong. But that's not why you're here."

From the backpack she'd set on the floor by her feet, she pulled out a folder and extracted the DNA report. "I wanted your opinion." She handed it to him.

He picked up a set of reading glasses from the table next to his chair. Settling them on his nose, he studied the report.

She leaned back on the sofa and waited.

"Son-of-a-gun. Leopold does have the genetic marker for double-muscled cattle. I've often wondered."

"What does it mean?" Piper asked.

"Over the last several years, ranchers have used DNA markers to improve their herds. One rancher might be looking for a bull to increase milk production. Others might be looking to increase the number of calves born each year. Muscle mass is another marker, which increases the sale price of the animal. More meat for the buck. In the past, it was guesswork. Ranchers had to rely on data after the calves were born. That's why DNA markers and artificial insemination have turned into a multi-billion-dollar business. Ranchers know upfront what they are getting."

"So, what is significant about double-muscled cattle?" Piper asked.

"A higher meat yield with less fat content, making the meat more tender. It has to do with a mutation of the myostatin gene that regulates growth. The mutation is actually two genes in the DNA marker. For the average rancher, breeding double-muscled cattle has always been problematic since many calves must be delivered by cesarean section. For rangeland operators, it's cost-prohibitive."

He looked back down at the report, shaking his head in amazement. "I wonder if Jennie knows how valuable Leopold is?" He looked back at Piper. "Studies indicate if the DNA marker only has one of the mutation genes, not two, the problem with the calves is eliminated."

Her mind raced as links dropped into place. "Leopold has only one gene."

"Yes. The better bulls can produce anywhere from 80,000 to over 100,000 doses every year. A straw, which is the term for one dose, typically sells from twenty-five to fifty dollars. Let's assume the lower end of the scale, 80,000 doses at $25. That's 2 million. At fifty bucks, it's 4 million. A straw for a bull with a single mutation marker like Leopold could easily sell for a hundred or more dollars."

"What I don't understand, Brad, is how someone could profit from stealing Leopold?"

"Since the bull is so well known, I don't know."

"What if his records were destroyed?"

A thoughtful expression crossed his face. "Never thought about it, but you might be able to create a new identity, especially with those DNA markers. That's what will sell his semen, not that he's won a bunch of awards. Some auction houses now include DNA markers as part of the auctioneer's spiel during a bull's sale. People forge new identities. Why not a bull?" He handed the report back to her.

As she stuffed it back into her pack, she said, "Could I borrow the books you lent to Jen?"

"Sure, let me get them. They're in my office."

While she waited, two words resonated in her mind, new identity. A sense of uneasiness built.

A few minutes later, he handed her two books. "If you have any questions, let me know."

She rose, slinging the backpack over her shoulder, the books cradled in her arms. She hesitated, then said, "Brad, do me a favor.

Forget you saw the DNA report. If anyone asks, you haven't seen it. All you did was give me a couple of books. Okay?" She stared at him with an anxious expression.

Brad gave her a sharp look of understanding. "It's a dangerous path you're traveling. You need help, you call."

She leaned over and kissed his cheek. "Thank you."

When she walked out, she made sure the books were clearly visible in case someone watched. She opened the passenger door and set them on the backseat. Piper slid behind the wheel, tossing her backpack across the console. She waved to the old man who stood on the front porch. He watched with a wistful look as he waved back.

On the drive into town, anxiety gnawed at her. Arnie certainly hadn't been optimistic about the outcome of a court case. Jen's word wouldn't carry much weight in a court of law against a signed contract. So why risk a second attempt? Why risk a high-profile murder of a federal officer?

According to Brad's calculations, Leopold could be worth millions. Was there more behind the attempts to kill Jen than the contract? If the plan were to totally erase the bull's identity, what about who owned the bull? Did the current owners, Jen, and by extension herself as the heir to the estate, have to be eliminated?

Another thought suddenly struck her, the value Jarvis had placed on the bull in the contract. Grady said Leopold was worth about two hundred thousand dollars. Why did Jarvis put it at one million? Was he only trying to jack up the contract's value, or did it have something to do with the DNA report?

Ahead, hospital windows gleamed from the light of the setting sun. Tony was still standing guard when she entered the room. She stepped to the bed to check on Jen.

"She didn't wake up again," he said, knowing it was what she'd want to hear first. "The doctor came by. He said to tell you this was normal, and she's a lot better."

Piper collapsed in the chair. As she watched her grandmother, she said, "I think I know why Leopold was stolen." She explained what she'd learned from Brad and her theory about a new identity for the bull.

"Makes sense," Tony said. "It sure puts a new twist on identity theft. Has Grady seen the pictures?"

"Yes, he thinks some of them were stolen from our ranch."

He glanced at his watch. "Davy will be arriving soon. I'll make sure he's brought up to date on everything."

She didn't stay long, wanting to get back to the ranch. As she pulled in front of the house, she felt the vibration of the phone in her pocket just as it rang. She braked to a stop and pulled it out. The caller ID said unknown. "McKay."

A low, raspy voice said, "I know where you can find your bull."

"Who is this?"

"I want the 25,000 in cash. I'll call in an hour and give you a location. Come alone. I see anyone else, I'm gone, and a chunk of that bull could end up on someone's plate."

Nerves tingling, she needed to stall for time. "It's not possible tonight. I want proof, something more than your say so. No proof, no money."

After a brief silence, the caller said, "I'll call tomorrow. Have the money ready." The line went dead.

At first, panic churned inside her at the thought someone would butcher Leopold. Then logic took over. It had to be a bluff. But why?

When she stepped into the house, she could hear voices in the kitchen. Hard to miss JT's booming voice.

"Piper, just in time," Grady said as she appeared in the doorway.

"Is that another pot of chili I smell?"

"JT and I got on the subject of chili. We've got a small bet going. I say it'll bring tears to his eyes. He's betting it won't. You want in?"

Piper's laughter erupted. "Oh, lord no. I'd never bet against a sure thing."

A wry look crossed JT's face. "That bad?"

"Oh, yeah."

Grady told her, "Go do whatever you need to. I'm ready to put it on the table."

It only took a few minutes, and Piper was back, prepared to burn the inside of her guts again. Fortified with a bottle of beer, she crumbled crackers into her bowl.

JT took one look and said, "That's cheating!"

"It's why I didn't take the bet. I love Grady's chili, but this is the only way I can eat it."

A wicked grin crossed Grady's face as he watched JT dish up a spoonful.

He stuffed it in his mouth and started to chew. While he made a valiant effort, he couldn't stop the rosy blush that stained his cheeks or the gleam of tears. Choking it down, he growled, "Good lord, what did you put in it, a whole field of hot peppers?"

Piper laughed again, holding out the package. "Crackers?"

In between bites, Piper brought them up to date, starting with the auction. "I'm convinced the ones with the missing ear tags were stolen."

JT said, "Easy enough to do. The tool to remove one is only about five or six bucks."

"I still have a hard time believing Grant is selling stolen cattle," Grady said after swallowing a swig of beer.

"The jury is still out on that one," Piper said. "I also believe I've found the motive for stealing Leopold, thanks to Brad. They would have been successful except for two reasons. First, Jen left a copy of Leopold's documentation with our attorney, and the DNA lab had a backup computer system. Neither of which they would have known."

While he listened, JT had refilled his bowl from the pot on the stove.

Piper said, "You're a glutton for punishment."

"Just took a little getting used to. Had to wait for my mouth to go numb," he quipped, setting off another round of chuckles. "Piper, your friend is right about the value of the bull. Interesting idea, creating a new identity."

"A man called about the reward for Leopold. Claims to know where he is." She spooned up her last bite of chili.

JT eyed her with suspicion. He'd worked with her for several years. Usually, that casual tone of voice, one meant to lull the listener into an indifferent state of mind, preceded one of her controversial ideas. He waited.

Grady unknowingly fell into the trap. "Who was it?"

"I don't know."

"What did he tell you?"

"Get the money, in cash."

JT chewed.

"Where are you going to meet him?" Grady asked.

"I don't know yet. He wanted to set it up for tonight. But I told him it had to be tomorrow, and I want proof."

Grady said, "Well, one of us will go with you."

JT thought, *here it comes.*

"That's the problem. I have to go alone. If anyone is with me, the deal's off."

Grady's spoon clattered into the bowl. "Jumping Jehoshaphat, girl!

You can't just go waltzing in there by yourself with 25,000 in cash."

Piper cast a look at JT, who quietly sat, chomping on his food, before she said, "Grady, I may not have a choice. This could be our only chance to find Leopold." She didn't want to mention the caller's threat that the animal might be slaughtered.

"What do you plan to do?" JT asked.

"I'm not sure yet. Depends on what I'm told tomorrow. In the meantime, I need to see if the reports ever showed up from Tanner's boss."

Parked between two cars, Cade watched the office. He'd seen Sloan and Giles arrive. Whatever the reason for the meeting, it hadn't taken long before the three men walked out the back door and left.

He waited. It would just be his luck to have Jarvis decide to return. Slumped behind the wheel, a dark shadow in the truck, the owners of the two vehicles next to him never glanced his way as they drove out.

Only then did he ease the door open and slide out. Edgy, he paused to let the sounds of the night settle around him. If he got caught, he'd blow the whole case and could kiss his career goodbye.

Cade's attire had undergone a radical change from his persona as Ron Pollard. Faded jeans and boots gave way to tactical pants and combat boots. The black jacket covered the Glock on his hip. Instead of the worn cowboy hat, a black ski cap covered his head. If necessary, it could be rolled down into a full-face mask leaving only his eyes and mouth exposed. His hands were encased in black gloves.

His pace fast but steady, Cade crossed the street and slipped into the alley. He checked the doorknob. This time it was locked. A twist of the lockpick, and he was in. Cade stopped at the end of the hallway, his gaze scanning the front windows before he stepped into the reception area and moved to Jarvis' office. He closed the door and pulled the small flashlight from his pocket. The narrow beam created deep shadows in the corners of the room. When it lit on a large, free-standing safe, Cade groaned. Safecracking wasn't one of his skills.

He dropped into the chair behind the desk. A single tap on the keyboard and a screen came up on the monitor. Damn, password-protected, another skill he didn't have. A vague hope it was written on the underside of the keyboard vanished when he tilted it.

In the center drawer, his fingers pushed aside pens, a small box of paperclips, another filled with rubber bands, as he searched for something that might have the password and safe combination. His hand slid under the drawer—nothing taped to the underside.

The large side drawer held several hanging file folders. Inside the first one was a desk calendar along with several pieces of correspondence. Cade laid the calendar aside. From a coat pocket, he extracted a small camera, not much bigger than a box of matches. Flashes of bright light illuminated the desk as he took pictures of the documents. The rest of the folders held purchase orders and catalogs. Nothing jumped out at him that was out of the ordinary.

The only item of interest in the drawers on the other side of the desk was a large checkbook. Cade quickly thumbed through it before putting it back. He didn't have time to mess with pictures.

Next, he turned his attention to the calendar, filled with entries of meetings, names, and telephone numbers. He snapped a picture of each page. It wasn't until Cade reached the last page that he hit pay dirt, two entries of unidentified numbers and letters. He'd bet one was for the computer and the other for the safe.

He was right. First, he accessed the emails. Evidently, Jarvis didn't rely on emails for his business dealings. Not wasting any more time, he pulled out a thumb drive from his pocket. A few quick clicks, and the files and contact list downloaded. He logged out, then looked at the second code. It had the correct sequence for a combination.

Cade stepped to the safe. His teeth gripped the small flashlight as he held the calendar in one hand. After noting the setting on the dial, he twisted it with his other hand. He took a deep breath, turned the handle and sighed with relief when it opened.

Inside was a stack of boxes. Cade grabbed the top one. When he looked at the label on the end, his gut twisted—Layton Ranch. He set it on the desk and flipped off the lid. Inside were pictures of the property, copies of the deed, bank and county tax documents, and contracts.

He didn't bother to read them. Instead, Cade quickly laid them across the desk and took pictures. After replacing them in the box, he grabbed the next one labeled Spence Ranch. It contained the same type of documents. His curiosity itched to check all the boxes, but his instincts told him he'd been here long enough. Get the hell out. Cade picked up the Spence box and set it on top of the one marked Anglin Ranch. The Layton box went back on top. Before closing the door, he took one last picture of the entire stack. Fingers spun the dial, making sure it stopped on the same number.

He replaced the calendar, then flashed the light around, checking for anything he'd left out of place. He'd just stepped into the reception area when voices echoed. Darting back, he barely escaped the beam of light that flashed around the secretary's desk and into the corners of the room. A cop rattled the doorknob.

Aw, hell! The back door. He'd left it unlocked in case he had to make a fast exit. Once the cop moved out of view, Cade charged to the back. No time to get out, instead he jabbed the button to lock the door. Pressed against the side of the wall, he waited.

Footsteps crunched. Fear raced through him. What if the door hadn't locked? There was no escape. Cade didn't dare move and even caught himself holding his breath.

The door shook and rattled, then the footsteps receded. Cade's body slumped with relief, though he wasn't out of the woods yet. He still had to get to his truck. After waiting several minutes, he eased the door open, stepped out, locking it behind him. He darted across the alley to the walkway between the buildings that he'd used before.

It wasn't until he was seated in his truck the tension in his body loosened. When he pulled out of the parking lot, his thoughts rolled around one question. Why did Lane Jarvis have a box of records for Jennie Layton's ranch?

When he stepped onto the porch, Cade checked for the piece of paper. It was still in place. Inside, he turned on the lights as he strode toward the kitchen. He retrieved his laptop from behind the fridge and laid it on the table before grabbing a can of beer. As he waited for the computer to boot, he drank, savoring the tangy taste of the cold brew. Still wired, he could feel the after-effects of the adrenaline dump.

Cade signed on and linked his phone to the computer. Once the transfer of the pictures was complete, he opened the file. He scrolled through them until he reached the photos for the Layton box. The first set was a contract. As he read each page, his disbelief grew. No wonder Piper McKay was hot on the trail of the cattle thieves. This was more than just a few stolen cows. Jennie Layton's cattle were slowly being siphoned off, and with each loss, the tab she owed Lane Jarvis shot up. Those losses, though, paled in comparison to the value of the stolen bull. He figured Jennie Layton owed the man close to three-quarters of a million dollars.

He leaned back, took another deep swallow of the beer. It didn't make any sense. Why would anyone in their right mind even sign a contract like this? Cade didn't know the woman, but she was an established and well-respected rancher from the comments he'd heard.

The cursor slid down the pictures until he reached the ones for the Spence ranch in Colorado. Sure enough, he found another contract. Somehow, he wasn't surprised to find the terms were almost identical to the Layton contract. He also discovered copies of the closing documents for the ranch's sale, the buyer, Lane Jarvis. It was the following picture that sent chills racing down his back, a death certificate for William Spence. He checked the dates and found Spence died after the contract date but before Jarvis acquired the ranch.

As the dots started to connect, his thoughts whirled at the implications. Two contracts and five more boxes. A ranch owner killed in a car crash, then the attempts to murder Jennie Layton and Piper. An unlikely thought nagged at him. He rejected it as impossible to pull off at first, but the possibility continued to tug at his mind. Were the contracts forged?

He glanced at the time on the computer. Too late tonight to call. Instead, he quickly typed up a report. It was attached, along with the pictures, to an email. He hit send. It would be waiting for his boss when he arrived in the morning.

Cade finished off the last of the beer, tossing the can in the trash can by the back door. A grim thought crossed his mind as he shut down the computer. His undercover operation had just gone from local cattle rustling to a deadly case of financial fraud involving at least two states. And Piper McKay was square in the sights of whoever was running the show.

Despite staying up late to read the reports she'd received from Rawling, Piper drifted in and out of sleep. Her brain didn't want to shut down. She finally gave up and crawled out of bed.

On her way out, she left a note for Grady that she'd be at the hospital. Arriving early had one distinct advantage. She could park close to the front door.

Missing was the usual hustle and bustle as she strode into the elevator. A lone nurse manned the nurse's station. She stopped and was told her grandmother had a peaceful night though she did wake up for a few minutes. Before entering, she lightly tapped to alert Davy.

As the door opened, he stood behind the chair, his hand resting on the butt of his gun. At the sight of her, a smile crossed his face. "What are you doing here this early?"

"Couldn't sleep," she said, walking toward the bed.

"She woke up for a few minutes last night, but I didn't have a chance to talk to her."

Piper stroked Jen's hand and kissed her cheek before stepping back to one of the chairs.

"So, what's going on?" Davy asked as he sank into a chair.

In a low voice, she brought him up to date. Like Grady, his eyes flashed when he heard she planned on meeting the unknown caller. Keeping an eye toward the bed, his tone soft, Davy said, "Don't go by yourself. It smells like a trap to me. Do you think they know you're onto their scheme?"

"It seems to be more than a coincidence that I'm spotted taking pictures at the stockyard, then get a call about Leopold."

"Who saw you taking pictures?"

"Ron Pollard."

"Looks like he just moved up on your suspect list."

Her face troubled, Piper said, "Yes, he has. I got the reports on the thefts in Cass County from Rawling, the supervisor at the association. I think it's all connected, those thefts, the auction house, and my grandmother's ranch. Plus, there was a rancher killed."

"We already know these guys are playing for keeps."

"Since a rancher was killed, I don't want to pull JT away from the ranch. That leaves you. Go get some sleep. I'll need you to be bright and bushy-tailed."

He chuckled as he stashed his computer in the small bag he'd brought with him. "Call! I don't care what time it is."

"I will. Now, get the hell out of here."

He waved and walked out the door.

Piper settled in the chair. Before leaving the ranch, she'd filled a thermos with coffee. She poured a cup and held it under her nose for a second, inhaling the rich scent before taking a sip. With a sigh of satisfaction, she set the cup on the small table next to the chair.

She pulled out her laptop, opened it, and clicked on the email from Rawling. As she slowly scanned each report, she couldn't get around the fact that an ugly picture emerged. Rawling had included the investigative notes from the sheriff on the shooting of the rancher. Based on what she read, he'd confronted the rustlers.

When she heard a faint moan, she looked up. Jen stared at her.

Piper bolted to her feet, dropping the computer on the chair.

"Grandma," she said, rushing to the side of the bed.

Even though her voice was weak, a faint smile crossed her face. "What's with this Grandma business?"

She cradled Jen's hand in hers. "Oh, it is so good to see you awake. I've been so worried."

Jen struggled to push herself up.

"No, Jen. I don't think you should be moving yet. At least not until the doctor says you can."

Jen's fingers reached to touch her head. "Why is my head bandaged?"

"Do you remember what happened to you?"

Her brow furrowed as she thought. "I was checking the fence."

"Did you get off Bess?"

"Yes. I had tied her to a tree. Something hit my head."

"Did you see anyone when you rode up?"

"No. Is that what happened? Did someone hit me?"

Though dismayed that her grandmother didn't know who had struck her down, she kept her tone even as she said, "Yes."

Her voice faint, she said, "A man …." Her eyes closed.

Sensing she was still awake, Piper waited. After a few seconds, Jen's eyes opened.

"A phone call, about the reward."

"What about it," Piper asked.

"Told me to meet him."

"That's why you were there?"

"Yes. Why?"

"I'm still working on it," Piper said. Until her grandmother was stronger, Piper wasn't about to explain.

"Who are the men I've seen in here?"

Piper smiled. "Your guardian angels."

Her voice stronger, she said, "What?"

"They're two members of my team. Davy Fenwick has the night shift. Tony Kline is here during the day. I expect Tony will be strolling in any time now. They've been making sure nothing else happens to you." Another fact she didn't plan to tell Jen, there already had been a second attempt.

"You really think someone will try again?"

"A safety precaution."

"Why would anyone want to kill me?" she muttered.

How about your ranch, cattle, and a prize bull, Piper thought. All she said was, "I don't have the answers yet."

"I expect you will. Sorry, sweetie. I can feel … slipping … again." Her eyes closed.

Head bowed, Piper let the emotion flow. Tears trickled down her face from the relief of hearing Jen's voice and her lucid questions. The opening of the door sent her spinning. It was Tony.

At the sight of her tear-stained face, he exclaimed, "What's wrong?"

Using the back of her hand, she wiped away the tears.

"She woke up, and I was able to talk to her."

A sympathetic look settled over his face. "Good news can be a huge relief."

"She didn't see who hit her."

"Damn, why is it never easy?"

She nodded toward the door. He followed her into the hallway.

"Someone called about the reward. Told her to meet him. That's why she was there."

His tone grim, Tony said, "It was a trap."

She nodded. "I didn't tell her about the second attempt or the contract. Jen knows who you are, so don't be surprised if she talks to you when she wakes again."

"Why are you here this early?"

She told him what she'd told Davy. Tony's reaction to the caller was the same. "It's a trap."

"I know. I told Davy to get some sleep. I might need him today."

"Good. Where are you going from here?"

"I'm stopping at the auction house, then it's back to the ranch. I want to talk to Luke and go back over the reports from Rawling."

"Keep me in the loop."

"I will."

After retrieving her computer and leaving Tony her thermos of coffee, she walked out. When she'd gotten the anonymous call, it didn't escape her notice that the caller knew the reward had increased. Grant was the only outside person she told. It was another link back to the auction house.

An early riser, Cade finished dressing before the sun even rose. In the small kitchen, the timer on the coffee pot dinged. He poured a cup, then pulled a skillet from the cabinet. Between gulps of coffee, he scrambled eggs and dropped slices of bread in the toaster. He balanced a plate piled high with eggs and buttered toast in one hand and pushed aside the computer on the table with the other. Cade glanced at the wall clock as he sat. By the time he finished, his boss would be in the office.

After pouring the last of the coffee into his cup, Cade quickly washed the dishes, leaving them to dry in the dish drainer next to the sink. Seated at the table, he tapped his phone.

Nick answered, "Yes."

"Cavalry. I sent you an email last night. You are not going to believe the contents. I included my analysis."

"I saw it but haven't had a chance to open it. Hold on."

In the background, Cade could hear the clicks of the keyboard.

"Good lord, did you do what I think you did to get these?"

"I don't think you want an answer."

"Why?"

In a mocking tone, he said, "Plausible deniability."

For a few seconds, Nick didn't respond. Then he cleared his throat and said, "A new report came in this morning. The count's over a thousand head. If Jarvis is the head of the ring, he can't be running that many head through Sheffield's auction."

"A lot of cattle to be moving around. Where and how? Did you find any record of eighteen-wheelers?"

"No, but I wasn't specifically looking. I will."

"In addition to the Layton and Spence documents, there are five other ranches. I listed them in my report. I'd like to know if you recognize any of them. I've got to go."

He disconnected, shoved the computer behind the refrigerator, and picked up the gun lying on the counter. On the way out, he gathered up his jacket, hiding the gun from view as he walked out. After stashing the gun in a lockbox in his truck, he slid behind the wheel. He didn't like not carrying it but concealing it while he worked was near impossible. Instead, he had to rely on his backup pistol tucked in the holster strapped to his ankle inside his boot.

By the time he arrived at the auction house, the place was already abuzz with activity. Even on off-sale days, everyone kept busy, cleaning up from the previous sale and getting the place ready for the next. As Ron Pollard, he planned to spend the day repairing a fence torn down by several steers during the auction.

He stopped by the office to grab a cup of coffee. His eyes lit up when he saw the box of donuts. From the large assortment, he picked out one glazed with chocolate and took a bite. As he chewed, he poured a cup of coffee. After chasing the donut with a swig of the rich hot brew, Cade turned to greet the two women. Not long after he hired on, he'd started a friendly interaction with them, hoping they might be a source of information.

Tina, the younger of the two, had started coming on to him from almost the day he arrived. She was cute, with a cheerful smile, and about eighteen or nineteen. Heidi, Grant's secretary, was married and had two grandkids.

As he walked over and propped a hip on Tina's desk, Heidi gave him an amused look.

He looked down at Tina. "You must be a morning person."

A gleam sparked in her eyes as she leaned forward. The motion pushed the front of her shirt open, showing the top of a lacy bra. "Now, why would you say that?"

"No one who isn't a morning person could look as cute as you do this early." He licked the chocolate from his fingers.

Her eyes dropped to his lips as she giggled. "Oh, I just bet you tell that to all your lady friends."

"Nope." He winked. "Just the cute ones."

Another giggle erupted.

A raised voice said, "Pollard!"

Taking his time, he leaned over and said, "You just keep that smile going."

A blush crossed her cheeks as he stood.

He shot a glance over his shoulder. "Morning, Boss."

"Need to talk to you." Grant turned and marched back to his office.

As Cade stepped inside, Sheffield told him to close the door. Wary, he shut it.

"I want that fence repaired today. I can't take a chance on any more cattle getting on the road. Can you handle it by yourself?"

"No problem. Where's Frankie?"

"Going to be late. I'm not sure when he'll get here."

"Okay. Anything else?"

"If you want to get friendly with the gals in the front office, do it on your own time."

"Reckon, I'll get on that fence then." He turned and walked out of the office. He wondered what had ruffled Sheffield's feathers. He didn't think it was his conversation with Tina. Where was Frankie? Yesterday they'd talked about starting on the fence first thing this morning. Something was in the wind.

She parked near the front entrance and hopped out of the truck. Across the way, she spotted Pollard hauling lumber from a building. As she stepped through the doorway, Grant walked out of his office.

"Piper. What brings you here this morning?"

"I wanted to talk to you about the new flyer for Leopold."

"Grab a cup of coffee. Heidi brought in donuts. Then come on back to my office."

After greeting the two women, she poured a cup of coffee but passed on the donuts. As she settled into a chair in front of Grant's desk, she took a sip, studying the man over the edge of her cup. She'd first met him not long after she came to live with Jen and found it difficult to believe he was involved in murder, financial fraud, and cattle rustling.

He leaned back, resting his crossed arms over his belly. "Now, what can I help you with?"

"The flyer. Who did you send it to?"

"Most of the livestock sales barns in the state are on my email list. It went out this morning. I requested they distribute it to their contacts. It'll get a lot of attention."

She took a sip. "I didn't know you had such a wide reach."

He laughed. "Just part of the job."

"How long have you been doing this?"

"I started working here when I was in high school. Back then, it was the Granger Auction. When old man Granger died, his son, who I'd gone to school with, had moved to California. He didn't want to have anything to do with the business. So, I bought it. Had to darn near hock my soul to the bank. But over the years, it's paid off."

"The other morning, I had breakfast at the café. Someone brought up the cattle thefts. Seems they are on the rise, and a rancher was killed." Her gaze never left his face. "What do you think is going on?"

"I don't know. The other day when Sheriff Horne was here, he mentioned it. According to him, the cattle seem to have vanished into thin air. No sign of them."

"While cattle rustling isn't my everyday sort of crime, I find it odd. How would a person dispose of stolen cattle? How could they be sold?"

"Nowadays, it's not that easy. Is this about Leopold?"

"Not just Leopold, Jen's been hit three times now."

"I hadn't heard about another theft. When did it happen?"

Though he acted surprised, his eyes never changed. "Grady discovered it yesterday, but we're not sure when they were stolen. Sometime in the last four or five days."

"What does Horne think?" He shifted in his chair.

"Grady talked to him. He hasn't come up with anything on the other two, so I doubt he'll have any luck with this last theft."

He fiddled with the pen on his desk. "He's still your best bet."

"Have you had any ranchers from out of state selling their stock?"

"Offhand, I can't think of any."

"How about from other areas of the state?"

"Piper, I get a lot of cattle run through here. While I know most of the local ranchers, I don't have contact with every seller or buyer. My staff handles the forms. Why the questions?"

"I'm dealing with a significant loss of cattle. Right now, I'm just trying to get a handle on the problem, disposal. Cattle don't just disappear into thin air, as Horne claimed. Where are they being sold?"

An over-hearty laugh erupted. "I still say Horne is who you should be talking to. By the way, how is your grandmother doing?"

"She regained consciousness."

"That's wonderful news. Has she been able to tell you what happened?"

She swallowed the last of the coffee. "Not yet, but her memory is improving." She stood. "I know you have other business to take care of. I'll get out of your hair." This time she didn't miss the look of relief that flashed in his eyes. "I appreciate your help with Leopold." On the way out, she tossed the cup in the trash can. Grant's nervousness had done nothing to dispel her suspicions.

Uncertain whether to stay or go, she slowly strolled toward her truck. Her gaze swept the pens as a truck backed a trailer loaded with cattle up to one of the ramps.

She stopped to watch. The driver and a passenger exited while Pollard dropped the gate. Since he was alone, the other two men helped. The animals pushed and shoved as they came out of the trailer. Piper looked each one over, no missing ear tags in this bunch. Once the trailer was empty, the driver pulled the truck forward. The passenger closed the gates while Pollard grabbed a clipboard hanging on the fence.

Though he glanced her way, he never acknowledged her presence. After scribbling on it, he tore off a page. The driver walked up.

Pollard said, "My count is eighteen. Take this to the front office."

The man glanced over it and strode toward the building.

Pollard shot another sharp look at her before turning to walk to the barn.

Piper stepped to the fence and counted—eighteen. How and when did the extra head get slipped into the sale?

A sense of disquiet tugged at her as she looked around the deserted lot. Grant certainly seemed uncomfortable with her questions. Pollard had an unfriendly look. She idly wondered what happened to the other man.

Back at the ranch, Piper grabbed a can of diet Coke from the refrigerator. For a few minutes, she stopped to stare out the kitchen window, enjoying the bite of cold liquid sliding down her throat. Pastures stretched as far as she could see. In the distance, Grady and JT moved a round bale into place.

Her thoughts drifted to the conversation at the auction house. One salient fact had emerged. The flyer had not been sent out until this morning which meant the caller had to be connected to the auction house. Was it Pollard? As she turned to head to Jen's office, she wondered if she'd get another call.

Seated at the desk, she opened her laptop to review the reports from Rawling again. She hit the print button. Once the printer finished spewing paper, she lined up the reports across the desk. Slowly, she studied each one. Over a hundred head stolen. Had they all been sold at Sheffield's auction? She suddenly realized the thefts were only in Cass county. What about the other counties?

Her phone rang. It was Luke.

"How's your grandmother?"

"Out of the coma."

"Does she know what happened?"

"No. All she remembers is getting off her horse, then something hit her. Someone lured her with a call about the reward for her stolen bull." Concerned Luke might believe Jen was out of danger of another attack, she said, "I'd still like to keep Davy and Tony on guard duty until we get to the bottom of this."

"I hadn't planned on pulling them back."

She heaved a sigh of relief. "I received a batch of reports from a supervisor, Nick Rawling, at the Texas & Southwestern Cattle Raisers Association. I forwarded his email to you. They're investigating the cattle thefts, not only of the ones in Hopkins County but also an adjacent county, where the rancher was killed."

"I'll take a look at them."

"Have you found out anything about the property in West Texas?"

"It's the Anglin Ranch near San Angelo. Jarvis used cattle as collateral for a loan, the ranch for a second loan. I'm waiting on a call from the previous owner."

"What about other properties Jarvis owns?"

"I should have a list today. Be watching for it."

"Last night, I got a call about the reward. The man claims to know where Leopold is."

"Leopold? Ah, yes, the bull."

"As it turns out, he's much more valuable than I knew." She explained what she learned about the DNA and money involved in artificial insemination. She added, "When you do the math, that could amount to several million dollars a year in sales."

"Good lord!"

"I told the caller I wanted proof before he'd get the money. He said he'd call and give me a time and place." Hoping to avoid what she knew would be a strong objection, she hastened to add, "The caller knew the reward was 25,000. The only way he could have found out was at the auction house. Yesterday I left a new flyer with Sheffield, who sent it out this morning to his contact list."

"What are you going to do about your caller?"

"I'm not sure yet. Depends on what he says."

"Is JT your backup?"

"No. I don't want to pull him away from the ranch. If I need someone, it will be Davy."

Knowing his agent, he said, "Don't go in by yourself."

"I'll work something out."

"Piper?" He breathed a sigh of frustration, one which Piper knew usually preceded his rubbing his forehead. "No hot-dogging on this. You've already been a target twice. It could be a trap, just like it was for your grandmother."

"I know. I'll be careful. I do think the caller is connected to the auction house. Pollard saw me taking pictures, and he handles the count on the number of cattle sold at the auction."

"He seems to keep popping up."

"Yeah. I don't like it. Did you ever find out anything more about his background?"

"No." He paused. "I've hesitated to mention my reservations to you. If he's one of the rustlers, he's likely involved with the attacks on you and your grandmother. I don't want you to lose sight of that. Still, I've hit a roadblock. In the past, I've only seen this when an officer goes undercover and assumes a false identity."

Shock rippled through her. "You're saying … he might be a cop!" Bits and pieces of trivia started to drop into place. The man who never called her back, his boss's attitude, even the reports she received. Just enough to keep her happy.

"Luke, do me a favor. See what you can find out about Cade Tanner."

"Isn't he the one who works for Rawling?"

"Yeah. Supposedly he's in a training conference. My instincts tell me he's Ron Pollard."

"For right now, this conversation is just between you and me," Luke told her. "My other line is ringing. Talk to you later."

As she laid the phone aside, she blindly stared at the papers strewn across the desk. Despite Luke's warning, deep down, she knew she was right. So much for her hotshot investigative skills. My god, she had him pegged as her number one suspect at the sales barn. While she mentally beat herself up, slowly, a spark of logic pushed aside her scornful disparagement.

The man was good, damn good. He had to be. Otherwise, he'd be dead. If he could convince her, it meant he'd fooled Jarvis and his men. She could also understand why he didn't tell her. It only took one slip.

Even more determined to find answers, she went back to her study of the reports. Financial fraud, cattle rustling, and murder all added up to big bucks for someone. She picked up the phone and tapped the number for the Association. After being transferred, Rawling answered.

"Marshal McKay. Did you receive the reports?"

"Yes, I did, thank you. I do have some questions if you have a few minutes."

"I do."

"Have you had any thefts in the San Angelo area recently?"

For a second, there was dead silence. His voice cautious, Rawling asked, "Just why are you interested?"

"I'm investigating the cattle thefts."

"Isn't it outside your jurisdiction as a U.S. Marshal?"

"Normally, yes. But in this case, I have a vested interest. Twice, someone has tried to murder my grandmother, the owner of Layton Ranch. I have had two attempts on my life. My ranch has been hit three times, the latest within the last few days. I believe the stolen cattle and the assaults are linked to Lane Jarvis, a cattle broker in Sulphur Springs."

"I have not received any reports from Sheriff Horne connecting any of this."

"Sheriff Horne made it abundantly clear he believed my grandmother's injuries were accidental. So far, I've not seen any evidence of an investigation beyond taking a report. Since I'm uncertain who else might be involved, I have no intention of discussing any details with him. The only reason I called you in the first place is because my grandmother had a note in her purse with a name, Cade Tanner, and a telephone number. I'd like to know how widespread the problem is. You only sent reports for Cass County."

"There have been a number of thefts in West Texas."

"How many head?"

"Around four hundred."

Shocked by the number, she asked, "How many were from the Anglin Ranch?"

Another long silence before Rawling said, "I'd have to check the reports. Why this ranch?"

"Lane Jarvis bought it."

"I'll find out."

"I'm also interested in any clusters of thefts in one area, either in Texas or Oklahoma."

"As soon as I have answers, I'll call you back." The line went dead.

Voices rang outside. She glanced out the window and saw Grady and JT had returned. Eager to share the news about Jen, she strode outside.

"Just in time to do some work," Grady said as she walked up.

"Looks to me as if you've already got it all done."

JT pulled off his leather work gloves, shoving them in his back pocket. "Nice spread you've got here."

"All the credit goes to my grandmother and Grady."

Grady snorted.

"I know. You don't like to be thanked. Jen woke up again. I was able to talk to her for a few minutes."

"Did she see who attacked her?"

"No. She remembers getting off Bess. Then something hit her in the head. She didn't see anyone when she rode up. Grady, she got a phone call about the reward. That's why she was there. I'm certain it's the reason her assailant took her cellphone. Unless you need me here for something, I'm going back to the hospital."

Grady said, "No, we've got it covered. I want to move another couple of round bales into the pasture before we call it a day."

"JT, you need anything?"

"Nah. I'm good."

"On Jen's desk is a copy of the DNA report on Leopold. I'd like for you to take a look at it. I'd be interested in your opinion."

Piper headed back inside, where she loaded her computer and the reports into her backpack. She grabbed her jacket. As she drove out, she honked as she watched Grady astride the tractor with a large round bale on the front fork head across the pasture.

As he finished up the repairs on the fence, Cade glanced at the near-deserted parking lot. Grant's truck was still parked in front, and to his surprise, nearby was Frankie's truck. Wondering what had brought the man back after taking the day off, he carried the leftover pieces of wood to the utility building. He made two more trips before he stripped off his gloves and meandered his way to the office.

Frankie walked out the door and stopped alongside his truck to answer his phone, unaware Cade approached. He held the phone to his ear. "I got them, four good pictures, but we only need one. I'll be there in a few minutes." He opened the truck door.

Cade ducked back behind the building. Once Frankie's vehicle was out of sight, Cade dashed to his truck. He followed him to Jarvis' office. He circled around to avoid passing by the front windows and parked on the side street where he could keep an eye on the place. In the parking lot across from the alley entrance, he spotted Giles and Sloan's trucks.

The rats were gathering, but for what reason? What were the pictures? He settled back, prepared to wait. Even though it was getting dark, if the trucks left, he'd see them. He might find out what they were up to.

Just as Piper stepped out of her vehicle at the hospital, her phone rang. The caller ID read, Unknown. Anticipation spiked as she slid back into the truck. This was what she'd been waiting for. "McKay."

"Do you have the money?"

"Yes."

"Then meet me—"

She cut him off. "Do you have the proof? I want to know the bull is alive and where to find him."

"I have a picture dated today, and I'll give you the location."

"Where do we meet?"

He relayed the directions, then said, "If I see anyone with you, the deal is off. You've got thirty minutes." The line went dead.

She pulled out her computer and typed in the directions. A map appeared. She clicked on the aerial tab and gazed at an overhead view of a church with a graveyard next to it. She zoomed out to see the surrounding terrain and didn't like what she saw. Her plan just went down the tubes.

She tapped the speed dial.

When Davy answered, he said, "Did you get the call?"

"Yes, where are you?"

"At the hospital."

"I'm in the parking lot," she said.

Her computer under one arm, the backpack slung over her shoulder, Piper rushed inside. When she stepped into her grandmother's room, her eyes darted toward the bed. Jen was asleep. She motioned, and the two men followed her outside. "Let's go to the waiting room. It's empty."

Seated, she opened her computer and pulled up the map. "The meet is at a church on a county road. I've got thirty minutes to get there."

Tony and Davy stood on each side of her, looking over her shoulder to study the screen.

Davy echoed Piper's earlier thoughts. "I don't like this. Too far out. I don't see a way to back you up without them seeing me."

"My plan to hide you in the truck and drop you off before I got there won't work. I can't stop. If you follow in another truck, you'll be seen." She pointed to the nearest intersection on the map. "Unless you have a better idea, you need to wait here. I sure wish we had comms with us, but our phones will have to sub. Just before I get there, I'll call and leave the line open."

Tony asked, "What about the money?"

"I don't have it. I'll take a look at the picture. If it looks sound, I'll set up another meeting and bring the money."

"He's not going to like it."

"Too damn bad. I still feel like this is a trap, but I have to let it play out." She glanced at her watch. "We'd better get going. Tony,

I'll call you just before I set up the call to Davy, to let you know I'm going in. If you don't hear from either one of us within fifteen or twenty minutes, call the sheriff's department."

His face grim, he nodded.

His phone rang. "Cavalry," he said.

"Where are you?"

"I'm watching Jarvis' office. Something's going down, but I don't know what." He told Nick what he'd overheard. "I've got a bad feeling."

"I got another call from Marshal McKay," he said. "She asked about the Anglin Ranch in West Texas. It was on your list. Jarvis owns it. You may need to break cover and contact her. We need to know more about those contracts. I can't find out. McKay will want to know how I learned about them. Just so you know, she doesn't trust the sheriff."

Mentally, he cursed but couldn't see a way out of it. "Okay."

Ahead, three men, illuminated by the street lights, walked toward the parking lot. Frankie hopped in his truck. Sloan and Giles into another. A few seconds later, truck lights flashed as Frankie pulled out.

"They're on the move." Cade disconnected and slid the phone into his pocket, then started the engine. Frankie turned one way, but Sloan turned to head out of town. Sloan and Giles were Jarvis' enforcers. Together, they spelled trouble. He followed them.

After his last attempt to follow the trucks that delivered the stolen cattle, he learned tailing a vehicle in the county was a far cry from a city with busy streets. To keep from losing them, he was forced to kill his headlights, relying on his GPS map and the faint moonlight to keep the truck out of the bar ditch. It made for a hairy ride. Brake lights flickered as Sloan turned again. When Cade followed, he saw headlights flash across a building. He pulled into the first driveway he came to and parked alongside an abandoned gas station where his truck was out of view of the road.

From the backseat, he grabbed his black ski cap and a dark windbreaker. He pulled on the cap, rolling it over his face before he slipped on the jacket. After shoving the Glock inside his waistband, Cade tucked an extra magazine in his back pocket. Then he set the phone on mute.

He eased around to the front of the gas station. Sloan's truck was backed up to a building. The headlights illuminated the parking lot and a circular drive. The outer edges of the beams faintly lit up a stretch of the cemetery next to it. In the glare of the headlights, the two men stood talking. What the hell were they doing at a church?

A driveway separated the building where he stood and one next to it. The sign on top proclaimed Bet's Thrift Store. Cade moved along the rear of the gas station, crossed over the driveway, then crept behind the store.

From his position at the corner of the building, he could see Sloan pacing, watching the road, and occasionally turning to stare at the cemetery. Cade's sense of foreboding intensified when he couldn't find Giles. Where did he go?

Once he left the cover of the store, he had to stay low. Even in the dim moonlight, Sloan might be able to see his outline. Cade dropped, belly crawling to the fence where he wiggled under the barbed wire. Bent over, he slowly inched his way closer to the church.

Sporadic moonlight shifted the black and grey shadows that shrouded the headstones. Since he had to watch Sloan, the second time he tripped over a grave marker, curses rippled in his mind.

In front of him, a narrow road divided the cemetery. It was as close as he could get. He spotted a large headstone rising above a grave and slipped behind it to watch.

Sloan shouted, "I see lights," and darted behind the open driver's door.

Cade glanced over his shoulder. A truck slowly approached. His heart took a nose-dive. He'd bet it was McKay.

Another glance in the rearview mirror reassured her that Davy wasn't far behind. The turn onto the county road where the church was located was ahead. She stopped and picked up the phone lying on the console. When Tony answered, she said, "Going in," and hung up. Davy had pulled behind her and walked up to her door. Her finger punched the button to lower the window, letting a welcome rush of night air cool her face.

"Did you call Tony?" he asked.

"Yes."

He reached in, tapping her shoulder. "*Don't* take any chances."

She nodded, and he stepped back. Once Davy was inside his car, she called his phone. When he answered, she hit the speakerphone before sliding it in the front pocket of her coat. "It's in my pocket. Can you hear?"

"Yes."

She pulled onto the highway and made the turn. "I see headlights in front of the church." She slowed, the truck barely crawling along the road. Her heart raced, each beat a hammer strike in her chest.

As she neared the entrance, she stopped. Her gaze scanned the building and parking lot, searching for places where a person could hide. The cemetery was on one side of the church, on the other a cluster of small buildings. The circular drive curved around a stand of trees and waist-high bushes. Easy for someone to hide there.

"A truck's backed in. Headlights are on. I don't see anyone, though the driver's door is open."

Piper pulled ahead. Instead of turning into the entrance, she angled the truck across the road.

She shifted into park and left the engine running. After lowering the driver and passenger window, Piper grabbed the gun lying on the console and jumped out. She closed the door and sidled up against the doorpost, then waited. From here, she could see the trees along the edge of the road and the truck.

A low, harsh voice hollered, "Step out where I can see you."

She recognized the voice, Jack Sloan. "If you've got the proof, bring it to me." Then, in a lower tone, she said, "Davy, it's Sloan. I don't see Giles."

Sloan shouted, "It's in an envelope on the hood of my truck."

Blinded by the bright lights, she couldn't tell if there was something on the hood or not. "Bring it over here. Toss it on the front seat." If they had proof, she wanted it before she hauled ass out of here.

"All right. I'm bringing it over."

His face covered with a black ski mask, Sloan moved from behind the truck's door. He picked up the envelope.

"Keep your hands where I can see them," she shouted, moving to the side of the hood. Over the barrel of her gun, she watched as Sloan slowly walked toward her, his hands in the air.

"Hey. I'm just trying to collect some reward money here. Do we have a deal or not?"

"Not until I see what's in the envelope."

A rustling sound alerted her. Her gaze flashed toward the stand of trees. *Giles!* With a gun in his hand, he leaned around a tree on the edge of the road. She swung the gun and fired. Startled, his shot went wide. She heard the ping of a bullet striking metal. She fired again, and he ducked back. Her head swiveled. She'd lost sight of Sloan.

Three quick shots echoed. Then Sloan shouted, "Someone's in the cemetery. Let's get the hell out of here."

Giles burst out of the trees. Piper shot over the hood of the truck. He stumbled but kept running. Sloan was shooting toward the cemetery as he raced back to his truck. He hopped in and slammed the door shut. The truck was already moving when Giles crawled inside. Sloan tore out of the driveway. The truck skidded as it turned, then raced away.

Davy's voice rang out. "U.S. Marshal! Stop, or I'll shoot."

avy stood at the edge of the road. His gun was aimed at a dark figure who stood motionless in the cemetery. He shouted, "Drop the gun. Now!"

Piper rushed to his side, her weapon raised to cover the man.

An object fell to the ground.

"Raise your arms in the air. Walk toward me," Davy commanded.

"Davy, he may be a friendly."

His arms raised, the man turned. Weaving around the gravestones, he slowly paced toward them. As he came closer, all they could see was his eyes and mouth.

A low Texas drawl sounded, "Marshal McKay, my boss told me to contact you. I didn't plan on such a dramatic entrance."

She knew the voice. Piper lowered her gun, pointing it toward the ground, though Davy still kept his aimed at the man.

Confused, Davy said, "Piper?"

"Take off the mask," she said.

He stopped. A hand slowly dropped, gripped the top and yanked. Black hair flew around his face.

Piper sucked in a deep breath.

"Do you know him?" Davy asked.

"Yeah, Ron Pollard. And I think I know what he's talking about."

Cade kept his eyes on Davy's gun, though a wry expression crossed his face. "I'm one of the good guys, though this is a hell of a dilemma. How do I convince you when I don't have any identification?"

"Cut the jokes, Pollard," Davy said.

"It's not a joke. My name isn't Ron Pollard. It's Special Ranger Cade Tanner."

Piper stared. "I'll be damned!"

"Piper? You know anything about this?" Davy said.

Just to be sure, she asked, "Who's your boss?"

"Nick Rawling. You talked to him earlier this evening. As a matter of fact, he thought you might be a tad bit upset with his lack of cooperation."

She shoved the gun in its holster. "He's a cop."

Davy did the same with his weapon. "Rawling. Isn't he the guy you've been talking to at the Cattle Raisers Association?"

"Yes."

When Davy lowered his gun, Cade breathed a sigh of relief. He trotted back and picked up his weapon.

As he climbed over the fence between the road and cemetery, Piper asked, "What are you doing here?"

"I followed two of Lane Jarvis' henchman, Giles and Sloan. I knew something was up, but not what."

"How'd you know?" Piper asked.

"I overheard Frankie on the phone talking about pictures. I followed him to Jarvis' office. When Sloan and Giles left, I followed them here. By the time I worked my way into the cemetery, Giles had disappeared. I didn't expect him to be in the trees." He looked toward her truck. "Smart move to angle your truck. Bet they didn't expect it. Probably saved your life."

Davy asked, "Who's Frankie?"

Cade said, "Frankie Hillard. He works for Sheffield. From what Sloan was shouting, I gather this was about your missing bull."

"I got a call about the reward. The caller said he knew where to find the bull. He told me to meet him here and bring the money."

"You brought it?" he said with a horrified tone.

"No, of course not. But the caller didn't know it. We suspected it was a trap."

"Who is we?"

"Ah, sorry, I didn't introduce you. Ranger Tanner, this is Marshal Davy Fenwick."

As the two men shook hands, Tanner said, "It's Cade."

Piper added, "Another one, Tony Kline, is at the hospital. Davy and Tony have been taking turns guarding my grandmother. There's another marshal at the ranch. That reminds me. Davy, you'd better call Tony before he sends in the cavalry."

Cade laughed. Both Piper and Davy stared at him.

"Sorry, inside joke."

While they talked, Davy stepped to the side of the truck to call Tony. Once he assured him everything was okay, and he'd give him all the details when he got to the hospital, he wandered over to where Sloan had parked.

"Piper," he shouted in excitement.

She hurried toward him with Cade right behind her.

Bent over, Davy stared at a picture on the ground. "It's a bull," he quipped.

Piper exclaimed, "I thought what he had in his hand was just a trick. Get me to walk out into the open."

"Be right back." Rushing to the car he'd left running in the middle of the road, he popped the trunk. When he ran back, he carried an evidence bag and rubber glove. After sliding on the glove, he picked up the photo by one corner, slid it into the bag, and handed it to Piper.

She stared at the picture through the clear plastic. A bull stood near a fence. Stuck to a fence post was a newspaper. It had today's date. "It's Leopold, but I'll have to take a closer look at it when I get home."

She handed it to Cade.

"Doesn't look like he'd be worth a million dollars," he said.

Startled, she looked at him. Where'd he get the idea the bull was worth a million? The only place she'd seen it was in the contract.

"Your boss is right. Where can we meet? We need to compare notes."

"Not anywhere around Sulphur Springs."

"Do you think you could get in and out of my ranch without being seen? It's located outside Sulphur Bluff."

"Is that where you are going from here? I'll need the directions."

"Yes. Davy, you need to be there."

"I'll call Tony and let him know I'll be late."

"Cade, I suggest you take the long route to get to the ranch. Just before you get to our driveway, there's a stack of round hay bales across the road. You should be able to park behind them and walk to the ranch. I'll turn off all the outside lights. Come to the back door."

She walked back to her truck and pulled a notepad from her backpack. After scribbling the address and her number, she quickly drew a map. "Oh, by the way, I think I hit Giles," she told him, handing him the paper.

Cade scanned it, memorizing the details, then handed it back. "I'll see if I can find out. Be an hour or so before I get to your place." He turned and headed along the roadway to where he'd parked his truck.

"Now, isn't this a kicker? Your lead suspect is an undercover ranger. Does he know he was on your hit list?" Davy said.

She laughed. "I doubt it, but I expect he'll find out before the night is over."

"Come on, let's get out of here," he said.

She took the lead as they left.

Anger swelled as the images of the ambush to kill Piper flashed in Cade's mind. When Giles started shooting, Sloan pulled out a gun and ran into the trees by the road. He didn't have a shot. All he could do was start shooting to get Sloan's attention.

His first stop was Jarvis' office. As he turned onto the side street, he spotted Sloan's truck. What happened to Giles' vehicle? He parked in the next block and sprinted to the parking lot. Piper was right. She'd hit him. Blood splatters ran from the side of Sloan's truck to where Giles had parked. *Must not be too bad if he could drive,* he thought.

He jogged back. No reason now to check out Giles' place. Instead, he wondered whether he could risk another trip into Jarvis' office until a truck pulled into the lot. Frankie exited and walked to the back door. What the hell was he doing here? He waited. It didn't take long before the three men walked out the door. Sloan left, but Frankie and Jarvis stood alongside Frankie's truck and talked.

Frustrated, all he could do was watch. Whatever was under discussion, Frankie didn't like. He leaned forward, his finger jabbed toward Jarvis' chest. Even from this distance, he could see the angry expressions. *Now, isn't this interesting?*

Finally, Frankie jumped into his truck and tore out of the parking lot. Jarvis stood motionless until Frankie's vehicle was out of sight. Then he went back into his office.

An ominous feeling settled over Cade as he pondered the implications of what he'd just seen.

Piper parked and stepped out of the truck. She waited until Davy exited his vehicle.

"Dang, I sure feel out of place around here with a car instead of a truck," he said.

She laughed. "It's why I switched to Jen's truck. I've already decided to get another vehicle. No more cars."

The front door opened. Grady stepped onto the porch, followed by JT.

At the sight of Davy alongside Piper, Grady's eyes narrowed, "Something happen to Jen?"

"She's fine. I had a slight detour when I left the hospital, and Davy was with me."

As Davy and JT greeted each other, JT said, "Figured something went down when I saw you."

"It did," Davy told him.

Piper said, "Let's get into the house, and I'll fill you in. Plus, we have another visitor who will be along shortly."

Both Grady and JT eyed her with a look of suspicion.

JT was familiar with her wide-eyed look of innocence. "Who is it?"

"I'll tell you inside. I don't know about Davy, but I'm starved. Anything in the fridge, Grady?"

"You know better than that. I've got a roast with potatoes, carrots and gravy warming in the oven. JT and I already ate, but there's plenty left over."

Her mouth watered at the thought as she followed the men inside. "Enough for three?" The torturous aroma of roasted meat, onions and spices greeted her. She dropped her backpack on the couch but kept the bag with the picture in her hand.

Grady glanced over his shoulder. "More than enough."

In the kitchen, she said, "Let's wait before you dish up the food."

"Okay, who is the mystery guest?" JT said as he sat. A creak echoed.

Piper had to wonder if Jen's chairs would hold up to the abuse as she sat and laid the bag on the table. "Ron Pollard."

Davy sat across from her and grinned.

"What?" JT protested. "I thought he was at the top of your suspect list."

Davy laughed. "Nope. Turns out her lead suspect is Special Ranger, Cade Tanner."

"I'll be damned," Grady said. "I know several of the rangers. He must be new because I sure didn't recognize him."

JT looked at Davy. "Tell us what happened since I know we'd get a watered-down version from Piper."

When Davy looked at her, she shrugged and stood. She grabbed a can of soda from the fridge. "Anyone else?"

Davy shook his head. "I'll pass, but a cup of coffee sounds good."

"I'll go for the coffee," JT said.

Grady turned and punched the button on the pot he had ready to brew.

"Piper got a call about the meet for the reward," Davy said as he settled back in the chair. "We decided I'd follow and hang back in case she needed help. It was a trap."

Grady looked at her, then Davy. The grim look on their faces told him more than Davy's words.

Piper picked up the story as she popped the top on the can. Her tone neutral, she said, "The caller said to meet him at the Hillside Church. When I got there, two of Jarvis' men were waiting. They planned to kill me."

For a few seconds, the only sound was the coffee machine's pump.

Grady broke the silence. "I know the place. It's in a remote area south of Sulphur Springs."

"Davy came flying to the rescue, but not before someone in the cemetery next to the church started shooting. It spooked them, and they hauled ass." She took a swallow.

Grady filled two cups, setting them in front of JT and Davy.

"Turns out it was Tanner," Piper said and gulped down more of the soda.

Davy said, "When I pulled up, I saw a man running in the cemetery. He had a gun. I thought he was one of the men trying to kill Piper."

As he took a sip, JT watched Davy. He didn't miss the bleak look that flashed across his face. He understood, as only one who had stood in the same shoes could, just how close Davy had come to shooting not only an innocent person but a cop.

JT asked, "Just how close did this come tonight?"

Piper glanced at Grady before answering, "They had their trap rigged, even with a picture. Good grief, how could I have forgotten? In their rush to leave, it got left behind." Hoping to shift attention away from what happened at the church, she picked up the bag with the photo and handed it to Grady.

"Well, if this isn't slicker than a greased pig. Danged if they didn't staple a newspaper to the fence. You know I've seen this stuff about proof of life in the movies, never expected to see it with a bull."

"Do you recognize the background?" she asked.

He carefully scrutinized the picture before handing it to JT. "No, can't say I do."

"Good-looking animal," JT said. "I looked over the DNA report. It's impressive. Big bucks there. Since that's a Dallas paper they used, the bull must still be in the area."

A knock sounded on the door to the mudroom. "I bet that's Cade," Piper said as she rose.

When she opened the door, he nodded, "Marshal McKay."

"It's Piper. Come on in. If you haven't eaten, we've got a roast with all the fixings."

"No, ma'am, I haven't. I can smell it from here."

"You can leave your hat and coat here," she said, motioning toward the hooks on a wall. Before walking into the kitchen, he picked up each foot, examining the sole before he followed her.

Three sets of eyes studied him as he walked in. Cade nodded to Davy before looking at the other two men. "Cade Tanner." He extended a hand to the older man first, who stood in front of the stove. "I've seen you a time or two at the auction."

"Grady Estes."

Stepping closer to the table, Cade said, "You must be the other marshal."

JT rose to shake his hand. "John Thompkins, though everyone calls me JT."

"Piper explained why Davy and the other marshal are here. But why are you?"

"Piper's already been hit three times with thefts. We're just making sure it doesn't happen again."

"Just so you know, JT's a cowhand we hired," Piper said.

Grady said, "Have a seat. Let's get this food dished up."

Piper grabbed plates and utensils and passed them around.

Grady set the pans he pulled from the oven on the table. "Got beer or soda in the fridge, and there is still some coffee."

"Dang, Grady. You didn't tell me you'd made biscuits," Piper said, her mouth salivating. When everyone opted for the coffee, she snagged another can of diet Coke from the fridge.

Seeing Cade eye the empty spots on the table, Grady said, "JT and I've already eaten."

As they dished up the food, Piper asked, "Any trouble on your way out here?"

"No, though I swung by Jarvis' office first."

She looked up in interest. "Oh?"

"That's where they headed when they bailed at the church." He scooped mashed potatoes onto his plate, then covered it with a ladle of brown gravy. "By the way, you did tag Giles. Found bloodstains in the parking lot."

Grady, a grim tone in his note, said, "I knew there was more than what you were telling us."

Before she shoved the chunk of meat dangling on the fork into her mouth, she said, "I'll need to get Jen's truck fixed before she comes home. It's got a couple of bullet holes."

"Hells bells, girl!" Grady exclaimed.

Holding a biscuit topped by a glob of butter, Cade motioned toward Piper. "She's been kicking in their sandbox, and it's got them pissed off."

Davy couldn't resist. "Hell, Cade, she had you pegged as a prime suspect."

He looked up from his plate. "Did she really?"

JT joined in the laughter. "That she did." He looked at her and laughed some more. "Yup. Grade A … number one suspect."

Piper groaned. She knew she'd be the butt of jokes at the office once word spread.

"It tells me my cover is damn good then."

Piper said, "All right, guys, enough is enough."

"I'm curious. At the cemetery, you weren't surprised. Why?" Cade asked.

She cut into the meat as she thought. The man saw more than

she'd realized—something to remember. "Earlier today, I talked to our boss, Luke Purdy. The possibility you might be an undercover cop came up in the conversation."

Davy exclaimed, "Why didn't you tell us?"

Not wanting them to know Luke asked her to keep it confidential, she said, "Never had a chance. Got the call about the reward."

Cade laid the fork down and leaned forward, a worried look on his face. "What gave me away?"

Quick to reassure him, she said, "It wasn't anything you did. It was my boss. I asked him to run you along with Jarvis and his band of thugs. While your criminal background as Ron Pollard held up, he was bothered by it. Luke's instincts are usually spot on. He mentioned the possibility. I started putting two and two together, the missing Cade Tanner, his uncooperative boss."

A look of relief spread across his face as he picked up the fork.

"Tell us what you know, then I'll add what we've discovered," she told him.

In between bites, he said, "I was a new hire, came in from Houston PD. Since I was an unknown face, my boss, Nick Rawling, decided to set up the undercover operation. The Association has been tracking the rise of cattle thefts. We hoped to get an idea of who was behind it at the auction house."

Grady nodded in agreement. "Good place to pick up on any rumors floating about the cattle business."

"What I didn't expect to find was the stolen cattle were being run through the sales. Additional cattle were showing up that weren't listed on the tally sheet. I've discovered the stolen cattle are brought in the night before the auction and are mixed in with the other cattle. I saw three men, Giles, Sloan, and Frankie Hillard. Hillard works for Sheffield." He looked at Grady. "Do you know him?"

Grady said, "Yeah. He moved into the area a few months back."

He paused. "Come to think of it, it was about the same time Jarvis showed up."

Cade said, "How did you snap to it, Piper?"

He does see too much, she thought. "A couple of the ranchers at the café mentioned an error in their receipts. The count was wrong. It got my attention. Then I spotted the missing ear tags. Every pen had one or more. I counted them, and it seemed excessive. During the auction, I was sitting next to Henry Miller. When his cattle came through, I already knew how many he was selling. There was one extra, missing the ear tag."

Grady said, "I'm surprised he didn't notice it."

"Grady, when you go to the sale, who do you watch when Jen's cattle are being sold?" Piper asked.

His hand rubbed his face as he thought. "Well, who is bidding and who buys."

She waved her fork at him. "You just proved my point. The ranchers want to know who is interested in their cattle. Not once did Henry look at the ring. He was watching the people in the seats. Once I started watching the other sellers, I saw the same type of reaction."

"I'll be damned," Cade said. "That answers one of the questions I had. I knew someone was falsifying the tally records. But I could never understand why the seller didn't notice the extra head. But from my position at the corner of the ring, I'm watching the cattle, not the crowd."

Cade swallowed the last bite of carrots. He sighed with satisfaction. "This sure hit the spot. I've been living on fast food for the last several months." He laid his napkin on the table. "Jarvis has more going on than stealing cattle."

"He does, but how did you find out?" Piper asked.

"Let's just say I had a chance to look at some of his records."

While Grady looked mystified, the three agents grinned at each other. In cop-speak, it meant Cade had searched the man's office.

"He has several boxes, one labeled Layton Ranch. It contained multiple documents, including a contract."

"That's where you came up with the value for Leopold."

At his questioning stare, she said, "At the church, you said the bull didn't look like it was worth a million dollars. The only place you could have seen it was in the contract."

He nodded. "I sure wouldn't have expected your grandmother would sign a contract that affected her entire herd."

"She didn't," Piper said. "It's a forgery."

"That possibility occurred to me after I saw a second contract, almost identical to yours for a ranch in Colorado," he told her.

"Spence Ranch?" Piper asked.

He nodded.

Piper said, "By the way, Jen's injuries weren't an accident, as Horne claimed."

"I know," Cade said. "I overheard a conversation. Giles is the one who tried to kill your grandmother. It's also when I learned they were coming after you again, but I wasn't sure when or where."

"You called to warn me!" she exclaimed.

"I couldn't take a chance on breaking cover. It's all I could think of. Why were you at the airport?"

Davy said, "Our unit in Oklahoma City is running a full-scale financial investigation of Jarvis. Piper flew to Colorado to meet with the widow of a rancher we think was killed by Jarvis."

"William Spence," Cade said.

At their surprised look, he said, "His death certificate was in the box."

"Davy found out about a complaint Spence filed against Jarvis," Piper explained. "Turns out, the contract showed up after the man was killed. After the Spence herd was stolen, Jarvis activated the contract's loss clause and acquired the ranch in the process. A handwriting expert has confirmed the contract, similar to the one my grandmother supposedly signed, is a forgery. And we found Jarvis owns another ranch in West Texas."

"The Anglin ranch?"

"Was it another one of the files you found?"

Cade said, "Yes. Not long after I got here, I'd asked Nick to start an investigation into Jarvis' holdings and financial background. But it wasn't until we had a chance to examine the pictures that we realized we could be dealing with a complicated financial scam. When you called Nick asking about cattle thefts in West Texas, he realized you were on the same track. It's why he told me to contact you."

Excited, Piper exclaimed, "Pictures! You took pictures? Can you send them to me?"

"I'll be damned." Grady looked at Cade with a look of approval.

Piper grinned, knowing he'd just put it together. Cade had broken into the man's office.

"I'll call Nick and ask him to send you the file since he already has your email address."

Davy spoke up. "You mentioned there were other boxes. How many?"

"Seven."

"Do you remember any of the other names?"

"No, but I took a picture of the boxes. Each one is labeled."

Piper's heart jumped. This was a gold mine. It would certainly jumpstart Luke's research. As her mind raced over the possibilities, it took a minute for Cade's next comment to register.

"The latest figure we've got is that over a thousand head of cattle have been stolen."

"Do you have any idea how many have been run through the auction house?" JT asked.

"Fifteen to twenty at each auction. It doesn't come close to accounting for all the missing cattle."

Grady exclaimed, "Good lord, where the hell are they stashing them, and how are they moving them?"

Piper said, "Luke is running down vehicle registrations for cattle haulers. They have to be using big rigs. I'm also waiting for a list of Jarvis' properties."

Cade said, "Nick is doing the same. Your boss and mine need to have a serious conversation. We're duplicating research and need to combine our resources. I'll call Nick after I leave here. Tell your boss to expect a call."

Piper nodded her head in approval. She picked up the plastic bag JT had tossed in the center of the table. "There must be a way to identify where this was taken. I'll scan it into my computer and enlarge it."

Cade said, "Any idea why the bull was stolen? I'd think Jarvis would have a hard time selling him."

"He can sell his semen."

"How? He can't advertise where he got it."

"He can use the DNA profile."

A thoughtful look crossed Cade's face. "Still, it would be easy to trace the DNA to Leopold."

"Not if Jarvis wiped out the records. When someone broke into the house to plant the contract, they also stole Leopold's file. Registration certificates, pictures, awards, DNA report ... everything gone. Then someone torched the DNA lab to destroy the sample along with the analysis. If it hadn't been for a backup system, the report would have been destroyed too."

Cade said, "Does Jarvis actually believe he can wipe out the bull's identification?"

"If he can create a new identity for the bull, Jarvis could market the semen," Piper told him.

"Nevertheless, it seems risky for just one animal."

Piper said, "This one animal could bring him millions each year."

Surprised, he stared at her.

"The bull has a genetic mutation that affects muscle mass." She explained what she'd learned from Brad, then added, "A straw can sell for double or more the going price."

Cade took a long considering look at her. "It wasn't about the reward money. The bull was the bait to set the trap. My take is they knew you would show up since you couldn't take a chance it wasn't valid. They were there to kill you."

Her voice somber, Piper said, "I knew. I'd already figured it out. You mentioned me kicking in their sandbox. It's more. Not only does Jarvis want to eradicate the bull's identity, but I believe he also intends to get rid of the two individuals who have a legitimate claim … Jen and me."

For a few seconds, an eerie silence settled over the table. Grady was the first to exclaim, "Damn their hides." The hand lying on the table clenched into a fist. "I hope I get a chance, just one," he muttered.

Cade glanced at his watch. "I need to leave. I sure appreciate the meal, an unexpected bonus."

"How can I contact you?" Piper asked.

As Cade pushed back his chair, he said, "Call Nick. He's the only one who has a way to contact me. I need to stay clear of you. I'm not certain what role Sheffield has in all of this, but I do know

Frankie's been watching you. From what I've seen, he's more than a flunky."

She said, "I'll keep it in mind."

He nodded to them before turning to walk out. Closing the door behind him, Cade stepped to the corner of the house. Earlier, he had waited at the edge of a hay bale, watching for any movement before he approached the house. Once he was sure no one was watching the place, Cade crossed the road, circling his way through the pasture to reach the door off the kitchen.

For the return trip, he took the same precaution. He darted from the side of the house to the barn. From there, he watched the roadway and fields, looking for shifts in the shadows, a betraying sound. A sense of déjà vu crept over him. For a moment, Cade was back in Afghanistan, where the smallest of mistakes could be deadly. Impatient, he shook off the unsettling feeling, focusing his attention on the here and now, not what had been.

When nothing stirred in the murky depths of the night, he slipped across the road. He didn't let down his guard on the drive back, keeping a close eye on the rearview mirror.

It wasn't until he pulled into his driveway that Cade began to relax. He stepped onto the porch, his eyes searching for the small piece of paper. Blown by the wind, it lay on the edge of the wood floor.

Cade quickly shifted to the side of the door as his hand jerked the gun from where he had shoved it inside his waistband. His back to the wall, he reached for the knob. It turned.

Cade shoved the door back and darted through the doorway, stepping sideways as his gun fanned the room. In the silence, nothing moved. Despite the empty feel of the house, he moved with soft steps, checking each room. Once he knew the house was clear, he surveyed the damage. Someone had tossed the place. Papers, magazines, and sofa cushions littered the floor. In the kitchen, drawers and cabinet doors were left open. When he looked behind the refrigerator, he sighed with relief, then pulled out the laptop, and laid it on the table.

In the doorway to the bedroom, he stared at the mess. Clothes lay tangled in a heap. Scattered across the tattered bedspread were the contents of a file folder. While he knew they wouldn't find anything except what he wanted found, a niggle of worry grew at the sight of the documents created for Ron Pollard. The timing was troubling. He had expected the house would have been searched before now.

He pulled his cellphone and tapped the number. A groggy voice answered, "Yes."

"Cavalry," he said.

"Give me a minute."

Cade waited, and a few seconds later, Nick's voice, stronger, asked, "What's wrong?"

"Jarvis upped the ante tonight. Tried to kill Piper McKay." He went on to detail what happened at the church before adding, "Three more marshals are in town. I met two of them at Piper's ranch tonight."

"I know. I inadvertently tripped across Luke Purdy during my research on Jarvis. He's the Supervisory Deputy in charge of the Oklahoma office where McKay works. We had an enlightening conversation."

"Good, I was going to ask that you call him. I take it you found out about Jarvis' scams on the contracts."

"Yes. I sent Purdy the pictures you took."

"Piper asked for a copy. I told her I'd have you send them to her."

"I will. I've also sent her another batch of theft reports. This latest development is very troubling. It makes three attempts to murder McKay. Any idea why?" Nick asked.

The phone tucked into his shoulder, Cade walked into the kitchen. From the fridge, he grabbed a can of beer.

"Not just Piper, but also two attempts to kill her grandmother. That's why two marshals are running round-the-clock protection. McKay thinks the reason is the bull that was stolen." He popped the top. "From what I gathered, the animal is worth millions. Something to do with the DNA code that affects double-muscling, a mutation gene is missing."

A short whistle echoed over the phone. "If it eliminated the calving problem, then she's right. Ranchers will line up to buy the bull's semen."

"Here's the kicker. After someone bashed in Jennie Layton's head, they broke into her house, planted the forged contract and stole all the documentation for the bull, along with the DNA report. Someone also torched the DNA lab, which would have destroyed the records if not for a backup system."

"Purdy mentioned the lab fire but didn't tell me about the significance of the DNA report."

"Someone searched my house tonight."

His comment was met with a short silence before Nick said, "We expected it might happen, but I don't like the timing. Do you think it's connected to the attack tonight? Were you spotted?"

"It's disturbing, but no, I don't. They were running too fast to get a look at me. I'm more inclined to think it's about Frankie's offer. Let's see what happens tomorrow. I told Piper to call you if she needs to contact me." He disconnected. Even though he had reassured Nick, the uneasiness persisted, like a lead rock in his chest.

Melodic Westminster chimes rang, signaling the bewitching hour, midnight. As Piper carried a cup of coffee into the dining room, she paused to listen. Shipped from Germany, the grandfather clock had been her grandfather's wedding present to Jen.

When the last tone faded away, a silence settled over the house. Grady and JT had left, taking the UTV to check the pastures. The widespread acres made it easy to load cattle and not be heard at the ranch house. Piper grinned at the memory of the argument between the two men when JT said he'd periodically patrol during the night. Grady had insisted on going with him. JT lost.

Seated at the dining room table, Piper sipped the hot brew and studied the new reports she'd received. A disturbing pattern began to emerge. The pocket of thefts in West Texas was similar to the ones near the Layton Ranch. Mrs. Spence had also mentioned the cattle thefts in the area. Was it possible they were a diversion? To make it appear the thefts were just part of a random pattern and not connected to the loss clause in the contract? Cade said he'd seen seven boxes. Would the pattern hold for the other four? Until she had the names on the other four boxes, it was idle speculation.

Earlier, she scanned Leopold's picture into the computer. A finger tapped keys, bringing up the image on the screen. She increased the magnification to study the background. Behind Leopold, a faint line appeared. Despite the blurriness, it looked like a creek or gully. It was the only identifying mark in the landscape. Not much to go on.

A beep sounded, an email alert. It was from Luke with an attachment, a list of the properties owned by Jarvis. Anticipation shot through her as she hit the print button. Maybe she could find the ranches without the pictures Tanner took. She rose, striding into the office to grab the paper as it shot out.

In amazement, she studied the document. Luke had listed each address and value of the property. Lane Jarvis was a wealthy man, eleven properties across Texas, Oklahoma, and Colorado.

Lacey Kirk, a fellow agent in Piper's unit, had followed the money trail. While at first, it appeared Jarvis only owned one company, Jarvis Livestock, Lacey located JR, Inc., a shell company with three assets, Macon Enterprise, Whitney Corp, and Jarvis Livestock. It had taken Lacey several days to peel back the layers and discover Lane Jarvis and Victor Reid owned the shell company, JR, Inc.

Who the hell is Victor Reid? Piper thought.

Jarvis Livestock owned six properties, including the Anglin and Spence ranches. What caught her attention were the five properties owned by Whitney Corp. Jarvis Livestock had initially purchased the properties, then transferred the titles to Macon Enterprise, then to Whitney Corp.

Luke had added a comment from Lacey that it was a high-dollar, sophisticated version of the old shell game; shuffle the shells, then guess which one hid the pea.

Piper's pulse raced. There was one reason why Jarvis would hide behind a dummy corporation and shuffle properties—launder money from the sale of stolen cattle. Was it also the answer to the disposal of the animals? Tanner had pointed out the limitation of selling stolen cattle, only a few at a time, through the sales barn. Were the ranches used as a holding area?

Sensing she was onto something, Piper walked into the office. In the file cabinet's bottom drawer, Jen kept odds and ends, catalogs, brochures, and maps. Piper grabbed a U.S. map and a black-felt pen from the desk drawer.

Spreading the map across the table, she marked the location of each property with a large X, then drew a circle around the X for the ones owned by Whitney Corp. Barely able to contain her excitement, Piper stared at a trail of ranches. Next, she marked the locations of the cattle thefts with a small x. The majority of the thefts were around the Texas properties owned by Jarvis Livestock. It certainly supported her suspicion the thefts were a diversion.

One of Luke's comments popped into her thoughts. Jarvis was using the ranches and cattle as collateral for bank loans. Yet, at the Anglin ranch, Luke hadn't found where Jarvis had purchased the cattle. Was Jarvis using the stolen cattle for the loans?

As she capped the felt pen, her gaze shifted to the Texas property in an adjacent county. Northwest of Lake Creek, it was only about thirty miles away. She sat down and typed the address into her laptop. Not only did the map appear, but also real estate ads for Sutton Ranch. One included several pictures. The house was in poor repair, but it did advertise barns and cross-fencing for the acreage. Was it possible this is where Jarvis stashed Leopold?

When she clicked on the aerial map, the house and two barns came into view. As she magnified the image, she leaned closer to the screen, searching for a creek bed or gully. She picked up the bag with the picture, her eyes darting between the two images. Disappointed, she sighed and laid it down. Even though she couldn't match the image on the screen to the picture, it didn't change the plan formulating in her mind.

She picked up the attachment to read the rest of Luke's comments. Luke said the handwriting expert confirmed the contract for the Layton Ranch was a forgery. She hadn't expected otherwise. It was the last entry that set off a surge of foreboding.

Luke had talked to the owner of the Anglin Ranch. He inherited the property after his grandfather was killed trying to stop the theft of his cattle. During the probate of the estate, the Jarvis contract was found. With the loss clause, the grandson had to sell the property.

Three contracts, Layton, Spence, and Anglin, and two of the property owners were dead. The body count was rising.

She sent an email to Luke so it would be waiting when he arrived at the office the next morning. She asked him to set up a conference call with Nick Rawling. He was in the best position to track the cattle thefts.

The sound of the backdoor sent her spinning on the chair. A voice shouted, "Piper."

"In the dining room, JT."

When he walked in, his gaze raked the table. "You've been busy."

"You'll be interested in what I've found. There's still some coffee."

"I spotted it when I walked in." He eyed her cup. "Do you want a refill?"

"No, I think I've had enough for tonight."

He nodded and walked out. When he reappeared, his large fingers were wrapped around the handle of a mug. He took a sip as he stepped alongside the table.

"Everything okay outside?"

"All quiet. Grady called it a night. Said he'd see you in the morning. I'll catch a couple of hours sleep, then make another run through the pastures." He motioned with the cup toward the documents and map on the table. "What'd you come up with?"

When she told him about the death of the owner of the Anglin Ranch, his face tightened. "How many more are we going to find?"

In a soft tone, Piper said, "I think at least four more."

"The other boxes," JT said.

"Yeah. But that's not all." She explained about the list of properties Luke had sent and what Lacey had found.

He grunted. "She's a damn good asset. Sure glad she decided to shift from the Treasury Department to our side of the house."

"Take a look at the map. The properties with an X are owned by Jarvis Livestock. The ones with a circle around the X are owned by Whitney Corp. The smaller x's are the locations where cattle were stolen." Then she detailed her suspicions regarding the thefts.

He bent over the table for a closer look. "You might be on to something."

"JT, how difficult is it to move cattle a long distance?"

"Federal guidelines say twenty-eight hours max, then you have to offload for water and food." He tapped the X for the Sutton Ranch. "From here, you could reach either the San Angelo ranch or the one in the Panhandle within hours. Same from the Panhandle to the Oklahoma ranches, from there to Colorado." He moved his finger to the ranch southwest of San Antonio. "Easy reach to West Texas, the Panhandle or the Sutton place."

He straightened. "Didn't Luke say something about Jarvis using the ranches for bank loans?"

"You're on the same track I am. Is he using the stolen cattle?"

JT said, "He's got ranches where he could legitimately run cattle. Jarvis could stash the stolen cattle until he's ready to dispose of them. It's a slick operation. And if he had to move them quickly, he's got a network of ranches where he can hide them."

Lacey's comments about the shell game flashed in her mind. Maybe it wasn't as much about the properties and more about hiding the cattle.

"Do you think Leopold is here?" His finger pointed to the Sutton Ranch.

"Yeah, I do. It makes sense."

He eyed her with suspicion. "You're not planning on checking this out alone, are you?"

"Not yet." Hoping to divert his attention, she added, "I sent Luke an email about a conference call tomorrow with Rawling. Before we can do anything, we need more information. I'd like for you to sit in on the call."

He let out a sigh of relief. "That's good. You don't need to go wandering up there by yourself. If the bull is there, I would imagine Jarvis has guards on the place." He swallowed the last of the coffee. "I'm off to bed. You'd better get some sleep too."

"Umm, I will. I want to check these reports one more time."

Once the sounds from JT's bedroom ceased, Piper walked softly to her bedroom. From her duffel bag, she pulled out black tactical pants, a black long-sleeved t-shirt, and the tactical gun belt. She quickly changed into the new attire and strapped the gun belt around her waist. Once the strap for the drop-down holster was fastened around her thigh, she shoved her Glock inside.

Outside, she slipped behind the wheel of the truck. What she planned was dangerous, and it had to be done at night. If there was any chance of getting evidence, she had to try. Too many people were dying. She'd debated whether to let JT know but finally decided one person had a better chance of getting in and out.

Hoping the engine's sound wouldn't wake Grady or JT, Piper drove out of the driveway. Even if it did, she'd left a note on the kitchen table telling them where she was headed and that she'd be back in about three hours.

Since the backroads were deserted, she made good time. Before she reached the road leading to the ranch, she switched off the headlights, relying on the faint moonlight. Piper slowed and turned. Her truck barely moving, she searched for the narrow driveway leading to a structure across the road from the house. She'd spotted it on the aerial map.

It turned out to be an old barn. After backing in, she turned off the engine. For a few seconds, she took deep breaths to slow the kick of the adrenaline dump.

As she slid out of the truck, she left the door ajar. Piper tugged the black cap tighter over her brow, making sure her hair was safely tucked inside it. Before stepping onto the road, she patted the pocket with her cell phone and a small flashlight. The only sounds breaking the deep silence were an occasional rustling of bushes and the stirring of cattle huddled in small groups in the nearby pasture.

A short distance ahead, the moonlight shifted across the dark outline of a house and barns. She wondered how confident Jarvis was. Did he have guards patrolling, or were the occupants asleep, safe in the belief no one would come snooping? Well, she was about to find out as she jogged toward a broken front gate that had been pushed to one side.

Piper paused, scanning the old ranch house, a single story with a small front porch and the two trucks parked at the edge of the long driveway. She glided up the road, stopping at the back corner of the house. When she leaned forward to take a look, her heartbeat rocketed. The source of her alarm wasn't the two trucks parked on the other side of the yard. It was the wide-open, sprawling expanse of ground, rutted and matted with weeds between her and the barns that were at least two hundred yards away.

She couldn't even see if an animal was in the corral next to one of the barns from where she stood. The thought floated in her mind that on the damn aerial map, the barns seemed closer to the house. There was no tiptoeing, easing her way across the yard. The longer it took, the longer she was exposed.

She took a deep breath and ran. When she reached the barn, she pressed against the side and looked back at the house. So far, so good. She slid toward the fence and looked over it.

Hot damn! She was right. It was Leopold. Even in the dark, she couldn't mistake his shape. Piper glanced over her shoulder. Reassured by the lack of lights, she pulled her phone from her pocket and took several pictures. Behind her, a shout echoed. Her luck had just run out.

"Someone's here!"

She looked back at the house. In the open doorway, a bare-chested man pulled on pants.

"Get me a gun," he shouted before turning and rushing back inside.

Trapped, she couldn't get to the road. Only one way to go. She shoved the phone in her pocket, grabbed the top of the fence and climbed over it. As her feet hit the ground, a stab of fear rocked her back. In the middle of the pen, a 1,400-pound mass of muscle and bone glared at her. Usually, Leopold was easy to handle. It came from all those stock shows. Not tonight. Spooked, Leopold tossed his head and snorted. Over the years, Jen and Grady had repeatedly warned her about the danger. Once, she'd seen a man trampled at one of the auctions. It was a sight she'd never forgotten. Despite the overwhelming urge to run, she couldn't alarm the bull any further. Her steps slow, Piper sidled along the wall, murmuring, "Easy boy, easy."

The same voice shouted, "Where is he? Where'd he go?"

A shot rang out.

"You fool, what are you shooting at? You hit that damned bull, you're a dead man."

The man hollered back. "I thought I saw someone in the pen."

"Hell, no one's that stupid. He has to be in the barn."

Never taking her eyes off the bull, she slowly moved toward the back fence. Further agitated by the sound of the shot, Leopold lowered his head, heavy breaths, almost like a growl, rumbled as he pawed the ground with a hoof. She braced one foot on a rail, hauled herself up and tumbled over the top.

Landing on her back, she knocked the breath out of her. For a second, she blinked at the dark sky before shouts sent her scrambling. Bent over, she ran toward a stand of trees. Now all she had to do was evade the cattle that surrounded her. The shouts and gunshot had them moving. Crouched down, she looked behind her. Lights flashed in the yard as men rushed in and out of the two barns.

She eyed the fence along the roadway and the stretch of pasture she had to cross to reach it. Once she left the safety of the trees, she'd be putting herself in the path of the cattle. In front of her, several agitated animals trotted, picking up speed. It wouldn't take much for the rest to follow. What seemed to be the safest route would take her deeper into the pasture, but there were scattered trees she could use for cover.

Ducking down, she darted from one to the next. When a group of animals raced toward her, she huddled against a tree, praying it was large enough to protect her. In a cloud of dust, they thundered by. Once they passed, she ran. Gasping for breath, she crawled under the fence and raced toward her truck.

A man hollered, "He's on the road." Shots echoed.

Piper jumped in the truck, slamming the door shut as she started the engine. Her foot hit the gas, and she spun the steering wheel.

Tires squealed when the truck skidded onto the road. In the rearview mirror, headlights flashed across the roadway when a truck drove out.

Thankfully, she had the foresight to come up with an exit plan before she left the ranch. She kept an eye on the GPS screen, watching for the road where she needed to turn. She waited until the final second to tap the brakes. Even then, the truck fishtailed. As soon as she had the wheels straight, she goosed it. The truck flew down the road. Another turn was coming up.

She eased off the gas pedal, killed her headlights, and kept her foot off the brake. Though she'd slowed, the speed was still too fast for the turn, pushing the truck dangerously close to the bar ditch on the other side. As she sped away, she watched the rearview mirror. Lights flashed on the road. The driver, unaware she had turned, went straight.

While she wasn't safe yet, she couldn't stop the sense of relief flowing through her. She flipped the switch for the headlights and sped up.

As the tension faded away and she relaxed against the seat, another problem worked its way into her thoughts. No, into her nose. The foul odor of cow dung permeated the inside of the truck. Damn, she'd stepped in a cow patty, probably more than once, in her headlong run across the pasture.

She'd just escaped from a ruthless band of killers, a raging bull, and god only knows how many stampeding cattle. What did she have to show for it—pictures and cow dung. Of the two, only the manure was a certainty. The irony didn't escape her as a gurgle of laughter erupted.

hen Piper pulled in, lights lit up the yard. *Damn*, she thought. She parked and hopped out. Nothing she could do but face the music. She detoured around the side of the house, where she slipped off the manure-caked boots before opening the door to the mudroom.

As she stepped into the kitchen, she was greeted with two angry sets of eyes. An irrelevant thought popped into her mind. Their glare was oddly reminiscent of Leopold's. She stifled the chuckle that rose in her throat.

"Damn it, Piper. What the hell were you thinking?" JT exclaimed. "I'd have gone with you."

"I know, but I needed you here, JT." She pulled out a chair and sat.

"Don't think you can get around me that easy."

"I'm not trying to, just explaining. I figured it was easier for one person to get in and out instead of two. I was right."

Grady spoke up. "I told him not to worry. You're just like your grandmother, hardheaded, but usually know what the hell you are doing."

She flashed him a smile. "Why, thank you, Grady. That's one of the nicest compliments you could pay me."

"Okay, what happened?" JT asked.

While she talked, she left out a few of the more salient details that would only add to their agitation.

"How many men were there?" JT asked.

"I saw four trucks, but there might have been five men."

"Did you recognize any of them?"

"No." She pulled her phone from her pocket, tapped the screen to pull up the pictures. She sighed in relief. The flash on the phone was strong enough to capture the image of the bull inside the pen. She passed the phone to Grady, who scrolled through the pictures before handing it to JT, saying, "That's Leopold. No doubt. So what do you do now?"

"We can't do anything without a search warrant. I'll check with Luke tomorrow, see where we stand on the warrants."

Grady, noticing the dark circles under her eyes, said, "Time to get to bed. Nothing more we can do tonight, and we all need sleep." He glanced at the clock on the wall. "Even if it is only four hours or so."

Piper didn't argue. After a quick shower, she collapsed in bed. Mentally and physically drained, she dropped into a sound sleep.

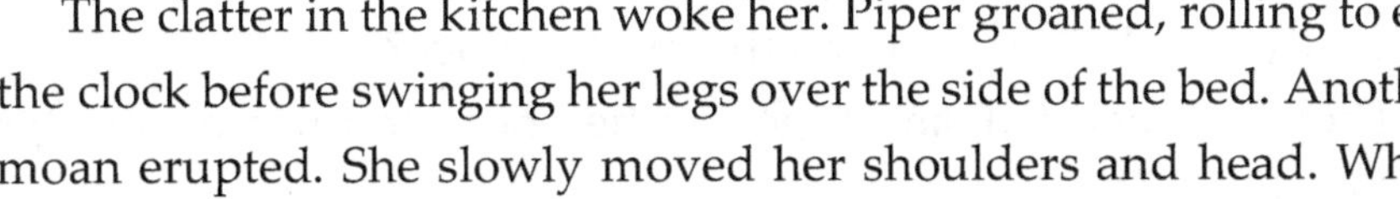

The clatter in the kitchen woke her. Piper groaned, rolling to eye the clock before swinging her legs over the side of the bed. Another moan erupted. She slowly moved her shoulders and head. While she couldn't see the bruises, she felt every one of them. Dragging herself into the bathroom, a hot shower eased some of the muscle aches, that is until she started to dress.

In the kitchen, she grumped a good morning to Grady and headed straight to the pot. Pouring herself a cup, she gulped down half of it, welcoming the intense, almost bitter taste. She topped off the cup before turning to look at Grady turning links of sausage.

He studied her face. Satisfied the circles had faded, he said, "JT's checking the stock."

"Anything I can do to help?"

"Nope. Once he gets back, we're ready to eat."

Feeling the jolt of caffeine, she began to perk up and discovered she was ravenous.

The backdoor opened, and JT strode in, bringing with him the smell of the cool morning air. He rubbed his hands as he inhaled. "That sure smells good."

He pulled out a chair. Piper held her breath as it creaked.

Grady dished up the links, pulled a large plate of scrambled eggs from the oven, and sat it alongside a stack of toast on the table. "What's on your agenda?"

"First is a phone call to my boss. I asked him to set up a conference call with Rawling. I'll stop by the café before I head to the hospital to talk to Davy and Tony. What about you?"

"I have to go into town for supplies. Once I'm done, I'll swing by to see Jen."

For a few minutes, silence reigned as they quickly ate. Swallowing the last bite of toast, Piper eased back with only a slight twinge in her muscles.

Grady stood. "You want a refill on the coffee?"

They both nodded, and Piper pushed her cup toward the edge of the table.

He poured the last of the pot into the cups. "I'll fix another pot and take care of the kitchen. The two of you get on with your business."

Piper stood and stepped toward him. After giving him a quick peck on the cheek, she grabbed her cup and headed to the dining room, where the documents she'd been studying still covered the table. JT followed.

After setting the cup on the table, she pulled the phone from her back pocket. Luke answered on the second ring. "Hang on, just walking into my office." When he came back on the line, he asked, "Where are you?"

Piper punched the speakerphone and said, "At the ranch. JT's here."

After exchanging a greeting with JT, Luke said, "Piper, I saw your email. Before I called Nick, I wanted to tell you about the interesting conversation I had with him yesterday. Turns out we were right. Pollard is an undercover cop."

"Yeah, we found out last night," Piper said. She went over the details at the church, and when she reached the part where bullets started flying, Luke angrily interrupted.

"Piper, I don't like what's going on down there. The deeper we get into Jarvis' activities, the more I'm convinced he's responsible for multiple murders. You knew it was a trap, and you went anyway."

She hastened to reassure him. "Luke, I didn't have a choice. We need evidence. Besides, I had it covered. Davy was with me."

"So, what does this have to do with Pollard, or I should say, Cade Tanner?"

"He followed Sloan and Giles, then snuck into the cemetery next to the church. When the shooting started, he jumped into the middle of it. It spooked the two men, and they took off. In the meantime, Davy got there and saw someone running in the cemetery and thought Tanner was with the two men."

Reading between the lines, he asked, "How close did he come to getting shot?"

"Let's just say it's good Davy doesn't have an itchy trigger finger. Tanner had no choice but to identify himself. We ended up having a meeting here at the ranch. Rawling had already told him to contact me." She told him about the pictures Tanner had taken.

"Rawling sent them to me, though I haven't had a chance to look at them. If you don't get a copy from him, let me know."

"Good. I want to see if the other four boxes match up to your list of properties for Jarvis Livestock."

JT spoke up. "Luke, the placement of the ranches makes it an easy run to move cattle around. They could be using the ranches to stash the stolen cattle, possibly even using the cattle as collateral."

"I'll add that to our research. What else?"

"Rawling is in a better position than we are to find other clusters of cattle thefts. I suspect Jarvis is killing two birds with one stone. He increases the cattle in his possession and uses the thefts as a diversion from his primary objective, the contract's loss clause. Who is going to take a close look when there are other thefts in the same area?"

Luke said, "Damn good point. I'll get Nick on the phone."

"Wait a minute. What do you know about the other man, Victor Reid?"

"Not much. I haven't found any pictures or even a driver's license. He may be a non-existent partner. But we're still digging."

"One more item. I found Leopold."

"How?"

"The proof I demanded turned out to be a picture. Sloan dropped it when the shooting started. Stapled to a fence post in the picture was a local newspaper, dated yesterday. It meant the bull was still in the area. After getting your list of properties, I keyed on the one located northwest of Lake Creek. This morning, I stopped by to take a look. Got a picture of Leopold in the stock pen."

For a few seconds, the line was silent. "You'd better explain … *stopped by.*"

As JT listened, his lips twitched upward. Luke's composed tone was the calm before the storm. If he didn't like what had happened at the church, he'd likely go ballistic when he heard the details of Piper's early morning excursion. He wasn't disappointed.

Even though she glossed over many of the details, Luke ranted. Piper scrunched her face, and when she glanced at JT, he shrugged his shoulders.

Once he wound down, Piper said, "Luke, it was a calculated risk, and it paid off. We need solid evidence that can tie Jarvis to the cattle thefts. You said it yourself, we're dealing with a ruthless gang that doesn't hesitate to kill. I bet when we look into the other four properties, we'll find out the owners were killed."

In a milder tone, Luke said, "I already have. Three were made to look like accidents, the fourth was shot. Send me the pictures. I've started working on warrants. I'll call you back once I get Rawling on the line."

Slumped in the chair, she hit the disconnect button. While Piper suspected what they'd find, she'd held out a hope she was wrong. A grim determination settled over her. This had gone way beyond stealing cattle.

She quickly connected her phone to her computer, downloaded the pictures she'd taken at Sutton's ranch, and attached one, along with the one found at the church, to an email.

As she hit send, an incoming email popped up. "JT, an email just came in from Rawling. I bet this is Tanner's pictures."

He scooted his chair closer to see the screen over her shoulder. As she scrolled through them, she stopped on the one of the seven boxes.

He whistled. "That's the inside of a safe. How'd he pull it off?"

"I can see why Cade glossed over some of the details. Breaking and entering isn't the best reference on a cop's resume," Piper said.

Enlarging it, she slowly scanned down the screen. By the time she reached the last one, she knew she was right. The names on the four boxes matched the ranches owned by Jarvis Livestock.

JT said, "I wonder how long it will take Luke to get a copy of the contracts?"

"Not long. The evidence is piling up against Jarvis. The only problem is we still don't know who else is involved."

Her phone rang. She answered, tapping the speakerphone.

Luke said, "Piper, Nick Rawling is on the line with us."

Piper greeted him, then introduced JT.

Luke said, "Nick, you should have received the files on Jarvis, his companies, and properties,"

"I've already studied it. Much of the information dovetails with what I've found. Now, what can I help you with?"

Piper spoke up. "Are you aware of the contracts Jarvis is using to gain control of the ranches?"

"Not until I saw the documents in the pictures Cade took."

Luke said, "We've found a third one, the Anglin ranch. Piper believes the cattle thefts are a way to divert attention from the ranches with a contract. Can you find out if there have been any other thefts clustered in one area?"

"I've already got it. As soon as I saw the list of properties, I spotted the connection. We've been tracking a pattern of thefts across Texas and into Oklahoma for several months. When it hit East Texas, and the incidents started to rise, we sent Cade in undercover. He began to suspect Jarvis not long after he was hired by Sheffield."

"How'd he get onto Jarvis?" JT asked.

"The two men who work for Jarvis, Giles and Sloan. They kept hanging around the auction house, watching the auctions. Cade couldn't find a legitimate reason for their interest."

Piper said, "On the property list are eleven properties. They could be using them as a holding area for the cattle. This morning,

I found the prize bull stolen from my grandmother's ranch at one of them. I've got pictures."

"Do I want to know how?" he asked.

"Let's just say a little judicious snooping. The bull is at the Sutton Ranch."

"I'm familiar with the place though I didn't know Jarvis had bought it. Did you see any other cattle?"

"Yes. There's a large herd. I'd bet they're stolen."

"Did you get any pictures?"

"Uh … no, didn't have time." She didn't think this was the moment to mention she was running for her life.

"I'll pass the information onto Cade. By the way, his place was searched last night."

A ripple of concern spread over her. "Is his cover blown?"

"We don't know. He's waiting to see how it plays out. Since you and your fellow agents are the boots on the ground, I thought you should know."

She glanced at JT. What she felt mirrored the expression on his face. They both knew how fast an undercover assignment could go sour.

Once they finished, JT headed outside. Piper shut down the computer and stuffed it in her backpack along with the files. It wasn't until she walked out to find Grady washing her truck that she remembered the damn manure.

At her approach, he turned off the nozzle. "Almost got it cleaned. Once I started, I decided to go ahead and wash the whole truck."

She chuckled in delight. "How'd you know?"

"The boots on the back porch. Hell, you couldn't miss the smell. I cleaned them too."

"Grady, what would we do without you?" she said, wrapping her arms around him, kissing his cheek.

"Hey, careful here, don't want to get water on you," he said as a blush stained his face. "Watch your back today. I hope no one recognized you last night."

She chuckled again. "Nah, I don't think so. They kept referring to me as a *he*."

"That's a good sign. Once I get cleaned up, I'll be leaving. Sure glad JT is here to keep an eye on the place."

As Piper strolled toward the front door, two men walked out of the cafe. One limped, his face contorted in pain as he eased his way down the steps.

Impatient, Sloan grumbled, "For chrissake, get a move on. We don't have all damn day." The moment he spotted her, his jaw tightened as a look of loathing crossed his face.

She stopped. Feet widespread, she hooked her thumbs in her jean pockets as she stared at them with a look of derision. "Aww … did someone fall down and hurt themselves?" she taunted.

Giles' head jerked toward her. His voice harsh, he said, "Bitch. Your day is coming."

She knew these men had tried to kill her and her grandmother. Still, she couldn't let the rage bubbling inside her spill out. Not yet. Instead, she said, "Won't be from you."

"You can't hide behind that badge."

"I don't need to. I don't have to be a cop to recognize scum when I see it."

Furious, Giles' hands fisted as he moved toward her.

Sloan grabbed his arm, yanking him back. "Not here." When Giles tried to shake him off, Sloan growled, "Not now."

After another angry look, Giles limped off. Sloan followed.

As they passed by her, Piper said, "Just in case you're interested, there is still a $25,000 reward for the return of my bull."

Inside, several tables were still occupied. Seeing Henry Miller, she ambled her way toward him, then spotted two men at a table by the front window. She changed course. Both men stared at her with a guarded look.

Piper extended her hand. "I haven't met you. I'm Piper McKay. I've seen you at the auction house."

He shook it, saying, "Frankie Hillard. Yeah, I've seen you there. Do you know Ron Pollard?" motioning to the man seated across from him.

"Yes. Grant introduced him. Hello again."

Cade nodded to her.

"That was an ugly scene outside. We were wondering if you might need some help," Frankie said. "What happened?" Over the rim of his coffee cup, he watched her.

"Nah, it wasn't a problem. One of them took exception to something I said. How did Giles get hurt? He seemed to be in a lot of pain."

"No idea." He looked at Cade, who shrugged his shoulders.

"Anyway, why I stopped is because both of you work at the auction. A bull was stolen from my grandmother's ranch, and there is a $25,000 reward for his safe return. I hoped you might help by spreading the word."

Frankie set the cup down. "Sure, be glad to. How do they contact you?"

"Grant has copies of the flyer if someone wants one, or they can call the Layton Ranch."

"I heard about your grandmother. I talked to her a few times when she showed up for a sale. A fine lady. How's she doing?"

He'd never taken his eyes off her. Piper didn't like his intense stare. Was he testing the water, wanting to see how she would react to his comment about Jen? For a moment, she looked back, never letting any of the anger that surged inside her show on her face. Her voice calm, she said, "Good, thank you. I need to let the others know about the reward before they leave. Nice to have met you."

She moved from table to table, visiting with the customers, until she reached where Henry was seated. The waitress walked up. "Just coffee," Piper told her as she eased onto the chair.

Henry said, "You've been busy. What's going on?"

"I wanted to get the word out about the reward for Leopold."

"You still haven't heard anything?"

"Nothing. I'm beginning to believe we might never locate him. I hate to have to tell Jen." She leaned back as the waitress set a mug of coffee in front of her.

"How is she doing?" Henry asked.

She'd taken a sip and set the cup down before answering, "Much better. When I leave here, I'm on my way to the hospital."

"Be sure to let me know when she can have visitors," he said.

While they talked, she'd kept an eye on the table where Cade and Hillard sat. Their heads leaned forward, the conversation seemed intense. She wondered what the hell was going on. Hillard didn't act like a man who knew he was talking to an undercover cop.

Once Piper was out of earshot, Frankie leaned his arms on the table. His voice low, he said, "That woman sure has caused problems for some people in town."

When she walked up to the table, Cade had felt his chest tighten. What was she up to? When she explained about the reward for the bull, he'd relaxed until Frankie made a comment about her grandmother. He waited with bated breath. Cade's respect rose when she didn't react even though she knew Hillard was involved.

Still, he didn't like Frankie's persistence about McKay or his comment during her confrontation with Sloan and Giles, indicating that she'd get her comeuppance one of these days.

But he couldn't afford to take exception to it. His tone nonchalant, Cade said, "I don't pay much attention to the local gossip, so I wouldn't know."

"Where'd you come from?"

"Up north."

"Where up north?"

Cade pushed his plate to one side. "Don't rightly think it's any of your business."

"I heard you did some time. Any truth to the rumor?"

Cade just stared at him.

Frankie threw a hand in the air. "Hey, doesn't matter to me. I've got some jail time in my past."

"Why the questions?"

"Since you've been so closed-mouthed, I just want to know who I'm talking to."

"Yeah, well, I'm still not interested in talking. Once I get a stake built up, I'm out of here."

"I gather you aren't interested in much except getting your paycheck each week."

Cade leaned back. Though his pulse raced in anticipation, his face held a look of disinterest. Was this the break he was looking for? All he could do was wait, not appear to be overeager.

"The job I mentioned. It would add to that grubstake if you're interested," Frankie said.

For a few seconds, Cade stared at him. "How much?"

A gleam of satisfaction sparked in Frankie's eyes. "Enough to make it worth your time. Let's get out of here. I'll discuss it with you when we get to work."

Across the room, Hillard and Cade were leaving. Piper said her goodbyes to Henry and followed the two men out the door. As they pulled out of the parking lot, her phone chimed. It was a text from Davy wanting to know where the hell she was. She grinned and texted back, telling him not to get his shorts in a wad. She was on her way. Though she couldn't blame him for his impatience since he probably wanted to get some sleep.

At the hospital, she stopped at the nurse's desk.

The nurse seated behind the counter said, "Ms. McKay, Dr. Henderson wanted you to know that Ms. Layton is doing exceptionally well."

"Oh, that is such good news," Piper exclaimed.

"We've all been pulling for her."

"I know you have, and I so appreciate all the care you've provided."

"We're getting used to having Marshals Kline and Fenwick here. They certainly have a way of livening up the place."

"That they do," Piper grinned as she headed toward Jen's room.

A roar of laughter erupted from inside the room as she opened the door. Tony and Davy were seated in chairs pushed close to her grandmother's bed. The bottles and tubes were gone. Jen was propped up, and a smaller bandage encased her head. Evidently, whatever she said, had both men laughing.

When Jen saw her standing in the doorway, her eyes lit up. "Piper," she said, lifting her hand.

Tears glinted in her eyes as Piper rushed to the side of the bed. Her fingers gripped Jen's hand, and she bent over to kiss her cheek. "Wow, just look at you. The nurse told me how much better you were doing, but I didn't expect to see you this chipper."

"I'm a tough bird to kill," she said, her voice still a bit raspy.

Behind her, Tony and Davy had risen. Davy pushed a chair toward her. "Have a seat. Tony and I are going to take a quick break." He leaned over to whisper in her ear. "She's been asking for you ever since she woke up this morning. I forgive you for the tacky remark about my shorts."

Piper chuckled as she turned her attention back to Jen. She didn't even hear the door close.

"Sweetie, you look tired."

"Ha, look who's talking. It's been a rough few days, but seeing you like this makes it all better."

"Tell me what's going on. I asked, but those partners of yours are tighter-lipped than Grady. Won't tell me a damn thing."

"Nothing for you to worry about," Piper said.

"That's the problem. Confined to a bed gives a body lots of time to worry and come up with all kinds of ideas, some not so good. I need to hear the truth."

Piper took a deep breath before asking, "Do you remember anything more about the day you were hurt?"

A grim tone crept into Jen's voice. "You mean the day someone clobbered me on the head?"

"Yeah. At first, everyone thought Bess had thrown you, and you hit your head on a rock. That was what Sheriff Horne concluded."

Jen sniffed. "That idiot. He couldn't find his way out of a paper sack if he had a map. Besides, what fool would believe Bess could throw me? Ridiculous."

Piper grinned. "Well, Grady didn't buy into it. After I had a chance to see where you'd been found, I didn't either. It's why Tony and Davy are here. Since someone wanted you dead, and you weren't, it was possible they'd try again." She still didn't want to mention the second attempt.

"What did Horne have to say?"

"Let's just say we had a difference of opinion. I basically told him if he wouldn't do his job, I would."

Jen laughed. "That's my girl."

"I'm still investigating, and so is my unit in Oklahoma City. We've come up with a lot of information about the cattle thefts around here. Right now, I can't share the details."

Seeing the mutinous look in her grandmother's eyes, she lifted a hand. "As soon as I can tell you, I will. The ranch is safe. Another marshal, John Thompkins, is staying there helping Grady. They've bonded over rodeoing. JT's been on the rodeo circuit as well as his daddy, who was a bull rider. Seems Grady saved his dad's life one time."

As a diversion, it worked well.

"Thompkins," Jen mused. "I think I remember him. I'll have to talk to Grady about it. Has he been here?"

Surprised at the unexpected anxious note in Jen's voice, she said, "Yes. As a matter of fact, we've both been bouncing in and out of your room."

"Really?" Jen said as a spark flashed in her eyes.

This is interesting, Piper thought. "Yeah. He's been here most every day." She looked at her watch. "He should be on his way."

"How do I look?" Her hand patted the bandage. "I haven't wanted to ask for a mirror."

Piper bit back the smile that threatened to erupt and simply said, "To us, you look wonderful. But, Jen, you have to promise me something."

"What?"

"Don't interrogate the man. I don't need you talking in your sleep about the investigation. It could be dangerous."

"Young lady, I have never talked in my sleep. But I see your point. Don't worry," she said, patting Piper's hand. "Besides, I trust you to do what's right."

"Okay, with that in mind, tell me about Jarvis. I found your contract about the sale of the ten head."

"Did you get a check?"

"Not yet. Was that the only dealings you've had with the man?"

"Yes, and it's the last time I'll do business with him. If he still hasn't paid, talk to Arnie."

"I already have."

"That's good. What about Leopold?"

"Nothing so far, but we're looking for him. Hard to hide a bull like Leopold."

"Did you find the DNA report?"

Not wanting Jen to know about the stolen records, she carefully phrased her answer. "I read it."

"Then you know what I found out. Leopold is worth a lot more money than even I realized."

"I saw Brad at the café one morning. He mentioned your interest. When I stopped by his place, I showed him the report. I hoped he could help me make some kind of sense out of it."

"Brad has been pushing me for months to get a DNA analysis."

"Jen, who else knew about the DNA report?"

"Just Grady. I didn't want to tell anyone until I had the new business up and running. Oh! There was someone else, Mack Huber at the bank. I planned to take out a loan for the startup costs. As part of the loan application, I had to give him a business plan. It included the details of the potential revenue. The DNA report was attached to support my revenue projections. All the paperwork is in a file in my desk."

A red flag went up at the mention of a business plan. There was no such document in the papers Huber gave her. Even as an ominous feeling rippled over her, she said, "I talked to him. The loan's on hold."

"He called when Leopold was stolen. I told him there was no point going ahead with the loan until I recovered the bull."

Outside the door, voices rumbled before it opened. Grady strode in, carefully carrying a large vase filled with spring flowers. Tony and Davy followed him.

Jen sighed in delight. "Oh, my."

He stepped alongside the bed. "Thought they might cheer you up."

"Grady, flowers? You never cease to surprise me. They're beautiful."

An uncomfortable look settled over his face as he glanced around.

Piper said, "We can set them on the small table by the chair. If we move it a bit, all Jen has to do is turn her head to look at them."

He shot her a grateful look and handed her the vase.

"How are you feeling?" he asked.

"Much better," Jen said. "Though, I won't be rid of this bandage for a while."

"Now, don't you go rushing it. Seems to me the Doc knows what he's doing. We're getting by just fine."

Piper touched his arm. "If it's okay with you, the guys and I will be in the cafeteria."

"That's fine. I'll just pull up this chair and have a nice visit."

Piper looked over her shoulder as she headed to the door. "Remember, Jen, don't be pestering him with questions."

"You just go on. We'll do all right here," her grandmother quipped back.

As the three walked along the hallway, Piper said, "New information. I didn't want to discuss it in front of Jen."

Once they each had a cup of coffee, and Davy had grabbed a plate of eggs and bacon, they settled at a corner table.

As he scooped up eggs, Davy said, "I updated Tony on what happened yesterday and about Cade Tanner. So what else?"

"I found Leopold."

Davy's fork stopped in midair as he stared at her.

"How the hell did you do that?" Tony asked.

"Luke sent me a list of properties Jarvis owns. One isn't far from the ranch."

Tony's cup clinked as it hit the table. "For cripes sake, don't tell me you went there?"

"Um … yes, I did."

"Did JT go with you?" Davy asked.

"No. Since I only wanted to take a quick look, I didn't want to pull him away from the ranch."

Disgusted, both men stared at her.

"What!" she exclaimed. "No big deal. I got in and out and have pictures." She wasn't about to share what really happened. "This morning, JT and I talked to Luke and Nick Rawling, Cade's boss." She explained what had transpired.

Tony said, "I think you're onto something. It makes sense to use the ranches as holding areas."

"Here's something else. We've been wondering who else was involved. I think a local banker, Mack Huber is part of it. Jen planned to take out a loan for the artificial insemination equipment. She had to submit a business plan. Huber knew about the DNA report. According to Jen, only one other person knew, Grady. I didn't discover Jen's copy of the loan application documents was missing until I talked to Huber. When I got a copy from him, it didn't include a business plan. He had an attitude at the time, a definite reluctance to give me a copy. He excused it as just being cautious."

Davy propped his elbows on the table. "How convenient to have a banker in the mix for the loans. I wonder how many have gone through his bank?"

"I don't know. I haven't had a chance to tell Luke."

"What's next?" Tony asked.

"I'm headed to the bank. I want to find out what happened to the business plan."

"You think it will alert Huber that we're suspicious of him?" Tony asked.

"Not if I play it right."

Davy stood. "I'm headed to the hotel. If there are any new developments, call. I don't care if I am asleep." A stern expression settled over his face. "Don't go off on your own again."

She gave him a half salute with her fingertips and smiled.

"Damnit, Piper. Ah, what the hell. I might just as well be whistling into the wind. I probably would have done the same. See you both later."

"I'll get back upstairs," Tony said.

"Tell Jen I'll be by later."

"She's going to want to know what's going on."

"I know. I've already had to duck several of her questions. I just hope she hasn't been successful in grilling Grady."

As they split up, Piper hit the speed dial for Luke. When he answered, she said, "Got another suspect for you," and filled him in on the details about Huber.

"I'll let Lacey know to look at the banks involved and who authorized the loans. We found two big rig cattle haulers. They're owned by Whitney Corp."

"I wonder where they are now?"

"Good question. I take it you didn't spot the trucks when you went looking for Leopold."

"No, just several pickups. No eighteen-wheelers. Are you feeding this stuff to Rawling, or do I need to call him?"

"I'm getting ready to call. I'll let him know about Huber."

"Ask him to contact Cade. I saw him this morning having a deep conversation with Hillard at a local restaurant. I'm curious what it was about."

"I'll try to find out."

"By the way, I also ran into Giles and Sloan at the café. Giles was limping."

A sardonic laugh echoed as she disconnected.

Piper pushed open the door of the bank. One of the tellers motioned toward her. As she stopped in front of the counter, she said, "I'd like to see Mack Huber."

"He just left," the teller told her.

"Do you know when he'll be back?"

"Probably not until early afternoon. He's headed to the Rotary Club's weekly meeting."

"How about his administrative assistant, Maisie? Is she here?"

"Yes. I'll call her. And you are?"

"Piper McKay. She knows me."

After making a call, the teller directed her to Huber's office.

When she stepped inside, Maisie glanced up, and a cheerful look lit her face.

"Marshal McKay, so nice to see you again."

"Please, it's just Piper."

"Mr. Huber isn't here, but is there something I can help you with?"

"In the loan papers he gave me, I've found there is a missing document, a business plan."

A disturbed look crossed Maisie's face.

"Any idea what happened to it?"

Maisie looked at the open door, then stood and walked toward it. She closed it. Nervous, her hands twisted as she looked at Piper.

"I'm not certain. When I realized it was missing, I informed Mack."

"When was that?"

"The day after your grandmother was hurt. I remember we'd been talking about her accident. He asked for her loan file. When he gave it back, I went through it to straighten up the documents. He tends to get them out of order. That's when I noticed it was gone."

"What did he say?"

"He said he'd seen it was missing and blamed me, that I misplaced it. I didn't. I know it was in the file." Her voice apprehensive, she said, "Are you going to ask Mack about it?" The woman looked downright scared.

"I had planned on discussing it with him. Why?"

"He said if I mentioned it to anyone, he'd fire me for negligence."

Knowing any further pursuit of the missing file would be futile, she said, "We'll just keep this conversation between the two of us. If you do come across it, please call me."

"Oh, I will," she said with a sigh of relief. "He'll want to know why you were here. What should I tell him?"

"I asked about the loan's expiration date. You looked it up and told me. If he asks why tell him you don't know. I never said."

A wan smile crossed her face. "Thank you. I can't afford to lose this job."

Her tone determined, Piper said, "Don't worry. You won't."

As she walked out, whatever lingering doubt she had about Huber had vanished.

Three men stood outside the church where the Rotary Club held their meeting. Jarvis said, "We had an intruder at the Sutton place last night, out by the bull's pen."

Huber asked, "Who?"

"I don't know."

A muscle by Huber's left eye twitched. "My god, this is getting out of control!"

The third man shot a disdainful look toward Huber before saying to Jarvis, "Was it McKay?"

"No one got a good look, but I can't see McKay sneaking around out there."

"She managed to put a bullet hole in one of your men."

Jarvis grunted. "It wouldn't have happened if she didn't have help. Did you ever find out who was in the damn cemetery?"

"It had to be one of the other marshals. Who else could it have been?"

"So, what are we going to do?" Huber's hand swiped the beads of sweat on his brow.

Jarvis said, "I've moved up the schedule. We're pulling out tonight. With someone snooping around the Sutton place, we can't take a chance. The herd has to be moved. It means we can't use both eighteen-wheelers for the Layton herd. We'll grab as many as we can shove into the trailer."

"Have you got enough men?" the third man asked.

"I'll use the men assigned to the big rigs, that's four more, plus I picked up another cowhand." At the questioning look on the man's face, Jarvis added, "Pollard."

"It's a bad idea."

"I had his place checked last night. Pollard's papers back up what you discovered."

"I still say it's a bad idea."

"It's not going to be a problem because I don't plan on Pollard leaving the Layton place alive. Since I'm also shutting down the Sheffield operation, he's the perfect patsy to seal the deal on Grant Sheffield. If McKay is suspicious, all the blame will fall on Pollard and Sheffield."

"I thought you weren't going to be ready for several more weeks to make the move," Huber protested.

Jarvis said, "Dick Crowley got a call yesterday about his application for the accounting job at the livestock auction house outside of Cuero. It's not far from the San Antonio property."

Seeing the blank look on Huber's face, he said, "I keep forgetting you don't know much about Texas. Cuero is southeast of San Antonio."

The third man asked, "When is Dick leaving?"

"He gave Sheffield his two weeks' notice this morning. Dick's already reconfigured the computer system, with just enough evidence to convict both Sheffield and Pollard."

"What about the bull?" Huber asked.

"Sloan's going to deliver it. Ramon's getting impatient, wanting to know when it will arrive. Since he's already deposited a half million into the offshore account, we can't hold off any longer."

Huber said, "I still think it's a mistake to get tangled up with some drug lord."

Disgusted, Jarvis said, "I'll be damned if I'm going to pass up a million bucks for one animal. Don't forget, Mack, you're going to get a nice chunk of change. The Mexico connection is another reason the Cuero location works to our advantage. Instead of sending the cattle north, we'll send them into Mexico."

The third man asked, "What about his insistence on the eradication of the bull's identity?"

Jarvis said, "I've assured him I'm taking care of the last two loose ends—Layton and her granddaughter. Even if I can't, they'll never find the bull once it disappears into Mexico."

Relentless, Huber said, "If you ask me, I think we should cut our losses. Move the cattle at the Sutton Ranch and forget about the Layton herd."

A malevolent gleam flashed in Jarvis' eyes. "It's not going to happen. I've spent too much time and expense to let it go. I want the Layton Ranch. To make sure it happens, the old lady has to lose enough cattle to activate the loss clause in the contract. Even though we can only fill one cattle hauler, adding in the loss of the bull, it'll be enough."

Huber nervously shuffled. "Yeah, but what are you going to do about the marshals?"

"Hell, two are staying close to the hospital. They won't be a problem." Jarvis looked at the third man. "Make sure you're there tonight. It shouldn't be too difficult to handle one woman and an old man."

"But ..." Huber started to say.

"Mack, if you're that damned worried, how about helping us tonight?"

The twitch around Huber's eye picked up speed. "No, you know

I can't. I don't know anything about rounding up cattle."

Cars pulling into the parking lot stopped the conversation.

Jarvis looked at the third man and said, "I'll see you tonight." He and Huber turned toward the door. Sunlight flashed across the badge pinned to the third man's shirt as he walked to his car.

His gaze on the end of a trailer, Cade's hand moved in a circular motion as he signaled to the driver. Once the trailer reached the gate, his palm flashed. The driver hit the brakes.

On the other side of the trailer, Frankie opened the gate. The driver, Dale Hanson, hopped out to help. This was the next to last batch of cattle for the day. Another truck waited to pull in.

While they worked, Cade knew Frankie watched him. During a lull of incoming trucks earlier in the afternoon, Frankie told him the job was tonight. Since then, the man had stuck to him like glue. Somehow, he had to get clear just long enough to call Nick. Inadvertently, Dale gave him a chance.

Once the tally was complete, Dale signed the form on the clipboard, then handed it back to Cade. "Do you mind dropping this off? On my way over here, I felt a slight pull in the steering. I want to check the tires before I pull out."

Cade's face had a look of indifference as he said, "Sure. Be glad to."

Frankie darted around the side of the truck. His gaze flicked toward Cade, then to the truck waiting to unload, before he said, "I need to go inside. I'll take it." He grabbed the clipboard and strode toward the building.

Keeping an eye on Frankie, Cade said, "I've got a tire gauge in my truck. I'll get it and check the tires on the other side." Once Frankie stepped inside, Cade pulled out his phone and hot-footed it toward his truck. His boss answered on the first ring.

"Cavalry. Hillard offered me a job loading cattle. It's tonight. He's been bird-dogging me, so I don't have long to talk."

"What did he tell you?"

"Not much, other than it is two different locations up north and will take several hours. It tells me this is more than just a few cattle in a stock trailer. When I asked where I should meet him, he said we'd leave from here. One shipment was ready to load, but the other would be later tonight. I didn't want to appear overly eager with my questions."

"Piper found the bull along with a herd of cattle at the old Sutton Ranch north of her place. Jarvis owns it. He also owns two cattle haulers."

"It's beginning to make sense why Jarvis needed another hand. The Sutton place must be one of the locations. I bet the other is the Layton Ranch."

"I don't like the idea of you going in without backup."

"I'm not exactly enthusiastic myself, but we don't have much choice. We need evidence."

Cade opened the back door to his truck. Before he leaned in, he glanced over his shoulder. The front office door opened.

"Got to go." He disconnected. As he reached to grab a tire gauge from the toolbox on the floorboard, he slid the phone into his pocket. He turned to walk back and saw Frankie trotting toward him. His eyes dropped to Cade's hands.

Cade ignored him and dropped to one knee alongside the front tire. Frankie stopped next to him.

Hanson hollered, "It's on this side, one of the trailer tires."

Cade stood and walked around the front of the truck.

Disgusted, Hanson stared at the tire. "I don't have a spare. It may get me home, though I sure hate the thought of breaking down alongside the road." He stripped off his gloves, slapping them against his palm. "Well, if I do, I'll call Henry and have him bring me a tire."

Once the last truck left, Cade headed inside, where he made a pit stop, passing Frankie on his way out the door. Outside, he ambled toward his truck.

Frankie caught up with him. "We need to get a move on. We'll take my truck."

"I'll follow you. I'm not leaving mine here."

Frankie glared at him. "I don't think you understand. We're staying together."

Cade shrugged his shoulders. "Forget it. I don't cotton to someone watching my every move, which is what you've been doing the last several goddamned hours." He turned to walk toward his truck. When Frankie hollered at him, telling him to hold up, the tension eased. His gamble had paid off, though when he turned, he stared at Frankie with a disinterested expression.

"Just stay behind me."

Cade nodded.

Occupied by her thoughts of Huber's complicity in the plot to kill her grandmother, she strolled into the hospital. When her phone rang, she stopped in the lobby, shifting the backpack to reach the phone in her pocket. She tapped the button and held it to her ear. "McKay."

Nick said, "Cade called. Hillard hired him to load cattle at two locations tonight."

The image of the two men talking at the café flashed in her mind. That's what the conversation was about. A man bumped into her, and she realized people were stepping around her. She walked back outside. "Does he know where?"

"Somewhere up north, and it will take several hours, which means a large herd. I told Cade you'd found the bull and where. We both believe the herd at the Sutton place is the first location. The other is your ranch. I'm putting together a team. But I don't know how soon I can get there."

The danger Cade faced set off a surge of trepidation. Her thoughts raced. "Is he going to call again?"

"He said Hillard was staying close to him. He doesn't know if he'll get another chance."

"If he does, tell him there's an abandoned barn across the road from the ranch house. That's where I'll be."

"What are you going to do about your place?"

"Protect it."

"Let me know how I can help." The line went dead.

Piper hit another speed dial, waiting for Luke to answer. When he did, she said, "I just got off the phone with Nick." She told him what Nick said before adding, "I think he's right. Jarvis is coming after the herd. It fits the pattern."

"I'll contact the FBI office in Dallas and get a SWAT unit."

"Good luck on that."

"Since the red tape's always a problem, I don't know how soon I can get them there."

"Nick's getting a team together but has the same problem."

"I'll contact him and coordinate the teams. You could be on your own."

"Once I get everyone at the ranch, we'll come up with a plan. I'll get back to you."

The next call was to Davy. It took a few rings.

His voice groggy, he said, "What's happened?"

"Meet me at the ranch as soon as you can."

"On my way."

Inside the hospital, she headed to the stairs. She couldn't waste time waiting for the damn elevator. Exiting onto the third floor, she trotted past the nurse's station, ignoring their surprised looks.

Inside, Grady sat beside the bed. Jen was awake, and her face alert as they spoke. Tony was settled into the chair with his laptop open.

Piper walked over and kissed Jen.

"Grady, do you mind holding down the fort while I talk to Tony?"

"Go ahead. We're fine here."

As they walked out, she heard Jen whisper, "Something's going on. I know that look."

"Don't worry about it. Piper knows what she's doing," Grady answered.

Once the door closed behind them, Piper explained what she'd learned from Nick. "Davy's on the way to the ranch. I want to get everyone there and decide on a plan."

"What about your grandmother?"

"It's a problem. I don't want to leave her unprotected, but I need you tonight."

"Can you hire a nurse?"

"Damn, that's a good idea." She headed to the nurse's station. After a few minutes of conversation, she walked back to where Tony waited.

"I've hired two. There's safety in numbers. I've left instructions that Jen is not to be left alone, though I suspect Jarvis' men will be too busy for me to worry."

"Since I haven't been to the ranch, I'll follow you."

Back inside, Piper stepped alongside the bed.

Jen looked up at her. Her eyes clouded with anxiety, she said, "Something's wrong. So don't try to bamboozle me. I feel so dang useless, just lying here, not able to help."

Piper picked up her hand, holding it between hers. "Jen, I've got a whole crew here to help, so quit worrying. As soon as I know something, I'll tell you. In the meantime, you're going to have new visitors."

After listening to Piper's explanation, Jen's emphatic protest that she didn't need someone to babysit her was rapidly overridden by both Piper and Grady.

"Quit getting riled up and let Piper do her job," Grady said.

Astonished, Jen stared at him.

He turned to Piper. "I'll stay here until the nurses arrive. Go on and finish this."

Piper leaned over and kissed Jen's cheek, then gave Grady a hug before rushing out the door.

When she drove into the driveway, Davy stood beside his vehicle, talking to JT. They both turned at the sound of her car. Behind her, Tony pulled to a stop.

On the way inside, JT asked about Grady.

Piper said, "I hired two nurses to keep an eye on Jen. Once they get to the hospital, he'll be here. Let's take this into the dining room."

The men grabbed chairs. Piper stood at one end of the table. "Hillard hired Cade for a job tonight, loading cattle at two different locations. According to Nick, the herd at Sutton Ranch is likely one of them. The other is probably our herd. We do know Jarvis owns two eighteen-wheelers."

JT snapped to the obvious. "He's going in without backup."

"That's another problem," Piper said. "I've got an idea, but first, Luke is contacting the Dallas FBI office to request a tactical unit. It's doubtful they'll arrive in time or the team Cade's boss is putting together. We're on our own." She dropped into a chair. "How do we stop them?"

JT mused, "The east gate is the farthest point on the property and can't be seen from the house. I expect they'll use it again. If they intend to steal as many as they can load, then they'll use the big rigs."

"How long would it take to load one of them?" Piper asked.

"Depends on what equipment they bring with them. Grabbing fifty or so head and loading them into an eighteen-wheeler is a lot different from a few in a livestock trailer."

Davy said, "They may have someone watching the house."

JT said, "I would if I were planning this. I'd come in during the wee hours of the morning when everyone is in bed. I'd have someone in place to stop anyone from interfering. It's probably how the rancher was killed during the heist in Cass County."

Tony asked, "When do we take them, while they're loading, or once they've finished?"

Remembering how the cattle reacted at the Sutton Ranch, she said, "I'd say wait until the cattle are in the trailer."

JT nodded in agreement. "Piper's right. If we go too early, it could cause a stampede. Better to wait."

Davy asked, "Then what?"

Since JT was obviously the expert at the table, everyone looked at him.

"The truck will be backed in. Easier to turn an empty truck around in a pasture than one loaded with 50,000 pounds or more of livestock. The driver will want a straight run to get out the gate. There will be other pickups for the additional men and equipment. Piper, how many men did you see?"

"I think five." Her lips curved upward in a wry smile. "But, I didn't have a whole lot of time to take a close look."

"Worst case scenario, we've got to assume that in addition to Sloan, Giles, and Hillard, there are at least five others. Since you shot him, Giles is iffy, though he could probably drive a truck and handle a gun or rifle. If they're using both cattle haulers, one for the herd at the Sutton place and the one here, there are the drivers and maybe passengers."

Tony exclaimed, "Damn! We could be looking at twelve men, all armed to the teeth."

"It's how I figure it," JT said.

Tony said, "Bad odds since we're outnumbered three to one."

"We are, but we've got an edge," Piper said.

Tony raised his eyebrow.

"We've got an inside ace, Cade Tanner."

Piper pulled her laptop from the backpack she'd dropped alongside her chair. She opened it, accessed a file, and hit print. As she stood, Grady walked in.

She said, "Pull up a chair and join the confab. I'll be right back. One of you bring Grady up to date."

When she returned, they were discussing how to stop the vehicles from leaving. She handed each of them an aerial map of the Layton Ranch.

Davy asked, "Anyone have an idea on how to disable the semi?"

Tony said, "What about a roadblock?"

"We'd be spread too thin trying to block the intersections on the road," Davy said as he studied his copy of the map. "The eighteen-wheeler would blow through anything we could set up."

"Good point," Tony said. "Which means we're back to stopping the trucks from leaving."

For several minutes, the agents studied the map. Grady stood and said, "I'll probably be more useful getting us something to eat. If you need me, I'll be in the kitchen."

Piper flashed him a look of appreciation.

"Any chance once they're finished here, they'll go back to the other ranch? Could we take them there? Nick or the FBI would have time to get there." JT said.

Piper said, "Good question since we don't know what they plan to do with the other eighteen-wheeler. Will they leave it there or bring it with them. The problem I see is whether we can take a chance they'll get on a highway. It would mean we'd have to stay with them."

Davy nodded in agreement. "If we did, they could spot the tail, and we run a risk of a chase or shoot-out. Jarvis may even have a truck trailing them for protection. The trucks could go in different directions. Any number of possibilities for something to go wrong. I don't think we can take the risk."

Tony shook his head in resignation. "We've got to stop them here."

"I agree," Piper said. "If this was only a few stolen cattle, it would be one thing, but it isn't. These men have killed and will kill again. They have to be stopped." Her finger jabbed the picture of the ranch. "That's here. How many weapons do we have?"

Davy said, "In the trunk of my car, I've got my sniper rifle, an M4, extra mags, and two cans of ammo."

Tony said, "Likewise, plus a 590 tactical shotgun."

JT nodded. "Same except for the sniper rifle."

Piper said, "I brought my sniper rifle and gear. Grady and Jen have several handguns, rifles and shotguns. We should be okay."

She picked up her phone. When Luke answered, she hit the speakerphone.

"Tony, Davy, and JT are here. Have you heard from Nick?"

"Yes. We're coordinating efforts on the takedown teams. He said he hasn't been able to pass your message to Cade. What message?"

"It's a plan to provide backup for Cade. I don't have all the details worked out yet. Where do you stand on the FBI?" she said, hoping to divert him.

A snort of disgust echoed over the line. "Still waiting for a call. What about on your end?"

"After considerable debate, the only viable option is to apprehend them here at the ranch."

"Any idea how many men?"

"A rough possibility is ten or twelve."

"It could turn into a blood bath!" Luke exclaimed. "What about weapons?"

"We're good."

"Damn, I don't like this. Keep me informed. As soon as I hear from the FBI, I'll call you."

She punched the disconnect button and laid the phone aside. The room had suddenly gone quiet. Three men eyed her with a look of suspicion.

Davy broke the silence. "What's *this* plan to provide cover for Cade?"

Knowing she couldn't dodge their questions, she said, "I'm going to the ranch." Her finger pointed to a structure on the aerial map. "It's an abandoned barn on the other side of the road. I'll be inside."

"Dammit, Piper," Tony protested. "You can't go in there alone."

A grim expression settled on her face. "One of us has to. First, we're assuming they'll be at the Sutton Ranch. What if they have some other game plan and aren't there? We need to know. If they are there, I can keep an eye on Cade and find out what we're up against. It gives us a head's up." Her gaze moved to each face. "This isn't open to debate. I'm the one who is familiar with the place. There's only four of us, and we need every advantage we can get."

From the doorway, a tray of sandwiches in his hands, Grady said, "Not four, five. I'm in this too."

"Grady, I appreciate your offer, but it's too dangerous for a civilian."

He walked up to her. His eyes gleamed with resolve. "I can shoot just as good as any one of you. I *will* help protect this ranch."

After a few seconds, she let out a deep breath. "Okay. But if you get hurt, Jen will never forgive me."

A grim smile crossed his face. "You just let me take care of your grandma."

"Well, dang." She grinned at him. "I will."

He set the tray on the table. "Be right back with the coffee."

As the pile of sandwiches grew smaller, they studied the map, tossing around ideas.

Piper was concerned about the house, believing someone might try to ensure no one inside interfered. Since Grady was the most familiar with the house and barns, he'd stay behind, armed with a handgun and shotgun.

There'd been considerable debate whether their sniper rifles would be effective since none of them were equipped with night vision scopes. Even with the full moon, would there be enough light? JT finally settled the argument. He expected there would be at least four or five vehicles, and they would use the headlights for illumination.

His argument made sense, and it was decided Davy would set up across the road. Since he would have the best view, he would take the lead on the communications. He'd also take out the tires—an iffy option at best since they had no idea how the vehicles would be parked.

JT and Tony would each take a UTV and park in a stand of trees near the back of the property.

"When they leave the Sutton Ranch, I'll call Davy," Piper said. She picked up the aerial map of the ranch. As she studied it, she spotted a narrow track, what might be a road or trail. It was some distance from the abandoned barn. She could leave her truck there and go on foot the rest of the way. It would let her approach the building from the back. Her truck should be far enough away so the engine's sound wouldn't be a problem.

Tony swallowed the last bite of his sandwich, followed by a swig of coffee. "What about communications? Looks like we'll have to use our cellphones."

Grady, in the process of picking up the plates, stopped. "I've got several handheld radios with earbuds. We use them in moving the cattle. Would they help?"

"Hell, yes!" JT said.

She glanced at her watch. "I've got to go. As soon as it's dark, I want to be in that barn." She headed toward her bedroom. Within minutes, dressed in tactical gear, she rushed out the door.

As Cade waited for Frankie to pull onto the roadway, he slid the phone from his pocket, setting it in a cup holder on the console. Once they were on the highway, he let Frankie pull ahead before he tapped the speed dial and speakerphone.

Certain that Frankie wouldn't be able to see his lips moving, he said, "Cavalry. I'm following Hillard. We're headed north on Hwy 19."

Nick said, "Then you're headed to the Sutton Ranch. You're going to have cover. Piper will be in an old barn across the road."

"How'd you manage it?"

"I didn't. It was her idea. Her boss is working on getting a SWAT team from the Dallas FBI. I'm pulling in officers for a team. I'm coordinating our response with Luke. I wanted to do the takedown at the Sutton Ranch, but we can't get there in time. It will have to be at the Layton spread."

"This may be my last call. If they're suspicious, someone may take my phone. Be prepared for a call. Any idea what Piper and her team plan to do?"

"When I asked, all she said was protect the ranch."

Ahead, Frankie slowed, letting Cade catch up. "Got to go." Focused on the truck in front of him, he didn't hear the soft whisper, "Good luck," before the line went dead. He picked up the phone and quickly erased the calls before shoving it into his pocket.

Frankie turned, and Cade followed. Against the fading rays of sunlight, a house and barns came into view. Trucks were parked along the side of the road and near the barns. Behind the house, a large group of men mingled.

Frankie pulled to a stop in the middle of the road, hopped out and ran back.

Cade lowered the window.

"Back into the driveway. We might as well use your truck."

Cade nodded. While he waited for Frankie to pull into the driveway, he studied the broken-down barn across the road, wondering how Piper planned to get inside without someone spotting her.

Once the roadway was clear, he eased forward, turning the truck to back in. Frankie had parked behind the house and stood near the driveway with Sloan at his side. Cade parked and stepped out.

Sloan stomped toward him. "Pollard, you armed?"

Cade stared at him with an unyielding expression. "What's it to you?"

"Give me your gun and phone."

Cade widened his stance. His fisted hands rested on his hips. "I don't like your attitude, and I'm not giving you a damned thing. You got a problem with it, then I'm out of here."

Frankie walked up. "Jack, back off. He's okay."

Sloan grumbled, "If you say so, but I don't like it."

"It's not your call," he said.

Cade felt the hackles rise on his neck. Since when did Frankie start calling the shots?

Frankie pointed to a collapsible chute on wheels. "Hook it up to your truck."

"Then what?" Cade asked.

"We wait. The cattle haulers haven't arrived."

Frankie walked off but didn't get far before Sloan stopped him.

"It's a mistake to bring in someone new, especially Pollard. I don't like him," Sloan said.

"We need another man."

"Maybe so, but there's something off about this guy. If I didn't know better, I'd say he smells like a cop."

"Not according to his background. Even the sheriff verified his criminal record."

"I still don't like it." Sloan glanced at the group of men in the yard. "I recruited every man here. I know them. I don't know Pollard."

Frankie smiled. "If it makes you feel better, Pollard's not leaving the Layton Ranch. When he's found dead, it will be another piece of evidence to tie Sheffield to the cattle rustling. A nice touch, don't you think?"

Sloan grinned. "I'd say so."

"No slipups this time. Make sure he's dead when we leave."

While he hooked the trailer to his truck, Cade kept an eye on Frankie. When Sloan stopped him, the angry glances Sloan shot his way made it obvious he was the subject of the heated discussion. When Sloan grinned, a chill raced down Cade's spine.

Finished, he stood and glanced toward the men clustered

alongside a pickup. Two were seated on the tailgate. No ordinary cowhands, these men had a rough, arrogant appearance. Tattoos covered thick biceps and neck muscles. Dressed in military-style gear down to their combat boots, each had a semi-automatic gun riding on his hip. Cade had encountered their types before, ex-militia, willing to do anything to make a buck.

He knew there was only one reason for the heavy armament, and it wasn't what was happening here. It was to steal the Layton herd.

Near the back of the house, Cade spotted a water cooler with paper cups stacked on top. He idly wandered over, ignoring the suspicious looks the men shot his way.

Using the cup as a prop, he took small sips as he studied each face, memorizing features and the occasional first name he heard in the low hum of conversation.

A commotion at the pen grabbed his attention. Sloan and another man were loading a bull into a trailer. *So that's the infamous Leopold*, he thought. Once they finished, they unhooked the trailer, and Sloan pulled his truck forward. The other man turned to walk around the side of the trailer.

Shock, followed by a sense of foreboding, whipped through Cade. It was Evan Clarkson, a deputy sheriff. On several occasions, he'd seen him at the sale barn with his boss, Sheriff Horne.

Outwardly unconcerned, Cade shifted his gaze away from Clarkson. A man stepped alongside the cooler and picked up an empty cup.

Cade said, "That's one damn fine-looking bull."

When the man straightened, he took a gulp of water and looked toward the pen. "I wouldn't mind owning him, but too rich for my blood." He took another drink.

Cade raised an eyebrow, saying nothing.

"Scuttlebutt is there's something unusual about him. The way the damn animal is treated around here, you'd think he's made of gold." The man swallowed the rest of the water and pitched the cup into a tin bucket.

Frankie shouted, "Pollard."

After tossing his cup into the same bucket, he ambled toward Frankie.

"Get in your truck. The cattle hauler is here. Follow it into the pasture."

The sound of an eighteen-wheeler engine intensified in the night air. The truck shuddered to a stop in front of the driveway. Behind it, a second one stopped.

Sloan trotted toward it and hopped on the running board. After a short conversation, he hung onto the side while the driver pulled toward a gate further along the road. Sloan jumped down and opened the gate as the cab swung out wide to make the turn. Inside the pasture, the truck pulled forward, scattering the cows as it circled and came about to face the gate.

Cade followed, towing the trailer with the chute. Once the truck stopped, he backed the trailer up to the rear end of the semi. Two men walked up and disconnected it from his hitch. Once he was clear, Cade pulled the truck out of the way.

By the time he walked back, men had opened the metal brackets, pulled out the extra walls, and were locking them into place. Clarkson stepped up and turned the winch to raise the chute's end until it was even with the trailer's floor.

Behind him, Sloan shouted, "Pollard, get a move on." He turned. Two dirt bikes shot past him. A UTV followed the bikers as they began to push the cattle toward the chute. Sloan handed him a cattle prod. He climbed onto the side as the first animal trotted up the ramp.

Tires jolted over heavy ruts in the dirt track meandering through the brushy landscape. It was slow going as Piper, even at this distance, didn't dare use her headlights. Instead, she relied on the faint glow of the rising moon. Lights on the horizon marked the Sutton Ranch. Once Piper had pulled even with them, she turned, praying she didn't end up with a flat tire. If she had to make a fast getaway, she wanted the truck pointed in the right direction.

Piper pulled her rifle from the case in the back seat and slung it over her shoulder. Attired in black, her hair shoved under a cap, she was near invisible as she trotted across the field toward the back of the old barn. Reaching it, she crept around the side. In front, rusted equipment littered the ground. Hunkered behind an old tractor, she had a bird's eye view of the activity across the road. She flipped out the legs of the bipod, setting the rifle alongside her. Instead of using the scope, she pulled out her binoculars.

Headlights on two trucks, parked next to each other, illuminated the eighteen-wheeler. Dirt bikes and a UTV weaved around the restless cattle, slowly pushing them toward a chute mounted to the back of the trailer. Piper searched for Cade and finally spotted him on the side of the chute, prodding the animals into the trailer.

She shifted her gaze to examine the second cattle hauler parked on the roadway before she looked at the ranch house. Floodlights lit the yard. She counted at least eight pickups, though there could be more on the far side of the house. A trailer with Leopold inside was parked in front of the pen.

A shout echoed, bringing her attention back to the loading. A man strode around the front of the trucks, followed by a second. Their faces harsh in the glare of the lights, she had no difficulty recognizing Hillard and Sloan. Hillard motioned, and another man broke away from the group around the chute and joined the conversation. It was Evan Clarkson, the deputy sheriff. More pieces of the puzzle fell into place.

She pulled her cellphone and tapped the screen.

Davy answered on the first ring. "I was getting worried."

"I'm in place," she whispered. "It took me longer than I expected. Call Luke and let him know I've confirmed they're here."

"How many men?"

A grim note entered her voice. "Twelve. One's a deputy sheriff, and he's not one of the good guys. We made a smart move by not contacting the sheriff. Something else, these men aren't your everyday ranch hands. If I had to hazard a guess, I'd say they're mercenaries."

Davy muttered a curse under his breath before he said, "Hired killers. Can it get any worse?"

"Any word on the FBI?" she asked.

"Not yet."

"They're already loading the herd. Leopold's in a trailer. They've got two dirt bikes, a portable chute, and a UTV. I've counted at least eight pickups plus the two cattle haulers."

"Any chance you can make contact with Cade?"

"Doubtful. Did you reach his boss?"

"Yes. What about weapons?"

"Handguns are all I've seen," Piper slipped the phone into the pocket over her heart. "Can you still hear?"

"Loud and clear."

"Do you have something to write on?"

"Go," Davy told her.

One by one, she read off license plate numbers before disconnecting the call.

JT was right. The process took longer than she expected. Once the last animal scrambled into the trailer, Cade jumped down.

Other men closed the doors, then buttoned up the chute. Cade backed his truck to the hitch.

Several of the men walked across the pasture, heading to the house. She recounted, but she hadn't made a mistake, twelve men against four marshals and a special ranger. No matter how she added it, it still came out the same. The odds didn't get any better. How the hell could they stop them and survive?

Cade finished hooking onto the trailer, then waited by his truck, watching the men head across the pasture.

"Pollard," someone shouted.

Cade looked toward the sound.

It was Giles, standing by the pasture gate. He motioned to him. "Park on the road," he shouted.

Cade nodded and slid behind the steering wheel. He drove out, stopping on the shoulder. He reached for his phone, only to shove it back in his pocket. In his rearview mirror, he saw Giles limping toward his truck. Cade exited and leaned against the side. He figured he'd acquired a guard as he gazed at Giles with a contemptuous look.

Giles turned to look at the pasture, acting as if he was only interested in watching Clarkson and another man muscle the dirt bikes into a truck bed. Once they were tied down, Clarkson drove out of the pasture and parked in front of Cade's truck. Giles never moved, except for the occasional glance over his shoulder to see what Cade was doing, which confirmed his suspicions.

The driver of the UTV had pulled through the gate and stopped on the road. Clarkson ran back, locked the gate, and jumped aboard the UTV. The driver hot-rodded it back to the house.

Since it appeared a meeting was going on, Cade decided to find out why. As he passed Giles, Cade said, "I'll be at the house, in case you're interested." Giles shot him a nasty look but didn't respond as he stepped behind Cade.

At the sound of an engine, Cade stepped to the side. A truck passed and whipped into the driveway. Jarvis was behind the wheel. By the time he reached the house, Jarvis and Sloan had their heads together in an intense conversation.

When Sloan spotted him, he growled, "Need something?"

"Water." Cade turned toward the cooler.

Frankie walked around from behind the trailer. Inside, the bull restlessly shifted from side to side.

"Pollard, what the hell are you doing here?" Frankie demanded.

Cade motioned toward the water cooler.

Seemingly reassured, Frankie said, "When we pull out, fall in behind the empty hauler."

"Where are we headed?"

Frankie hesitated, glancing at Jarvis before he said, "The Layton Ranch."

Cade frowned. "You expecting trouble there?"

"Why are you asking?"

"If I'm going into a shitstorm, I'd like to know ahead of time, that's all. A damn marshal lives there."

"She won't be in a position to interfere."

Inside him, the tension ratcheted, though his voice was flat. "Good enough for me."

"You've got a passenger. Get ready to leave." He turned.

Cade's voice stopped him. "When do I get my money?"

Frankie glanced over his shoulder and scoffed. "Don't worry. You'll get paid."

A malignant laugh erupted from Sloan.

Cade grabbed a cup of water and gulped it down before ambling back to his truck. Damn, he didn't like the idea of someone riding with him, but there was nothing he could do about it. Frankie was keeping him on a short leash. He glanced over his shoulder. Giles had disappeared. Once he stepped onto the roadway, his hand slid into his pocket, and he surreptitiously pulled out the phone. His thumb punched buttons.

On the other end, Piper's voice echoed, "Yes."

In a low voice, almost a whisper, he said, "Headed to your ranch."

"We're ready."

"How many officers?"

"Four."

Even in the moonlight, she couldn't miss the look of shock that rolled over his face. "Weapons?" she asked.

"All I've seen are handguns. One man's a deputy sheriff."

"I saw. Behind you." The line went dead.

He quickly punched buttons to erase the call, then dropped his arm to slide the phone back into his pocket. Voices grew louder. He glanced back as he opened his door. Clarkson was headed to his truck. Beside him, a man limped, trying to keep up. He should have known his passenger was Giles. Still, the thought of Giles couldn't push aside the trepidation that roiled in his gut. Jarvis' arrival made thirteen heavily armed men. How the hell were four marshals going to stop them?

The sound of an engine firing overrode the bellows of the cattle inside the big rig's trailer that was still parked in the pasture. Headlights on the empty eighteen-wheeler lit up the road.

A pickup pulled out of the driveway several minutes later, followed by another towing a trailer loaded with the UTV. Once they were on the road, the semi lurched forward, slowly picking up speed. As the convoy passed Cade's truck and the one with the dirt bikes in the bed, they fell in line behind it.

Piper grabbed the rifle, slipped around to the back of the barn, and ran. Even using the shortcut she'd discovered, it was iffy whether she'd make it back before the trucks arrived. Though the heavy combat boots braced her ankles, her feet twisted and turned as she landed on the edges and in the holes of deep ruts.

Back on the road, she called Davy. "Cade called to warn me. My ranch is next. They just left, four trucks hauling dirt bikes, a UTV, and a portable chute. There's one big rig. They left the other semi here. What's the status there?"

"JT and Tony are in place. I'm in position across the road. Grady's inside the barn. Can you contact Cade?"

"No. Giles is in the truck with him. What about the FBI?"

"Not going to get here in time to help us."

Muttering curses, she punched the disconnect button. Once she hit the paved road, she goosed it and hoped she wouldn't cross paths with a cop or the convoy.

In the driveway, she screeched to a stop and slid out. Grady trotted out of the barn with a shotgun cradled in his arms and a gun in a holster on his hip. A bandolier, the loops filled with shotgun shells, hung across his chest. Binoculars dangled on a strap around his neck. "How far out?" he asked, following her inside the house.

"I'm not certain, but they're close."

He picked up a portable radio from a table near the door and handed it to her. "It's on and set to the right channel."

Piper hooked it to her belt and settled the attached earpiece in place. She keyed the mike. "Davy. I'm here."

"Everyone copy?" he responded.

Clicks sounded as JT and Tony keyed their mikes.

Piper said, "Shut off all the lights. Let's make it look like we've gone to bed. Where'd you park Tony's car?"

"I moved it into the barn. Not much I could do to hide JT's truck and trailer."

"As soon as we get outside, open the gate."

Piper dashed into the bedroom and pulled a spare magazine from the duffle bag. She had two in holders on her belt. This one she stuffed into her pocket. She flipped off the lights behind her as she raced to the door.

Grady had the gate open. She started the engine, engaged the four-wheel drive, and drove through the gate, heading across the pasture toward an outbuilding where they stored extra grain and supplies. Parked alongside it, her truck was barely visible in the shadows of the overhanging roof.

She keyed the mike. "In place," she said, then grabbed the binoculars she'd tossed on the front seat. The few clouds had dissipated, and beams of light from the full moon spread over the fields. She looked to the north but didn't see Tony or JT. Lowering the windows to listen, all she heard were the distant yips of coyotes.

Piper could feel the rising tension. In her mind, she played a dangerous game of second thoughts. Was there another way, one less risky? Here the ruthless gang was contained, whereas on the highway, they weren't.

Davy's voice, "They're coming," shut down the debate in her head. Right or wrong, they were committed.

"It's showtime," Davy added.

Other than a grunt from Giles when he heaved himself onto the seat, the only sound since leaving the Sutton Ranch was the hum of the engine. Jarvis had split off shortly after leaving the ranch. Probably headed back to his office. He wasn't the type to get his hands dirty, let everyone else do it for him. Still, it was one less man. Frankie had also disappeared. His truck wasn't in the convoy.

Cade played out various scenarios in his head. None, from his perspective, had a good ending. All he could hope for was that Piper and her team had a workable plan. In his experience, though, tactical operations usually went down the crapper from the get-go from uncontrolled risks. This whole deal was loaded with them.

A phone rang. Giles answered, "What?" He listened for a few seconds, then said, "Yeah, I got it." He slid the phone into his pocket. His head swiveled toward Cade. "Boss says when we get there, get a hustle on to get that chute unloaded and in place."

When Cade didn't respond, Giles growled, "Did you hear me?"

Cade never looked his way. "I heard."

"Arrogant bastard," Giles muttered.

The semi signaled for a turn, and the brake lights on Clarkson's truck flashed. Cade slowed. The eighteen-wheeler, swinging across the road, turned and drove in. The pickup hauling the UTV was already inside the pasture. Cattle scattered as the big rig crossed the field to loop back.

"Stop," Giles said. He opened the door and slowly climbed down. "Once you're clear, move your truck out of the way."

Giles limped to the back corner of the cattle hauler. He waved until Cade reached the right spot, then flashed his palm. Another man walked up to help Giles unhook the trailer.

Once his truck was free, he drove forward, turning to park on the driver's side of the semi.

Piper had swung the glasses toward the gate. When Cade's truck pulled in, she warned the others. "That's Cade's truck with the chute, but I only see three pickups. Four left the Sutton place."

"I don't see it. It's not on the road," Davy answered.

Visible in the bright headlights, men rushed to unload the UTV and bikes. Once they finished, the truck that had carried the bikes and the one towing the UTV trailer were driven a short distance away from the semi. The drivers angled the trucks, pointing the headlights toward the eighteen-wheeler and the chute. When the two drivers exited, they carried rifles. The trucks had effectively formed a barrier between the house and semi. The men would see anyone driving across the pasture and could use the trucks for cover.

"Two men with rifles by the trucks. One is the deputy," Piper said.

Davy responded, "The way the vehicles are angled, I can't see the men. Another truck's coming in."

When Piper shifted her gaze back to Cade's truck, he'd turned. His truck disappeared behind the semi, and so did the latest arrival.

The bikes and UTV were on the move. The bike riders started at the outer edge moving the small groups of animals into a larger one. They circled and pushed the cattle together, their movements similar to a man on horseback. *Motorized horses,* she thought. The UTV kept the herd moving toward the chute.

Davy said, "Once they close the trailer gate, I'll take out the tires."

Piper answered, "As soon as we hear your shots, we'll move in."

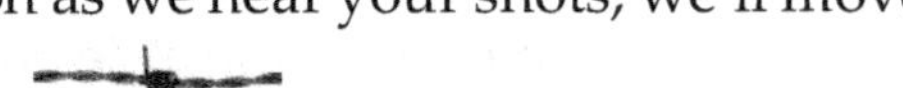

Cade parked along the driver's side of the eighteen-wheeler. He grabbed the spare magazines for his Glock from inside the console, shoving one in each pocket of his jacket. The gun rode in a holster in the small of his back. He stepped out and headed toward the chute. Headlights flashed. Another truck drove through the gate. Cade shot a look over his shoulder. Frankie had arrived.

After turning the truck to face the gate, Frankie stopped alongside Cade's truck. Sloan hopped out, followed by Frankie. As they walked past him, Sloan gave Cade a hard look. Ignoring him, Cade reached to lock a side panel into place.

In the distance, Cade heard the rumble of the bikes. When he looked up, cattle were slowly drifting toward the ramp. It's when he realized Clarkson and the man towing the UTV had moved their trucks. Now they were angled, so the headlights illuminated the semi and chute. The two men, holding rifles, watched the pasture on the other side over the hoods.

A chill raced over Cade. Located on the opposite side of the property, the house and barns were out of view. If someone did hear and came to investigate, they were easy pickings. He figured the marshals would approach from the direction of the house, and they didn't know about the rifles. When they charged in, they'd be sitting ducks. He had to get the rifles out of play, but how?

The sound of hooves on the ramp broke into his thoughts. As Cade looked around, he realized no one seemed interested in him. He'd been surprised when the truck driver shut off the engine as it took several minutes to restart one. Was it possible he'd left the keys? If so, Cade could stop the semi from leaving. It was worth the risk to find out.

Cade stepped back into the dark shadow cast by the eighteen-wheeler. He slipped along the side until he reached the driver's door. After a quick glance over his shoulder, he eased the door open and stepped onto the running board. Keys dangled in the ignition. Cade leaned forward to grab them, sliding them into his pocket. As he started to step back, he spotted the cattle prod on the passenger seat. He reached across and picked it up.

When he jumped down, a hand grabbed his shoulder.

26

Cade twisted, knocking the hand aside. It was the driver of the semi.

The man leaned forward. "What the hell are you doing?"

Cade lashed out, striking with the cattle prod. Startled by the jolt of electricity, the man staggered. Cade dropped the prod. His fist rocked the man's head back, and he fell to the ground.

Cade quickly looked toward the chute. The animals stomped and bellowed as they trotted up the ramp, covering up any sounds from the brief confrontation. Focused on keeping the cattle moving, the other men never glanced behind them. Cade rolled the body, shoving it just far enough under the cab that it was out of sight, then picked up the cattle prod.

One less threat, Cade thought as he moved back to the side of the chute. He wondered how long it would take before someone discovered the keys and driver were missing. Damn, where were the marshals? When did they plan to make a move?

From across the road, Davy hunted for the men with the rifles. He still couldn't see them. He swung the barrel toward the semi. A sinking feeling flowed through him. He had the same problem. He couldn't see the men clustered around the chute. Cade's truck and the last one to arrive were in the way.

While he cursed the gods of misfortune under his breath, Cade appeared. He sidled along the side of the semi until he reached the cab door. What was he doing, Davy wondered. Then Cade climbed inside. Was he after the truck keys? Tension spiked when another man headed toward him—no way to warn Cade. The crosshairs settled on the man's chest.

When the man grabbed Cade, Davy tensed. Before he could reposition the crosshairs, the man lay motionless on the ground. *Damn good reflexes,* he thought.

As Cade walked back toward the chute, Davy keyed the mike. "Cade might have grabbed the keys to the semi."

Piper clicked the mike along with Tony and JT to acknowledge. She swung the binoculars away from Clarkson and the other man, looking toward the chute. Driven by the dirt bikes and UTV, animals trotted up the ramp into the trailer.

A movement near the front of the truck caught her eye. Astonished, she saw a man crawling out from under the semi. He shouted, "Where's the new man? Find him," and opened the passenger door. He reached inside. When he stepped back, he had a gun in his hand.

Cade heard someone shout and recognized the voice. It was the damn driver. Before the men around the chute could react, Cade darted toward the front of the semi. Dropping the prod, he grabbed the gun from under his coat. When he rounded the front of the truck, the driver spotted him.

He shouted, "There he is," and raised the gun he held.

Cade was faster. He fired. The driver fell. *Crack,* another sound ripped the night air, followed by three more quick shots. *Who was shooting?* Cade twisted, looking for the men with the rifles.

He watched Clarkson run around the end of the UTV trailer and disappear. His buddy dove into the bed of the truck. There had to be a sniper, but who? Cade could only hope it was one of the marshals and not one Frankie had set up.

A bolt of fear had raced over Piper when Cade ran into view. Then Cade shot, and their plan went down the tubes. They couldn't wait. Davy reacted, firing at the tires. Men darted behind the semi.

Even as she threw the glasses aside and started the engine, she heard JT's booming voice through the open window. "U.S. Marshals. Drop your weapons. Walk out with your hands in the air." Shots rang out. Cattle bellowed and ran.

Piper stomped the gas pedal. The truck bounced over rocks and plowed through grass and brush. In front of her, a man jumped into the bed of the truck. Clarkson was running toward the back of the trailer used to haul the UTV.

Another shot echoed. This time, someone was shooting at her. The windshield cracked. She spun the steering wheel, throwing the truck into a skid. Once she was crossways, she slammed on the brakes, the transmission grated as she threw the gearshift into park, then grabbed the door handle, and tumbled out. When Piper hit the ground, she rolled to her feet, jerking the Glock from its holster.

Over the hood, she fired at the man in the bed of the truck. He ducked down. Her eyes shifted, searching for Clarkson. Instead, she saw Cade charging across the pasture toward the two pickups.

From somewhere toward the back of the field, Cade heard one of the marshals shouting. A truck raced across the pasture, headed straight toward the pickups. His chest clenched. It was Piper. The man in the bed of the truck had his rifle pointed at her. Cade aimed but couldn't shoot. Piper's truck was in his line of fire.

A dirt bike shot past him, heading toward the gate. Another rifle shot cracked. The bike's front wheel came off the ground, then rotated in the air as if in slow motion. The bike went one way, the rider the other. When the man hit the ground, he lay motionless.

Two down, Cade thought. It also answered his question about the sniper.

When he looked back, Piper's truck was crossways in the pasture. From over the hood, she was shooting at the man in the bed of the truck. He dropped down, but Cade didn't think he was hit.

Then an engine roared. Cade shot a quick glance over his shoulder to see Frankie's truck racing toward the gate. Another rifle shot echoed, but he didn't bother to look. Instead, he took off at a dead run, zigzagging across the pasture toward the two pickups. Bullets from someone shooting at him kicked up dirt and rocks near his feet.

Where was Clarkson? Then Cade spotted him running toward the back of Piper's truck. From her position, she wouldn't be able to see the man.

Cade bolted around the end of the trailer, firing two quick rounds as he ran. Clarkson fell. Cade whipped around. The man in the bed of the truck had his rifle aimed at Piper. Before Cade could shoot, Piper fired. The man fell back. This time he didn't get up. *Four down.*

Cade sprinted to Clarkson's body. He shoved his gun inside his belt and leaned down to pick up the rifle. A bullet whizzed by, hitting metal. Bent over, he darted back to Clarkson's truck.

As he looked toward the semi, cattle ran, kicking up dirt as the gunfire drove them back. An animal was crossways at the top of the chute. Inside the trailer, bellows and thuds of hooves striking the metal sides resounded from the trapped cattle.

The rest of the gang had taken cover on the other side of the eighteen-wheeler, shooting toward the pasture. Cade shouldered the rifle. Resting his arm on the hood of the truck, he peered through the scope, searching for a target.

In the gap between the trailer and cab, he saw Sloan lean forward. Sloan popped off two fast rounds at Cade, then ducked back. The bullets pinged as they struck the truck.

Cade positioned the crosshairs at the spot where he'd seen Sloan. When he leaned out again, Cade was ready. He pressed the trigger. Sloan sagged, then dropped out of sight. *Five down.*

Gunfire still echoed from behind the semi and somewhere in the pasture. Cade still hadn't seen the other two marshals. He started to move the rifle toward the field when a gunman ran out from the front of the semi. As he dashed toward the bike lying on the ground, he kept up a steady stream of fire toward Cade, forcing him to take cover against the side of the truck. A sharp crack sounded, and the man stopped firing. Cade leaned forward for a quick look. He was on the ground and not moving. Chalk up another one for the sniper. *Six down.*

He moved the rifle back into position, this time searching the pasture through the scope. Cattle ran in every direction. The UTV used by the rustlers sat in the middle of the frenzied mass of animals. The driver was slumped over the wheel. *Seven down.*

In between animals, Cade caught a glimpse of the passenger snugged against the side of the UTV. Cade recognized him. It was the man he'd talked to at the cooler. A short distance away, he spotted two UTVs, stopped side by side. They had to belong to the marshals.

The animals split off, racing toward the back of the pasture, giving Cade an opening. As he steadied the crosshairs in place, the man started to rise, his gun pointed toward the marshals. Cade pressed the trigger. *Eight down.*

In the distance, the sound of a helicopter grew until it hovered over the field. A bright spotlight flashed on, lighting up the pasture. Over a loudspeaker, a voice said, "FBI. Throw down your weapons. Walk out with your hands in the air."

The firing stopped as abruptly as it had begun. Three men, arms raised, walked out from behind the eighteen-wheeler, one limped. Vehicles zoomed through the gate and came to a screeching halt in front of the semi. Agents with FBI emblazoned across their vests jumped out.

Two UTVs pulled forward with JT in one. Cade didn't recognize the other but guessed it was Tony. Their jackets identified them as U.S. Marshals.

Cade placed the rifle on the hood and raised his hands in the air before walking around the truck.

An agent ran toward him. "Put your hands on the hood, spread your legs."

"I'm Special Ranger Cade Tanner," he said as he complied.

"I need to see your identification."

With a wry chuckle, Cade said, "It's a bit difficult. I've been working undercover. The marshals can vouch for me."

"Until they do, don't move."

Since the agent had an MP5 pointed at him, Cade was damn sure he wouldn't even twitch.

A man walked up with a Special Ranger badge sewn on the front of his jacket. "I can vouch for him. He works for me," Nick Rawling drawled.

Much to Cade's relief, the agent immediately lowered his weapon.

Within a few minutes, the agents had the remaining suspects handcuffed and on the ground. The helicopter landed, and the pilots joined the melee.

Piper walked over to him. "Cade, nice to be able to greet you officially." Then she turned to the other man. "I'm Piper McKay. You must be Nick Rawling."

He extended his hand. "I am." Nick motioned to the hubbub in front of them. "Doesn't look like you needed us after all."

"Not true. I have to say, Cade Tanner was a force to be reckoned with. Hell, he was a one-man wrecking crew." Her face grim, she eyed the handcuffed men. "I didn't think we'd come out of this unscathed. Eight dead or injured, and thankfully not one of us."

Tony walked up and was introduced. "Piper, an agent wants to talk to you."

"Okay, but first, I need to call Luke." She stepped away from the men and pulled out her phone. Luke answered on the first ring.

"Is everyone okay?"

"Nary a scratch. Though I can't say the same for the other side." While she filled him in on the details, she watched the FBI agents talking to Cade and the other marshals.

Luke said, "Send me a report tomorrow." He cleared his throat. "Hell of a good job."

"Most of the credit goes to Cade," she told him.

"I'll make sure Nick knows."

Piper had to smile as she disconnected. It wasn't often Luke passed out accolades.

Grady walked up. He'd driven over in his truck once all the hoopla, as he called it, was over. His arm encircled her shoulder. "Everything okay?" he asked.

"Yeah," she said as she leaned into him. "From this point, it's all paperwork, reams of paperwork."

It wasn't until sometime later, she remembered Leopold. She didn't know how long everyone would be tied up here. They were still waiting on the county coroner to arrive and the FBI crime scene unit. It could take hours before the FBI was finished.

As she headed to her truck, Davy walked up. "One of the agents is waiting to talk to you," she told him.

He groaned. "Damn, it starts. Reports! Where are you going?"

"To get Leopold." She waved her hand toward the FBI agents. "There's no telling how long this will take. I don't want to leave him in the trailer."

"Do you need any help?"

She grinned. "You're not going to get out of talking to the agent. You might as well get it over with. Besides, all I have to do is hook up to the trailer and haul him back here."

She looked at the cracked windshield, deciding she could still drive the truck, that is if the tires hadn't been damaged. Once she cleared the pasture and the wheels were on solid ground, everything seemed to be working okay. She headed out the gate.

This time, the trip was a lot less stressful. She welcomed the silence, needing the time alone to decompress. Her body still hummed from the adrenaline that had poured through her. She knew she would be reliving what happened for days to come.

When she arrived, she backed in. It wouldn't take long since all she had to do was hook up and pull out. She'd be on her way back home.

When Davy spotted Cade and another man talking with JT and Tony, he strolled toward them. Cade introduced him to Nick. Davy spent several minutes answering Nick's questions.

An agent shouted, "Does anyone know what happened to the keys to the cattle hauler?" Cade pulled them from his pocket and tossed them to the man.

Davy said, "You did get them. I was watching and saw you climb in the cab but couldn't tell."

Nick asked, "What happened to Piper? I don't see her."

Davy said, "She left to get her bull. It's at the Sutton place."

A look of alarm crossed Cade's face. "Hillard's the one that got away in the truck."

He turned and ran. Agents shouted as he opened the truck door. Ignoring them, he jumped inside, started the engine, and tore out the gate.

Piper slid on the lightweight leather gloves Jen kept in the driver's door pocket, then jumped down from the truck. The outside lights still lit up the large yard. The ranch had a deserted air, despite the trucks the gang members had left behind. Even the cattle inside the cattle hauler had settled down. The only sound was the occasional hoot of a nearby owl. At her approach, Leopold tossed his head, his massive body shifting uneasily.

Her hand on the rail, in a quiet tone, she said, "Easy boy. Time to take you home."

A harsh voice said, "I don't think so."

Startled, Piper spun. Fear clawed its way into her brain at the sight of the gun pointed at her. "Hillard!"

"No, my dear. Not Hillard, Victor Reid."

Shocked, she stared at him. "You're Jarvis' partner."

"So you found out about that. You know more than we thought. I've been watching you. I warned Lane to be careful. But then, Lane always tended to underestimate a woman."

"You can't get away. We've arrested your men."

"Oh, but you're wrong." His lips twitched with a scornful smirk. "I've prepared for this eventuality. I have a new identity and will soon be over the border. Even Lane won't know where to find me. No turning state's evidence for him. For you, it's the end of the line."

"Killing me won't help you. All it will do is trigger a massive manhunt."

His flat, empty eyes stared at her. The fear rippled through her.

"You just don't get it, do you bitch?" he said. "Revenge, my dear. It's all about revenge. Jarvis and I had a damned good venture going until you landed in the middle of it. I'm going to lose a lot of money because of you." Reid motioned toward the open doorway of the barn. "Move."

When she turned, he took a step back, making sure he was well out of her reach.

He waved the gun toward the trailer. "Once I'm done with you, I'm taking your bull with me. A man in Mexico is waiting for him. It won't be a total loss."

Anger washed over her, pushing back the fear as she walked past him. Her gun still rode in the thigh holster strapped to her leg. Why? Was he that confident? Keep him talking, she told herself.

Equipped with large double doors, the wooden structure was a good-sized barn. The odor of hay and grain filled her nostrils as she stepped inside. "Whose idea was it to use the forged contracts? Jarvis?"

The light from the yard only extended a few feet, deepening the shadows toward the back and corners. It took a few seconds for her eyes to adapt.

Reid scoffed, "Jarvis! You give him too much credit. He's nothing but a pitchman, a high-pressure salesman. I'm the brains in this outfit."

Her steps slow, Piper moved toward the back of the barn, going deeper into the darkness. Her gaze swept the place. Near a worktable, bags of grain were piled along one wall. At the rear were odds and ends of equipment. On the other side, stacks of square bales leaned against the wall. Several had broken open. Hay littered the floor.

"Turn around. Put your hands on your head."

When she turned, she managed to take several small steps backward. Reid had stopped in the light. A slight advantage as he'd be looking into the darkness, but not enough she could risk going for her gun. Not with one pointed straight at her.

"Do as I say. I don't want to put a bullet in you, but if you make a move toward your gun, I will."

She raised her arms, placing her hands on top of her head. Why didn't he want to shoot her? "How did you set up the signatures?" Her mind raced as she looked for any opportunity. "Even our handwriting expert couldn't tell the difference."

"A man in Mexico is considered one of the best in the business. You must admit the contracts were truly brilliant, especially the loss clause. We'd get the owner to sign a contract for the sale of a few head of cattle. Then we'd transfer the rancher's signature onto the second contract."

He stepped to the side, picked up a red metal can, and set it in front of the doorway. His gun never wavered. He sneered. "I don't need to worry about that massive manhunt. There's more than one way to kill someone."

From the broken bales on the end of the row, he shoved hay onto the floor, scuffing his foot, pushing it into small piles in front of the doorway. "This will look like a tragic accident. No one will ever suspect me. It's why I let you keep your gun. I'm sure you've been wondering about it. But you see, if it was missing, it might raise suspicion."

Piper readied herself, all her concentration on his gun. "Were you responsible for the murders of the ranchers?"

He preened as he said, "Another of my brilliant ideas. Sloan and

Giles were so very good at that sort of thing." He eased down, his gun and eyes on her, his hand fumbling to unscrew the cap on the can. He straightened and kicked the can over. Gasoline gushed out. "This old building will go up like a pile of dried timber."

Horrified, Piper watched as he pulled a lighter from his pocket. Terror engulfed her, paralyzing her mind and body.

"Never thought an addiction to cigars would prove so beneficial." He flicked it open, a small flame lit. He tossed it onto the gasoline-drenched hay. Tendrils of fire shot up, gaining in strength as it spread along the pile. It raced toward the stack of hay in the corner.

He was right about the building. The dry hay was a perfect conduit for the flames. Piper still couldn't reach for her gun. Reid stood outside the doorway, where he'd stopped to watch his handiwork. A malicious laugh echoed over the crackling flames.

The fire crept up the walls and across the floor toward her, gaining strength from the hay that littered the floor. Dense black smoke boiled in the air. Her lungs burned. Faced with the blistering heat, Piper instinctively stepped back, though she had nowhere to go.

She didn't have a choice. She'd rather face a bullet than being burned alive. Piper ripped the gun from the holster and charged, racing through the fire. Flames licked her body. Diving toward the doorway, she hit the ground with a thud. Rolling onto her back, she brought the gun up.

Reid had stopped alongside the trailer. At the sound, he turned. Piper double-tapped. Two rounds hit his chest. A look of astonishment filled his face as he stared at the gush of blood before he fell to the ground.

Pain stabbed her body. Her clothes were on fire. Piper rolled over and over until the dirt smothered the flames. Her hands batted the few remaining sparks before she stripped off the burned gloves.

Over the sounds of the fire, she could hear bellows of fear from Leopold as the heat and flames built. There wasn't enough space to open the trailer gate and let him loose. She had to pull the trailer from the barn before it crashed down, but she was running out of time.

In the distance, Cade could see flames shooting into the sky. Turning onto the road leading to the ranch, he fought the wheel to keep the truck from sliding into the bar ditch. He screeched to a stop in the driveway and was greeted with a scene from hell.

Flames climbed the walls and shot through the roof of the old barn. Dense smoke roiled. Though Cade saw both Frankie and Piper's trucks, where were they? A fear, unlike any he'd ever felt, flooded his senses. Gun in hand, he vaulted out of the truck and ran.

"Piper," he shouted. When she darted around the front of her truck, the relief came close to dropping him to his knees.

"Cade, help me," she screamed. "I've got to get Leopold away from the barn."

Then he saw Frankie's body lying on the ground and started toward him.

"He's dead," Piper hollered.

He shoved the gun inside his waistband. "Get into the truck. I'll hook up the trailer."

Dodging falling pieces of burning timber, he ran to the back of the truck. Embers fell through the gaps in the trailer's roof. Inside, the maddened bull bellowed and kicked the metal sides. For several hair-raising seconds, Cade's hands fumbled before he could connect the hitch. Once it was in place, he waved.

Piper hit the gas, pulling the truck and trailer down the driveway before she stopped and turned off the engine. Her body shook as she gasped for breath, sucking in the air. She carefully stepped out. Her legs wobbly, Piper leaned against the side of the truck.

Cade ran up to her. Soot and burn marks covered her face and clothes. "We need to get you to the hospital," he said.

"No, I'm fine. Nothing a bit of salve won't fix. Is Leopold okay?"

"He's got a few cuts on his legs from kicking the side of the trailer, but that's all."

Another shiver rocked her body as she coughed. "Is there any bottled water in your truck?"

"I'll get it." When he returned, Cade had two bottles, one he'd already opened.

Piper gulped down the entire bottle. With the back of her hand, she swiped her mouth.

He grinned. "You may start a new fashion trend. Smeared soot in place of lipstick," he said, then laughed.

She gave him a snarky look. "God, I love a good compliment."

He handed her the second bottle of water. This time, she sipped as she told him what happened and that Hillard was actually Victor Reid, Jarvis' partner. "What made you follow me?"

He nodded toward Reid's body. "I knew he had escaped, and Davy told me you'd left to get your bull. I just had a feeling he would head back here."

She tipped her bottle. "Here's to your intuition. If you hadn't arrived, I'm not sure I could have gotten Leopold away from the building."

In the distance, sirens sounded.

Piper said, "Here comes the cavalry."

A belly laugh erupted from Cade.

She stared at him.

He just laughed even harder before he said, "Inside joke. I'll tell you about it one of these days."

EPILOGUE

Two weeks later

Piper slowly turned into the driveway. Despite the assurances from both her grandmother and the doctor that it wouldn't hurt Jen to ride in the truck, Piper was still careful. Jen wasn't entirely happy, though, since the doctor had told her to stay off a horse for another two months.

As she rolled to a stop, Grady stepped out the front door. Spiffed up in new blue jeans and a starched white shirt, his face lit up with a smile. Piper glanced at Jen as she reached across to undo her grandmother's seatbelt. Jen had a similar smile on her face.

When she realized what Piper was about to do, she swatted her hand. "I'm perfectly capable of unhooking my own seatbelt."

Piper grinned. "Yes, ma'am,"

Grady opened the door to help Jen step down. Once on her feet, she took a deep breath, then looked around. "It's good to be home."

As they stepped inside, Jen said, "Good lord, did you buy out the flower shops? These are beautiful." She gazed at vases filled with assorted flowers on the tables and mantel.

"It's a special day," Piper said, with just a hint of tears.

"Now, don't go getting all emotional. We got through this, and both of you helped put away a whole band of murdering thugs. I did manage to worm details out of those other agents before they went back to Oklahoma City. Which is more than I got from the two of you."

She turned and marched into the kitchen.

"Jennie, don't you need to lie down and rest?" Grady said as he hurriedly followed her.

"Humph. I've been lying in a bed for weeks. It's time to get up and get moving. Besides, I smell coffee."

As they settled around the table, Jen asked Grady about the herd, which miraculously hadn't been hit by any stray bullets flying around during the pasture shoot-out, as it had been titled by the news media. It wasn't going to take long for her grandmother to get back into the groove of running the ranch, though Grady might have a thing or two to say about it. She pondered whether she should play matchmaker or stay out of it. Since she'd be headed back to Oklahoma City in a couple of days, it was best to let them work it out.

The doorbell rang. "I'll get it," Piper told them.

As she opened the door, there stood Cade, holding a vase of flowers with both hands. He stepped into the room, glanced around, then quipped, "No wonder I had a hard time finding these."

He looked a lot different from his days as Ron Pollard. Gone were the scruffy whiskers. His hair was neatly trimmed under a white straw Stetson. A starched, white long-sleeved shirt, crisply pressed blue jeans, and full quill ostrich Lucchese boots replaced the worn jeans, shirt and scuffed-up boots. A cocked and locked 1911 Colt rode in a Davis Leather, Taylor Omega holster on a matching leather gun belt. Not that she recognized it. JT was the one into serious gun leather and spotted the holster during a meeting with Cade and the district attorney. Later, JT couldn't stop talking about it. Still, Piper had to admit it was an impressive rig, especially with the Special Ranger badge on the side of the holster. A duplicate of the one pinned to his shirt.

While as Ron Pollard, she'd been enticed by his dangerous, rakish air, Piper preferred this look. Since Jen and Grady were western movie buffs, she'd been exposed to the old-time western stars. Cade reminded her of one of her favorites. Albeit much younger, he had the air of a Gary Cooper, confident without arrogance. Though, Cade Tanner was the real deal. No matter which way you threw the dice, he was a hell of a lawman. He'd walked into the middle of a gang of killers. He did what he had to do and never looked back.

Suddenly, she realized she was standing there staring at him. As he gazed back, his deep eyes gleamed with a sensual look. Heat flooded her body.

Then he grinned, breaking the intense moment. Cade motioned with the flowers. "I heard your grandmother was coming home."

Ignoring the thrum of longing, she said, "She's in the kitchen."

When they walked in, Jen looked up. A smile of delight crossed her face. "Cade, I was hoping you'd stop by."

Astonished, Piper said, "You know each other?" While over the last couple of weeks, she'd seen him, she had no idea he'd met her grandmother.

"Oh, yes. He came by the hospital a few times." Her gaze shifted from one to the other with a sly look of satisfaction.

Piper eyed her with suspicion. What was she up to?

Cade handed Jen the flowers. "Looks like you can start a flower shop."

She buried her nose in the bouquet. "These are wonderful. Thank you. This was very sweet of you."

Grady said, "Grab a chair. Can you stay for supper?"

Cade shot a quick glance at Piper, then said, "I'd love to stay."

"Jen, let me have those. I'll put them in the living room," Piper said.

It wasn't until after supper that they had a chance to talk. She walked outside with him. They wandered to the pen where Leopold placidly chewed a chunk of hay. As they approached, his eyes rolled, and he snorted, then turned, so his rump faced them.

Cade laughed and propped a boot on a rail as he leaned his arms on top. "You'd almost believe he's pissed at how he's been treated." He looked around. "Kind of quiet around here now."

Leaning against the fence, she said, "We've got almost everything wrapped up. The rest of the warrants were served two days ago. The last I heard, Jarvis and Huber were trying to outdo each other in turning state's evidence," Piper said.

Cade nodded. "Between your boss and mine, the phone calls and reports, it's been hectic. Getting the financial records on all the companies put the final seal on the indictments. What surprised me was learning Dick Crowley, Grant's bookkeeper, doctored the books and sales documents. The buyer's copy was different from the seller's copy. It's how Jarvis and crew were able to sell the stolen cattle and cover up the fact ear tags were missing. Grant knew something was wrong, but Dick kept telling him it was a computer problem."

"I had Grant on my list of suspects." She chuckled. "But so were you. You were pretty convincing as bad guy Ron Pollard."

"Not an experience I would care to repeat."

Her voice turned somber. "Yesterday, I called Edna Spence. I told her Jarvis had been arrested. I also told her there would be restitution for the theft of her ranch. While she thanked me for letting her know, I could still hear the grief in her voice."

Cade said, "What she lost can't be replaced."

Piper shuddered at the thought of how close she came to being in the same position. She turned and nodded toward the bull. "Did you know Huber is the one that started the business with Leopold? When he saw Jen's business projections and the DNA report, he told Jarvis. They were going to sell the bull to the head of a drug cartel in Mexico."

Cade laughed. "Nothing like having a banker in your hip pocket. Huber was in a perfect position to funnel money from the cattle sales into the offshore accounts, as well as to set up the loans."

"I even got a visit from the sheriff. He swears he had no idea one of his deputies was involved, even though Clarkson managed to derail the investigations into the cattle thefts and the attack on Jen. Clarkson was also Reid and Jarvis' pipeline in the sheriff's department. Horne still had an attitude. I stopped by the café the other day. From the discussions, there is a lot of dissatisfaction with him. Horne may have a problem when he comes up for reelection."

"Since I'm going to be living here, it's probably a discussion I'll steer clear of," Cade said.

"It would be wise."

"When are you headed back?" His gaze skimmed over her face. Under the light of the setting sun, her hair gleamed with russet highlights. When he remembered how she looked after the fire, he could still feel the fear. Piper McKay was one gutsy woman.

She shifted to lean back against the fence. "Day after tomorrow."

He cleared his throat. "Are you aware Special Rangers are commissioned in Oklahoma as well as Texas?"

She glanced up at him. The look in his eyes warmed her. "When I went looking for Cade Tanner, it seems I remember reading that."

"Well, I was wondering … if we could get together."

"I'd like that."

He grinned. His fingers reached to lightly brush her cheek.

From the front window, Grady and Jennie watched. A smile crossed their faces. Grady reached for Jennie's hand. She looked down, then tightly gripped it.

THE STORY BEHIND THE FICTION

SPECIAL RANGERS

Faced with heavy losses to rustlers, in 1877, forty Texas ranchers signed an agreement in Graham, Texas that created the Stock-Raisers' Association of North-West Texas, the forerunner for today's organization, the Texas & Southwestern Cattle Raisers Association, with over 17,500 members.

In 1893, Special Rangers became the enforcement arm for the Association. Just as the Special Rangers fought the battle against cattle rustling in the late 1800s, they carry on the same tradition today.

Thirty Special Rangers are spread across Texas and Oklahoma. While all of the Rangers are commissioned through the Texas Department of Public Safety, Rangers based along the Texas and Oklahoma border have a dual commission through the Oklahoma State Bureau of Investigation.

This unique group of officers is backed by market inspectors who collect the distinctive brands and other identifying characteristics on 4 to 5 million cattle sold each year at Texas markets. The details are then entered into the nation's largest livestock data retrieval computer system, an invaluable resource for the Special Rangers in locating stolen cattle. Each year, Special Rangers investigate approximately 1000 agricultural crimes and recover an average of $5 million in stolen cattle and other assets.

For more information on a truly exceptional organization and dedicated officers, please visit the Texas & Southwestern Cattle Raisers Association website: tscra.org.

U.S. MARSHAL SERVICE

The U. S. Marshal Service was the first federal agency in the United States. Formed in 1789, 3700+ men and women continue to occupy a unique position as they protect individuals within the Federal Judicial System. In addition, they apprehend federal fugitives, manage and sell assets illegally obtained by criminals, house and transport federal prisoners, and operate the Witness Security Program.

CATTLE DNA

Genetics plays an increasing role in cattle production and the sale of bulls. Many auction houses include a bull's DNA profile during the sale of the animal. In February/2021, a bull in Nebraska, Poss Deadwood, sold for $900,000. According to the owner, he'd received 4500 orders for the bull's semen before the sale. In 2019, SAV America sold for $1.51 million.

The double-muscled DNA marker is just one of several markers that can enhance a bull's market value. Double muscling is a result of a mutation in the DNA myostatin gene (GDF8).

ABOUT THE AUTHOR

Anita Dickason is a twenty-two-year veteran of the Dallas Police Department. She served as a patrol officer, undercover narcotics detective, advanced accident investigator, tactical officer and the first female sniper on the Dallas SWAT team.

Her fictional works are suspense/thrillers, and her plots are drawn from her extensive law enforcement knowledge and experience.

I hope you enjoyed ***DEADLY BUSINESS***.

Best Wishes
Anita Dickason

<u>anitadickason.com</u>